The Lost Lady

Amelia M. Brown

First Printing: January 2019   Second Edition: July 2020

Ordering Information:

Special discounts are available on quantity purchases by corporations, associations, educators, and others. For details, contact the publisher.

U.S. trade bookstores and wholesalers: Please contact our representative at Tel: (209) 663-3044 or email ambrown984@gmail.com.

DEDICATION

This is dedicated to my Sister and Grandmother. For always pushing me forward, for being there when I fall, and for the hands you hold out to help me back up. With my everlasting love and gratitude.

**Other Titles By
Amelia M. Brown**

Ties of Fate

The Chronicles of Odde:
The Beast of the Ruin

Coming Soon:
The Chronicles of Odde:
Of Riddles & Ravens

CONTENT

"Learn to win a lady's faith
Nobly, as the thing is high;
Bravely as for life and death –
With a loyal gravity."
~Elizabeth Barret Browning

ACKNOWLEDGMENTS

Thank you to the people at National Novel Writing Month (NaNoWriMo). Your programs and enthusiasm help motivate me and so many others to turn our dreams into reality. Thanks to Dianne G. and Kriston for reading the manuscript at the last minute and being so into it that you made me blush. You are the reason Part Two was completed in record time. Thank you, Meredith, for the feedback and for letting me rope you in despite your words to the contrary.

A special thanks to my readers. I wanted to thank you for your grace. I have had listened and edited the novel again. I don't expect it to be flawless, but I hope the story shines through.

Part One

Lander's

Keep

Amelia M. Brown

Chapter 1

The little cares that fretted me, I lost them yesterday
Among the fields above the sea, Among the winds at play.
~Elizabeth Barrett Browning

The wind moved through the branches overhead. Sunlight fell in golden patches on the forest floor. Life here was verdant and peaceful, Luveday sat calmly on her gnarled root and let the minutes tick by. Her more practical wool jacket cushioned her seat, momentarily forgotten. Her mind refused to take in her situation, deciding to examine her surroundings instead. It was beautiful here, a mix of amber light and deep shadows, cool breezes and warm earth. Luveday pushed a strand of tawny hair behind her ear as she reclined against a massive oak to watch the sunlight dance through its leaves. She felt a slight breeze, but the feeling couldn't penetrate the numbness shielding her mind.

Glancing down, she still wore the flowing cobalt skirt with matching blouse she had put on that morning. A single digit idly traced the gold swirling pattern over the deeper blue of the embroidered vest. It contrasted so well with the brown and green of her surroundings that she was dazzled by it. She remembered she had saved this look for a special occasion, packing it on a whim. She'd only worn it today because she'd run out of clothes on this business trip. Thanks to a client's clumsy personal assistant, she'd lost her two best shirts to the dry cleaners the first day. It seemed a shame to waste the outfit on her day off, but she'd had nothing else to wear but the sweats she'd brought for the cold New England nights. She'd not be caught leaving the hotel looking like a college student who just rolled out of bed, so the wispy skirt it was.

Her ever-present backpack purse sat at her feet. The extra-large tote resting beside it was full of gifts and the odds and ends she'd purchased during her walk through the quaint east coast town. She had fit in rather well with the patrons of the Celtic fair, not that she'd planned it. That morning Luveday set off for her staid version of an adventure: window shopping. After all, she was on the other side of the country. The shops lining the narrow streets had put forth an effort to draw in customers, and she'd excitedly perused them.

Luveday was an administrative assistant, ranked number two of three. The number one, the enigmatic Sarah, had become ill and left an opening on Mr. Lawrence's business trip. Being the only one without any prior engagements or social life to speak of, Luveday had gotten the go-ahead by default. It was not that she couldn't do the job; no, she was excellent at it. It was more that the boss, handsome middle-aged man that he was, usually went for Sarah, to impress the male clients, or Matt if he needed a macho presence. Luveday was short and curvy, not that her looks really impacted her job, but she was usually relegated to organization, scheduling, and research, which all entailed a good amount of time behind a desk. That life seemed far away from here, wherever here was.

Cogs began to turn in the back of her mind. Luveday recalled the events earlier that morning. In her mind's eye, she was back in the little New England shops. She saw the people mulling up and down the streets, laughing and dressed in bright costumes typical for any Celtic fair. Her mind felt an echo of the longing that had pinged in her heart at their laughter. Being alone was no fun, but she didn't belong back with her boss either; mingling was not her forte. Mr. Lawrence was a suave businessman, and she was a quiet bookworm.

Luveday stuffed a recent purchase in her tote as she stepped off the curb, stumbling over a pebble on the cobbled street, and barely caught herself before she hit the pavement face first. She flung out an arm for balance and met a sturdy tree. Eyes closed in mortification; she exhaled a sigh of relief, taking a moment just to breathe. No one called out to her, asking if she was alright, which she hoped meant no one had seen the near incident. Ready to move on, she opened her eyes, only to meet the hues of a wood, not the busy brick and stone streets. Noticing how quiet it had suddenly become, it took her mind a moment to realize what she was seeing, a forest, a deep wood and not anything resembling civilization. Confused, disoriented and more than a little scared, Luveday moved away from the tree, not realizing she was still using it for support. Spinning in a circle proved fruitless; retracing her steps did not make the mirage disappear. By all rights, she should have been standing in the middle of the street, not lost in the woods. Luveday retraced her steps, waving her arms like a mad woman while looking for any sign of something familiar.

Fighting down panic, she sat down under a large oak tree whose roots looked like a good spot off the forest floor. And there she had sat for the last fifteen minutes or so, debating what had happened to her. Was she hallucinating, in a coma, or maybe… dead? Was it the sample that street vendor had given her? What exactly had she eaten? She'd tasted unusual spices, and it had gone down a little rough, but she'd not felt any aftereffects, and it had been at least a half hour ago. She checked her watch, make that forty-five minutes. Were full-on hallucinations this real? Or had she stumbled into on-coming traffic and somehow missed her own demise? She remembered everything up to finding herself here so clearly; there hadn't been a blackout or a dizzy feeling, no light show or sci-fi sequence, just her usual clumsy self, tripping over her own feet. There was nothing at all to point her toward any answers to the questions swirling in her head.

The bark under her fingertips was rough and all too solid. The leaves under her feet crunched as she stretched out her legs; all signs that her surroundings were, indeed, real. Perhaps she was in a coma somewhere. Luveday kept reminding herself that she'd always had a vivid and overactive imagination. She was a daydreamer, and some of her flights of fancy had been realistic, though never to this extent. There were two other possibilities, she mused. One, she was dead, and this was a piece of heaven, though that seemed unlikely, but who was she to say what heaven looked like. The second option was that she was exactly where she thought she was; that while improbable, she had been transported somewhere else in the blink of an eye. Her laughter rang through the wood. "You've been reading too many romance novels." She chastised herself, trying to shake these thoughts from her head. *Yep*, and now she was talking to herself.

She didn't know whether to laugh, scream or cry. "This is ridiculous!" She looked around and knocked on the root under her. Yep, it was solid, and the sting in her hand told her the bark had just removed a bit of skin from her knuckle. Sighing she asked, "What now?" But no one was there to answer. So, she sat and waited a moment more, but all she heard was the life of the forest continuing as if she weren't even there.

A rhythmic sound came from afar. Luveday rose to her feet, her current situation forgotten as hope and fear blossomed inside her. She knew that sound, but how? It was a slow sort of jingle, metallic with a steady tempo. A moment later, a whistled melody joined the beat as her frantic mind put the dots together. Someone was there; it was someone on a horse. Should she call out or run and hide? She couldn't decide, so she stayed where she was and watched the rider meander through the trees, coming towards her. At the first sight of him, she sat down again, her legs giving out.

It was a knight in armor who looked as if he had seen a long, hard journey. He wore dark brown leather armor on his chest with chainmail on his arms and thick gloves. He was dark, rugged and from what Luveday could tell, rather large. He looked to be straight out of one of the BBC period pieces; that is to say, 100% authentic.

Luveday didn't move, didn't speak, and just watched in wary awe as he came steadily closer. For a split second, she thought she should have hidden behind the tree, but she realized that he had yet to spot her. Like a deer scenting danger, she froze where she was. He startled her as he broke out into song. The deep timbre of his voice was pleasing. He passed not twenty feet away, and when he came into her direct line of sight, he stopped, finally spotting her. They looked at each other in shocked silence, until he dismounted and offered aid.

"My Lady? What are you doing out in this wood?" Leading his horse closer, Luveday was all too aware of how large a man he was; well-over six feet, she guessed. She sprang to her feet sparing a glance at her backpack and the pepper spray that was somewhere in its depths. What should she do? Her mind raced for answers. He had called her Lady, which was a title she was not sure any of her ancestors had ever possessed. She could correct him, but then she doubted that that would go in her favor. Luveday did not realize that her baring and dress did more for her status than anything she could have said. Her back was as straight as a rod, as she tried to act with the poise and courtesy she was used to employing as an executive assistant of a large firm. It was hard as she fought her turning emotions, past the constriction in her throat. His accent was British, though she heard something else under the cultured demeanor. Had she come so far? How? Why? When? Forcing down her panic, she couldn't speak and looked at him with pleading eyes.

She could see soft brown eyes, looking at her with great concern and felt a weight leave the pit of her stomach. "I am afraid I am lost, sir." She looked away from him, not sure what more to say. How much should she reveal? A part of her knew that this was real and that speaking about it to the wrong people could cost her dearly and, yet she hesitated to lie. She had never been any good at it.

Seeing her distress, he offered his name. "I am Sir Gregori of Brooke Abbey, on my way to Lander's Keep, Home of the King's Champion. I am happy to assist you there; perhaps we can find your people." He offered, looking at her garments, and the few possessions at her feet. "It is the nearest castle or village of any size." His eyes were kind and curious.

"Lander's Keep?" She asked, hesitant to reveal her ignorance.

"Yes, not much farther through the wood." He offered her his hand. "If you don't mind sharing a mount, we can make good time." It seemed that chivalry wasn't dead. She had a knight to prove it.

She didn't argue, just nodded her head. "Thank you."

He began talking to her in a quiet and smooth voice as if he were afraid she'd bolt like a skittish animal. He gathered her belongings and tied them onto the back of his saddle. "I have just returned from King's Point, where My Lord De Lane, the Wolf of Lander's Keep has been campaigning. I will be happy to see a proper night's rest." Once finished, he turned to her. "If I may, My Lady?" He held out his hand again, and Luveday realized she was clutching her jacket to her as if it might protect her from harm. She loosened her grip and handed it over. He threw it over the horse's neck and picked her up as if she were no heavier than a sack of flour. She was positioned sideways on the front of the saddle, and with a fluid motion, the knight mounted the horse again, settling behind her. "If you will excuse me, Lady..."

"Luveday." She answered in a clear voice.

"I'll need to hold you a little closer if we are both to stay on the horse." He rearranged her gently, and a moment later they were on their way, with Luveday wrapped securely in the arms of a wandering knight. He smelled strongly of sweat, horse and, of all things, rosemary. Somehow, she found the last comforting.

Crumbling stone, a strange odor on the breeze, and piles of trash littered the corners around the muddy courtyard. Suffice it to say that the castle of Lander's Keep was not what Luveday expected. Gregori handed her down off the horse, and she stood a moment in awe while he handed over her meager belongings. She was full of wonder, but not at the sight of an authentic medieval castle. No, she was shocked by the ruin that was visibly beginning to take hold of the once beautiful buildings.

The village they had passed through was little more than a collection of peasant cottages and sheds; though made of stone they hadn't fared much better than the castle. They had passed a lively inn as they met the road but did not stop with their destination so near, and Luveday was grateful. There was little to recommend the Boar's Head to her. The castle loomed off in the distance, growing larger as they approached. From afar it had been a truly massive structure, but on closer inspection seemed to be badly neglected, and rather forlorn. Where were all the people, she wondered. Weren't castles like mini cities? Where was all the activity? But it looked like the keep hadn't been full for a long time, and Luveday suddenly doubted the good luck of being so quickly rescued.

Luveday took in every detail. It was a well-fortified castle, with a thick outer wall of sandy colored stone. It had a gatehouse, battlements and all the trappings one might expect, but underneath all that, there were some rather beautiful designs, like the coat of arms carved over the main gate and the vines over the keep's main doors. And that's what made the neglect so sad. Someone had put a lot of thought and love into this castle only for it to start to crumble toward ruin.

"This way, Lady Luveday." Having to get her attention, Gregori was polite as he ushered her into the main hall. The massive wooden doors were banded in sturdy iron. Though rather plain, they looked like they could hold back a siege. She guessed that was comforting to some.

Inside looked much better, but only because there wasn't much to see in the dim light. It took a moment for Luveday's eyes to adjust. Two long tables sat side by side, taking up the main space to her right. A dais sat at the opposite end of the room, a single step up, where the smaller head table lay perpendicular to the rest. Before her, a large space on the back wall was open to a massive hearth, with a small sitting area before it on another dais. The dining hall was dark, though the fire roared with life. The massive chandelier overhead might as well have been unlit for all the light the few candles gave off. There was no ornamentation, no decor other than two sturdy looking chairs before the fire. The walls were bare but for the unlit torches.

People seemed to be going about their tasks though there wasn't the bustle she had expected. A few men stopped to give her a strange look. They looked clean for the most part, though rough around the edges. Even the women looked a little harried, though they were even fewer in number than the men.

Like Gregori, the men had full beards and wore leather armor prepared for battle at a moment's notice. But that made sense from what her rescuer had said on the way there, the lord's men were more accustomed to the hardships of battle than living in a comfortable keep. Men at arms manned the walls, but the majority of Lord Iain's men were with him on campaign. *Tournaments*, Luveday thought and wondered what that might be like, images of the Celtic fair flashed through her mind.

The dreariness of her surroundings deflated Luveday's growing sense of hope. She was at heart an optimist, though a practical turn kept the trait from being too obnoxious; there was only so much it could take in a single day.

Gregori called out, as a young woman appeared through a far door with a large wooden tray in hand. Behind her was another lady, elegant in a silvery gray gown and well past middle age with silvery hair to match. "Ah, little Elli. Lady Emmalyn." The knight bowed to the women.

"You have brought home a lady, Sir Gregori." At the older woman's curious tone, the young woman's face lost its happy demeanor.

Gregori chuckled. "It seems so, My Lady. I found her in the wood. She has lost her way; her companions have abandoned her, and she had nowhere to go." He gestured to her. "May I present Lady Luveday of Sacramento. I fear she has come a long way."

The Lady Emmalyn looked her over, and Luveday returned her smile shakily. "You are welcome to our hospitality; it being what it is." She gestured around her clearly aware of what was lacking about the keep.

7

"Thank you, Lady." Luveday felt more at ease, though not comfortable in their presence.

A door slammed somewhere overhead causing most of the room to jump and look toward the source of the sound. Elli started so that the cups and pitcher on her tray dipped dangerously to one side.

The young Ellie grimaced while Emmalyn offered her a comforting smile. The girl headed toward the stairs but was met by another harried looking woman whose black attire added a severe air to her wrinkled face. "What is taking so long, child?" Her appearance reminded Luveday of a nun, but her manner was kinder than her scowl implied. "My Lady is growing impatient for her refreshments." She looked worriedly up the stairs.

"I am sorry, Mistress Adela." She started up the stairs, but the woman stopped her and took the tray.

"Best stay here child, My Lady is overly tired from the journey." There was an undercurrent to that statement, and Elli let the tray go without a fuss. The older woman headed back up the stairs with everyone watching her steady progress.

Gregori watched the exchange with as much interest as his new guest. A puzzled expression crossed his face. Elli and Emmalyn exchanged a look once their companion was gone. "I take it the Lady Christabel has arrived."

"You are astute as ever, Sir Gregori," Elli said with more than a hint of sarcasm, but the knight didn't seem to take offense.

His expression turned troubled. "He will not like that she has arrived so early." He rubbed his chin and spoke to no one in particular.

"No, he won't." Emmalyn agreed but seemed to shake herself. "Now, young Lady, come sit by the fire and tell me a bit about yourself and what misfortune has befallen you." The Lady's kindness overwhelmed Luveday.

Luveday followed without thought. She was happy for the chance to sit down, but she'd never been any good at lying, and the vague details she'd given the knight were little more than that. Trying to come up with a plausible story to explain an extraordinary and unexplainable event was beyond difficult. What had all those time traveling heroines said? For once her mind went blank, and she could not remember a single line.

Of one thing, Luveday was totally sure. She was completely alone. It was a first for her. She was close to her family, though their busy lives and long hours at work often left little time to see each other. Phone-tag was often a game they played, but she knew that if she needed them, her family would be there in a heartbeat. What was she to do now? The tears that filled her eyes were not contrived, she blinked them away, but Emmalyn had already noticed.

Lady Emmalyn had a sense about people, or perhaps it was her age and experience, but she felt that this woman had come to them for a reason. Her generous spirit was more than willing to take on a companion and helper. The Creator knew Lander's Keep needed all the feminine influence it could get. "Now come, dear. Tell me what has befallen you."

And they sat in the two large carved chairs before the fire. Luveday rested her belongings at her feet, afraid to lose sight of them completely. She gazed into the fire, trying to gather her thoughts. She'd told Gregori little, as he had done most of the talking on the journey, no doubt to distract her. The warmth of the fire was comforting. The hearth was almost as tall as she was and twice that in width. It looked as if a whole tree burned within, in an attempt to take the chill out of the great stone structure.

Glancing over at Lady Emmalyn, Luveday had an urge to unburden her mind, but she quickly squashed the feeling. She didn't know exactly what happened to mentally unstable people in this time, but she was sure it was a fate to be avoided at all costs, and her tale was strange at best.

Clearing her throat, Luveday tried to weave believable facts into the truth of the matter. "My family is gone. I was on my way to a distant relative who has been kind enough to take me in, but I think... I am not sure. I believe that was all a lie." Luveday stumbled over her words, not knowing how credible a job she was doing. "We traveled far, farther than I've ever gone in my life, but I think it was all for the goods and little coin I had with me. The men seemed distant, and I had a feeling about them, but I thought it was just my imagination."

"That is often the case. The heart sees more than we may comprehend." Emmalyn nodded as Elli arrived with large earthenware cups full of a steaming liquid. The Lady took one, and Elli offered Luveday the other.

Elli's eyes no longer held an edge of disapproval, they now overflowed with sympathy and Luveday, not for the first time, wondered at the life of a young woman here. The girl looked to be around sixteen, yet there was something in her eyes that spoke of experience.

"My father's estate, everything, went to a distant relative. My only hope was traveling. I don't know how I ended up in the woods. I woke up in a clearing, far from the road. Lost in an unknown land."

"You must have been frightened," Elli said.

"Truthfully, I couldn't understand what was going on. I did not believe it. I didn't have time to be afraid. Sir Gregori appeared and brought me here." Luveday held the warm cup in her hands.

Emmalyn nodded, "A blessing." She sipped her tea and looked the young woman over. Yes, the woman was here for a reason. "Everything is gone?" She asked not overly concerned; they could provide something suitable for a simple Lady.

"What little I have is in these bags." She looked down at the gray backpack taking a brief stock of her possessions. She'd bought the pack a few years back because it looked more professional. It was the adult version of a backpack that was able to carry her laptop, which was back in the hotel room, yet still able to stash all the personal items she might need on the go. Annalisa, her eco-friendly, all natural, English teaching older sister had called it her mom bag. Annalisa had two beautiful girls, Abigail who was five, sandy blonde and in charge, just like her mother, and Seraphina who had just turned three and had the darker coloring and logic of their father, Mark. Annalisa had laughed because out of the two of them her own pack was truly a mom bag, with the plastic baggie full of Cheerios and the random happy-meal toys in comparison to Loveday's pack.

Luveday hadn't been insulted by her sarcastic remark because she knew it was closer to the truth than anyone realized. She organized with makeup bags and pencil cases. Thanks to their mom, she had a super-duper upgraded first aid kit along with dad's version of an emergency survival kit. Though what dangers they thought she might encounter in Sacramento, California was a mystery to her. She wasn't really suited for the zombie apocalypse, had never even touched the emergency kit that lived in the bowels of her pack and had only pulled out two band-aids from the first aid bag. Her parents lived by the motto, *be prepared*. Mom was a nurse and Dad owned his own construction business. He was a man's man and had taken the family fishing and camping in her youth, both activities Luveday had never really enjoyed for themselves. All things considered, a survival kit wasn't that ridiculous a thing to have she supposed. They might even come in handy, lost as she was.

The rest of her "mom bag" was full of the usual purse items: makeup and feminine products, some toiletries she'd thrown in for the trip, she'd had to mail them to the hotel via UPS to get around the flight regulations. There was also her wallet and day-planner, her cell phone and I-pod. What else might be floating around in there she didn't know.

The tote was a separate issue. Luveday had been window shopping on her day off in that lovely New England town and picked up two outfits at a trendy thrift store to replace the stained and damaged items that hadn't survived two days on the business trip. She'd found a cute pair of gray flats to match the new outfit of a gray blouse and vest she planned to pair with the full-length black skirt she'd also found. She'd picked up a white blouse and a navy long skirt, with a pair of Victorian looking half boots. The stop at the thrift store had been very lucrative; she had even bought the tote to carry it all in. Everything for under twenty dollars, she'd mentally patted herself on the back at the time.

Walking along the shops she had come and gone on a whim, she'd picked up some books from an old bookstore, some small items from vendors along the street. All in all, her worldly possessions didn't add up too much. The practical voice in her head said that it wouldn't get her far. She didn't want to end up like Jane Eyre, failing to sell her gloves for a round of bread and starving on the moor. She didn't have much hope for the charity of others, though looking at Lady Emmalyn she thought she might be wrong.

Luveday's mind was jostled from her thoughts as she realized that Lady Emmalyn was speaking again, though it seemed she was talking to Luveday, her voice rose several degrees, and she realized Gregori and some other men were drawing near. "Lady Luveday has agreed to stay with us. Elysant and I need the companionship." The lady stated matter-of-factly, looking between the group of women. The serving girl, Elli or Elysant, looked pleased. Luveday looked at the younger girl's kind eyes and thought she might have just found a friend on this otherworldly adventure.

The gray pea-coat landed on the arm of Luveday's chair. Startled, she looked up into the smiling face of Sir Gregori. "Welcomed news." His deep voice was sincere. "Welcome, Lady Luveday."

Smiling awkwardly at both of them, she said with all sincerity and no small amount of relief, "Thank you, Sir Gregori, Lady Emmalyn. Thank you very much. I will never forget your hospitality and generosity."

Lady Emmalyn blushed. "Oh, come now, dear." She rose and set her empty cup aside. Turning to Elli who had taken up a stool at the edge of the hearth, she wondered aloud. "Where to keep you?" She and Elli exchanged another look. The young woman's face was full of concern.

Gregori spoke first. "The guest chambers are open."

"That's no place for a lady, Sir Gregori," Elli commented, which only puzzled him.

The knight looked to the men behind him, who were listening to the conversation. They looked away without a word. "We do not have any guests at present..."

"The rooms are a disaster." It looked as if Lady Emmalyn had trouble getting the words out. "They are not fit for a dog." The sigh that came for the lady was matched in intensity by the scowl on the knight's face.

The men, giving up on whatever reason had made them linger, were suddenly scarce. Gregori watched them flee; his expression growing darker. It seemed they had momentarily forgotten about Luveday as they spoke. "The villagers have not returned?"

"A few women have come, but most avoid the keep as if they will catch the pox." Elli chimed in wiping a curling strand of brown hair behind her ear.

The knight ground his teeth. Emmalyn spoke to smooth the situation. "Can you blame them? After the folly with Steward Keen, there is no love lost between them and this castle. We are lucky Agnes, and the others work so diligently." Emmalyn straightened her gown in a nervous habit. "Truth be told, we don't have enough people to get anything done, and Elli and I know not where to start."

Gregori nodded solemnly. Luveday suddenly understood. There was a rift between the castle and the village, and nothing the lady did was helping. Luveday got the impression both women had not been in residence for long, and whatever Steward Keen had done, he was the major cause for the current strife.

Gregori turned to their new guest. "Perhaps she might stay with you, lady."

"I'm afraid that won't do, boy. I have given my room to Lady Christabel and her maid. Elli and I share the far room. Henna sometime sleeps in there as well. She cannot stay with the women in the sewing room."

Elli shook her head in agreement.

Luveday decided to speak up. "I do not need anything grand. A small space would be fine."

A light seemed to turn on in the Lady's mind. "A small room, yes." She turned to Elli who seemed to be on the same page.

Nodding the girl smiled, her light blue eyes shining. "My Lady, the room does have a window. There is a bed in there; we just need the men to move some of the other things out."

"Yes, it will work." Emmalyn declared.

Gregori looked at them with a smile. "How may I be of assistance, Ladies?"

The chill was slowly fading thanks to the brazier in the corner. The bed was low to the ground, solid wood with a rope grid to act as springs. The headboard was wide and plain, but the bed and linens were clean. The straw mattress was fresh and smelled of lavender. The rest of the long narrow room was bland being made entirely of stone. The one good thing was the gothic arched window with its heavy shutters at the far end situated over the bed. The single bed took up the width of the room, situated in the only place it could, at the back of the room beneath the window. There was also a wooden chest that looked as if it had belonged to Black Beard himself, a three-legged stool, and a carved chair, sans a cushion. Some pegs stuck out in the gaps between the stones that made up the walls, pegs to hang up her clothes, she guessed.

Luveday surveyed the room with a sense of accomplishment. Gregori looked doubtful, while Elli and Emmalyn looked tired.

"Are you sure you wish to stay in here?" The knight asked for the third time.

"It is lovely, Sir Gregori. A room of my own is no small thing." The two other women agreed, pleased with Luveday's response.

Emmalyn leaned against a table in the crowded hallway. Though Luveday would have loved to keep more furniture in the room, the large scale just didn't make it practical. Fifteen feet long and a little over six feet wide, the room's dimensions leant themselves toward minimalism.

The men returned to the top of the stairs and took the next item down. Gregori had been less than pleased when they had opened the storage room beside the Lord's solar.

Elli watched in wonder. "Where did all these pieces come from?" She had asked as they began clearing out a storage room. The women had clearly had their eyes on its contents for some time but had yet to tackle the task of looking through it. Who could blame them? The small room was packed ceiling high with furniture and odds and ends. The thick layer of dust told her this room had lain untouched for a long while.

While the men waited in the hall, the ladies wrapped large cloths around their middles like aprons. Luveday rolled up her sleeves and took off her jewelry and stashed it in her backpack nearby. No one made a move, looking at the task before them, so Luveday stepped in and started handing out anything she could reach. Gregori and two men-at-arms, one Durstan who was gruff and rather crass, and Archer who was young and clean-shaven, were there to help. Luveday had taken charge after the women seemed at a loss on how to proceed.

Furniture was pulled from the darkness of the room, piece by piece, and what was too heavy for the ladies was handed over as the men stepped in.

As the excavation had progressed, Elli and Emmalyn told her something about themselves and the lord of Lander's Keep. Emmalyn was the lord's aunt and recently widowed. "My nephew has not stayed long at the keep since it fell to him. He's always been more at home on the battlefield than here." The sad look she gave an ornately carved chair as she handed it over to one of the men spoke volumes. "I was surprised when he asked me to come to lend a Lady's presence to the Keep." She strained a little as she took a small chest from Luveday but continued. "I have been in residence for over a season, but there hasn't been enough light in the day to get everything done."

Elli commented as she sagged under the weight of a square side table. "Not with the villagers refusing to help." Gregori took the table from her with little effort while Emmalyn called her full name to chastise the child.

"I gather there is a rift between the castle and the people of the village." Luveday prompted, her natural curiosity making her a little bolder.

"A rift?" Emmalyn seemed to like that. "A chasm; 'tis a good description.

There might as well be a canyon between us and the village." Emmalyn sighed and sent up a plume of dust that sent several of them coughing. Once the dust settled and breathing became easier, she continued. "Iain has been gone for a long time. Being the King's Champion has kept him on the road, and he left the keep in the hands of an untrustworthy man."

Luveday handed Elli a large potbellied ceramic vase. "Easy there." She warned, but the girl had it. "Was he a cruel man?" She asked, imagining a man who looked like Friar Tuck and acted like Prince John.

Gregori answered as he stepped between Luveday and a large hutch and shooed the women out of the room. "No. He hid his greed well. If he had not, perhaps we would have found out before he disappeared."

Emmalyn started to wipe her brow with her apron and thought better of it. "Steward Keen seemed a kind man, diligent and hardworking, but it was a lie. He was not cruel to the villagers, but he was not overly kind to them either. Iain sent him the spoils of his tournaments, and the goods the King bestowed upon him." Emmalyn seemed wary of the tale, so Elli took it up.

"Keen kept the coin for himself and let the castle and the village rot. He acted as if Lord Iain had abandoned them. There was no coin for repairs or to pay merchants. The villagers looked to the steward as the mouth of their Lord while Iain was away. Keen continually told them that there was left nothing for improvements, nothing to ease their burden when the winter was hard, and the crops were poor."

"And they grew to despise him," Luveday stated flatly.

"They care no more for him than they think he does for them," Emmalyn said in equal defeat. "They pay their taxes, give their crops, but they give only as much as is lawful and no more."

It was understandable, but it seemed that whatever the Lady had tried to do to mend the situation had not been enough in the eyes of the villagers. Or was it the case of too little too late?

"And the steward disappeared." Luveday's statement was to herself, but it sounded more like a question.

Durstan, a gruff and dirty looking man-at-arms spoke his mind as he came to the top of the stairs once again. "The blither took off when word came that Sir Gregori and some of the lord's men were returning home. Took the coin and the good ale and fled. Didn't realize anything was amiss until Sir Gregori started demanding answers." The man laughed though not exactly happy. "Didn't know the skinny pole had it in him. He's probably to King's Point by now, drunk off his arse and tupin'...."

"Durstan!" Gregori growled in warning as he stared the man down.

Almost managing to look chagrinned, he apologized. "My 'pologizies Ladies." He turned away carrying a chair, at the landing a few steps down where the door to the Lord's solar met it at an odd angle, he stopped and looked back at them. "But you know my meanin'." He nodded at them, as Gregori came out of the storage room to glare at him in warning.

While Elli looked shocked, Lady Emmalyn looked resigned, and Sir Gregori continued to scowl at them. This was when Mistress Adela and her lady, Christabel, made their appearance. The noise coming from the hallway drew the two women.

Elli spotted them first, as they waited outside of the Lady's chamber that by all rights had been Emmalyn's. "My Lady Christabel, Mistress Adela!" Her voice was pitched to carry and warn the others of their unexpected guests.

Christabel was beautiful in that thin and pale-skinned sort of way that teenage models could attain. She looked to be around sixteen, eighteen at most. Her hair was the shiny black of a raven's wing that looked as if it would curl if not braided around her head so intricately. Her eyes were dark as well, but they were not kind. Her mouth looked like it tended towards poutiness and had a slight downward turn. The Lady was clearly unhappy though she contained it within her frame with an elegant grace.

It was Adela who spoke. "Lady Emmalyn, young Elysant. What is going on here?"

The women looked at each other. In their excitement to see what treasures might be hiding in the depths of the storeroom, they had forgotten that Lady Christabel's chambers were right next door. No one had been concerned for the guests, and no one thought to make an effort to keep the noise down. Both women were at a loss; it had taken them less than a day to find out how changeable Christabel's temperament was.

Emmalyn looked to Luveday searching for some excuse to pacify the young lady. She introduced Luveday buying time but didn't know what else to say.

"It is my fault, dear ladies." Luveday addressed Adela and her Lady, trying to copy Emmalyn's style of speech. "I have arrived unexpectedly. Lady Emmalyn wished to find me a good bed for the night. Her graciousness led to this endeavor. The storage room seemed the best place for a simple woman like me." She paused to look at the other women who waited almost impatiently. "I sincerely apologize if we have disturbed you. The task has proved to be more than it at first seemed."

Both women looked at the furniture crowding the hallway; many were in a semi-state of cleanliness. Men continued to trek up and down the stairs redistributing the furniture. Adela looked to her lady, who examined the furniture more than the women. She smiled slightly and nodded. "Carry on Lady Luveday, and Welcome to Lander's Keep." Christabel retreated into her chamber; Adela paused to look at the three women curiously. She looked Luveday over thoroughly, nodded as if she approved and then followed her mistress, closing the door behind her.

Elli and Emmalyn left out their breath in a whoosh that sent more dust swirling. Gregori had remained within the storage room, out of sight, a shadow among shadows listening to the conversation. He could see the curve if Luveday's right shoulder as she leaned back against the door frame, and Emmalyn leaned against the wall opposite the opening. He noticed when she stood taller, and when her jaw took on a hard edge. Christabel had been an attraction at court, she was a spoiled child in Gregori's eyes, but perhaps her arriving before the allotted time was not a mistake as he had supposed. There was something more to her presence, though from what he had gleaned, the lady loathed being here. A thought struck him. What if there was more than her father's eagerness to solidify the ties to Lord Iain that brought the lady here before her groom, but what good would it do to anger the Wolf?

Emmalyn and Elli both smiled at Luveday. "Well done," the lady said.

Luveday merely smiled back.

Now that the room was finally clean, Luveday unpacked the tote by dumping its contents on the bed as neatly as she could. Her new clothes were folded at the bottom, she shook them out and placed them on the hooks in the wall. Elli looked on as she unrolled a light fleece blanket that was a plum purple. She'd picked it up for her mother from a street vendor. The throw was secured by a printed brown cardboard wrap around the middle. The craft vendor had embroidered flowers around the edge, turning a five-dollar piece of material into a pretty blanket. She sat the shoes down beside the chest and sat the books on the stool. Upon seeing the volumes, Elli moved closer. There were a few wax-paper bags of jewelry. A few pieces for Annalisa who like the natural, energy-centered quality of real stone. There was also a bag of costume jewelry she'd picked up for the girls. Abigail loved playing dress up. She looked to Elli who had inched closer still.

Luveday smiled at her. There wasn't much more she could do under her companion's watchful eye. The backpack was full of odds and ends that it was probably best to go through later where medieval minds wouldn't be confused by modern day tech. She needed a distraction to get them out of the room.

As if on cue, Luveday's stomach growled. Elli laughed, only for her own stomach to make itself heard. They smiled at each other. Luveday was about to comment that she was hungry enough to eat a horse but stopped herself. Other than being un-lady-like she thought it might be possible that they actually ate horses and so kept her mouth shut. Her understanding of medieval cuisine was limited, and so it was better to be safe than sorry.

Elli solved her dilemma by offering to take her down to dinner. "The evening meal should be about ready. We should go down. Together?"

"Thank you. Together." Luveday closed the shutters on the window and then the door behind her as they left.

"Elysant. That is such a lovely name." Luveday thought it was beautiful, much like the girl. Elli blushed but smiled happily at her.

"Everyone at the castle calls me Elli." She said as if to clarify. Elli had a light complexion with light brown hair braided like a crown around her head. It was a simple style that was popular with the women back home in Luveday's time. Her face was heart shaped with a slightly pointed chin, and her nose had a small upturn at the tip. She reminded Luveday of a pixie, and the girl's wit and mischievousness only added to the image.

Luveday sat at the head table, Elli to her right, Emmalyn to her left. Gregori sat on the other side of the Lady while two places sat empty on the other side of him. Lady Christabel and Adela were taking their meals in their room for the second day in a row. In fact, they had only eaten one meal in the hall since their arrival, which Luveday learned, had been just as unexpected as her own.

The meal before her was not recognizable, and while everyone ate, they did not do so enthusiastically, even though many had worked up an appetite. A few men dined in groups of three or so at the long tables, but their presence only emphasized how empty the castle truly was.

Dinner consisted of a roundish, slightly burnt piece of flatbread that acted like a plate, a hunk of meat, and a pile of salad greens that looked half weeds and half herbs with a few flowers thrown in for color. There were bowls of something that looked like gravy, something that smelled like vinegar and looked like pickled eel. Luveday's stomach turned at the sight. The bread soaked up the juices from the meat and was rather tasty though most of the food was served cold, the meat was still warm but rather bland. Luveday ate with a strange two-pronged fork and a knife one of the women had given her. After serving the high table the women went to their own meals, either joining the men or disappearing down a flight of stairs to the kitchen. The conversation was minimal, and while Luveday answered all the questions they asked of her, she was beginning to feel the weight of the day.

Men got up to return to their posts which seemed to signal the end of the meal. Emmalyn ushered them over to the fireside, but even she seemed worn after the day's events. It was with a lighter heart that the three women said goodnight to each other. Luveday watched Emmalyn and Elli disappear into their room down the hall before closing her own door.

Making her way carefully to the window, she knelt on the bed to pull open the shutters. The castle was dark and cold, but the light from the moon was strong enough for her to see a bit more of the room. She pulled out her pack, opened it and started to go through the contents. The cell phone still had power though, not surprisingly, no signal. It was a work phone and had its own hotspot, but there was still nothing for it to connect with. She made sure it was on silent before stashing it in a space behind her headboard. It might be good to count her time here. She hid her I-pod in easy reach of her pillow. She pulled out a pair of boxer shorts, a long-sleeved cotton top and the spare socks and underwear she kept in the bottom of the laptop holder. Not only did they cushion her laptop, but they were there for emergencies. They made convenient nightclothes.

Undressing was the least of her worries. She took off a pair of gold flats and the blue tights she'd worn for modesty and slipped on the shorts. Her skirt was high waisted, and the vest gave her more of a Victorian feel than the velvets and wools that the other women wore. Luveday wore a sports bra over her pushup bra to keep the latter from moving around. She put on the white cotton shirt, it was baggy, and she had bought it a few sizes larger just to be sure it fit. She wouldn't consider herself fat, but she wasn't skinny either. Losing some weight recently had made her feel better about herself but hadn't made a big impact on her wardrobe. She hung the clothes up and stored her bra in the tote that hung from its hook.

She sat on the bed, turned on her wind-up emergency flashlight and began sorting through her backpack. Makeup bag. Check. The toiletries included her crystal deodorant, animal-friendly perfume and all-natural lotion, all courtesy of Annalisa. Check. Okay, the other bag of toiletries which included a toothbrush with paste and nail kit. Check. Hair Supplies. Check. Emergency kit. She sat that aside to go through later. First Aid Kit. Double Check. Bag of medications. She thought about taking an Aleve but decided against it. Her headache wasn't that bad. Waste not, want not; she chimed to herself. Altogether her supplies were rather impressive; one might even say she had planned for something like this, and perhaps they were right.

Along with her items were things for work. A few notebooks of different sizes, her day planner, pencil case with a bevy of supplies. There was the folder with the meeting agendas and hotel information. She found some snacks; a few protein bars, some fruit leathers, three half-empty packs of gum, two tins of mints, and two large handfuls of individually wrapped ginger candy that had migrated to the bottom of her bag. Two more books joined the pile on the stool. The first was the complete works of Elizabeth Barrett Browning. Annalisa knew her soft spot for romantic poets and old books, while the other was a romance novel she'd picked up at the airport after she'd finished the two she'd brought on the plane. She looked at the titles of the other three books, The Bloody Chamber by Angela Carter was a collection of retellings of the old fairytales. Luveday had read it in college and found it at the bookstore for a few bucks. There was a journal, the sticker price tag labeled it the celestial journal, which she had purchased to add to Annalisa's birthday gifts. The cover was an exotic and beautiful shade of blue that had made her think of the deep Indian ocean. A color she imagined coming out of some hot, arid climate on the back of pack horses along the silk road. Embossed on the cover was a swirling pattern of gold that reminded her of a Persian rug. A gold clasp held the book closed. She'd picked up a quill and ink set to go with it, rounding out the gift set. It looked like Luveday would be using it instead.

The light began to fade so Luveday spent a minute winding up the lever on the flashlight. The final book was another gift for Annalisa; The Complete Medical Herbal by Penelope Ody. Annalisa had asked her to keep a lookout for such books to add to her growing home remedy collection.

She stashed her solar charger, another gift from her dad, in the pouch that held her travel chargers and extra electronic add-ons and stuffed them down with her phone. The work stuff went back in her bag; she'd put it in the trunk later. Toiletries went on top of the chest for in the morning. With the bed now clear, she pulled back the covers and did a once-over before laying down. The decorative blanket was over the thick wool and linen sheets. They weren't smooth like her cotton ones at home, but they were comfortable.

Turning off the light, she looked out the window, no glass just open air. She was loathed to close it, even though the breeze was cold. Luveday had a habit of going over her to-do lists before she went to sleep, but tonight that proved unsettling rather than a comfort. There wasn't much she could plan for with all the unknowns. She doubted she would somehow wake in her own bed and hoped to make the most of her current situation. The best she could do was hope that she could be useful here. Useful meant she wouldn't be forced out into the world with nowhere to go. Useful meant a roof overhead, food in her belly, and a chance at finding out why she was here and how she could get home.

What-ifs and doubts assailed her. Concerns for her family, friends, her condo, her car. Her life in the other world and what would happen the longer she was lost in this one. She shut down her thoughts, focused on the things in front of her. *Tomorrow, you must learn about Lander's Keep, learn about this country, learn about its people. Be useful, be helpful, be someone they can depend on. And don't lie, lies will trip you up.* That was about all she could do. Luveday turned over, facing the wall below the window she looked up, perhaps the deep windowsill would be a good place to charge her phone if she found something to conceal it. She then promptly shut out the rest of the world and fell asleep much sooner than she would have believed possible.

Life at Lander's Keep was everything that Luveday had imagined and then some. Living without running water or electricity was okay for a weekend; modern inventions made it fun to go camping in nylon tents with eco-friendly everything packed into your lightweight, waterproof, space-saving pack. Life in a medieval castle had the trappings of civilization and none of the amenities.

A woman appeared with a pitcher of water, luckily Luveday was an early riser, or the woman would have walked in without preamble to find her sleeping. That thought disturbed Luveday a good deal, but there was no latch on her door, and she felt it wasn't her place to ask. Not yet at least.

Privacy was a non-issue, meaning no one thought about it a wit, except Luveday. A brief trip to the garderobe was as disgusting as she imagined, at least state parks had that blue liquid to help with sanitation. She shuddered to think of the smell in the summer. Once back in her room, Elli arrived with a handful of garments.

"Your clothes are very fine but too light for this time of year." She laid out a gray wool gown, white undergarments, and a shift. Elli chatted while she helped Luveday dress. "Lady Christabel is a late riser, but she has barely left that room since she arrived. I guess the castle was not what she was expecting, though we weren't expecting her arrival until late summer when the betrothal time had started; that the King had given the Lady a choice was probably Lord Iain's doing. He had plans you see, plans to get the castle restored before she came."

"Is that why Sir Gregori said he would not be pleased?" Luveday asked as she was laced up from behind.

"That and the fact that he wanted to give her a proper welcome. No one was there to greet her. There was no fanfare as is fitting the lord's bride. It's a sad start to things." Elli turned her around admiring her work. "There, all done."

Luveday looked down at herself. The gown fit her in most places. It was a little long, but not too much. The gown's quality fell somewhere in between Lady Emmalyn's serviceable velvet and Mistress Agnes from the kitchen with her coarser wool. The fabric was soft, and the gown well made. She felt as if it would help her to fit in better and that was nice in itself. "Thank you, Elli."

"You are welcome, Lady Luveday." She smiled and rushed to open the door. "Lady Emmalyn wanted to see you in the kitchens if you were awake."

Luveday grabbed a pair of gray fingerless gloves and her yellow scarf from the pocket of her jacket before following the girl out.

The kitchen was a massive affair, something befitting the castle, though dark and rather quiet. Agnes spoke to Emmalyn as a few women did busy-work around them. Both turned as Elli and Luveday entered the room.

The women greeted each other. Luveday was as polite as she could be, but she was distracted and looked around in wonder. The kitchen indoors? She hadn't realized she had spoken aloud until Emmalyn answered her.

"Aye, not many of its kind. We bake the bread in a separate house, but most of the cooking is done here. Easier to get it to the table hot."

"Yes, that is wise. Do you worry about fires?" Luveday asked.

Agnes answered in her gruff voice. "We keep a good watch and if tended well nothing will get out of hand." Luveday thought the cook's words had a double meaning, but she wasn't sure.

Luveday was eager to prove herself. "What can I do to help?"

Agnes eyed her sharply. "You wish to help, lady?" The cook seemed wary, but Luveday couldn't tell if it was because she was an interloper or a lady.

"I will earn my keep," Luveday stated honestly.

Agnes and Emmalyn exchanged looks, while the cook's expression did not change, Emmalyn smiled happily. "Good girl. We have plenty of work to go around."

Emmalyn gave her an apron and set her to chopping this or that. Luveday cleaned off the area where she was to work and taking up the basket of vegetables, she found them still covered in dirt. So, she went in search of water and found the well in the bailey out the side door of the kitchen. She brought in two buckets of water and returned the pails to the well before washing the fruit and starting to chop. The knife she used was large and thick with a wicked looking edge that certainly got the job done. She worked fast having grown up in a household where everyone pitched in.

Emmalyn gave her a cup of tea in a large earthenware mug. While it wasn't as good as her coffeepot at home, the hot liquid worked wonders as it flooded her insides with warmth. "Lovely," was all she said as she got back to work.

The women stopped for breakfast and served the men as well. Gregori was glad to see Luveday up with the rest of the ladies, though Christabel's continued absence clearly displeased him. Luveday got the notion that he was not upset for himself, but on behalf of his friend, Lord Iain. Apparently, this was not the behavior of a proper wife.

"Back to work." Elli proclaimed after her porridge was gone.

Luveday followed while Emmalyn talked to Gregori. The bits of conversation that carried over to her seemed to be about the future lady of the keep. Luveday had too much to think about to wonder about someone else's problems. The day moved on at a grinding pace. She met three other women in the castle, Henna, whose red hair looked glorious on her and was similar in age to Elli. A slip of a girl was supposedly the best seamstress around. Beatrice was a dark-haired, buxom beauty, wearing a gown with a daring neckline. The woman reminded Luveday of a lusty barmaid; the comparison was rather stereotypical of her, but she couldn't shake the connection. Beatrice didn't seem to care for Luveday on sight, though they barely spoke two words to each other. Last was Paige who was friendly enough. She kept her head down and did her work and didn't really talk to anyone. Her traits reminded Luveday of a country mouse from those children's stories, but in a flattering way.

Luveday scrubbed pots and pans with lye soap that stung her hands and whipped off tables and swept floors but there was little improvement. As soon as one thing was done, it was time to start the next.

By the end of the day she was exhausted and ready to find her bed. Emmalyn and Elli had been right beside her. Mistress Adela had been the gopher for her lady who, yet again, refused to leave her chambers for more than a brief walk in the sunshine.

Though proud and beautiful, Luveday got the impression that Christabel was terribly unhappy, more so than just a childish refusal to join the rest of the group. Something troubled the lady. And for some reason, Luveday cared.

The next day dawned bright. Luveday washed in a bowl she'd received from Agnes. The woman had appeared and handed her a wooden bowl and a pitcher full of water with only the words, "For your room." Then turned and walked away. Luveday suspected that was her seal of approval, as she carried the new items up to her room. The water was welcome, though Luveday missed a proper shower, she hesitated to ask about a bath.

Dressed all by herself, she felt a sense of accomplishment as she met Elli on the stairs. "Good morning, Elysant."

The girl smiled and changed direction, clearly going up to retrieve Luveday. "Good morrow, Lady Luveday." She was just as cheerful this morning. "Lady Emmalyn asks you to meet her in the kitchen again."

"On my way. Thank you." The girl turned back to her as she called out. "Oh, and Elli, you can call me Luveday." Elli smiled wide, as Luveday was about to stride away across the hall Sir Gregori greeted her.

"Good Morrow, Lady Luveday. Up bright and early, I see." He smiled at her but watched Elli. "Good Morrow, Elli."

"Good Morrow, Sir Gregori." Both women said in unison, causing all three to chuckle.

"It's good to see you lovely young ladies in such good spirits." He said off handedly and excused himself. "I have some exercises for the men this morning."

"Until later, Sir Gregori," Luveday replied and walked off, noticing that Elli started and rushed off to catch up with her.

The day progressed much like the last, but Luveday was given different assignments, a few of which she had to ask about before completing. Kitchen work was roughly the same no matter in what era one lived.

Luveday didn't keep her questions at bay. She asked about the herbs they cooked with, went out to see the spring garden. She asked about candles and cooking meals. She asked about sewing garments and tending crops. They seemed happy to answer her questions, mostly because she listened intently to everything they had to say. Usually, it only took one time for them to explain something and Luveday had it down.

By the third day, the kitchen was in decent order, though the garden was looking poorly. Luveday knew a bit about a lot of things including gardening, and more recently organic gardening thanks to Annalisa. In the warming air, the women went out to tend the raised beds. Instead of stone containers, wood held in the dirt for the beds. Wooden stakes were driven into the ground every few feet and twigs woven through them like a great wicker basket. The natural structure did its job, creating raised garden beds.

Emmalyn and Elli worked on each side of her, pointing out what was edible, what was medicine and what could be weeded out. A good deal of things she would have tossed had medical properties; other things she would never have eaten ended up on the castle's table. Emmalyn seemed pleased with her interest.

"And what is this?" The lady asked, holding up a green stem with rows of unopened flowers.

Luveday thought a moment and recited back what the lady had said earlier. "Figwort. Used for the cleansing of abscesses and poisons in the body. Good for cleaning the skin. Used to make tinctures, infusions, and washes. Helps with redness and dots on the skin."

Emmalyn smiled, "Good. And this?" She held up a twig with a flowering top that reminded Luveday of yellow baby's breath. This one was easier to remember as she's heard about the plant before. "Elder. Good for coughs and throat mucus, fever and chills. Brewed in infusions, creams for chapped hands, tinctures for fever, and washes for inflammation. Berries are good for..." She had to think a minute. "Syrup and wine to help with coughs."

Elli smiled at her.

"Very Good, Lady," Emmalyn commented.

Elli plucked a few things to add to her basket. "Are you sure you do not know of healing plants?" The girl asked.

"My sister is..." Luveday paused before correcting herself. "My sister was the one to learn about healing herbs. I listened but paid her no mind." Luveday smiled sadly. Thinking to herself, how long would it be before she went home? A part of her worried how easily she fitted in here.

Trying to comfort her, Emmalyn patted her on the shoulder. "You learn fast, girl. That is good."

Agnes growled at the plants before her. "Look at this." She held up a puny looking plant. Luveday couldn't tell if anything was wrong or not. Emmalyn clucked in disapproval.

"Lady, the garden is doing poorly this year. Second year in a row. What will we do when summer comes, and we are overrun with guests?"

"We will meet that task when it gets here and not before, Agnes." The Lady said.

Agnes glared at the garden as if she could intimidate it back to health. Mumbling under her breath, she took her basket back inside. The women continued to putter around the beds. Luveday took a closer look, curious and ready to put some of her know-how to use.

The beds weren't infested with any pest that she could see. There was some bug damage, but without pesticides, there would be. The plants were spaced apart, well-watered but the soil quality looked poor. It was not the dark, rich earth one bought in bags at the local home improvement store. There was little green matter. Thanks to one semester of plant and soil science and Annalisa's all-natural food crisis, Luveday knew what to do about it. She shoveled up buckets of ash, and chicken manure and began mixing them into the soil around the plants. She watered afterward. The women gave her wary looks but let her do as she wished.

Satisfied she returned to the keep with the rest of the group.

"Well, what do you say, Luveday?" Emmalyn asked.

Luveday was caught off guard by the suggestion. Learning to heal was a skill that would be more than useful. It could be life-changing. She had more than a basic idea of standard medical practices thanks to her mother. She was good at learning new things and retained knowledge like a sponge. She was even surprisingly good at handling blood, which she'd found out when Annalisa split open her foot after stepping on some glass as a teen. She had a certificate for CPR from babysitting, not that her mom hadn't already taught her basic first aid and the Heimlich maneuver by age twelve. There were cons. Definitely, plague and death were the first to pop into her mind, but realistically she might be able to handle it. Taking a deep breath, she heard herself say, "It would be my honor to learn from you, Lady Emmalyn."

The lady smiled at the formality. The girl had an odd way of phrasing things, and her accent was strange, but Emmalyn had yet to find a reason to dislike the girl. In fact, the last few days had proved her first impressions to be sound. "I don't know how much of an honor it will be, child. But if you are diligent, I have a feeling you may surpass even my skills."

Elli looked on happily. "Another healing woman will be a good thing for the village." Elysant had jumped at the idea when Emmalyn had suggested it last night before bed. Luveday was a strange lady, like none Elli had ever met, not that she had met many, but she liked the new lady, much more so than Christabel, though Elli was trying to give the young lady the benefit of the doubt. She knew court ladies would find the keep a disgrace, far from the lavishness they were used to. Even at its finest, she wondered if the castle would ever suit its future lady.

The next day was more hard work with its own challenges and the evening was quieter than usual as the women waited for Luveday to talk about her short stay with Lady Christabel. Elli looked at Luveday, wondering what the two ladies had talked about earlier that day. Elli had brought up refreshments in the afternoon, only to find Luveday at the court lady's door when she knocked.

Luveday knew that Elli was curious, but she need not have been concerned. Lady Christabel was little more than a child. Not in age, where she had confirmed her seventeen summers and to Luveday that was nearly an adult, for medieval times that might be getting on to middle-aged.

Earlier in the afternoon, after dropping her jacket off in her room, Luveday had been startled to find Mistress Adela in the corridor waiting for her. "My Lady wishes to speak with you for a while, Lady Luveday."

Surprised did not begin to describe Luveday's feelings. "It would be my pleasure, Mistress Adela." She closed the door behind her and straightened her gown.

Adela smiled in reassurance. While stern in appearance, Mistress Adela was more of a hen protecting her chick then a bear. Luveday got the idea that the woman was trying to smooth things over between her lady and the castle, but the woman could only do so much. The Mistress ushered her in, announcing her as she closed the door behind them.

Luveday had not seen the interior of the chamber before, but it was everything she had imagined a medieval lady's room to be. Tapestry's hung on the walls, velvet curtains on the sturdy looking bed, cushioned chairs and footstools, large chests and hefty side tables lent the room a rich and full feeling. There was no fireplace in this room, but a brazier kept it from being chilly. Looking at the lady, she bowed slightly, not quite a curtsey, but Luveday acknowledged the fact that Christabel was above her station. "My Lady. It is a pleasure to meet you finally." Luveday opted for formality, not knowing the protocol of court, she thought it was the safest bet.

"Lady Luveday, Adela has told me something about you. Please sit." A sort of sitting area was before the large open brazier. The fire was rather lively, though not emitting a lot of heat as Luveday took a chair next to the lady. A small side table rested between them. Luveday noticed the chairs angled toward each other for better conversation. "I have heard of the misfortune that brought you here." The lady seemed deeply concerned. "I am so sorry that such a fate has befallen you and so happy you have found your way here. Fate could have been much crueler." The lady's eyes grew distant, and Luveday wondered if something hadn't marred Christabel's fortune. "But please, on to happier things. You are settling in well I take it."

"Yes, Lady, I am happy to have found such hospitality and such a generous lady as Lady Emmalyn," Luveday spoke matter-of-factly, not wanting to gush in front of another woman.

"I hear you have come from afar." Christabel prompted.

Luveday had been building her back-story, converting her life into medieval terms that these people could understand. "Indeed. The journey took many days; it seemed we had been on the road forever. I cannot tell you where home is from here, but it is far away."

"Over the sea, or so I am told. The way you speak is very unusual." Adela coughed catching the ladies' attention. Luveday thought it might have been a warning to the lady, but for what she couldn't say.

"Yes. The journey was rough at times, but I was not overly troubled by sickness."

"Lucky. I have heard that wave sickness is hard on a woman. Some of the ladies at court have been terribly ill on such voyages, or so they profess. Lady Ann said she would rather die than undertake such a journey again." Christabel looked at Luveday as if she suddenly realized something and seemed to change directions. "Did you have a chance to visit court, Lady Luveday?"

Luveday smiled, not wanting to give away anything. "I have not had the pleasure, Lady Christabel. I hear it is a marvelous place. "

"Oh, indeed." Christabel warmed to her subject and began to recount everything from food and dress, to parties and funny antics of court life. The quick visit Luveday had hoped for was turning into something much longer. Luveday tried to listen attentively, not because she was overly interested in court affairs, but because she realized that Christabel needed someone to talk to. With Emmalyn being in the enemy camp, as it were, and Elli being somewhere between a servant and a lady, Luveday was the only one to fill the position of an acceptable companion. So, she listened, aware of how much being cooped up in this room was probably driving the young lady mad with boredom.

It was with a sense of relief that she heard a knock at the door, and offered to answer, letting Adela continue her needlework. Elli had brought up the Lady's afternoon drink, with some cheese and fruit, Luveday took the tray from her and had the urge to beg the girl for some excuse to leave. The look she sent her had left a confused expression on the girl's face as she thanked Elli and closed the door again at Christabel's behest.

Declining to join in on the refreshments, Luveday made her excuses and left, telling the lady she would be happy to talk with her again.

Later that evening the events of that stay were the talk of the castle. Lady Emmalyn had not seemed offended that she had not been invited to chat with the young lady, though Luveday thought the woman knew more of what was going on with Lady Christabel than anyone.

Gregori joined them at the fireside and began whittling away at a chunk of wood. Luveday could see it taking shape but had yet to identify its new form. It was he that broached the topic of the secluded lady. "Has Lady Christabel health improved this afternoon, Lady Luveday?"

Luveday looked on as a few of the women hovered to hear her reply and could barely contain her smile. "I was unaware that Lady Christabel was feeling ill. She merely wished to ask about how I came to the castle. We talked for a bit. She told me a lot about her time at court."

Elli and the women seemed intrigued, all except Lady Emmalyn and Agnes. Elli moved from her stool by the fire to sit near Luveday. "What did she say court was like?"

Thinking back to all she had learned from the other lady, Luveday recounted a few funny tales, things she thought would entertain the women. The tale of a courtesan that had snuck into the King's carriage to hide under one of the benches, only to be trapped there, was the first that came to mind. Even Lady Emmalyn laughed. "And the King left none the wiser."

"So, Lady Hanna and her dog were both stuck in the carriage all day?" Elli asked clearly entertained, and Luveday nodded, happy to make her new friend laugh.

"I don't imagine she'll make the same mistake twice." Lady Emmalyn chuckled to herself.

"One would hope not. I suppose these court ladies will do anything to be noticed." Luveday could imagine the sort of antics they could get up too and almost shuddered.

Sir Gregori chimed in, "Aye. Some have gone to unusual lengths to gain the favor of the King. Though they have calmed down since he took his Queen."

"Queen Augusta will not put up with their tricks. She is a strong and sensible Queen." Emmalyn seemed to have respect for the woman. From what Christabel had said, Luveday thought the royal couple was rather young though they had four sons.

"It sounds wonderful!" Elli sighed longingly. "Don't you wish you could go, Luveday?"

"No," Luveday stated a little too vehemently.

"Why not?" The girl asked, clearly shocked. To Elli court was a magical place, Luveday could see the wonder shining in her eyes. For Luveday, it represented something else entirely.

She spoke bluntly. "I shouldn't be comfortable there. Who am I compared to those fine ladies? I wouldn't know how to act. No doubt I would insult half the court before the first day was through," She laughed in self-deprecation. "Then where would I be?"

Lady Emmalyn laughed, but Elli just shook her head. "You would do fine, Luveday. I know you would."

Luveday was touched by the girl's faith in her. "Thank you, Elli. With you there, I am sure it would not be so terrible."

Lady Emmalyn rose to her feet, as the bell from the abbey tolled the hour. "Town is not so pleasant a place, youngling. It is full up of people, foul air, and foul tempers, and yet it can be a magical place. Men come from across the sea to speak with the King, merchants from distant shores sell their wares. You will never see so many colors of fabrics in your life, nor so many different people to match them. But enough of that now, it is time for bed. Off with you!" She waved them away.

Gregori rose and bowed to the women wishing them a good night. Emmalyn stopped to talk to Agnes before she too headed off to bed. Luveday went to sleep imagining herself lost in a ballroom full of brightly garbed men and women, dressed to the nines, and dancing in a kaleidoscope of color. She looked for a familiar figure but could never catch more than a glimpse of a tall and masculine form, though she tried all night.

Chapter 2

Measure not the work until the day's out and the labor done...
~Elizabeth Barrett Browning

The days formed a routine. Luveday was up a little after dawn and worked beside Elli and Lady Emmalyn to make the castle more hospitable. Though they seemed to make little headway, they persevered. A few more women had arrived to work at the castle having heard of the ladies' diligence, but there was still so much to be done. Over a fortnight had passed since her arrival when Luveday learned of Lady Christabel's departure.

Mistress Adela stuttered as she handed off a small trunk waiting to go on the wagon. "My Lady has an old acquaintance at the Abbey, within the Cloister of the Heavenly Maiden. A fortnight is not so long a stay."

It was clear to Luveday that Mistress Adela was making more excuses for her lady. The woman looked as if she thought leaving now was a foolish idea, and yet was helpless to change the girl's mind. Over the last few days, Christabel had shown herself to be a gracious lady one moment and a spoiled brat the next. She was a lady who had obviously always gotten her way. When the women could not provide what Christabel asked for it was up to Mistress Adela, and more recently Luveday, to shield the others from the young woman's temper.

"The journey is not long," The Mistress continued as a large trunk was removed from the hall. "We will be there this afternoon."

Luveday watched as all of the pair's possessions were carted downstairs then loaded onto their wagon. For a short journey and a quick visit, was it not odd that they took everything with them? Luveday had nothing to say on the matter; it wasn't her place.

Elli was upset for Lady Emmalyn as they waved farewell to the departing women with all the fanfare Christabel believed she deserved. Elli's smile did not last as long as some of the other women who were, in fact, happy to see the lady go, if only for a few days respite. "Took everything." Elysant huffed as she picked up her skirts and marched back into the keep. "As if we'd take something of hers when she left it behind."

"Now, Elli..." Lady Emmalyn tried to placate the girl's temper, even if she secretly agreed with her pique. "I am sure Lady Christabel meant no insult. She is not used to a strange place like this, and perhaps she will dine with fine lords at the Abbey. You know they often stop there to take a night's rest and visit the Mother Superior." Emmalyn's voice dropped, and Luveday got the impression that the Lady did not like the Head of the Cloister of the Heavenly Maiden. "The fine ladies there will be better company than we three, and with the Lady absent we can focus on what needs to be done." Emmalyn finished matter-of-factly as they headed back into the keep.

"You mean instead of taking care of her every whim!" Elli was not going to let go of her anger just yet. "Emmalyn, you did not hear what the Lady said to Luveday before she left." Her small feet stomped across the great hall after the lady in question.

All eyes turned to Luveday who was clearing the morning tea off the table before the hearth. She looked up startled by the sudden attention and a little guilty. She knew exactly what Elli was talking about. The List. Luveday had hoped to wait and discuss it with Lady Emmalyn before anyone else got wind of it. Obviously, she was not going to be so lucky.

"And what did the lady say to you, Luveday?" But she didn't get the opportunity to answer Emmalyn's solemn inquiry; Elli did it for her.

The young woman was building up to being irate. "She left Luveday with a list! A list of chores! What did she say...?" Elli's face turned sour. "Yes, I remember. As the future lady of the keep, she should see that these things be done before her return. As if we didn't know what needs to be done!" Elli took the tray of tea items out of Luveday's hands and stormed off to the kitchen muttering to herself all the way.

Luveday had never seen the cheerful girl so upset, especially on behalf of another. She hoped Elli would calm down somewhere between the kitchen and coming back.

Emmalyn shooed the women away and gestured for Luveday to take a seat. The deep and weary sigh that escaped the lady as she sat down reminded Luveday that Emmalyn was under a good deal of pressure at the moment. "I am sorry that the lady has burdened you with so much, Luveday."

Protesting Luveday countered, "It is not so much, and the lady is very lonely."

Emmalyn nodded. "Elli is right to be so upset; it is not a good sign that Lady Christabel did not stay. That she took everything with her and doesn't trust us to look after her belongings, is even worse. The women will be hard to handle after that. And yet Lady Christabel is in her rights as well. She will be the lady of Lander's Keep; she is its lady in everything, but name, now. The betrothal is sealed." Emmalyn mumbled to herself, but Luveday was able to catch the words. "What was that boy thinking." A delicate hand raised to rub her brow. "We will get someone to read the list. Sir Gregori is good with letters; perhaps he would be so kind..."

Luveday pulled the roll of parchment from a pocket and looked at the list. She was not sure if the lady or Mistress Adela had penned the lines there, but the handwriting was a little better than chicken scratches. Luckily, Luveday's boss had horrible penmanship as well and deciphering the words had only taken her a few moments. It was not a list as Luveday would describe one, there were no numbers or neat rows, and it was more like a paragraph of short, misspelled items. Unfortunately, the items on the list were rather, well, selfish. Not that Luveday should have expected more from Christabel, though for some reason, she had. "The lady doesn't want anything too extravagant, though where we are to find most of these food items I haven't the foggiest. Perhaps the Boar's Head might have something. Otherwise, it is mostly chores like airing her mattress, sweeping her room, stitching new cushions for her chair and what not." Looking up, she found Emmalyn looking at her with a strange expression.

"You can read the list?" She asked quietly.

It never crossed Luveday's mind that the ability to read was something she should perhaps keep to herself. "Of course, though the handwriting is very poor." Luveday smiled at the older woman and was confused by the lopsided smile she was given in return until it bloomed into a full-fledged grin. Something flashed in the other woman's eyes, and Luveday got the feeling that something was about to change...

Luveday addressed the women in Lady Emmalyn's absence. The two had planned the next few days well, and God willing, much would get done to repair the rift between the castle and their lord. With all of the calm she could muster, Luveday gave the women their marching orders. Emmalyn had given her full discretion as she left to join Lady Christabel at the Abbey. The elder woman's trip was not to visit, but to procure some of the goods left behind by the women who joined the cloister and gave up their earthly possessions. Mother Superior got the pick of the best items to furnish her sitting rooms, but the rest went into storage. Over the years of neglect, the keep was stripped of most of its furnishings, and it was in dire need of sprucing up. Emmalyn hoped she could negotiate a fair trade from her old nemesis, Mary Odilia, now Mother Superior, while Luveday managed the work on the keep.

A letter had arrived the night before, accompanied by a small band of men. The King had sent masons and three wagons of supplies to help repair the weathering stones of Lander's Keep. A nearby query would provide the necessary raw materials.

"Good morning to you all." Luveday looked around at the expectant faces; even a few men had gathered to see what was going on. "As Lady Emmalyn departed this morning, she has news from the Lord De Lane and Lady Christabel, the future Lady of Lander's Keep." There were mumbles and some groans but mostly looks of interest. "The castle is in need of your help." More mumbling, Luveday took a deep breath and pushed on. She hoped to appeal to their pride in their home and wondered if it would help to cancel out their hostility to their lord. Perhaps they might even take pity on him. She realized this was a bit of underhanded manipulation, but whatever would get the job done. "Lord De Lane is to be married before fall, and the celebration is to be here. As the King's Champion it wouldn't be farfetched to think we might be graced with a royal guest!" Now there was some excitement in the group. "We must work hard and diligently to make sure the castle and village are ready for such a visit." The excitement dimmed as they looked around at their few numbers. "I know how hard you all have worked, day in and day out, and you are right, there is not enough of us to meet this task." No one interrupted her, but Luveday paused to take a deep breath. "So, Lady Christabel has offered this promise to you, her future people." Luveday briefly wondered if they could tell she was lying through her teeth. "Should the village rise to help their lord in this time of need, she too will help the village. One week of labor in the castle and the lady has said that the village will get the help it needs to repair the cottages and to build a village garden to rival what the castle's garden once was. The daily meals will be prepared here at the castle for those who work. All are called to come." There was some more mumbling, and many turned away for quickly whispered conversation to their fellow women.

"Anyone may come and help clean the castle, and will be fed?" Henna asked warily.

"Anyone old enough to work will be fed for their efforts, and once the week is done, the village will be repaired as well. All in preparation for the coming wedding." Luveday replied and was happy to see that the women were pleased. So, she continued. "Your men may take a break from their fields. I ask only that you give a full day's work. We have much to do, and summer is nearly upon us. We start with the first bell tomorrow morning."

Agnes nodded at her as the women disbanded and went back to their tasks. Elli was excited and chatted with Gregori as they watched the women go. Gregori turned to her, a twinkle in his eyes. "A fine speech to rally the troops, Lady Luveday." The knight observed.

"I hope so, Sir Gregori. I hope the castle is teeming with people tomorrow." Luveday joined them by the large doors near the bottom of the staircase. "Is there any news of the missing mason?"

The knight's expression darkened. The Lord's letter had said a good deal more than Gregori had imparted to the ladies. One of the more interesting bits of news was that the King's masons were to join a head mason already in residence. It appeared that he had been sent to them before the last steward had disappeared. From the sound of it, Lord Iain believed the man had been hard at work since he arrived several months ago. The only problem was that none of them had seen heads nor tails of a mason, especially not a master builder. Gregori had been angry ever since he had read the news, taking it as yet another betrayal of his friend's trust. He had spent most of the morning trying to track down the man's whereabouts. Sir Gareth, a friend, and trusted knight swore he had delivered the mason safe and sound into the hands of the steward himself; what happened after that was anyone's guess.

"I have yet to lay eyes on the man, but many remember a well-dressed young man who arrived around the time of Sir Gareth's visit. He was last seen around the castle and village, but none remember much more. No work was begun on the walls, or we would not be in this state now." Gregori looked out the open door to the group of masons unloading their tools and beginning to measure the task at hand. "The men are hesitant to start without a master to guide them. They were assured Master Alexander would be present; many looked forward to working with him." The knight's voice dropped to a growl. Another reason for Gregori to detest the steward.

Elli, with her eternal optimism, smiled and offered a ray of hope. "I am sure you will find him, Sir Gregori, and tomorrow we return Lander's Keep to its former beauty!" Then she promptly excused herself and left for the kitchens to check the mood of the women there. Both smiled as they watched her go.

"I am sure Elysant is right." Luveday turned back to look up at the tall knight. "Can the masons not start on the minor repairs without the master's supervision? Surely there is something they can do until we find him..."

Gregori nodded and squared his shoulders. "I will see what can be done. Good day, Lady." And the knight was gone again. Luveday had gotten used to his brisk ways. It was not that he was a hard man, just rather quiet and to the point. He was educated, having spent his youth in a monastery, under the watchful eye of his elder brother. At some point, he had met the young lord of Lander's Keep and decided to become a knight. He enjoyed reading, practicing his skills with a blade, was always chivalrous to the ladies regardless of station and had a great love for one pixyish young woman who ran around the castle. This love was not unrequited as Luveday was sure that Elysant was just as head-over-heels for him as he was for her, though they didn't seem to see the longing looks they gave each other. Luveday shook her head and sighed. It was no use daydreaming about such things; the young couple would figure it out eventually; Lady Emmalyn would see to it if no one else did. Right now, there was work to be done.

The next morning dawned clear and crisp. Breakfast was light and served from the fireplace in the great hall. Luveday spent the previous afternoon collecting tools, supplies, and information about what work needed to be done. The list seemed to grow ever longer. She knew a good deal of the work ahead because much of the repairs were obvious. Anyone could see the dirt in the hall, the garbage in the outer bailey, or the crumbling mortar on a few sections of the walls. It was the things she didn't know to look for that were piling up; not to mention the repairs for the village and preparations for their garden. Luveday had thought it a generous and important gift that the villagers would take to heart. What better way to help them then by feeding them, and providing for their future? Lady Emmalyn had thought it a good idea before she left, though neither really understood the scope of such a task. Now she almost wished she could take it back, but what else was there to offer in return?

The morning had arrived. As Sir Gregori opened the keeps main doors, Luveday's heart was filled with trepidation. She feared the courtyard would be empty, that the villagers had once and for all abandoned all hope in the keep. Almost afraid to look, Luveday took a deep breath and moved outside. Gregori had stopped in front of her, his massive frame blocking the courtyard from view. He stepped aside and turned to smile down at her. It was such a full, and joyous smile that she momentarily forgot about anything else until he turned back to the yard.

Confused and curious, Luveday looked out too and was at a loss for words. The courtyard of the inner bailey was full of people. Young and old, men, women, and children. Suddenly, Elli was at her elbow holding on so tight she feared the girl might take off her arm. They grinned at each other like idiots, but they were too happy to care. The village had come.

People looked on expectantly as Luveday moved forward to address the crowd. She introduced herself, thanked them for coming to her aid and split them into groups. She spoke, so her voice carried over the yard, and she spoke for so long her throat began to ache, but what she said she couldn't remember. She had the feeling she did well, that her words reached the people, but she couldn't have repeated it if her life depended on it. As she fielded more questions and set people to their tasks, first Elli, then Agnes was at her side telling her what a good job she had done. Luveday thanked them and kept organizing groups and handing out supplies.

Children helped to scrub floors while men constructed a wooden scaffold to reach the highest and darkest corners of the Hall. The first day focused on the kitchen and great hall. Food was collected the night before, and cooking moved to the summer kitchen outdoors as women began scrubbing and polishing every surface of the massive kitchen. Luveday pitched in where she could but stopped often to answer questions. Did they need to move this or that? Did they need more help in this area? Did they have more rags, more lemon, and vinegar? Time flew by as they worked together with amiable chatter.

As Luveday stopped scrubbing a particularly stubborn stain to answer another question, a man appeared at her elbow. She recognized one of the masons, as they had shared a few meals since their arrival, though she couldn't remember his name. "My Lady, we need you in the yard if you are not too busy. We have some questions concerning the walls."

The blank look she gave him didn't seem to bother him. Luveday sat down her rag and wiped her hands on her apron. Turning to Agnes who was in charge of her kitchen, Luveday didn't even have to say anything. The woman waved her away saying, "We have it in hand, girl." So, she followed the mason through the corridors and up the stairs and out the hall.

The man continued, but Luveday stopped as a man leaning heavily against the wall yelled orders to the masons. They completely ignored him. "Not there you fools! Shore up that scaffolding before you fall on your fat heads!" He tried to leave the stability of the wall, only to stagger and fall back to its steady support. "Bloody fools!" He spat.

Stale ale and unwashed body, the odor radiating from him was enough to turn her stomach. He was drunk. When not yelling at the masons, his mumbling was slurred and rather coarse. Though rough looking, his speech was rather refined and Luveday puzzled at the man. His clothing looked as if it had been of fine quality at one time. Definitely above the common wardrobe, and he yelled at the masons as if he were a man used to being in charge. Luveday's interest piqued though she couldn't say what specifically had caught her attention. Had this man come only for the meal? Luveday was about to leave the steps and talk to the masons when she suddenly turned back to look at the drunkard.

He steadied himself and gave her a wobbly bow, belching a deep, "My Lady." His clothes were dirty and had a few good holes in them. The beard on his face was scraggily, and unkempt which reminded Luveday of the homeless on the streets and yet something about him was nagging her. She would usually ignore such men as she was not one to want a confrontation, but as she looked into his bloodshot eyes, something clicked into place.

"Master Alexander?" She took a step closer and stopped not wanting to get another whiff of the man.

His thin frame seemed to straighten. "At your service, Lady Luveday." His attention seemed to focus on something behind her, and his eyes widened. Stumbling past, he started yelling at the masons again. Luveday cringed at the smell and the language he used. Luveday watched his disjointed movements across the bailey and was surprised when he made it to one of the mason's wagons.

Sir Gregori came into view and was heading for the head mason with a dark look when Luveday was able to grab his attention. She waved him closer, and he reluctantly changed directions to meet her while keeping an eye on the drunk. "My Lady?" It was more a question than a greeting.

Luveday smiled at him, not sure how he would take the news. "I have found your head mason, Sir Gregori!"

The knight's smile was broad, but not entirely happy. There was a tightness around his eyes that spoke of anger. "And where is he now, Lady?" Gregori asked looking behind her into the darkened keep as if he would emerge from the shadows.

The lady merely raised a hand and pointed across the yard. Gregori's smile disappeared completely. He swore under his breath; something Luveday was sure she was not meant to hear. They watched as Dunstan and Archer headed for the man in question, but Gregori halted their movements with a wave and a dark look. "What do we do now, Lady?" The knight turned back to her.

"We sober him up, clean him up, and hope that when we are done the man has enough brains left to lead the Masons." She spoke bluntly, sure the situation called for it. Gregori smiled at her serious expression. The lady was ready for a fight.

"We may have some ideas on how to make him human again." Sir Gregori stalked off, toward his men. After a brief conversation, the trio surrounded the head mason. One minute he was yelling and the next laughter and then more yelling as Dunstan grabbed one arm and Archer the other. They dragged the man away, and Luveday wondered what they meant to do to the poor fellow and then thought it best if she didn't know.

The masons were none the wiser about the whole affair. Their queries made little sense to her, and so she walked them through their issues and in the process helped them answer their own questions. It seemed that as they struggled to explain the situation to her, they also clarified things for themselves. Critical thinking was all it took. From what Luveday gathered the walls were in good shape, but that would change if they were left much longer. The masons were hesitant to start not knowing what they should do first but soon decided that shoring up the steps would be the main priority as the staircase acted as a brace for a large section of the curtain wall. After which they would begin on the high wall and check the merlons on the battlements and the wall walk for signs of erosion. They were already mixing large batches of mortar to finish the minor repairs on the inner bailey. A group of men and a few masons were at the quarry cutting a few stones for larger repairs. With a direction firmly in place thanks to their talk and a bit of advice taken from Master Alexander's rantings, the masons began their task. Luveday missed some rather devoted looks from the masons as she returned to the castle to help where she could and check on the progress of the midday meal.

Supper was as congenial as lunch had been. There were a few scuffles between the workers, but only the usual sort of 'my way is better' arguments. Luveday assigned tasked and mitigated arguments by hearing both sides before deciding. She was still surprised when people listened to her and took her words as orders. She imagined it would take some time before she became used to the mantle of authority.

Luveday sat with Elli and Agnes as conversation and laughter rolled through the hall. A commotion at the doors drew everyone's attention. Gregori was up and greeting the newcomer before anyone recognized him. The knight embraced his companion; they spoke quietly as Gregori ushered him toward the women. As the pair approached, the mysterious man threw back his hood and removed his cloak. Luveday stood to greet the newcomer, recognizing his simple garments as a man of the cloth. He was not old, and yet not young. Luveday guessed he was in his late forties, but there was something about him that vibrated with vitality. Perhaps it was the happy crinkle at the corner of his eyes or his kind smile. "Lady Luveday," Sir Gregori's deep voice was full of mirth as he made the introductions. "May I introduce Father Nicholas Quinn, an old friend."

"It is my pleasure, Lady Luveday." He bowed over the lady's hand. His brown hair was graying around the temples and cut short to match his neatly trimmed beard.

"Please sit, Father." Luveday offered him a chair next to her, as she turned to Henna. "Please bring our new guest a trencher and another flagon of ale." Henna rushed off to the priest's words of thanks. "Have you traveled far?"

Gregori took a bench next to the priest and answered for him. "Father Quinn has just returned from the Abbey."

The two men shared a smile that spoke of long acquaintance and some shared humor. "Aye, I rested a few days with the good ladies of the Abbey and was surprised to see Lady Emmalyn and fair Lady Christabel in residence." Father Quinn looked questioningly at her, and Luveday got the feeling that he and Emmalyn had exchanged a good deal of their plans, but how much she wasn't sure. "The lady sent me here, with a full wagon and some ideas about the village garden." Twinkling eyes looked into hers, and she knew without a doubt that she was talking to a friend.

"Your help is needed and greatly appreciated." Luveday smiled ruefully at him. "I am afraid I barely know where to begin."

Elli chimed in from her customary spot next to the fire. "Lady Luveday has done well, Father Quinn." Elysant beamed at them as her praise made Luveday blush. "There hasn't been this much excitement since I was a child." Luveday sometimes forgot that Elli had grown up in the keep, before leaving to join Emmalyn and returning before winter had set in.

"There is much to be done, Father. And I am sure you were sent to us for a reason." Luveday looked at him in earnest.

He laughed. "I could say the same for you, My Lady."

The days progressed slowly and with much effort. There was only one incident that rattled Luveday's composure, though she later learned that it had solidified her presence in the eyes of the people. Beatrice, the buxom serving woman, had been a thorn in her side since her arrival. They had not liked each other on sight, though Luveday had worked to be polite, Beatrice made no mistake about her dislike of the new lady.

Truth be told, the serving woman was jealous of how easily the newcomer was accepted into the castle by Lady Emmalyn. Sure, the woman worked hard, but what was there to her? She was little better than the rest of them, a poor lady was nearly no lady at all, in Beatrice's opinion. And why should another woman take up so easily at Lander's Keep when the rest of them had worked so hard? It wasn't fair, and Beatrice made sure everyone knew her thoughts on the matter.

Luveday was aware that Beatrice's dislike was about more than just her unexpected arrival, but lately, the woman's grumblings were upsetting the other women as well. Luveday had overheard Agnes chastising the woman, but a good talking to had not improved her disposition. In fact, it seemed to have made it worse.

Beatrice nagged and insulted and joked, trying to find an ear among the women, and while some might laugh at her crude jests, her pettiness towards the new lady did not go unnoticed. Her boldness often attracted someone's attention, but Beatrice couldn't find many who would agree with her about the lady that had schemed her way into the keep.

It all came to a head on day four as the women prepared to clean the garderobe. It was a task left undone too long, and while Luveday shuddered at the idea, it was better to do it now in the cool spring air than wait for the summer heat to make the issue known. Luveday had discreetly asked about the process of removing the offending matter, which she tried not to think about too much. She found out that it had helped to have straw and dirt dropped into the garderobe from above, and so it was done. Herbs were mixed in to help with the smell. The women wore a cloth over their hair, and the fabric that covered their faces had drops of essential oils to help block the noxious odors. The women were happy to take Luveday's suggestion about the oils and were even more surprised to see the lady dressed similarly that morning. If Luveday had learned anything, it was that people in positions of power should never send someone else to do something they were not willing to undertake themselves. If she were to gain these people's trust, she had to wade in with the rest of them.

As the women gave her appraising looks, Beatrice who had yet to mark her arrival, loudly voiced her opinions about this particular task. "A lovely way to start the day!" She growled sarcastically. "I've no doubt Lady Luveday is enjoying her tea this morning while we shovel shit!" Luveday listened in silence and watched several women slowly inch away from the angry woman. "Ya think she was the lady of the Keep the way she's been giving orders in Lady Emmalyn's absence. Says the Lady Christabel orders this and that. Ha! That Lady won't care to know how this castle is run as long as she gets her spoiled way." The men started to gather and listen as they waited to cart away the refuse. "Lady Luveday's just a mouthpiece, nothing more. Trying to gain favor with Lady Emmalyn before the Lord returns. Steppin' in like this! Lady Christabel is too much the court lady to get her own hands dirty, Lady Luveday too."

"Be careful how you speak of your future lady, Mistress Beatrice!" Luveday's voice was pitched low, but it carried across the opening before the wall. The outside space before the pit's door was shaded by the castle walls, but even in the dim light, she could see her nemesis stiffen. Beatrice turned to her, taking a defiant stance planting her hands on her wide hips. The serving woman's confidence wavered as she recognized Agnes as the cook came to stand beside the Lady.

"You're no Lady of Lander's Keep, Mistress Luveday!" Gasps echoed around the group as women began to move towards the walls clearing the space; such disrespect was unheard of.

"I may not be your lady, Mistress Beatrice, but Lady Emmalyn and Lady Christabel have left me in charge of this Keep while they are away, and I mean to have these tasks done, and a proper Keep awaiting their return." She took a step toward the woman and spoke directly to her. "You are either my help in this endeavor or a hindrance, and if you are a hindrance, like any thorn in my shoe, you shall be removed."

Sputtering in anger, the woman took a step closer. "How dare you? The likes of you, threaten me?" She laughed venomously forgetting who was watching. "A little homeless upstart of a lady, taken in by the charity of others. You ungrateful, ignorant girl!" Beatrice took a swing and made a grab for Luveday, missing both times. "Emmalyn was a fool to let you..." The serving woman had missed the wooden shovel her opponent carried, and as she made another attempt to lay hands on the lady, Luveday sidestepped stuck out the shovel and felled the other woman. Swatting her on her arse as she fought to get back up sent Beatrice face first into the dirt of the courtyard. Laughter rang out through the crowd.

"Misters Durstan, Archer and Warin, please escort Mistress Beatrice outside of the castle gate. Her presence is no longer needed here." Luveday pulled all of her frazzled nerves together and tried to act the part of a lady rather than hit the daft woman over the head with her shovel, repeatedly, as she wished to.

"With pleasure, Lady." The men laughed and dropped their tools beside the wagon, to help Beatrice to her feet.

As Luveday turned away, Beatrice was manhandled until she regained her footing. Seeing an opportunity to break free, she lunged for Luveday again, but the lady heard the gasps before a proper warning could be given. She turned ready to use the shovel as a weapon and accidentally connected with Beatrice, hitting her in the chest hard enough to throw her back and knock the wind out of her. The men collected their unwilling companion and dragged her out of the courtyard, no longer amused at the fight between the women. A spat between women was one thing, trying to harm a lady was something altogether different.

Suffice it to say, once Beatrice was removed the women were able to work in relative peace and harmony.

And so, the days turned into a week and by their end the castle, though still rather bare, gleamed with renewed splendor. There wasn't a room that was left untouched. From the Lord's solar to the deepest storeroom and darkest dungeon. Luveday and the women waded through a decade of dust and cobwebs, but every inch of the castle was cleaned, including the men's barracks and outbuildings. Men worked to repair roofs, and furniture while the masons did their own work. By the end, Lady Emmalyn had still not returned though several wagons had appeared bearing her name and goods for the Keep. It seemed that what little coin the lady had taken with her had produced much. More wagons came from the Abbey baring cuttings and plants along with greetings from Lady Christabel and Mistress Adela. It seemed that Lady Emmalyn had moved off to visit friends nearby and would return in a few more days.

As the week came to an end, the village waited expectantly for their turn. Some doubted that this new lady would keep her word, but as the first day dawned clear and bright, the masons, men-at-arms, serving women and Lady Luveday met the village men in an opening between the cottages. The mason's wagons were followed by others as they brought out supplies to start the repairs. People began to leave their homes and help unload the wagons.

"Father Quinn, good morning! The Creator has blessed us with a good day!" Luveday chatted excitedly. This was her chance to help rebuild the trust between these people and the Keep. She could almost feel the chasm closing between them.

The father was up and ready to work. He had assured the lady that he was happy to oversee the building of the village garden; there was nothing he would enjoy more. "A good day indeed, Lady Luveday."

"I wonder if I might ask you to bless our endeavors again today, Father." Luveday knew they would need all the help they could get.

The man smiled as people gathered around. "It would be my pleasure." Many bowed their heads as the priest asked for the Lord's blessing. When he had finished chatter broke out around her, but soon fell silent again as many looked to her for where to begin. Speaking to the people had almost become a familiar practice for Luveday.

"If the masons will begin on the cottages closest to the road and work this way. If you could please clear your hearths and let them look at the chimenies. Warin," She looked to the salt and pepper haired man-at-arms, "you know what repairs need to be made, please help the masons." She turned to Henna and Agnes. "Mistress Agnes, Henna," both women smiled at her, "Please set up a cooking area at one end of the cottages, we need enough space to feed everyone." There was some mumbling and happy jostling as they realized the Keep would be helping to feed them again. "Sir Gregori," he approached with an "Aye, My Lady" and a smile. "Where would you like to work today?" The knight had many skills, and Luveday was unsure where to put him, so she left the choice in his hands.

"I will help Father Quinn with the garden, if that is alright with you, My Lady." Sir Gregori smiled again.

Luveday couldn't help smiling back. "That would be wonderful! Thank you, Sir Gregori."

The knight walked away, and Luveday heard him laugh as he threw the words over his shoulder. "The pleasure is mine, lady."

Elli appeared at her shoulder and looked at her expectantly. Luveday knew what she wanted and had trouble not laughing at her eager expression. "I think your skills would be best used in the garden as well, Elli."

Some of the women overheard and laughed, but the girl didn't mind. She just beamed at Luveday, and said, "Yes, My Lady." Before running off to chatter at the knight. The women smiled and started to work.

Luveday approached the first house and waved over some women. The masons were already at work with a wagon of thatch pulling up to help repair some of the roofs. Luveday has started collecting the needed items for the village a few days in advance to have things at hand, rather than wait for them.

The first house was larger than most but other than that; the village was rather nondescript. The stone and thatch cottages were all whitewashed with their color fading, stones separating, doors hanging ajar. Repairs were visible, but not well done. The buildings were spaced haphazardly with the main thoroughfare dividing them roughly in half, perpendicular to the main road. The majority of the cottages lay to the right of the road with a hand full off to the left. Some had small gardens between, but they looked barren and unkempt. There were more homes scattered across the countryside, and she had every intention of seeing them as well, but the main focus was the main body of cottages.

Looking inside, Luveday spotted Cassandra, Warin's wife, the village healer, and midwife. The woman looked frazzled by the activity in her home. Cassandra saw the lady and came out, leaving the men to fix her hearth and home. "My Lady, can I be of service?" The older woman asked. Cassandra was strikingly beautiful. Age had not diminished the beauty of her long dark hair, her tall and fair build, but the woman was known for being as kind as she could be stern.

"That is what I wish to ask you." The women gathered around her looked confused. "While the men work on the stones, is there anything else you wish to do?" With her look of confusion, Luveday saw she had to elaborate. "Do you need linens washed, or floors swept?"

The women got the hint. "Oh, Lady we couldn't..." They exclaimed.

"What better time, then when we are all here to help?" The women stopped a moment and then smiled at her.

And that was how it began. Soon women were in and out of every cottage. Wash-pots were out, and laundry lines were strung between buildings. Groups of women cleaned each cottage after the masons and thatchers finished making their mess. Luveday worked beside them, learning more about these people. She could not help her growing feelings, the sense of belonging and as if her life here made a difference. Looking around at the little houses and laughing families she could not help but miss her own. The busy, noisy mess that had been family get togethers. The familiar smell of the house she grew up in. This place was nothing like it, yet as she looked around, she couldn't help the way the laughter and comradery seemed to ease the sharper pangs of loss. Home was where the heart is. She thought, watching Warren tease and flirt with his wife. Ellie and Gregori stood, heads bent together talking intimately over garden beds and flower clippings. The pain in her heart sharpened for a moment. Was this her future? How was she to bare going home, and not miss them, or stay and long for the other? Someone called her name, and she pushed her own feelings aside. As always, there was more work to be done, and nothing quieted her inner doubts like hard work.

Days passed, and the garden was already taking bloom in the spring sunshine. The little gardens were weeded, bushes and vines pruned, and the lanes raked and cleared. The cottages were whitewashed and almost finished by the time the campaign arrived.

At first, Luveday thought Lady Emmalyn had returned there was such a commotion until she heard the pounding of a multitude of horses. Sir Gregori rushed out to see what the uproar was about; he had been helping to repair a roof and at the noise rushed back to his knightly duties. The castle gates lay open, and only two sentries manned the walls, but there was no reason to fear. The standards of the galloping horde bore the silver wolf of Lander's Keep.

Women and men flocked to the road excited as the horses rode on. Sir Gregori ran for the keep as if the hounds of hell were after him, in order to get there before his lord. Elli was excited, chattering beside Luveday and hanging off her right arm, but Luveday had a sudden chill slip down her spine. Fear left an unpleasant taste in her mouth.

Lord Iain De Lane was an enigma, one she had hoped to face with Lady Emmalyn beside her. The man these people spoke of was in turns a charming youth and a battle-hardened champion. Sir Gregori told tales of his prowess on the battlefield, and the women whispered about his prowess in bed. Supposedly he was a legend at court. Lady Emmalyn and Elli had spoken of a man they remembered as being responsible and loving, kind even, but Luveday knew that he was not the man from their stories. The true man had yet to make himself known. On his first visit home in nearly a decade, would he find a lone lady more of a burden than a help? Luveday couldn't help but worry.

Elli pulled her along as the crowd cleared. A group hurried to the castle as many returned to finish their work. There was no one to greet the lord on his monumental return but Gregori. Men took horses and helped down knights as they entered the inner bailey behind the entourage. Luveday received many strange looks from wary and bedraggled men as she approached Sir Gregori and a gruff looking man as they spoke in a lively conversation. She assumed this was Lord Iain and he did not look happy. Although, he did not look as if he were in a rage either. As the two women drew near, Sir Gregori turned and smiled reassuringly. As he opened his mouth to introduce them, the Lord strode into the keep without a glance backward.

They caught the concerned look that flashed across Sir Gregori's face as he turned to follow. Elli turned to Luveday as her steps slowed to a stop. "Don't worry, Luveday. Lord Iain is a good man; his return is what we were expecting."

"Yes, in a month or two hence." Luveday countered. "He does not seem pleased to be here." She looked at Elli who shared her concerned look. Agnes and the women bustled passed. Luveday and Elli picked up their skirts and followed them to the empty kitchen. The fires had been laid low to last the day, but the kitchen was cold as the castle's occupants had been working in the village the last few days. They had plenty of food brought up from the stores in preparation for feeding the village, so it wasn't difficult to shift gears to feed the lord and his men. Women carted out more food as men opened more barrels of ale and caskets of wine. The lord was home, and they meant to show how much they had done. Pitcher after pitcher was filled with cool liquid and even Luveday helped carry items upstairs.

A tray full of sliced meat and cheese to break the Lord's fast was held securely in Luveday's hands as she approached the fireplace. She sent Elli a look as the girl poured out goblets of wine. Setting the tray down, she stepped aside, not wanting to interrupt the conversation flowing between the group. Men she did not know conversed and joked around the fire, obviously weary from their journey.

As she let their words flow around her, Luveday looked over the castle to gauge what Lord Iain might have thought on his first glimpse of the keep. She looked around with pride in the work that they had done, but perhaps he would not know how they had scrubbed the floors for two days and repaired the wall sconces. He would not care that the chandelier was scraped clean and the candles were all new. So, she looked for flaws, things that he could say were left undone. *What was there to find fault with?*

Thanks to Lady Emmalyn's journey the Keep had some new furniture and a few more pillows to soften their hard edges. The keep was clean, the furniture sparse, but comfortable. They had found more items in the storage rooms and dark corners, but even with the new additions, it was not enough to fill the hall. The walls were bare, but Luveday had some ideas to help fix that, and Lady Emmalyn had suggested starting a tapestry once the spring sheering was done. With a bit more time they might have even made the place feel cozy, and lived in. For now, it was clean, fresh smelling and as good as it was going to get.

"A fortnight!" The Lord spoke with such force that the whole hall went still.

Luveday's attention was brought back to the conversation before her. They had been talking about Lady Christabel and her unexpected arrival and subsequent departure. It seemed that Iain's return had been prompted by Gregori's last letter informing him of his betrothed's presence. Gregori had previously informed him that the lady was visiting the Abbey. He had only just learned how long her stay had been and was clearly not happy about it.

"Lady Luveday has had things well in hand, Iain." The knight assured him.

"Where is this lady you speak of?" He sat back and sipped his wine with an angry scowl made fiercer by the thick beard and long hair that moved like a dark brown cloud about his head. His eyes looked hard, but Luveday couldn't tell his demeanor through all that hair and grime.

"I am here, My Lord." Luveday stepped forward and curtsied as best she could. She had been practicing each morning as she got dressed for just this occasion.

"And I take it we have you to thank for this warm welcome." His voice was hard, but she could not tell if that edge was pointed at her or at the situation, he had found waiting for him. Clearly, he had expected Christabel to be in attendance, to welcome him home as was his due. Instead, he had gotten an empty castle. *Drat, the man's timing.* Two more days and the work on the village would be complete, Lady Emmalyn would be home and perhaps even his wayward bride, though Luveday secretly doubted the lady would indeed return as she had claimed.

"Welcome indeed, Lord Iain. I am sorry you did not find the keep as you had hoped." She said with all sincerity.

He laughed at her. "I had hoped to find that the roof doesn't leak, and our meals remain un-chard." He took another gulp of wine. "I have yet to see if either has been improved upon since your arrival." Sir Gregori sat forward in his chair, clearly annoyed by his friend's attitude.

Gregori was not sure of Iain when he was in this sort of mood. He had spoken of Lady Luveday in his letter, and while he had not known her long enough at the time to give his lord a true impression of the woman, he had spoken of her in kind and honest words. The lady was a blessing they had not expected, and he would tell his friend so as soon as he could talk to him in private.

"I am sure you will find both to your satisfaction." Luveday was not impressed by this man, at least not by his prickly disposition. From all the stories of him, this was not what she expected of the King's Champion in words, actions, or looks. He was perhaps a handsome man under all that hair. He was tall with wide shoulders, a narrow waist, large hands, large feet and a gleam of hard intelligence in his eye.

He grunted in acknowledgment of her words and counted with a snide comment. "My satisfaction has yet to be seen too." He smirked behind his goblet and shared knowing smiles with the men at his side.

Luveday was not ignorant of the double meaning and might have slapped him if it did not look as if Gregori would do it for her.

Elysant stepped in unaware of the tension, meaning only to help her friend. "You cannot blame Luveday for that, uncle! She has worked hard to restore the castle. I don't know what we would have done without her."

At calling him uncle, Elysant reminded Luveday of her delicate situation. Elli was the bastard child of Iain's older brother. The eldest De Lane had been killed in a skirmish while fighting for the King. Several years later a child had arrived bearing his name, and though the woman accompanying the young Elli had sworn that she was a legitimate heir, no record of a marriage could be found. The woman had disappeared with what little coin Iain was willing to hand over, though there was no doubt in his mind that Elysant was indeed his brother's child. Her place had been a precarious one, and when he had left to champion the King, Iain had also left Elysant with his aunt knowing that she would care for the girl.

"And what would the lady have done without us, I wonder." He pondered aloud, his eyes resting on her.

Gregori growled a warning that surprised his lord. "Iain..."

"No, it is all right, Sir Gregori." Luveday stepped forward, and the knight sat back down. She leaned down a little to look Lord Iain in the eye which seemed to startle him even more. "My Lord, I am fully aware of what my fate could have been if not for the kindness of Sir Gregori and Lady Emmalyn, of Elysant and the people here." She looked at him with a hard eye. "I am not here to be a burden to anyone, if you think I do not earn my keep, then tell me plainly and I will go, but do not sit there and make suggestions about my character. You do not know me." She straightened and took a step back. "My actions will speak for themselves." She picked up the empty tray and turned to leave and in a pleasant voice called over her shoulder. "If you will excuse me, My Lord... I will go see how the preparations for the evening meal are progressing." She didn't wait for an answer.

The meal progressed in stony silence. The women had heard of her confrontation with Iain and wished to protest the only way they could, by serving an inferior meal, but Luveday would not let them. She reminded them that this meal was his first at the keep and any shortcoming would reflect solely on her. So, in opposition, the women produced a meal the likes of which rivaled that on the King's table. It was a shame that Luveday couldn't enjoy it; she had lost her appetite as soon as she was seated between Sir Gregori and De Lane.

Conversation flowed around the high table like water around a stone. The knights seated on either end tried to engage their fellows in conversation, but the middle of the table was uncooperative. Father Quinn had arrived to say grace and had joined the knights at the lower tables. Gregori looked as if he wished to join him but was loathed to leave Luveday and Iain alone. The women were on their best behavior; they made special trips to see if the lord or lady needed anything. Luveday nearly laughed at how sweet and attentive they were. It made Iain uncomfortable which gave Luveday a small bit of satisfaction.

The sun was setting as the doors opened to admit one weary traveler. Half the head table was out of their seats upon spying Lady Emmalyn. Iain had missed his aunt, Luveday had missed her friend, and the rest longed for her calming influence to navigate the tension between the two. The knights were at a loss of what to do.

Unbeknownst to many, Iain and his men had made a trip to Lander's Keep before installing Lady Emmalyn there. They were all aware of the transformation the lady had performed, and though their lord was in a dark humor, they could not bring themselves to dislike her, though many tried to reserve their judgment for later.

"Dear Aunt," Iain called as he reached her first, his demeanor so different from what it was a moment ago that it brought Luveday up short. The two hugged and laughed as they greeted each other. The lord complimented his aunt's eternal beauty, causing the older woman to blush profusely. Luveday was confused; here he was almost charming.

"Lady Luveday!" Emmalyn looked around in wonder. "I knew you would do wonders, child!" She affectionately cupped both of Luveday's cheeks in her hands. "Thank you!" They hugged, and Luveday smiled happily, trying to say that it wasn't her, that the village had done the majority of the work. "Now, now, dear. I know you are too modest to take credit for all the hard work." She stepped back and looked between Iain and her friend. "Has my nephew been charming you in my absence? I knew you two would get along splendidly." The group surrounding them was suddenly noticeably quiet.

Iain shifted uncomfortably.

"Has he regaled you with stories of his valor? No, well I'm sure that's to come." She laughed and patted Luveday's arm as they walked arm-in-arm up to the high table, Emmalyn still unaware of the tension.

"How was your journey? The pieces you send were wonderful, and I do not know what we would have done without Father Quinn." Luveday let the lady take her chair and sat in the chair on the other side of Gregori, luckily the seat had been empty.

"The trip went well, though I must say, I do not enjoy traveling as I once did. These old bones prefer to stay at home." She took a sip of wine and smiled at the setting before her. "What wonders you have performed in a fortnight, Lady Luveday."

Sir Gregori sat and smiled at the two women, his mood much improved. "Indeed, she has, Lady."

Luveday blushed at their praise. "I was merely following orders." She countered.

Elli made a comment to Iain that didn't reach Luveday, but whatever had been said caused him to look at her peculiarly.

The rest of the meal progressed with happy chatter. The mood of the Hall was greatly improved. Emmalyn, tired from her journey retired early, Elysant went with her to help her unpack and get ready for bed. It had been a long day for all.

Luveday went about her duties. She and Agnes rearranged and reviewed their plans for the meals for the next few days. She had been satisfied knowing that the village had been well fed in their absence. The knights and men-at-arms were more than satisfied with the evening meal, though many jokingly complained that a few more meals of that caliber and they would no longer fit into their armor. Luveday was happy with the banter, and while the knights treated her cordially, their lord remained silent.

Luveday took the tray of wine up to the solar, unable to put it off any longer. She had already seen to other preparation for the lord, hot water, clean linens and the like. She wouldn't have him say that they did not know the meaning of hospitality. She trudged up the stairs, knowing that this encounter had to take place, she was solidifying her position here, but she didn't look forward to it. A part of her expected him to throw her out of the castle at any moment. Taking a deep breath, she opened the outer door to the solar.

A boy of about thirteen sat in the small anteroom that transitioned from the castle to the solar. The room was small, little more than a pass-through with a built-in wooden bench taking up the left wall. Above it were three small square colored-glass windows near the top of the low ceiling, the only glass windows in the castle save the chapel. The boy sat on the bench which had been covered by his pallet. Obviously, it was where he would be sleeping, as he cleaned bits of leather and armor. He looked up and nodded shyly at her. Luveday stopped to look at him.

"You are Coll, Lord Iain's squire?" Luveday asked quietly. The boy looked happy for the recognition.

"Yes, Lady Luveday." He answered clearly, his mop of sandy blonde hair nearly covering his icy blue eyes and long lashes.

He was cute, but Luveday tried to remind herself that a boy of his age was no longer a child. Children in this time did not get a childhood as she had known. "Did you enjoy supper, Squire Coll?"

"Oh yes, lady. 'Twas the best we've had in ages." The boy beamed.

"Good. If there is anything, you or your lord need, please tell me." She offered, more for the boy's sake than his master's.

"Yes, My Lady." Coll looked up to her with shining eyes and then returned to his task.

Luveday pulled open the second door, hearing voices inside. She looked sharply to her left and saw that Gregori and Iain sat before the large hearth in the room. She had placed two large chairs before the fire, but looking now, she thought they could use a larger table.

Both men looked to her. Henna was collecting the dirty clothing for washing. While Luveday had seen to her duties around the castle, several serving women had helped the lord bathe. It was a quick affair that improved his disposition and smell. Setting down the tray of wine between them, she helped Henna collect the garments and was going to help the girl carry them down when Iain asked her to attend them.

Everyone was very polite if brief with each other. "The wagons and the rest of my men should arrive in a day or so." He spoke to her without looking at her. "There are some spoils of my tournaments among the wagons. Perhaps you will find something useful."

"Perhaps... We will see it settled." Luveday replied ready to leave.

Sir Gregori tried to fill the silence. "Lord Iain plans to visit the Abbey in a few days." Iain gave him a hard look.

Luveday smiled to herself. He was going to collect his bride. She secretly wished him luck, Luveday had the feeling that Christabel would be more of a challenge than he expected. "Please tell Lady Christabel that I hope she has enjoyed her visit and that I hope she is doing well." Iain looked as if he was trying to gauge her sincerity, but Luveday was not trying to be polite. She knew firsthand what it was like to be far from home. "If that is all, I bid you both a good night, My Lord. Sir Gregori." She curtsied, little more than a bend of the knee and a bow of the head, but she thought it was more than enough. He didn't seem to be the sort to worry about formal etiquette. That was good, because at that moment Luveday didn't care if he was insulted or not. She was tired and sought her bed at the first opportunity.

Chapter 3

A woman's always younger than a man of equal years.
~Elizabeth Barrett Browning

In the several days since his arrival, Lady Luveday proved to be everything Gregori said she was, which irked Iain to no end. It was not that he disliked the lady, there was just something unusual about her that he couldn't place. He looked for ulterior motives but could discern none. She seemed to have installed herself in his home with ease. In fact, she was constantly at his Aunt's side learning the ins and outs of the keep and even the healing arts. Iain had the strange feeling that every time he spoke to her, it was a test of wills and wits. It was an unusual situation. Not that he doubted the intelligence of the woman, it was that he had never met one with brains that seemed to equal his own and that unnerved him more. She looked him in the eye when she spoke, she listened intently, and she spoke only when she had something worth saying. To put it plainly, she intrigued him, and that would not do. Iain thought of his future wife and scowled as he chose his attire with care. Today was an important day, and he needed to make the best impression. He was leaving for the Abbey, and he would return with his bride. It would be the first time his people would see them together. It felt like the future he had dreamed of was finally at hand.

Luveday helped to mend the Lord's clothes as she sat with the women in the sewing room. It was more like a gallery, a long and narrow room on the second floor with two large shuttered windows that overlooked the garden. It was also a room where some of the women occasionally slept. After being cleaned and some furniture arranging within, the room was actually very pleasant and often had a nice breeze that came in through the open windows. She sat repairing a leg of some hose with straight, uniform stitches and contemplated their owner. Iain's clothes were very fine, but many of them had seen better days. Months spent on the road had taken their toll, not to mention numerous skirmishes and what have you. She had only a vague idea of what a champion did. Luveday thought that it was not so glorious a title as one might imagine. There must be a good deal of fighting and going where the King sent you. That did not seem very appealing to her.

Lord Iain had ridden out that morning saying goodbye to only his aunt. He had taken a few men with him, as they had business of some kind at the Abbey, but what it could be she couldn't guess. Luveday had been in the kitchen checking on the castle's stores. With so many men in attendance they all worried about having enough provisions to go around. Most of the meal was made from the harvest last fall and the stores were running low until the first crops were ready. It was clear that a hunt was in order and Luveday was hesitant to learn how to skin and dress an animal. The fish and fowl were something familiar to her, but beef and pork fresh off the hoof made her stomach turn. Even thinking about it as she sat mending a pant leg, was enough to make her uncomfortable. There was bound to be a lot of blood and gore and Luveday didn't know how she would respond.

She had a bit of her mother's clinical eye, mostly because as a nurse's daughter she had inherited, by proximity, her mother's training to not freak out when someone came in covered in blood. As a teen, Luveday had spent some time in the hospital where her mother worked. The opportunity to be a docent was an eye opening one. She remembered enjoying working with the patients and visiting people to keep them company, but she'd never truly been privy to the turmoil her mother often faced in the ER or in the operating room. Medicine in her current world was something altogether different from what her mother practiced. She'd dealt with a few minor injuries under the steady eye of Lady Emmalyn and even with the help of Cassandra, the midwife. Between the two women, she had a wealth of healing knowledge, and thanks to the Medical Herbal she had picked up for Annalisa, and her mother's mandatory first aid classes, she was a few centuries ahead on medical technique. She had the knowledge, now she was gaining the experience.

After little more than a month, Luveday still marveled at all of the new things she was learning. Emmalyn had been impressed with how quickly she was catching on, while at other times wondering why she didn't know something simple in the first place. Things that were everyday occurrences in the castle were new to Luveday, and yet she had taken to this life like a fish to water. The more she learned the more she wanted to do.

Elli burst into the room scattering her thoughts. The girl took a moment to catch her breath as Henna plied her with questions. "Elli is something wrong?" They were all relieved when she shook her head no, but the girl was still too winded to speak. "Does Lady Emmalyn need us?" A nod and an excited smile were their only answer as Elli went over and grabbed Luveday by the arm to drag her out of the room. The women followed chattering all the way.

They descended the stairs to see men bustling back and forth carrying all sorts of things. Men dropped items here and there to Emmalyn's dismay. The women stopped to marvel at the chaos when Lady Emmalyn spotted them. "Don't just stand there, I need your help." She addressed them all but looked straight at Luveday. "Lady Luveday, they are making a mess of our beautiful hall."

These must be the wagons Iain spoke of, she thought. Luveday started opening chests and untying wrapping. The items she found ranged from the everyday to the exotic. Men continued to bring in more and more, a never-ending procession bearing gifts. Colorful bits of armor were heaped in a pile just inside the door. Chests were stacked haphazardly, rolled rugs and bundles of cloth, and a great metal circle were leaned against whatever might keep them upright.

Luveday nodded to herself as Emmalyn fretted and tried to order the men around. She spotted Coll looking on from a corner as they brought things in. "Coll, come here." She called, and the boy weaved his way through the men to reach her.

"Yes, Lady Luveday?" The boy looked around eagerly at the commotion.

"Do you know what belongs to Lord Iain?" The boy looked confused by the questions.

"All of it, My Lady. 'Tis the spoils from his campaigns and tournaments." They moved aside as a pair of men sat down a large iron-bound trunk. "Lord Iain is good about trading if the men didn't have the coin." The squire was proud of his lord; not all men were so fair.

Taking a deep breath, Luveday tried again. "Are any of these things his personal items? Things we should move up to the solar?"

"Oh, no lady. We brought everything with us. These are all ransoms." The boy smiled widely, and Luveday couldn't help, but smile back.

She remembered something about ransoms. Knights holding ransom the armor and belongings of their defeated enemies until the man, or house, could pay some fee to have the items released. It was a lot like winning the jackpot and having to strong-arm your fellow players for your winnings. Luveday was unsure of how she felt about such practices, but about one thing she was sure, Lord Iain De Lane had done very, very, well for himself.

"Alright. Open this trunk, please." She straightened and began giving orders in a no-nonsense tone that garnered swift obedience "Please take any spices and foodstuff to the kitchens." Women helped direct the men as they revealed hidden treasures and carried them off to their new homes. Luveday called the men by name when she was able and learned many new ones in the process. "Not there, carry it up to the solar, please." She waved the men toward the stairs, ignoring their groans. "Henna please see that the cloth and other sewing items are put up in the sewing room." She moved to examine the rugs and a large round metal object that Luveday couldn't quite identify. Everything had a purpose, and a giant silver dish had to have some use that she had yet to discern. It was beautiful and about as large in diameter as she was tall. The circle had a lip around the circumference that was about an inch tall, the surface of the piece was lightly etched in a complex and circular design that she couldn't quite see. The light from the torches and candles reflected off its polished surface obscuring the pattern.

An idea popped into her head. Luveday thought she might have figured out what the metal was for, light. If they could find some way to hang the piece over the fireplace, not only would it nicely fill the wall, it would help to illuminate the hall. She had them set it aside along with a large carved wooden platter and some pottery.

By the time the hall was nearly empty, the men were winded, and the women were cooing over the lord's spoils. All that was left was a pile of armor, mostly shields that had served the knights as calling cards, a whos-who to announce their presence in the tournaments. Most of the shields were for ceremonies only and hung outside tents or on the boards to show their prestige. They were beautifully painted, and Luveday was loathed to store them in the armory or toss them into some dark corner as the men suggested. Luveday had come across some more shields as they had cleaned the castle and was mulling over some way to make them decor pieces in the hall.

Luveday called for cool wine and trays to be dispersed among the men, and they were happy to be rewarded for their hard work. The women were still putting away the spoils as Luveday took a moment to stop and rest. Emmalyn came up beside her. "Well done, child." She sat down, and Luveday joined her if only for a moment. "I was sure we would not get it all done tonight." She took a goblet from Paige whose quiet demeanor often left her overlooked. Luveday had learned little about the young woman though she had tried. Her thoughts were interrupted as Emmalyn continued talking. "The boy has done well for himself, that is for sure."

Accepting a cup, Luveday looked at the wall above the hearth in thought. "Yes, very well." She doubted any other man had gone home with such a bounty and Luveday thought that one or two of the chests the Lord had brought with him must be full of coin. *Very well, indeed.* Luveday didn't have time to be impressed at the moment. "Excuse me, Emmalyn. I must check on the women. I want to make sure everything is put away properly." She drained her cup and headed for the sewing room. She had been right to worry; the women were too busy looking through the chests and items to have gotten much done. Luveday put them to work again, before heading to each and every area in turn. By supper time that evening, everything was in its proper place except for those few items Luveday wished to install in the hall, but for that, she would need some unlikely help.

Luveday had yet to meet the blacksmith of Lander's Keep. The man was reputed to have such skill that Iain had taken him with him, preferring to have his talent close at hand. The smithy was in the outer bailey not far from the barracks and had been cleaned during the massive undertaking. It had clearly not seen any activity in years, though no one would know that looking at it now. The blacksmith, a Master Barth, was a large man, several years older than his lord, perhaps in his mid-thirties. He had short deep brown hair and was dressed in thick leathers to protect him from the flames. Luveday thought that such attire would be terrible in the heat. The man was working at the hearth when she appeared and watched him work for a few moments. He was shaping a horseshoe with a few well-placed strokes. Luveday thought her presence had gone unnoticed until he startled her by speaking. "What can I do for you, Lady Luveday?" A deep and quiet voice flowed through the space.

Startled was putting it mildly, Luveday was momentarily confused and forgot what exactly she had come to ask. Shaking her head, she moved closer, and the blacksmith put down his tools and turned to her. She didn't go near the fire, even in the spring chill the heat from the forge was strong. "Good morning, Master Barth." The blacksmith arched one eyebrow at the greeting. He knew she wanted something from him. Looking at him, Luveday threw out the speech she had planned and spoke plainly. "I know you are a busy man, but they say you are also clever, and while I may be underutilizing your skills, I need your help."

Interested, the blacksmith moved them out into the open air. "What can I help you with, My Lady? I have not the hands for delicate work." He opened his large hands and showed them to her. She saw the scars and burns from a lifetime spent forcing metal to one's will.

She placed her small hand in his and grasped his fingers which seemed to startle him. Looking into each other's eyes, she smiled. "I do not need delicate work. I need a sharp mind." And instantly a friendship was forged.

The castle had settled into a routine. Luveday sometimes missed the quiet. It had seemed that the stones were wrapped in silence on her arrival, but she reminded herself that Lander's Keep was never meant to be empty. Lord Iain had not returned nor sent word about what kept him, though many suspected his lady was being difficult. Many would have liked to be a fly on the wall for their first meeting, Luveday included.

She saw a good deal of the blacksmith and a few of the masons, who were still working on some of the cottages, the mill and looking at a manor house on the edge of the land's that lay well within the wood. Barth was helping her to find a way to hang the shields and large silver dish without damaging them or the walls, the later issue caused them to consult with the masons.

Master Alexander had proved to be as good as his reputation, though sobering him up had been a challenge. He and Gregori had conversed at length about what the mason remembered of his arrival there, and more specifically, the wayward Steward. Gregori had recounted some of what happened, though not all. Luveday got the impression that the knight had made it his mission to find the steward and bring him to justice. She shuddered at the thought, Gregori's would be a hard justice.

After the chores in the castle were done, Luveday's eyes had looked for other tasks. Cassandra and even Elli sometimes joined her and Emmalyn as the women taught her more about their art. They had a small journal passed down from one of Emmalyn's foremothers, but the book was so old that she had trouble reading it. Not only were the pages faded with time, but the handwriting was also poor and the language difficult to decipher if it was in English at all. Emmalyn did not read well, and what she knew about the book was mostly taught to her verbally or by example. She could still recite her lessons as if it were yesterday. Still, many of the book's secrets would remain unknown. Hours were spent learning about plants and brewing in the healing shed, as Luveday had come to call it, was not enough to fill her days. So, her eyes turned to the women. They had been happy to accept some of the ointments and unguents she had made, and when she suggested they try this or that, or she made a comment about their appearance, they were happy to try something new there too. The women started washing regularly, as Luveday did. They braided their hair and wore bits of color to contrast their serviceable gowns. As a whole, they seemed happier, even when Luveday took the scissors from her backpack and offered to trim their hair.

It was only a matter of time before the men started to notice and while they might take more care with their garments to catch a woman's eye, their hair was still unkempt, long and straggly. They had talked amongst themselves and had decided to ask for the Lady's help, but no one was comfortable broaching the subject of bathing with the lady, so they found themselves a spokeswoman to champion their cause.

Agnes cleaned her hands on her apron, a nervous habit no one had seen from her before, as she approached Lady Luveday while she sat alone at the hearth. It was unusual for the cook to be upstairs, preferring to spend her time in the kitchen or its garden rather than in the bustle of the hall. Many of the men that loitered about gave her knowing looks, and she nodded her understanding. It was time to talk to the lady. "Lady Luveday?" The woman asked knowing that many of the men had put a great deal of stock in her relationship to the new lady. Agnes liked the girl, talked to her a great deal and respected her because Luveday respected others in return, but she didn't think that she, as a cook, could ask much of a lady, even Luveday, so she hesitated.

The lady looked up, startled from her thoughts and smiled at the cook. Rather than getting up, Luveday asked the woman to sit, and as Agnes rested her feet it felt as if a large weight had lifted from her shoulders, and so the cook found she was unburdening herself on the lady and couldn't stop talking though she tried. "Lady, you have worked wonders in this keep, and it has not gone unnoticed. I was cooking the morning meal a few days ago, and the women came in laughing and singing and looking like spring chickens and the men stopped to ask me what they were doing that made them look so fare. The women heard and said 'twas you who helped them. And the men have watched the girls these last few days, and they like what they see, and they think that if they might bathe and have their hair cut they too would be better off, and I think it a fine idea. Many of the men looked like they've not seen a comb since they left here, and the bath is ever so nice though saved for the Lord and noble guests, we've yet to open it again. The men asked me to talk to you, lady, and ask if they might use it and soap and your scissors to be presentable. After all, we might have a royal guest sooner than we think and ..."

Luveday laughed never knowing the woman to talk so much and held up a hand to slow her down. Agnes stopped the flow of words from her mouth with visible effort. Luveday got the gist of the situation, and while she had heard of the bath and knew it was cleaned with the rest of the castle, she had not yet seen it. A community bath had been unappealing to her, so she had not thought to look farther into it. "Mistress Agnes, I see the men have asked you to champion them." Those standing near enough to hear her words scoffed under their breath while Agnes blushed. "I do not see a reason why they cannot use the bath. We will assemble what's needed, and they may bathe this afternoon, perhaps they might even let Lady Emmalyn and myself look them over. Some have been complaining of pains but have yet to call on us. We can kill two birds with one stone." Luveday got up, and Agnes joined her. Thanking her quickly, the cook hurried to return to her kitchen. The men only nodded at the lady and went off to tell their fellows that the bath would be ready.

And that was how Lord Iain found the women prettifying his men upon his return.

Luveday focused on cutting the hair of Sir John Templeton of Alric. The man was in his early forties and chatted at her as she once again asked him to keep still. "Yes, me lady," was an automatic reply, little more than a breath in the middle of his tale. Truth be told, Luveday had no idea what the man was talking about. She was trying to cut his facial hair and was sure she would take out an eye if he didn't stop moving. Luckily, she had just taken a snip when Iain's voice boomed far too close to her.

"What in God's name is going on here?" The Lord shouted above the happy chatter.

Panicked eyes turned to Luveday as she was the one giving orders. Closing her eyes briefly to gain some composure, she took a deep breath and turned to meet De Lane. "Good day Lord Iain. I see you are safely returned from your visit abroad." Someone chuckled behind her and Luveday thought she might be in trouble as the man's expression suddenly turned from stormy to calm. It was not a good sign.

"Good day, Lady Luveday. Would you mind telling me," he stepped closer, and Luveday had trouble standing her ground, but she refused to budge, "why my men are in the hall, pampered like courtesans readying to see the King?" His tone was sickly sweet with a biting edge under it.

"Certainly, My Lord." She turned slightly to look at the scene behind her. There were several stations where the men were being seen to after exiting the bath. Currently in use, male laughter and some feminine giggles rolled out with the steam. Emmalyn and Cassandra were before the hearth; they saw to injuries both great and small. Occasionally, they called Luveday over to test her on some ailment or another. Henna sat mending garments as Paige helped the men shave and Elli cut hair. Both girls had proven to be remarkably talented in their respective departments. Men lounged scattered across the hall, some chatting in groups and others talking to the women as they waited for their turn. The last group of men had just entered the bath and would be exiting shortly. Luveday took the time to gather her thoughts before turning back to her impatient Lord. She realized that she could not say that the men had asked for such treatment, there would be no end of teasing. So, she shifted the truth a little. "Your men were looking slovenly, and we women had had enough." Men grumbled to each other, but many caught on to her and were grateful.

"You had enough, had you?" He asked between clenched teeth.

"Yes. They looked little better than beggars. I would wager they'd not seen a proper bath in months." She made it clear that she thought it was his responsibility. "I'm not sure if any of them even remembers what their clean faces look like."

Sir John commented, "I do remember I had a nice chin. The ladies liked it at least." Men laughed and joked about it. Some were ribbed about their baby faces. John joined in. "I bet Sir Gregori won't lose his beard lest they mistake him for a squire."

The man in question stepped forward having gone to the Abbey that morning; he had missed the day's activities. "I can straighten out anyone who makes that mistake, John."

John laughed. "Aye and right quick too!"

Iain stepped closer without Luveday noticing and spoke quietly to her as his men continued to chatter around them. "Now, Lady, what is going on?"

Luveday looked him in the eye and sighed. "I apologize if we have used the bath without your permission. It is my fault." His expression didn't lighten at her apology. "Since your return, your men have not been seen to, and if a bath was what it took to get our hands on them then so be it." His eyes narrowed, and Luveday thought she could have phrased that a little better. "Their health is my major concern. You have been on the road for a long time, and many of the men have ailments and injuries that should have been seen to before now." She watched his eyes flicker out to the laughing faces and back to her. "You had no healer with you, and this has let us see the state they are in. I am surprised there wasn't more trouble." Another hard look made her sigh again. "Besides, do they not look handsome all cleaned up." She asked changing direction.

"Like shiny coins, My Lady." He said resigned. He had come home expecting a welcome but had gotten something else yet again. The woman never ceased to surprise him. He was not upset at the use of the bath, what good was it if it went unused. What upset him was the men encircling the women like a pack of wolves. He knew the men were on their best behavior with the ladies but some of them were getting too familiar with Lady Luveday, and that irritated him. His men had ribbed him about his rudeness to the woman, trying to get to his problem with her. She wasn't his type, so they did not worry for her virtue, but they liked the lady and were annoyed with him that he couldn't admit he liked her too. She was a good lady, and they were quick to remind him when his temper flared unexpectedly.

He left her abruptly, heading straight for the solar. He was tired and dirty from the ride, which soured his mood more than usual.

Luveday watched him ascend the stairs and heard rather than saw him slam the solar door shut. A few moments later, Coll came running down the stairs and smiled at her as he headed for the kitchen, most likely to get Iain something to drink. The chatter was silenced for a moment, but with the slamming of the door, everyone went back to what they were doing. Gregori and the two knights that had accompanied Iain looked at the bath with longing. Luveday smiled then nodded, and the men ran off to get their things. Sir John resumed his story, which Luveday now had the feeling was definitely inappropriate for a proper lady, but the man's happy conversation was sort of soothing to her. She finished trimming his beard without a single eye lost.

Supper was a happy affair for everyone except the Lord of the keep. He looked over his men and noticed, not for the first time, how well they looked. He had not seen Sir John smile for over a month. Cornell Reeves, a rather shy knight, was flirting with one of the serving women who reminded him of a door mouse. Everyone at the high table was having a grand time except for himself. Iain admitted he was being stubborn. Coll had returned to the solar with drinks and a tray of fruit and cheese, but what he really wanted was to talk to Luveday. He wanted to ask about his men. Was Perivale's tooth well or did it need to be removed? Had Gregori's arm healed well from his last skirmish? Did Cornell need something for his foot? He knew his men had suffered through their time on the road. Healers were, more often than not, just looking for quick coin, so the men had learned to take care of themselves as best they could. Being warriors, they muddled through, and if they survived their wounds then it was God's will, and if they didn't, that was His will too.

Laughter caught him off guard for the second time that night. He leaned forward to look around his aunt, and Sir Gregori, who had become a fixture at the head table, to see Lady Luveday trying to stifle her laughter. She was blushing a pretty pink and tried to hide her smile behind her hand. He realized he had not heard her laugh before tonight and found it was a nice sound. He also couldn't remember seeing her smile openly. Sure, she smiled at the men, and politely at him, but never showing teeth. He wondered about that as he watched her. She shook her head at something one of his men had said and quickly took a sip of wine. She smiled at him even as their eyes met down the table. Humor sparkled in her gaze, and he sat back and turned to Elysant who sat on his other side.

"You don't have to look so fierce, My Lord." He gazed at her in confusion and realized he was scowling. Schooling his features, he tried to look indifferent at the very least. "She is lovely once you get to know her, and she has worked hard to make this keep a proper home for all of us." He was about to comment that he was sure she worked hard, but that *his Lady* would be returning shortly, and they should not count on Luveday so, but thought better of it. Elli finished her meal and looked him straight in the eye, something she must have picked up from her friend. "Please give her the benefit of the doubt before you judge her." And with that, the little pixie was gone.

Before he knew it, the whole table was clear, and he sat there watching his men, but not really seeing them. How could he say that his irritation wasn't with her; it was with the situation. He had judged her upon her arrival. A woman alone in the world with some sad tale was nothing new, and at first, he had wondered what the woman wanted by coming here. That Gregori had rescued her from the wood was odd, but not so odd knowing his friend's character. Every day he watched her and looked for some hidden motive, expected her to make overtures to his person at the quickest opportunity. As the days passed, he saw what the others saw; a kind-hearted, hardworking *Lady*. She surprised him and puzzled him, she made him angry, and she made him envious of how quickly she had taken the hearts of his people.

What could he say? He didn't mean to fight with her, but every time he looked at her, he saw what his bride was lacking. It should not be some lost lady that won the hearts of his people; it should be his future wife. Lady Christabel should have seen to the castle, making it a home for them and their children. Christabel should have seen to the village and started the preparations for their wedding. It should be that lady who saw to the well-being of his men, who greeted him in the morning and was the last face he saw at night. Even though they could not yet share a bed, he and his betrothed should be using this time to get to know each other, to show their people that they were a good match. Instead, his woman was cloistered in the abbey, and it was Lady Luveday who cared for his people.

He emptied his goblet in a single long draft and finally headed for bed. He removed his shirt to wash in the basin of warm water and looked at his surroundings, Luveday's presence was everywhere he looked. She had filled his room with rugs and pillows, warm furs and rich textures. The room had been sparse and clean when he arrived. His things had added a bit of interest, but with each day the lady added something to brighten the space. From a pitcher of flowers to a small silver mirror that now hung on the wall. The space felt lived in, more importantly, it felt like home.

He could find no fault with her. Luveday did not act like the lady of the castle. She did not flaunt her power over his home, but sat and talked with his people, eagerly sought them out to help or get answers to her many questions. It was her manner that had endeared her to them, and Iain had a hard time not being angry about it. Looking at his reflection in the polished metal of the mirror, he was faced with the reality of his situation. His rough face looked tired, even covered by the mop of his beard. The truth was he had made a monumental mistake. He had let gold dictate his actions. Lady Christabel was a beautiful and charming star at court. She was exciting, young and vibrant, but she was not the lady for Lander's Keep. For a single moment, he wondered what it would be like if he had found a lady like Luveday, what his land and people could become under her care, but only for a moment because it could never be. Iain had signed the contract, had signed away his life for the gold Christabel's father, Lord Henric Sumerland of Stonegate, would provide as a bride-price. And it was no revelation that he still needed the coin, not for him but his people. He dreamed of what his home had once been and returning it to its former glory. Today, the stores for the castle were nearly empty, the orchards and fields had produced poorly the last few years, and his livestock were few in number. One hard winter and his people would suffer. Sickness among the cattle would devastate his lands. He needed the coin to ensure their future, and that meant that he needed Christabel. So, he set all else aside and focused on how to win the unwilling young woman.

The knock on his door was not unexpected. The lady he refused to think about any longer that night stuck her head in and softly called his name. He stood shirtless before the fire, his left arm resting on the mantel and his head resting atop it. He turned his head only enough to glance at her from the corner of his eye and caught the widening of her eyes.

"Yes, Lady Luveday?" He prompted, no longer looking at her, but into the heart of the fire. Iain thought he heard her shake herself before she answered and almost smiled.

"My Lord, is there anything else you have need of tonight?" She quietly asked as she stepped fully into the room, but no farther.

"No, nothing, Lady... unless... unless you have some way to make my barren orchards yield fruit this spring?" He mocked himself, as he shared a glimpse of his troubles with her.

She paused a moment to ponder him before saying good night. "I am afraid I don't, My Lord. If that is all, I will wish you a good night's rest."

"And to you, Lady." He replied. He had no way of knowing that she would ponder his words long after they both found their beds that night.

One of the men dropped a shield causing a peel like a bell to ring through the hall. Luveday nearly jumped out of her skin at the unexpected noise. Barth, the blacksmith, glared at the clumsy man, Mace, a man-at-arms only smiled back at him and apologized to the lady. It was in the middle of their project that Lord Iain arrived. As usual, he made a beeline for her to ask what was going on. Luveday was tempted to answer sarcastically because it was rather obvious what was going on, but she didn't. Her temper was short thanks to her helpers. The men had been eager at first, but they proved more of a hindrance than a help. "We are decorating the hall, Lord Iain." She looked across the room to see the large polished dish he had brought back from his travels as it gleamed in its place above the hearth. Light reflected in its surface illuminating the hall with a cheery glow. She was overjoyed at the improvement it made. She had hung the wooden tray on a protrusion of the massive stairs and sat a small table under it. Now they were working on the shields. "Master Barth," she began as the men greeted each other with a nod of the head. It was a common greeting between men that set her teeth on edge. *Could they never just say hello*? "Master Barth," she began again, "has devised a rope system to hang the shields in the hall." The men eyed the ropes hanging down the walls.

The Blacksmith explained his creation. "Lady Luveday came to me with the idea of using the shields as decoration for the hall." He pointed to the multitude of ceremonial shields spread across the nearest of the two long tables. They covered the benches on this side and a good bit of the floor. "She wished to display them on this wall without having to hammer in a spike for each piece; she worried that it would damage the structure."

"And rightly so," the Lord commented though, in truth, he wasn't sure what that might do.

"So, she asked if I might know of a way to display the shields, using chain or rope." Barth looked up again and pointed. "I've place spikes with rope loops at the top of the wall. The rope is run through the loops and down the wall where its knotted and tied to another spike at the bottom." Barth touched the ropes, which were taught and didn't budge. "More rope is tied around the rafters in the ceiling to help carry some of the weight of the shields, so in case of some mishap the ropes won't snap and bring the shields crashing to the floor."

"And what are the wooden blocks on the ropes for?" Iain asked. Tied and evenly spaced over each length of rope as it ran down the wall was a series of wooden blocks, completely level with the next block on the next rope over in six lines of six. Each block was about ten inches long, five inches wide and five inches deep with a groove chipped out of the length of the top. The groove was slim but deep as if something were to fit into it.

Luveday took over the explanation as she picked up a shield. They were thin since they were not meant for battle, but still quite heavy. "The blocks will hold the shields. Six shields per rope, six ropes in all."

Barth took the shield from her with little effort. "Look here, My Lord." He turned the shield around and showed them the arm loops where the knight would hold the shield. A bar had been added to span from one loop to the other. "This," he grabbed the sturdy bar he had added to each shield, "this will slip into the notch on the top of the block, and its weight will hold the shield in place." He demonstrated with the shield he held. "There is also a peg we can put in place if the Lady is worried about the shields coming off the wall." Barth looked at Luveday, and the lady smiled brightly at him. It had been a brilliant collaboration between the two. Luveday mentally congratulated Barth and herself.

Turning to Iain, Luveday looked at him expectantly; they had put a lot of time and effort into this project. "I am sure you will be pleased with the outcome, My Lord." Several shields had been hung as they talked, and one could get the idea of what it would look like when finished. Luveday was already happy with the outcome, now if only Iain would be too.

Iain looked at her for a moment too long, and Luveday thought he was going to tell them to take it all down, but "carry on," was all he said before striding out the doors.

Barth and Luveday did just that. They tested the ropes once again after putting on the first row of shields. Luveday had Elli, and Lady Emmalyn help her choose which shields to display and in what order. All in all, thirty-six shields decorated the one wall. There were only a few left so Luveday had them hung around the castle; some in the back hall the knights had taken over as a sleeping area and used as storage.

The back hall was a rather dark place that ran the back of the castle on the main floor with the sewing gallery above. The knights slept in there as the barracks were small and already full, with the exception of Sir Gregori who bunked in the rooms of the castle's chapel in the base of the tower in one of the curtain walls. She had tried to make the dungeon-like space comfortable for them, but they assured her that it was paradise compared to what they had endured on campaign. Luveday took their word for it.

Chapter 4

Meek leaves drop yearly from the forest-trees
To show, above, the unwasted stars that pass…
~Elizabeth Barrett Browning

A breeze ruffled the leaves above their heads, and Luveday stopped a moment to enjoy it. The days were turning warmer; there was more than a hint of summer on the air. The small group of women talked amongst themselves as their male protectors scanned the area for signs of trouble. The men took turns looking vigilant and bored beyond measure. They were not happy to be assigned this particular task, preferring to participate in the contests of skill that had sprung up between the men as of late.

Luveday sympathized with them. The contests were impressive to watch, and the knights' skills were so good that it rarely ended in injury. She had watched a few of the pairs locked in combat and wondered if it wasn't Lord Iain's need to expel some of his pent-up emotions that prompted these exercises.

Perhaps he felt as stifled in the castle as she had. Emmalyn, seeing Luveday's unrest, had suggested they take an outing in the woods to replenish some of the castle's supplies. They hunted for wild berries, mushrooms, and herbs. Cassandra and Emmalyn taught her what to look for and how to harvest items without killing the plants. It was all about sustainable collecting, though they didn't call it such. They cautioned about taking too much, as both had seen areas plucked clean of common healing herbs that left a community in danger. Luveday listened to their warnings with care.

The women stopped at midday to eat a light meal before heading back to the keep. Luveday's spirit felt lighter after the outing, and as she looked across the fields, she spotted an evenly spaced cropping of trees. She shielded her eyes against the sun and looked out to see men walking under the barren branches. Spring was in full swing though many of the trees were not yet thick with leaves. Turning back to join the women she gestured toward the grove as she asked Lady Emmalyn about them. "What are those trees opposite us? There are men out there."

Emmalyn looked out to see if she recognized the figures. "That is the orchard." She sighed heavily. "What's left of it. There are more fruit trees behind the castle, but they look the same."

"I take it they are doing poorly?" Luveday picked up a piece of dried fruit and wondered for the first time where it had come from.

"And have been for many years," Elli added.

Cassandra nodded as she sat on her wrap under the shade of the trees. "The man who cared for the orchards died several years ago; they have not been doing well since."

Elli leaned back as she munched on a bit of fresh bread. "They produce less and less fruit each season. I heard the men say that they might be sick, and we might have to burn them, but that was a few years ago."

Luveday was shocked. Diseased trees were no small thing. If the castle depended on their fruit, replacing those trees would mean importing new stock from somewhere else, when and if, they could kill whatever plagued these in the first place. Not to mention the fact that it would take years before the new trees were old enough to bare a good yielding of fruit. Did Iain have the coin to purchase a whole orchard of trees? No wonder he had been so concerned.

Sighing to herself, the image of the orchard stayed with her, not only as the women gathered their belongings and headed back to the castle, but through the following days. Luveday had a basic knowledge of fruit trees, which was probably more than most people in her time had. She liked to tell her family that she knew a little about a lot of things, but not very much about anything useful. Annalisa had always agreed with her, but it was Luveday her sister turned to if she needed help with anything. Being a researcher by trade meant that she knew where to gather the knowledge others were looking for. Thanks to her sister's organic homegrown philosophy, Luveday's whole family had started to garden and plant their own produce. Their father had a small impromptu orchard, an orange tree, apple, peach, plum and an old pecan. Trees were planted over the years, though like the castle orchard, they had never produced a bountiful supply of fruit, at least not in Luveday's memory.

That was until her father got it into his head to prune the trees. Luveday was roped into helping him as Annalisa was a busy mom. They had gotten a little carried away, and by the time the pair was done the trees look as if there had been a massacre, leaving Luveday to wonder if they would survive the devastation. Unexpectedly, they had lived, and not only did they grow new limbs, but they also produced so much fruit that her father had to remove most of it before it was even ripe to keep the new shoots from breaking under the heavy weight.

Luveday walked the orchard a few days later. She was alone and looked at the trees for signs of infestation or fungus, but didn't see any, though she hoped she remembered the signs correctly. It had been at least two years since she worked on the fruit trees with her father. They had had some pest problems and a little mold but had caught it early. These trees looked healthy though old, there were signs of insect activity, but it didn't look like an infestation. What did one expect without pesticides anyway? She thought.

Warin wove through the trees to reach her, not knowing that the lord of the keep was hot on his heels. "Lady Luveday!" He called out to her. Cassandra's husband was a nice man, a good man-at-arms and always polite and friendly to the women of the keep. "Lady!'

"Warin! What are you doing here?" Luveday asked as she checked a low hanging branch for signs of life. She broke the branch to see the green inside and was relieved that the trees were still alive though not yet budding.

"It's not safe to be out here alone, Lady!" Warin was breathing heavily by the time he reached her.

She turned to look at him, perplexed, "Not safe?"

Her companion looked away at the castle in concern as if he had said too much. "'Tis best to take a man with you if you go out. Just in case." He looked at her, hoping she would catch his meaning.

"Aye, just in case." Luveday agreed, concern flooding her system and causing her nerve endings to tingle. Looking at the twig she held in her hand, she switched topics as Warin ushered her back the way he had come. "Do you know who cares for the orchard, Warin? Cassandra said the man had died years ago, but someone must look after them."

Warin spotted his lord, but Iain gave him a look and followed at a distance. It was strange behavior, but then Iain was strange where this lady was concerned. Lord Iain had made several trips to the Abbey but had yet to persuade his bride to leave its comforts or its protection. Turning his thoughts back to the Lady, Warin answered as best as he could recall. "I do not think anyone cares for the trees, a few of the village men look after them, but they have no skill at it." He paused. "Archer spent some time with the old man, 'twas a friend of his father's, perhaps he will know something about them."

Luveday smiled. Archer was a young and rather handsome man-at-arms. He had a new bride, and they shared a cheery little cottage near the forest. "I will ask him about them when we return. Thank you, Warin."

"'Twas nothing, My Lady," Warin spoke little on their way back, concentrating on his breathing and getting them both inside the walls as soon as possible. Lord Iain shadowed them for a good distance. It was his Lord's expression upon hearing that the lady had gone outside on her own that had caused Warin to go after her. There were signs of men in the woods, men not part of the village. Perhaps they were just passing through, as the road before the Abbey was a busy one this time of year, but perhaps they had other plans. As Warin had said, better to be careful; just in case.

Archer was happy to walk with the Lady in the orchard and tried to answer her many questions. Archer had spent a good deal of his youth beside Grummand, the foreigner, who had taken care of the castle's orchard and gardens for many years. The man could grow anything, and when he passed the castle had suffered. He had been quiet, a lot like the trees he cherished, and no one knew how much Grummand had seen to until the tasks went undone. Now the lady was making him think of things he had not thought of in years, certainly not since he took up his position in the castle.

"The trees have not been cut in many a year." Archer looked at the mass of branches overhead and was sad to see them bare, like long bony fingers. If memory served, they should have been full of leaves and new buds beginning to bloom. "Grummand, the man who took care of the trees, he would cut them every other year, I think. Called it shaping, like he was carving something out of the branches."

"Yes, that sounds about right. So, it has been years since they were cared for?" Luveday had made a list of everything that she could remember about caring for the trees, but she was still unsure of herself. So, she had decided to experiment. She would try out her ideas on a few of the trees, five to be exact and see if her project produced any results. The rest of the orchard would be her base group, the unbiased measure of her success or failure.

With many ideas in mind and Archer at her side, she recruited several men to help since no one was willing to let her do it herself. Over the next few days, the group's notoriety wore off, and villagers stopped dropping by or taking notice. The group started by pruning the trees and cutting off any branches that pointed straight up or down. On two trees they cut off the tops so that the trees would grow out rather than up. Any major cuts were patched with tar and left. They dumped several buckets of fertilizer, a mixture of water and chicken manure, and watered some more to let it sink into the roots. Mounds were built around the base of the trees creating little moats to hold in the water. It took a few days of hard work with Luveday supervising and occasionally showing the men how she wanted things done, but soon it was time to wait for their work to bloom.

Luckily, the lord was gone again for this time, and Luveday was able to work without having to look over her shoulder. What was it that character had said? Annalisa quoted him a lot when she wanted something, she knew she would get in trouble for doing. *Right!* Better to ask forgiveness than permission. For once in Luveday's life, she wholeheartedly agreed.

The Abbey of St. Lucas housed the Cloister of the Heavenly Maiden. It was a beautiful compound with multiple buildings of dark gray stone, extensive gardens and a rich air about it. Father Quinn guided her through a tour of their gardens as he filled Luveday in on some of the Cloister's history. Luveday took it more as a warning than idle gossip. "Fine ladies from all over the kingdom come to the Abbey to take their vows. It is perhaps the most sought-after of all the cloisters." He looked out over the blossoming garden, but the sight didn't make him smile as it usually did and Luveday turned her thoughts from what ideas she could implement at the Keep to the Father's serious tone. "Mother Superior is a powerful woman, with a keen eye. I suppose she must be to become what she has."

Luveday knew that many powerful men came here, not only to visit their relatives in the abbey but to talk to the woman in charge. Emmalyn had commented that if Mary Odilia had been born a man, she would have been a force to be reckoned with, instead she was Mother Superior, and thank God for that. The lady rarely said an unkind word to anyone, and Luveday believed the animosity between the two women went back a long way. She thought that perhaps Father Quinn could shed some light on the matter.

The pair turned down a side path deep within the garden, Luveday thought the man looked for a place where they would not be overheard. "Mother Superior has done very well for the Abbey and her sisters, but her eye is always looking for something to make things better. A jewel in her crown as it were."

"Do you not take oaths that say your treasure will be stored up in heaven and not on the earthly plane?" Luveday commented.

He looked taken aback for a moment but smiled at her. "Yes, but Mother Superior is now concerned with leaving behind a legacy worthy of the abbey." The Father stopped to examine a grouping of flowering plants that Luveday recognized as chamomile. "To secure a happy future for the Abbey would entail the acquisition of a generous benefactor, who would lavish money on the Abbey and its endeavors." He watched her out of the corner of his eye as they heard footsteps swiftly approaching.

Sister Gaynor had welcomed the small group to the Abbey that morning. Her appearance now did not look so cheerful. The woman was out of breath, and flustered, but she tried to compose herself as she addressed them. "Father Quinn, Lady Luveday. Lady Christabel is now ready to see you. Mother Superior has asked her to take refreshments in the sitting room and asked that you join them, Lady." The summons clearly did not include the priest in the invitation to the inner sanctum.

He gave Luveday a sharp look before turning back to Sister Gaynor with a bright smile and a cheerful comment. "That would be wonderful. I will continue to look over the gardens. We can meet at the front gate when you are ready, Lady." With that, he shooed away the women and continued on his path through the lush green rows and manicured beds.

Sister Gaynor asked the Lady to follow her, but Luveday had trouble keeping up with her shuffling scurry. It seemed the good sister was in a hurry and afraid of being late, or perhaps of keeping Mother Superior waiting.

The sitting room was exactly what Luveday was expecting, down to the gilded mirror and velvet cushions. The furniture was sumptuous and rich with dark woods and polished surfaces. It was a place she entertained important guests. Luveday attributed her presence to curiosity. Obviously, the woman had heard something about her, from Christabel or any number of other sources and wanted to meet her; it was curiosity and nothing more.

Mary Odilia was a sharp contrast to her surroundings, the simple but fine garment she wore was not the traditional black of her modern counterparts, nor the plain tawny wool of her fellow sisters. Her garment was a beautiful pale blue that reminded Luveday of the color of the Madonna's gowns in many traditional paintings. The wimple she wore was a crisp white and also a sign of her status as most were made of the course unbleached linen. The top of the wimple was a piece of darker cloth that acted like a hood which was a deeper, cobalt blue. Looking at her, Luveday saw that her eyes were as pale a blue as her gown and held an icy intelligence. As Luveday was introduced to Mother Superior, she revised her opinion of why she was there; it was more than curiosity. The Mother Superior wished to size her up. Friend or foe, Luveday thought that it would depend on what the woman wanted from her, because sure as day, Luveday knew that the woman wanted something.

"Lady Luveday, please join us." Mother Superior gestured with an elegant hand. Thanking her, Luveday took a delicate looking chair at the table were Lady Christabel also resided. Mistress Adela was nowhere to be seen. "Lady Christabel has told me of your amazing journey here; to think what could have happened." She sounded sincere in her concern.

"The Creator has blessed me with good fortune and helped me find my way, Mother Superior. My fate could have been a sorrowful one, but I thank the moment Sir Gregori found me." She stated simply. Truthfully, Luveday had had a few nightmares after arriving at the castle. She knew exactly what could have befallen her and thanked the Lord each night that she was safe, with new friends in this strange place, even as she waited to see what her purpose here was.

"He gives, and he takes away," her eyes narrowed as she looked at Luveday as if she looked too deep. "He has plans for you, child. Good plans. Noble plans." She said it almost as one might expect a fortune teller to impart a glimpse of the future. Luveday wasn't sure if she should believe the woman or not, but the Mother Superior's words seemed to carry a weight that settled within her. It didn't lighten her spirit or make her feel at peace, it was a heavy weight of expectation, of things to come.

Christabel broke through the brooding air as she looked at Luveday and commented on her appearance. Christabel had been gone from the keep for a little over six weeks, and the change in Luveday was noticeable. Gone was the dull tawny hair and in its place, was a head of gold. Gone was the sallow complexion and in its place a happy glow. The woman had lost a stone or more and looked almost pretty without a bit of rouge or powder. A spark of jealousy flared to life in her breast but was quickly extinguished. *After all, what did a poor lady like Luveday have in common with the likes of her?* No, Christabel chose to pity her instead. No amount of prettiness could raise her state or stature. The woman was still on the round side, and her gown was a borrowed monstrosity they had tried to make fit her shorter frame. Yes, the lady was to be pitied, and so Christabel let lose what kindness she possessed.

"Lady Luveday, you look improved since I last saw you." She smiled kindly, but not without the pity showing through. "Lord Wolf has said the castle is much improved. Mother Superior was gracious enough to accommodate Lady Emmalyn's offer to buy some of the furnishings from the Abbey." Christabel looked gratefully over to her protector who nodded and smiled softly at the young lady.

Luveday thought some words of gratitude were expected of her. "Thank you for your kindness, Mother Superior."

While they seemed to talk of trivial things, Luveday watched the mother for signs of interest. The only sign of emotions was the widening or narrowing of the woman's eyes. Her small smile was constant and reminded her a bit of the Mona Lisa. *The Mother knew something she was keeping to herself.*

Luveday spoke of the improvements or at least tried to, but Christabel was clearly uninterested. She asked if anyone had arrived at the castle, perhaps expecting a royal guest as the lord and his men were nothing special in her opinion. The conversation turned quickly to court, and it was Luveday's turn to listen carefully. Luveday added the conversation to what little she knew of the King's court. Christabel's father was a powerful man, who seemed to want this marriage for his daughter. The King's Champion was a powerful ally, and a connection Lord Henric wished to capitalize on. Mother Superior spoke of Christabel's father with soft awe, and respect she did not use when mentioning De Lane. Luveday did not know if she was sincere or if her words were for Christabel's benefit.

Conversation slowed to a stop, and Luveday took the opportunity to take her leave. Mother Superior looked as if she wished for Luveday to stay, but Christabel was getting bored with the country lady and wanted to head back to her room.

Mother Superior was about to say something more when Sister Gaynor appeared and announced the presence of a *visitor*. The two women shared a look between them that even Christabel did not miss. Gaynor hurried off as the Mother Superior quickly said her goodbyes then left them. Christabel looked to Mistress Adela who was waiting in the shadows of a nearby door. The look on the nurse's face was one of pained patience.

"Lady Luveday, good day." The older woman looked pleased to see her.

"Good day, Mistress Adela. I hope you are well." Luveday greeted her. Christabel was done with pleasantries and announced to everyone within hearing that she was tired and would be resting in her room until supper.

Mistress Adela smiled at her charge. "That is good, My Lady. I will accompany Lady Luveday to the gates." And without further ado, she grabbed Luveday's arm and walked away leaving Christabel pouting behind them.

Luveday wondered at the woman's haste and the iron grip on her forearm. Luveday didn't say a word but let Mistress Adela pick the time and place. It did not take long before they were out of the area the sisters used and into the common spaces the guests frequented, where the sisters did not usually linger. They slowed and seemed to take a serpentine path to the gates.

"Lady Bella, I mean Lady Christabel, and I have enjoyed our stay at the abbey." She stated a little too matter-of-factly. Luveday didn't answer as it looked as if her companion was deep in her own thoughts. "Mother Superior has been extremely gracious in allowing us to stay so long." The mistress gave her a hard look; she made it clear that in her opinion they had stayed too long. "My Lady has grown fond of the place; it is *very* comfortable for a lady such as herself."

There was something more to her words, that reminded her of Father Quinn's warnings. She was trying to say something without actually saying it. Luveday hazarded a guess. "It seems that the Mother Superior is happy to let you stay with the women."

"YES!" She looked relieved that Luveday had understood her. "The Mother would not mind if we stayed a good while longer, but I am eager to see the changes Lord Iain spoke of. I am sure the castle is much improved. I hear that while under your care it has blossomed. Lord Iain even mentioned the spoils of his campaign, no doubt to impress My Lady. It sounds like Lander's Keep will be a jewel among the country lords." Mistress Adela guided her down another corridor. They must be close to the gates by now, Luveday thought.

"Indeed, such riches I had never imagined. Lord Iain has done very well for himself. I am sure even the King will be pleased by the transformation." Luveday hoped she was giving the woman some ammunition to fire against Christabel's seeming indifference.

"I will tell My Lady you said so." They were finally before the gates, were Father Quinn waited expectantly. He smiled upon seeing the lady but did not move to meet them. "Thank you for visiting, and please tell his lordship that we look forward to his next visit as well." Mistress Adela gave her another lingering look.

Luveday was growing weary of the intrigue but smiled politely at her not knowing who else might be watching. "I will relay your message. Good day, Mistress Adela."

"And to you, Lady Luveday." And without another word the woman was gone.

As Luveday came abreast to the priest, he looked her over and smiled at her tired and confused expression. As they walked through the gate and headed for the road that would lead home, Father Quinn asked a single question. "An enlightening trip, My Lady?" She knew he asked about more than just their reason for coming, a look at the gardens.

Sighing heavily, Luveday answered enigmatically. "Indeed, Father Quinn. In more ways than one." The walk home was long, but she had never been so happy to see the great doors as she was that evening.

Luveday relayed Mistress Adela's message. Lord Iain got the undercurrents in her words. He did not ask her opinion of what had transpired but discerned it by how she chose to word her recounting of the conversation. It was no surprise that Iain was gone the next morning to visit the abbey. While many asked about the visit, only Lady Emmalyn seemed to know what the situation was. It did not seem to surprise her either.

The day carried on like any other. Luveday was mentally expanding the castle garden to rival the abbey's as she performed her duties when a commotion like she had never heard roared in from the bailey. Screams and cries, nearly stopped Luveday's heart as she ran not towards the commotion but for the healing supplies. Lady Emmalyn was as white as a ghost when Luveday arrived with several women who brought clean linen and hot water. The lady was in shock and would be no help to her, so Luveday asked someone to run for Cassandra as she weaved her way through the group of men, to a small, unused room under the stairs.

A small cot had been placed inside the room, and a man covered in blood and sweat lay in the bed so ashen that he looked almost dead except for his shallow breathing. Candles had been brought to lighten the room, but there were too many people in too small a space. "Clear out everyone." The men protested, clearly this man was a friend, but they were no help to her. "I need only two men, two men with strong stomachs." They cleared out, and Luveday prayed she would hold up under strain. She had never done something like this and shook at the idea of doing it alone. The men turned pale, but not as pale as the injured gentleman. She looked back over her shoulder as she blocked the door, he was still breathing. Looking out at the men no one stepped forward. The women deposited their items inside the room with only quick glances at the cot and left in a hurry. Luveday had no time for this, so she chose two. "Sir Gregori," who only nodded solemnly, "and Sir Perivale." The second man looked as if he might be ill but stepped up just the same.

Back in the room, she had the men move the bed away from the wall, just enough to allow one of them to get to the other side of the cot. There wasn't much room to work with. Luveday washed her hands and kneeling on the floor beside the low bed, she began to hunt down the source of the blood. A piece of cloth was pressed to the wound until the bleeding had stopped. There was a gash in the man's right thigh that looked as if someone had tried to cut it to the bone. Luveday worried about the main artery there, but she was sure he would have bled out by now if anything had nicked it. She used the warm water to soak the cloth before she removed it to get a better look at what they were dealing with. The blood was thick and dry, and Luveday worried at how fast infection could set in.

She worked diligently, issuing orders and not thinking about how quickly they were obeyed. Emmalyn and Cassandra both joined them, but neither woman interrupted. Cass held onto the lady as Emmalyn cried quiet tears. Time passed without Luveday being aware of it. She worked smart and utterly focused on the task at hand as if she had been doing this all her life. She didn't hesitate as she sliced off bits of shredded skin. She soon had the wound cleaned enough to see the damage properly. There was no way for her to tell if the man would be able to use the limb again when he healed.

Muscle lay open to the air, and already the skin around the wound looked wrong. Blood poisoning was not a pretty way to go. Luveday focused on what she could do, not the distant future. She did not let herself believe anything, but that this man would live. There was still debris in the wound, she could see clumps of dirt in the gash in the muscle. It looked like someone had tried to cut off his leg but had somehow missed, laying open a shallow furrow from groin to knee. The majority of the wound was not deep but laid open from the top inside of his thigh, almost at his groin, to extend down the inner thigh and turn out to finish over his knee. There was a piercing wound on the inside of his upper thigh, only a handsbreadth from his groin. She prodded the hole left by the blade that had done this. It looked as if he were stabbed with the blade, a puncture wound about the width of her first finger went deep into his leg. If the blade had been a little farther in, she was sure the artery would have been severed. As it was, the wound was starting to bleed again, she thought that was a good sign.

"Get me some more boiled water and tell Warin to bring that horrible drink of his. I need a mug of it."

One of the men outside laughed at her call for spirits. "Aye, we could use a drink too." Her two helpers nodded but said nothing. She continued to clean the wound as best she could but couldn't tell them what she planned to do with the strong alcohol. They would never help her otherwise.

The spirits arrived first, and Luveday set them aside and washed the wound with water again, not caring that liquid ran down in rivers, soaking her skirts as she knelt beside the bed. The gash looked clean, but to be sure it was free of infection she had to do this next part and prayed that her patient would remain unconscious a while longer. Luveday retrieved what she would need from the healing supplies and dropped the threaded needle into the spirits and let it set a few moments. Moving to her feet, Luveday issued her orders without so much as a hint of the doubt that ate at her stomach. She had a feeling this was going to be bad, but it had to be done. Cassandra had prepared an ointment that she could put on the wounds once the gash was sewn closed, but it would keep infection out, not treat something left within. "Gregori hold his shoulders, and Perivale his legs. Put your weight into it." Luveday fished the needle and thread from the bottom of the cup. The ladies exited the room, and the door swung closed behind them. Without thinking it over again, Luveday dumped the contents of the mug onto his leg and the most horrible scream she had ever heard rang through the tiny room. Gregori and Perivale held their friend as he writhed in pain, both men looking at her in horror. No one outside dared to open the door to see what was going on.

Luveday used a clean cloth to wipe away the excess liquid and spoke as calmly and soothingly to the man as she could as she began sewing up his leg. He settled and watched her a moment with hooded eyes before succumbing to oblivion again. Luveday didn't know what she said to the man, she spoke of things from home, of happy summers and comfort, and wasn't sure it made any sense to anyone, not even herself. By the time she was done sewing, she was done talking. The ointment she applied was noxious and burned a little, but it would keep the suture clean as it healed. Already the redness around the wound looked faded. Gregori looked at her sweaty face in the glow of the candles and only nodded to her. Perivale staggered around the bed and out of the room. She stopped Gregori as he pushed passed her. "What is his name?" She finally thought to ask.

Gregori just looked at her. "Lord Benedict St. James of Lion's Head," came a haggard voice from behind her.

Luveday turned to look into the face of Lord Iain and knew that he had been present for that scream, and that like her, it still echoed through his mind. She nodded past the lump in her throat.

Iain did not enter the room as Luveday called for the women to help her clean up. The women worked quickly, removing the ruined garments and washing the blood from his body. Benedict moved and moaned but did not awaken even when they brought another cot and lifted him to remove the soiled one. They covered his naked form with a sheet of clean linen and placed blankets and furs at the foot of the bed. Someone placed a pile of belongings outside the door not wanting to clutter the tiny room. The floor was cleaned, Luveday scrubbed it herself. Her gown was already ruined, there was no need for the women to fuss over it. Someone offered to bring incense, but Luveday asked that they burn a candle in the chapel instead, the room was too small for the thick aroma.

The day passed into night with Luveday keeping watch. Emmalyn came and sat with her for a while, relaying some of her patient's past and identity. Benedict was a companion of Iain's, more like a brother. He and Gregori were always at De Lane's side. They had grown from long-legged youths to knights together, a small band of brothers. Benedict was the charmer, always a smile and a joke to contrast Iain's foolhardiness and Gregori's quiet demeanor. Through tournaments and fierce battles, the three of them could be found side by side.

Emmalyn had watched the boys grow, taking them in as her own after her own young sons had died so suddenly. Lady Jane St. James was the man's mother and Emmalyn's dearest friend. Seeing him hurt and so pale sent her mind racing to things she had hoped to forget. Her heart broke as if it were her own son once again. The lady quietly apologized for not helping, but Luveday just took her hand and held it for a while. Neither noticed Iain's presence or when he left to find his bed. The lady left soon after, urging Luveday to find her bed for a few hours at least. "Change your gown and wash up. One of the women can keep vigil for a while."

Reluctantly, Luveday finally took the advice and was happy to find that the water in her room was still warm when she stripped to only her underwear and a shirt to lay down on the bed. If she could, she would pour some of her own strength into the knight to heal him. In fact, it felt as if she had done just that.

The night had not been kind to Benedict. Sometime in the wee hours, a fever had started to take hold. Luveday found him flushed and restless a few hours later when she returned from her brief rest. Henna watched as she took a candle and heated the glass vile that contained the willow bark syrup that Cassandra had taught Luveday to make. It was easier to manipulate when warm, and the chill in the room had caused the sticky substance to harden. Luveday used the candle to liquefy the honey like medicine so that she could dispense a spoonful down the young man's throat. The syrupy concoction was made to taste better than its tincture counterpart and was far more potent. A little was enough to help bring down his body temperature and help with some of his pain. Luveday checked the wound again, though still raw looking the coloring was good. She had stitched the skin closed in strategic places in case there was a need to reopen the wound. She laid the cloth back in place and took up her stool beside the cot never noticing when Henna left a little while later.

When she emerged from the room a few hours after dawn, she was surprised to find that Iain and a handful of men were already gone. Elli retold what news they had heard from the men. A traveler had found Benedict on the road, not far from the Abbey. At the time, the young Lord was still conscious and had asked to be brought here. Gregori and some men had come across them as they went to the Abbey to talk to Father Quinn and Lord Iain. Elli let it slip that they were there to talk about Lady Christabel, but a look from Emmalyn had her back to the subject at hand. Benedict didn't make much sense as he tried to talk to his friend. Gregori had sent a man to the Abbey to fetch Iain, and the rest had helped to transport the injured young Lordling to the keep. St. James's horse had arrived on its own not long after its master had been settled and Iain had arrived not long after that. At the news, De Lane had ridden out of the Abbey as if the very devil pursued him.

Supposedly there was talk of foul play in the woods. Iain had left at first light to examine the scene. They were to collect the traveler from the Abbey, and he was to show the men where he had found the wounded knight. Elli's recounting had all the drama and dire tones of a horror story, but Luveday knew there was a real danger here. Someone had tried to kill that man, and more than likely they would try again. Luveday returned to her patient and sat talking to him about the world outside of his little windowless cell though she was unsure if he actually heard her.

Two days passed before Luveday looked up from her sewing and found Benedict looking back at her with intense eyes. Her song stuttered to a stop, and she poked herself with the needle as she dropped her work into her lap. Benedict had opened his eyes on and off through the last two days, but when they tried to speak to him, there was no recognition, no understanding. He'd close his eyes again as if he wished to sleep for a hundred years, which wasn't so outrageous to Luveday. His golden hair and bright blue eyes with their long lashes reminded her of a Disney princess, though the rest of him was decidedly male.

He leaned up against the wall at the head of the bed, how he had gotten in that position without her noticing she couldn't guess. He shifted his weight and grimaced. Luveday got to her feet and offered him a drink.

"I am Lady Luveday, and you are safe in Lander's Keep." Luveday thought he would be relieved by the news, but the look he gave her over the rim of his cup clearly said, 'I know,' as if he had spoken the words aloud. Luveday waited until he finished the drink which was laced with a bit of the willow bark to help with the pain and inflammation.

The first word out of his mouth was, "Iain?"

"Gone for two days to hunt the countryside for whoever did this to you." Luveday didn't know what to expect, but his reaction finally showed the relief she had thought to see earlier. He nodded, still tired and threw back the edge of the blanket that concealed him to remove the heavy cloth that covered the upper half of his right leg. The edges of his skin where healing together nicely, even Emmalyn and Cassandra were surprised at how well he was doing. Another day or two and they would bind the wound closed with a proper bandage, a week or so after that they might remove the stitches.

He stared at the long line twisting down his thigh for several minutes in silence. Luveday watched the flicker of his eyes until he sighed and returned the linens to their former place. He looked at her and in a clear and steady voice said, "'Tis not as bad as I had thought."

Luveday smiled at him, and he returned it. "No, it's not."

Over the next week, Iain spent more time roaming the countryside than at home. His bride was momentarily forgotten as he searched for the villains who had dared to attack his blood-brother. Iain was filled with such rage that if he had found the culprit during those first few days, he would have killed the man with his bare hands. Luveday sent men out with supplies every few days, Iain believed it was more to update him on Benedict's condition than because she thought he was unable to fend for himself. He admitted that the food and messages were very welcome.

After nearly a fortnight the men returned home. Iain was wary and tired of chasing shadows. If this attacker truly meant Benedict harm than it was only a matter of time before he tried again. Better to plan and wait for his prey to come to him. It was late afternoon when he entered the hall and headed for the room under the stairs. The door was ajar to let in air, and laughter rang out from the small space, male and female laughter. Iain couldn't help but smile as he recognized the mumbling voices, but that smile soon turned to a frown as he approached the door. *What were those two talking about*? Rather than let his presence be known, he waited to listen at the cracked door.

Stifled female laughter. "He didn't!" She tried to catch her breath between laughs and gulps of air.

"Yes, he did! And got up and did it again, the bloody fool!" Benedict laughed heartily, then groaned aloud. Iain opened the door to see Luveday leaning over Benedict examining his leg.

"Careful now!" She reprimanded; all humor gone.

Benedicts smiled at her bent head when she could not see him. The light in his eyes annoyed Iain, it was a look of affection. "When will I be able to leave this bed, Lady?"

Straightening Luveday smiled at him, it was a question he had been asking every few hours for the last couple of days. "Walking is out of the question, but..." she paused and looked at him. Her eyes narrowed as his smile widened. "But perhaps we can move you to the hearth for a little while this afternoon."

"Lady!" Benedict swooped forward to grab her hand, meaning to kiss it, but Iain's voice cut through the happy moment.

"Lady Luveday! Benedict!" The Lord's happy demeanor held a false quality that Benedict was familiar with. Iain was angry and yet wanted to appear as if he had just arrived and was happy to greet them. Benedict wondered how long he had been waiting to come in. "Benedict, you look well!"

"All thanks to this lovely lady." Benedict teased her with the play on her name, but Luveday didn't think he meant anything by it. She knew she was not lovely, no matter what her name implied. She felt that Lady Christabel, Lady Emmalyn, and even Elli were far prettier than her, and Benedict was just an incorrigible flirt.

"Do you think it is wise to get him up, Lady Luveday?" Iain filled the doorway and rested his hands on each side of the casement. Benedict wondered why he was posturing so, making himself look bigger, then smiled. His friend was jealous. Benedict realized the truth and humor settled in. He would not let Iain have all the pretty women of the castle, and so decided to make an effort to win this lady, even if he had no intentions of bedding her. Iain wouldn't know that, and so it would be a good game between the two. He thought Luveday would be a good sport, she was a compassionate lady with a sharp wit and lively sense of humor.

Luveday looked over her shoulder at him and then turned sideways on the stool so she could turn her head and see both men easily. "I don't expect him to walk, but we can move him into the Hall." She turned back to her patient and looked at the grimace on his face. He didn't like the notion of being carried. "Sitting by the hearth for a while should tire you out well enough."

"Oh, I see. You just want me to rest." He said. "Always rest."

She was familiar with this joke. "And stop asking questions." She countered.

"Is that how it is?" He asked in mock offense.

"Just so." She laughed at him as she got to her feet. "I'll let you two talk for a bit while I see about moving our guest."

"Guest!" Benedict huffed at her retreating form. "More like prisoner!" His raised voice echoed through the halls with her laughter. He smiled at Iain as his friend took the vacant chair. "Any news, brother?"

"No." De Lane felt exhaustion settle in as he sat down. "We saw where you were attacked and followed a trail back through the wood, but lost it." He ran a hand through his hair and over his rough beard. "We hunted down any sightings of a man matching the description you gave Gregori, but to no avail." He looked Benedict in the eyes, for once his friend wasn't laughing or smiling or making jests. "If he means to finish the job, he'll have to come here."

"That was what I was thinking." Benedict sat back, suddenly tired. "Better to wait for the enemy than chase our tails around the countryside."

"Aye." Iain looked at him sharply. "How are you feeling, other than giving the ladies grief?"

Benedict laughed at him. "The ladies love me! You know that." Iain grumbled. Benedict leaned in as if he were imparting a secret. Iain leaned in as well. "Besides, Lady Luveday fancies me!"

"Like hell she does!" He spat, rocking back.

"No, she spends most of her day here keeping me company, checking the leg." He wiggled his toes. "She fancies me!" He grinned.

"Stay away from Lady Luveday, Benedict!" He growled before rising and heading toward the door, but his friend's words caused him to turn back with a glare.

"It's I who is stuck in this damn bed," he chuckled. "'Tis easier to tell her to stay clear of me!"

Iain bumped into Luveday as he turned away from Benedicts grinning face. He had to grab hold of her to steady them both. They looked into each other's eyes, momentarily startled. Without a word, Iain let go of her, stepped back and then brushed past on his way to the solar. Luveday watched him stomp toward the stairs and a moment later heard the solar's outer door slam against its frame with a loud bang that echoed through the hall.

She moved to see Benedict had witnessed the exchange and laughed merrily to himself. She asked him in confusion, "What was all that about?"

Benedict continued to laugh heartily. "Nothing lady. 'Twas nothing." She gave him a dubious look as she set the fresh pitcher of ale beside the bed. He looked at her and thought happily, *Let the game begin!*

Chapter 5

God answers sharp and sudden on some prayers and thrust
the thing we have prayed for in our face, like a gauntlet with a gift in it.
~Elizabeth Barrett Browning

Benedict's wound healed fast and well; it was only a short time until he was a permanent fixture before the hearth. The man was eager to use his legs but listened to the women and settled for the chair before the fire though they knew they couldn't keep him in it for long. His presence lightened the mood of the castle, even Iain was seen smiling a good deal around the hall. One night when they were gathered around the fire after supper, Iain came down from a bath, clean shaven and smelling fresh. The last few days had seen him to the Abbey and back several times, and the man looked rougher than usual after each trip.

Luveday had gotten up to pour another round of drinks and looked up at hearing the solar door open. Feminine laughter emerged as Coll came down and behind him a very handsome man. Luveday's brain froze. A part of her knew who she was staring at, but another part couldn't believe that a man that handsome had been hiding under all that hair. The women had said he was a fine-looking lord, more so than most men, but some of them had a vastly different notion of what was pleasing to the eye; quite different from Luveday's tastes, at least.

He smiled at her, a small quirk of his lips as if he knew what she was thinking and Luveday was shocked back into her body. She looked down sharply to find that the mug she was filling was near to overflowing with ale. Luveday checked herself, embarrassed. *How long had she been staring at him?*

Benedict looked around his chair to see what had caught the lady's attention and grinned. So, Iain had shaved and cut his locks. It was about time. Benedict couldn't help but comment. "Finally bathed, have you? I had forgotten what an ugly face was lurking under that pelt."

Iain laughed. "I've not heard the women complaining about it."

"The ladies are too polite, I'm sure." Benedict looked at Iain's clean-shaven face and couldn't help but cause trouble. Iain sat next to him, closer to the fire and watched Luveday as she refilled mugs of ale. "Lady Luveday, do you not think my friend is handsome?" Benedict asked playfully. Emmalyn called his name, but her laughter softened the warning. She knew what he was up to, what he had been up to these last few days. Luckily, Luveday's head wasn't turned, she took the teasing and flirting as a jest, and occasionally gave as good as she got.

Luveday smiled, as she looked over her shoulder at the two men. Benedict wore his charming grin, and while Iain smiled his eyes were narrowed as he awaited her reply, "Aye, Lord Benedict. He is handsome, I am sure many women have told him so."

"Aye, a few men as well." Emmalyn and the men laughed at his jest.

"My nephew has quite the reputation, or so I'm told." The elder lady did not look upset, she smiled mischievously at her nephew across the way.

He looked uncomfortable for a moment but smiled heartily back at her. "Nothing that needs concern you, Aunt. And who have you been talking to, to hear of such things?"

"Never you mind, lad. Never you mind." Iain looked perplexed at his aunt's answer as she sipped her drink.

"Quite a few fights have started over that face." Benedict continued. The men laughed, and Iain scowled.

Luveday laughed as well, quoting under her breath, "the face that launched a thousand ships."

"'Twas an excuse, the fight started long before they saw his face," Gregori added.

"Yet, I quite distinctly remember them complaining about it." Benedict laughed. Cursing Iain's handsome face had been a game for them. Anytime anything had gone wrong, they reverted to blaming it. More than one fight had started with some yelling, "Damn your comely face," just before someone tried to rearrange it for him.

"I remember them complaining about other things as well," Iain looked knowingly at his friend.

"Damn," Benedict mumble under his breath, but Luveday was at his elbow, and he looked up startled. She had heard him. "My apologies lady, but my friend is not playing nice."

She readily countered that comment. "I did not think you two played nice with each other."

Benedict gasp in mock hurt. "Never say so, lady. We are the best of friends. This *is* our nice."

Luveday smiled at them and chuckled. "If this is nice, I shudder to think of you playing dirty."

Humming under his breath, Benedict caught the speculative look Iain gave Luveday's remark. "Yes, I suppose it would be something to see, Lady; besides being so much more fun." Iain glared at him while Emmalyn called a halt to their banter.

Luveday finally handed Iain a mug and filled it with cool ale. She did not look him in the eye but concentrated on her task. Iain took a moment to look her over in the firelight. The woman had changed a good deal since her arrival. She was pretty with blonde hair and changing eyes. She wasn't a great beauty, but there was something kind and trustworthy about her, or perhaps that was only what he had come to see.

Benedict interrupted his thoughts. "So, brother, what is the occasion? Why shave a year's worth of hair from your chin?" They glared at each other, Benedict with his cocky grin and Iain with a light of his own.

Iain smiled wide. "Tomorrow I am to head back to the Abbey," he paused a moment for effect, "to escort Lady Christabel home." He stated in triumph.

There were gasps from the women and a good deal of hearty joking and congratulations from the men. Luveday, who stood amongst them with her back to the fire looked to Iain startled, smiled strangely at him, looked to Lady Emmalyn perplexed, who nodded at her, and then rushed for the stairs that led to the kitchens. Iain watched the exchange with confusion and a bitter taste in his mouth that the ale did not wash away.

Luveday and the ladies worked deep into the night to prepare for the arrival of Iain's bride. They were determined to present themselves as they should have the first time, if not for the lady, then for their own honor. Luveday and Emmalyn changed around the menu to surprise the lady with fine food. The important items on her list had been taken care of a month ago, her rooms cleaned spotless and bedding aired. All that was left was to make sure the rooms were still clean and to do the little touches that would please any young woman. Fresh flowers were picked the next morning, plates of dried fruit and cheese ready to greet her. Luveday raked her brain for anything that might help to win the lady's heart, but she could think of nothing to add.

When the afternoon rolled on, and the procession finally made it to the castle, both Iain, and Christabel were in a fine mood. They looked as if they might have been arguing the whole way, but the castle, in full, was present to greet her. The people quickly dispersed as Iain glared daggers at them and their future lady ignored the welcoming party entirely.

Christabel watched until the last item was unloaded from the cart before entering the hall. She was met at the door by Luveday and Emmalyn who had retired inside its shadow to watch the scene in the courtyard unfold with concern. The lady swept by the two women, took a look at the hall, sniffed delicately, and headed straight to her room. The slamming of her door echoed through the hall for what seemed like minutes. Luveday turned to look at De Lane as he marched up the few stairs to the great door. He stopped to look at her, then up at the staircase. When his gaze returned to her, it was hard, and Luveday forced down the urge to step back by straightening her spine.

"Is there anything I can get you, My Lord?" She asked in a calm, clear voice that did not reflect the turmoil inside.

He looked as if he were about to say something and then changed his mind. "No, Lady Luveday. I *need* nothing." The way he said *need* made her think that he put a good deal of meaning behind the word. She wished she knew him better to be able to understand the intellect behind his, sometimes, mercurial moods. Luveday knew there was a great deal on his mind. His responsibilities were vast and to throw a bride on top of trying to rebuild his estates was adding to his burdens. "Money," Luveday whispered to herself as she watched him ascend the stairs. "You can't buy happiness." She thought ironically, considering the situation. There was talk of Christabel's bride price and the money needed to restore the lands. Iain was marrying for money, not love. She thought Christabel might be more of a burden than a help in the times to come and wondered if, in the end, it would be worth it.

Christabel settled in, much as she had before. Her demands were at times absurd and Luveday was often called upon to mediate by Mistress Adela. The castle was coming to despise their future lady no matter what Luveday, Adela or Emmalyn did to help. The lord of the castle tried to charm his lady; his handsome face was only a momentary distraction. It was clear that Christabel did not wish to be there and had many wondering why she stayed.

Iain spent as much time with his betrothed as he could stand. Luckily, duties called him away. He was grateful for the respite as he rode across his lands and surveyed the improvements. The masons were hard at work on the mill and had done a fine job on the cottages. The men were back in the fields and greeted him kindly. He tried not to be upset when they followed the polite questions about his health and the weather with inquiries about Lady Luveday or wishing him luck with his reluctant bride.

"Damn the woman!" He whispered under his breath, but Gregori, who had decided to accompany him on this outing, heard.

"Which woman?" He laughed, as Iain cursed his exceptionally good hearing.

"All of them... none of them... why can't they just... just..." He growled under his breath as he ground his teeth. Gregori laughed until he had tears in his eyes. It was so unusual to see Iain perplexed by the fairer sex.

His friend had always seen women in certain lights. He put them in place in his mind, once in a camp, he no longer worried about them. There were the mothering types like Lady Emmalyn and Lady Jane. The Courtesan types, like Lady Katherine who wanted only the handsome face or the notoriety of sleeping with the King's Champion. There were proper ladies suitable to take to wife, like Christabel and other court flowers that expected all the chivalrous customs of a knight. Below them were the serving women that worked at hand and could be bedded if he had a mind to. His were simple, straightforward categories that influenced his behavior concerning women, yet now he had two women that no longer fit into his view of the world. Christabel had changed categories to become something he had only vague notions of what such a woman must be like, his future bride. Bride was not a category he had ever spent much time thinking about, and the fact that a court beauty had suddenly taken up the single position was not heartening in the least. On the other hand, there was Luveday who refused to fit into any category and instead decided to confuse him by jumping around from one to another as it pleased her. His moment of fancy had briefly placed her in the bride category which still confused him as he tried to ignore the images it conjured and his growing appreciation for the woman. "Damn these women!" He said again causing the few men with him to laugh harder.

Gregori leaned over to slap him on the shoulder. "Don't worry, my brother! There is always a good way to handle the fairer sex!"

Iain looked at him, seeing the amusement in his friend's eyes as Gregori lightened his mood. Women had never been a problem for him in the past, and by God, they wouldn't be now.

The tinker made his way slowly up the road, his passage wasn't slowed by pain or fatigue, but by his examination of the scenery. He had heard that Lander's Keep had recently blossomed under the care of a young lady and the return of its lord. The King's Champion was known far in wide for his skills on the battlefield, and it was also well known that he had not been home for some years. The tinker, Thom Little, had made the familiar journey a number of months earlier to find the Champion's aunt, the fair Lady Emmalyn, had taken residence in the hall, but to the tinker's mind, it had been no place for any lady. That was no longer the case.

Flowers blossomed, adorning the newly whitewashed cottages in a rainbow of color. The new village garden flourished in contained chaos. The people who greeted him were smiling, and women rushed out to check his wares, and barter trinkets with him. As he finally made his way into the courtyard of the keep, he was surprised at the transformation.

A group of elegantly dressed people emerged to greet him.

"Lady Emmalyn, a pleasure to see you again." The tinker swept off his hat and bowed in a flourish.

The lady smiled, as she looked to her female companions. "Tinker Thom. Good to see you back again."

"It is always a joy to stop at Lander's Keep." Thom let down the legs on the cart so the ladies could take a look.

Emmalyn called to the others. "Lady Christabel, Mistress Adela. Tinker Thom Little has the best merchandise in the country. Come and take a look. Lady Luveday!" Emmalyn looked around. "Where is Lady Luveday?"

Elysant dragged a reluctant woman from the keep. "I have her, Lady Emmalyn!"

"Alright Elli, I'm coming." The last lady was not much to look at compared to Lady Christabel's dark tresses and thin frame, but Thom liked the look of her. He had heard of Lady Luveday, and of the trouble, the young Christabel had caused the keep and its lord. There was something cold and hard about the court lady, but Luveday was a summer daisy, and Thom took to her as she started a conversation with him and only glanced at his wares.

"Tinker Thom Little. Lady Emmalyn speaks highly of you." Lady Luveday watched the women coo over jewelry and other bobbles but took no interest in them herself.

The tinker blushed as Lady Emmalyn nodded. He wasn't a young man, nor was he old, but he blushed like a young girl at the compliment. "Tinker Thom is the best tinker north of town, that is for sure, Lady." He said of himself and gave her a bow.

She smiled, showing a pretty row of white teeth. "You travel far and wide, or so I'm told." She paused in thought. "Do you visit all the keeps of the land?"

Thom wasn't sure if the lady was fishing for some news. "Every town and keep both great and small, Lady. I trade with them all." He said proudly.

Lady Emmalyn examined some fine ribbon as Elysant looked at strands of beads hung from the rack in the middle of the cart. Lady Christabel found a bottle of perfume that she liked and turned to Lord Iain who had come out after them. The tinker remembered the man. He had seen the King's Champion at one of the many tournaments in the land, though the Lord had taken no notice of the likes of him. Thom had a sixth sense when it came to people. He could tell the good from the bad just by looking at them. Watching the Lord and his future lady talk a moment in private, he got the feeling that they would not fit together, that both of their edges were rough. They'd fit poorly and grind against each other and wear the other down like iron against iron. They'd dull each other until there was little left. He shook his head; these noble marriages were never about the important things. Money was little comfort in a cold bed with a cold woman that bore only one son. In his tinker's mind, a warm bed, a soft woman that was willing to bare you lots of barns was what marriage was all about. A helpmate, a friend, and partner were worth much more than a chest of silver and a plot of land, but he was a tinker, not a nobleman. Some nobles didn't have the sense God gave a goose.

Lord Iain nodded a greeting at the tinker and moved to Lady Luveday's side. She chatted with the tinker asking about the places he had been. The crops and other things, and laughed at Thom's jokes, until the Lord appeared at her elbow and her laughter stopped.

"Anything you would like, Lady Luveday?" The lady's brow furrowed as she looked at the cart.

"I have no coin, My Lord." She whispered to him.

He looked down at her and Thom thought he saw something soften in the knight's eyes. "Consider it a boon from your lord. You have worked hard and healed Lord Benedict. You may have whatever your heart desires." He stated magnanimously. The women looked on in wonder. Christabel looked displeased for a moment, but the women urged Luveday to look, holding up items they thought she might like.

"What about this scarf?" Mistress Adela offered her a blue piece of raw silk. "Or this Perfume; 'tis rose oil? Or this green ribbon, it would look fine on your gown!" Elli said as she rounded the cart. "Here is a fine comb! Or a kirtle of blue for you?" Emmalyn offered.

The lady looked at her companions and smiled. Christabel held up one of his finer pieces, a gold necklace with a fine amethyst stone. "What about this Lady Luveday? The stone is large and lovely." It was an expensive piece for sure.

The lady smiled and looked to the Lord. "I may have anything I like?"

Benedict walked stiffly arriving late to stand beside Sir Gregori and the other men that watched the women. "What is going on here?"

Gregori leaned down to whisper at his friend. "Iain has offered Lady Luveday a boon. Anything she wishes..." He said raising his eyebrows. Benedict looked startled.

"Trouble afoot." He whispered back. Instead of interrupting, Benedict decided to see what would happen. While the women continued to offer up items, the men all watched Luveday who finally took a step closer to the cart.

She looked to Thom, who knew right away that the lady wanted nothing in his cart and smiled at her. She smiled back, and he thought she had gotten his meaning. He was not insulted that she did not wish to purchase anything, for he got the feeling that what she wanted was something better than trinkets and bobbles.

Luveday looked at the cart and the women who looked on so expectantly. Nothing appealed to her, mostly because she had many of these items in the chest in her room, though none but Elysant knew they were there. Luveday thought the items best stayed put away, until a time when they were needed. No, nothing in the cart appealed to her, but there was something that she wanted.

"I may have anything I like?" She turned to ask Lord De Lane, and he nodded, so she stepped closer to the cart, examining it to play along a little. She smiled at the tinker, which he returned, and she could tell that he knew she was not going to choose one of the items in his possession.

She turned back to Iain as Elli offered up a pot of some herb or spice. "Does this boon come with a time limit?" His head turned slightly to the side as he looked at her quizzically, so she rephrased her question. "Is your offer only for this moment, only for the items in Tinker Thom's cart, or does it extend further?"

He seemed to get her meaning and looked concerned but didn't recant his offer. "Anything you wish." He stated, and Luveday thought she could hear the hesitancy in his voice. The men mumbled among themselves.

Luveday turned back to the tinker. "Thank you, Tinker Thom Little, but I will not be buying anything from your cart today." The tinker smiled once again while the women looked on with expressions ranging from disappointment to curiosity.

The lord paid for the women's purchases and even bought some of the spices for Emmalyn and Luveday. He worried about what he had done. Especially when he later asked Luveday if she was sure there was nothing she wanted, and the lady had said, "I am saving my boon for something special." *What had he gotten himself into?*

Luveday knew exactly what she wanted. This boon was a godsend, and she was not going to waste it on bits of glass and metal. What she wanted would take a good deal of time, but she was sure it was a practical wish. So, the next morning she entered the stables to find the stable master, Farrier Wells. He was a grisly old man who had cared for the Champion's horses through the fanfare of royal tournaments and terrible battles. He had taught the lord how to ride a horse, and if he could teach an eager boy, Luveday thought, could he not teach a reluctant woman?

Iain had not asked her what she wanted, merely watched her the rest of the evening. She would have told him if he had asked, but instead, she watched him brood over her puzzling statements. She could see he was worried about what she would ask for and even the men whispered about it. The women looked at her with a critical eye. Agnes had even told her she was a smart girl, though the woman did not know what she would ask for.

Farrier Wells was cleaning out a stall while a lad wiped down the Lord's mount. It was early yet, but the lord had already been out riding. The lad saw her and cleared his throat to get his master's attention. Wells looked at her startled. Of course, he knew who she was, especially since she worked with Barth the Blacksmith, but she had never entered his stables before.

"Lady Luveday, good morrow." He set down his rake and anxiously wiped his hands on the leather jerkin he wore. "Can I help you, lady?"

She smiled at him, and Wells felt himself smile back, though he knew his smile wasn't anything as pretty as hers. He could tell what the fuss was about, this was a good lady, not like the Lord's bride, beautiful though she may be.

"Yes, please, Farrier Wells." She looked over her shoulder at the boy who held the rope to Iain's great gray destrier. The animal was slightly smaller than the draft horses but could run a good pace. Benedict's mount was much smaller, near an Arabian if Luveday guessed right and was as quick as lightning. "I am sure you have heard that Lord Iain has offered me a boon?" The man nodded and looked suddenly concerned, and Luveday wondered why men always seemed to jump to the worst possible conclusions. "I have decided... that is I would like..." She tried again and took a breath, "to learn to ride a horse." She paused a moment to clarify. "I know this will take you away from your duties as most of the men are in the fields this time of year." The man looked relieved enough to fall over. Luveday wondered if she should offer him a chair, then wondered about just what he had imagined she would ask for. She suddenly realized she didn't want to know.

"Ye wish to learn to ride?" He asked grinning.

She nodded. "I have never had the opportunity to learn, and I believe it is a good skill to have." She looked at the horse that suddenly came to nuzzle the waist of her dress. She turned and offered it her hand. It smelled it and gummed it a moment but didn't bite her. She patted his muzzle, and he leaned into her shoulder as she stroked his neck. Luveday had no experience with horses. Being a fan of my little ponies and watching the Lord of the Rings trilogy didn't count. She thought she would be scared of such a large and powerful beast, but she wasn't, then again, she wasn't going to have to ride him either. She imagined it would be a different story should she have to mount him, or God forbid, Benedict's Arian. It might be smaller, but that speed would terrify her.

"He seems to like you, Lady. Gus, finish muckin' the stall and put Ironwood away." The boy nodded curtly and say, "Yes'um," before getting to work. "You're not afraid of the big brute. That's a good sign. Them court ladies don't much care for the animals." He looked at her. "You say you've never ridden?" He asked.

"Never." She stated flatly. She still stroked the horse's neck.

Wiping his hands on his shirt, he looked her over. "Well, I guess we have a lot to do."

They started by choosing a mare, one of the pack horses who was steady and calm. Luveday spent the day learning about a horse. How to feed her, and brush her, and clean her hooves. By afternoon she was exhausted, and she hadn't even been on a horse yet. Wells had assured her that they would take it slow and that he could teach her to ride astride and side saddle, which was exceedingly popular in town.

By day three she was saddling her own horse, and Iain had finally found her hiding place and what had captured the attention of his stable master.

Today's lesson was about tack and how to tie things on a saddle. Luveday had learned how to hobble a horse and was working on knots. Wells had given her a piece of rope and sat her on a stool to practice while he finished his own duties, and that is where De Lane found her.

He watched her for a moment before making some noise to alert her to his presence. Luveday glanced up, too focused on her task to much care who had entered the stables until she saw that it was him. They looked confused at one another and just stared for a moment until Wells returned to greet his lord.

"Lord Iain. Do you need your horse saddled? The boy has been doing a fine job, has he not?" Wells asked. Gus had only been helping in the stables for a few months, but Wells could see the boy had a gift with horses.

"Aye, he's been doing well, though he doesn't know how to saddle Ironwood like you. He'll learn."

"That he will, My Lord, that he will." Wells agreed and was happy that De Lane thought well of the boy. He watched the lord as he watched the lady work. "Here now, Lady. How does it fare?" She showed him the length of rope, and he took it and tested the knots. Her work was good. She learned quickly and listened well. The men and boys he had taught always thought they knew how it was done, even though they'd not spent a minute on a horse's back. Not this lady, she listened and waited for him to instruct her. She didn't show any fear, and when she said she wanted to know everything about caring for and riding a horse, she meant it, not shying away from the hard and dirty work. His estimation of her grew each day, and he could see why so many spoke so highly of her.

"What is going on here, Lady Luveday?" Benedict and Gregori, John and Perivale all entered the stable in search of their lord and curious why Lady Luveday had been spending so much time away from the keep.

Luveday seemed surprised that they had not heard of her current endeavor. "Farrier Wells is teaching me to ride. Right now, we are working on knots." She stated simply as she rose to her feet.

"Well done, lady. Those are fine knots, sure to hold tight." Wells handed back the piece of rope. "Keep practicing until you don't have to think about tying them. It's a skill that has saved me life a time or two." He added as he passed the men to yell something at Gus.

Iain looked at her confused. "Riding, knotwork?" He asked as she walked by him.

Luveday smiled. "You did say I could choose anything I liked for my boon..." She commented and greeted the men.

Benedict laughed heartily at how wrong they had all been. The men had argued and bet amongst themselves about what exactly the lady would ask for. She had not been swayed by trinkets, and the men worried that she would have a sharp eye out for finer and more expensive game. Instead, she had fooled them all.

"And what's so humorous, Lord Benedict?" She looked at him annoyed but had trouble not smiling. The man's laughter was infectious.

The men smiled at her, all knowing the reason for their friend's humor. "Oh, Lady." He took a deep breath and grabbed her about the waist to swing her around. She gasped and laughed at his antics. "You never cease to delight."

"Oh, stop you!" She laughed. "Mind your leg." Shaking her head, she untangled herself from him and stepped aside. Her lessons were done for today, and she had work to do in the keep. She walked away, but the men heard her words clearly. "It's enough to turn a woman's head if she's not careful!"

Later that evening, after dinner, a group sat around the hearth sipping wine. Lady Christabel and Mistress Adela had joined them on this rare occasion, while the usual people were in attendance. Lady Emmalyn and Lady Luveday shared a padded, high backed bench beside Gregori facing the fire, Lord Iain sat to the left of the coffee table before them. Elli sat on her stool beside the fire working on her sewing though Luveday warned that the dim light was not good for her eyes. Men came and went, and some stayed to momentarily take up the spot next to their lord, recently vacated by Lord Benedict, to chat about some matter while Christabel and Adela sat across from De Lane and tried to ignore everyone else. Gregori, who sat closest to the women had tried to converse with them, but the ladies didn't seem up to it. Many wondered what drew them to the fireside until Christabel addressed Luveday directly.

"I hear you are learning to ride, Lady Luveday." She stated with a lofty air.

Luveday wondered where this conversation would be going as many eyes turned to her. "Yes, Lady Christabel. I have never learned and thought it a good skill to have."

"Yes, a very good skill, but a waste of your boon if you ask me." The lady looked around and at Luveday in particular. She seemed to look her over, and many hackles rose as she commented, with no small amount of contempt, about Luveday's appearance. "If I were you, I would have asked for a new gown and some shoes, or perhaps a few as you only have the two." The Lady ignored her nurse's looks and attempts to chastise her.

Luveday looked passed the lady's shoulder to shake her head almost imperceptibly at Elli who had come out of her seat, ready to defend her friend. Luveday was not one to pick fights and certainly not over her attire. Her hackles didn't rise at the remark because it was the truth. While she knew Christabel had meant to wound her with the statement, Luveday couldn't say she cared a whit about a spoiled child's opinion and let it pass. There was nothing she could do about it anyways. She had had three sets of clothes as gifts from Lady Emmalyn, but one gown had been ruined tending to Benedict that first day and Luveday would not ask for anything else. The Lord and Lady had been too generous as it was.

"Of course, Lady Christabel, but I have no need for dresses as fine as yours." She looked at the girl's ruby velvet and had not one iota of envy for it or the fancy embroidery. "It would be impractical. I should be too sad when it got dirty or ruined. No, nothing like that for me." She looked to Emmalyn who continued to sip her wine. "I should think that riding is worth much more than a gown or a shiny bobble. I will get much more enjoyment out of it in the long run." She took a sip and watched the girl pout. "It is a skill for a lifetime." She added silently to herself, *teach a man to fish and all that*, she thought.

It was not surprising when the two women excused themselves shortly after. Mistress Adela made sure her lady did not see the look of apology she earnestly gave Luveday. Luveday didn't fault the nurse for remaining silent. Christabel was a handful on the best of days.

The remaining women finished their wine and then excused themselves to finish their duties for the night, all under the watchful and thoughtful eye of Lord Iain.

The days turned warmer still as summer took hold and Luveday finally started her lessons in the saddle. Wells said she took to riding as if she had been born in the saddle, and Luveday thought the charming old man was just trying to ease her nerves. Riding was both more and less than she expected. It was easier, but then her mount did most of the hard work while Wells bellowed out instructions. It was less frightening, there again her teacher and mount helped with that too. They moved from walking around the bailey to taking short trips through the town, to trotting across the countryside. While Luveday longed for the freedom to fly over the fields in controlled abandon, she knew her skills were still new and hesitated to urge old Nell into a full gallop.

Her time spent riding each day helped to build her endurance in the saddle and lightened her heart. There was something freeing about being in the saddle as if a road of possibilities opened up before her if she would just give her mount its head. But she didn't gallop toward some far horizon, not in a world unknown to her, yet still, there was the gleam of freedom should she choose to take it, and that was enough for her.

Weeks turned into a month and a month into a season as summer was finally underway. The crops were growing full, and even Luveday's trees were bearing fruit while their brothers struggled on. Father Quinn and several farmers made the trek to the keep asking her what she had done for the trees. Some were having trouble with their crops, and Luveday promised she would visit their fields, but warned that she could only do so much.

It was after one such trip that she found herself resting in the field before the castle. She had walked, deciding that the trip was too short to saddle a horse. The basket she had carried on her back as a sort of pack was filled with a notebook and pencils. Setting it down and pulling out the water skin and the blanket she carried, she decided here was a good place to stop and have a snack.

The warm sun was not too hot, though she didn't worry with her small supply of sunscreen. She watched Archer, her escort as he stopped to talk to some men a distance away. As long as she didn't wander too far, he was happy to let her be. She didn't think Warren or one of the other men would be so lax, but that is why she had chosen Archer to go with her. They had stopped to talk to his wife for a few moments. The woman was spinning thread, and Luveday offered to let her use some of their dyes, which pleased her a good deal. Though the woman was pregnant, she was not too far along, and Luveday hoped a visit to the castle would not be too much for her.

Warmth soaked into her bones and Luveday enjoyed the sensation. The castle was cold, even as the temperature warmed, and while she was sure in later months, she would be happy about that fact, at the moment the sun was a pleasant change. Reclining a bit on her arms, she closed her eyes and let her head fall back soaking up the rays, but her peace was interrupted by the laughter of children as she watched a group race towards her, led by Coll and Gus. Luveday watched them come, not getting to her feet. If there was trouble, someone would have sent one of the men. More than likely, Emmalyn sent the boys with a message to stop by the chicken coops or the bakehouse before coming back. The boys ran right up to her and dropped on the ground next to her outstretched legs. The rest of the group slowed and approached more slowly.

Luveday handed over the water skin, and the boys took big gulps as they tried to catch their breath. The wind had decided to pick up, and the children, near ten in all, looked out across the field as the tall green grass waved in the breeze.

Coll caught his breath first, or perhaps Gus let him speak as it was the squire who had been charged with carrying the message. "Father Quinn has come to the Keep and wished to talk to you this afternoon. He is looking at the castle records right now, and Sir Gregori says they will be a while yet." The boy looked at the others around him as they started to sit down in a semi-circle before the lady.

Gus decided he had waited long enough and spoke before Coll could do more than open his mouth to take a breath. "Lady Emmalyn also asks that you pick some willow bark before returning to the castle as your stocks are low. Elli says that some dandelion root is needed too, and would you stop to speak with Cassandra about her tea, on the way back." Gus looked pleased with himself, while Coll frowned at him.

The children were mostly silent as the wind picked up and tossed their hair and garments about. Luveday got an idea in her head and looked at the children who seemed to mirror the mischievous look in her eye. They smiled at her as she smiled widely back. As she got to her knees, she looked at Gus and Coll. "I will do all that, but first, I need your help." The children looked at each other and then back to her nodding. "We need to hunt for a few items, but I think we can do it." She hoped the weather would continue to be obliging. "Now what I need you to do is..." And the children listened closely to what she had to say, most did not believe her, but were up to helping anyway, especially when she pulled some sort of treat, she called candy, from her pocket and gave them each a piece. It was payment enough for them to help the lady do anything she asked.

The wind rushed by in spurts and long gusts. It was not unpleasant but not the sort of thing they saw until late summer. Iain sat on his horse and looked out at the village. He had ridden his lands to check on the watering of the fields and had taken the back way to reach the castle again. His men had informed him that Lady Luveday had yet to return from her visit that morning, but wherever the woman was, Archer was still with her. That did little to ease his mind as Benedict, Gregori and Father Quinn, who, he was told, had arrived in his absence, were also gone for some time and no one seemed to know where or why. So, he had turned his mount back to the countryside.

As his eyes scanned the village for her familiar form, something caught his eye high above the yellow thatch rooftops. At first, he thought it a bird, until it turned in the wind. It did not look like any creature he had ever seen, and he could swear there was a rope tying whatever it was to the ground. He took off to investigate.

In one of the unused fields on the other side of the village was a group of men that watched the sky. They chatted together and pointed but made no other move. His missing men were among their number as they turned their gaze to earth and looked across the field. Iain finally saw what it was they watched. Luveday, surrounded by a group of children held a thin rope that was carried aloft by some red cloth that floated in the stiff breeze high overhead. A boy, which one he could not tell, stood before her as she handed over the rope and leaned down to give him some words no one else could hear. The boy smiled and pulled back on the string. The diamond of fabric dropped suddenly, and all eyes turned to the boy. Luveday moved out of the way and spoke some instruction to him, but the wind took her words before they could reach the Lord's ears. Iain watched in fascination as the boy moved across the field and the object rose higher. The wind died a bit, and the boy repeated the maneuver to save the deflating cloth. De Lane realized it was like the sail of a ship, which was carried aloft in the strong wind. Men and boys alike seemed to be enjoying the process.

Dismounting, he joined his knights and the Priest. "What is that thing?" He asked.

Father Quinn looked to him with the twinkle bright in his eyes. "The Lady called it a kite." He raised his voice to speak over the wind. "The children helped her make it."

They watched a few moments until another child came forward and the kite was returned to Luveday as she instructed the next one on how to keep the kite in the air. Iain saw that only Archer was in the field with the children. "What is he doing there?" He pointed to the man-at-arms.

Gregori was the one to speak up this time. "When the wind dies, or the child loses control of the kite, and it falls to earth, Archer helps the lady get it aloft again." He never took his eyes from the field as he spoke. "They've lost it twice so far." The men commented on its supposed construction and how a lady might know of such things. Iain glanced at his men and noticed that Benedict didn't comment but watched the goings on with a sharp intent.

Iain was about to ask what was on his mind when he took off across the field. The men looked at each other, strangely hesitant to follow; all but Iain. He took off after his brother gaining ground until they both met the woman smiling so brightly in the field.

Luveday's golden locks had been blown free, and her cheeks were pink from the sun and wind. Iain was not about to let Benedict charm the lady and was about to ask her something when Benedict interrupted and surprised him from his train of thought. Startled by the other lord's question, Iain couldn't help but stare, wondering how he had misjudged the situation.

"Can you teach me, Lady Luveday?" Benedict asked earnestly.

The lady only smiled at him and nodded. She looked to the boy who held the string. "Of course, but we will have to wait until Ollie has his turn." Turning back, she looked at the two men. "Have you ever flown a kite before?"

Iain wasn't sure what to do or say, and luckily Benedict answered for him. "I have not. I have never seen such a thing before." He looked up at the sky, clearly fascinated. "How does it work? How did you learn to make it?"

"Children play with such things where I come from." The wind blew her hair into her face as she spoke and Luveday raised a hand to her forehead to keep her hair out of her eyes and to shade them against the sun as she watched the kite. "Pull back a little, Ollie." She called to the boy, who did as she said, but the wind continued to die down. He let go of the loose string as another gust grabbed the kite and tore it from his hands. The kite sailed for a moment, and Luveday feared it would end up in the trees, but the wind died again. The kite tried to recover some altitude before falling to the ground.

Archer ran and picked it up, but his expression said that something was wrong as he approached to return the kite to Luveday. Benedict tried to examine the kite and how it was made as the lady looked it over. One of the branches had snapped on impact with the ground. Setting the kite down, Luveday sat too and began to unwind the string that tied the sticks together and the thick fabric to the branches. Suddenly the wind stopped, and Luveday looked up to see that she was surrounded by people. It seemed the men had finally given in to their curiosity and come to see what she was up to. They didn't say anything as they watched her repair the kite with another branch that the children had collected, but she hadn't used. Retying everything, the kite was once again ready to go.

Benedict, who had been crouching in front of her to get a better look, helped her to her feet. The crowd parted as she handed the kite back to Archer who took up his position as she got the kite back into the air. As soon as it was stable, Benedict appeared at her side. She gave a few instructions and handed over the string. The young lord was as fascinated with the kite as the children had been. The kite flew for another quarter hour before the wind finally died, and the group headed back to the castle. The children said their goodbyes before scattering, clearly happy with the day's activities.

Benedict chatted her ear off on the walk back, but she kept looking to Lord Iain who watched them with an expression she couldn't quite name. Every time their eyes met, she felt that something passed between them, something that confused her to no end.

That evening she found Father Quinn in the steward's rooms. It was a sort of office with ledgers for the keep. A record of harvests and a record of grievances were kept for the lord and taxes for the King. While the books seemed to be in order, it was clear that a good deal of the entries puzzled the priest.

Luveday didn't bother trying to look at them, she wasn't sure she'd be able to decipher them anyway. Father Quinn seemed happy for the interruption as Gregori had left him to work. "The evening meal will be ready in a short while, Father. There was something you wished to talk to me about?"

He set the book aside and looked at her in the candlelight. "Gregori said you had some questions about the Lord's marriage. Anything I may help you with?" His eyes held an expression of kindness and softened when they looked at her. Luveday thought she saw something like sorrow there, but she couldn't think why he would look at her with such an expression in his eyes.

Luveday was hesitant to ask too many questions on this subject, but her knowledge was lacking, and she could never stand not knowing something. She was worried about what changes were in store for the keep and especially for herself. "I know almost nothing about marriage vows and contracts. I imagine it is a rather complicated affair. Other than the feast and ceremony, what other customs should I expect? Will the King's presence change things?"

Father Quinn laughed at her troubled expression. "It is not so serious a matter, Lady Luveday. The wedding date will be announced all over the Kingdom, and people will no doubt be arriving early for the celebration. As the King's Champion, De Lane has a reputation to uphold, so expect a good deal of feasting, perhaps even a month's long celebration." He watched the lady pale and smiled at her. He supposed it would mean a lot of work for her and the women, but didn't the fairer sex usually rally together in this sort of thing? "Many will bring gifts; a good amount of food and wine is customary to help the couple feed their guests. Then there are the games and the village feast before the day of the ceremony. The Binding will be said in the chapel in the morning and more feasting and merrymaking until late into the night. The traditional flying of the sheets with a good deal of ribbing the next morning and the festivities usually come to an end after a week or so."

"So, the celebration could last a few months?" Luveday watched the Father nod and felt a sort of weight drop to the bottom of her stomach. De Lane had yet to set a date for the ceremony, but all talk pointed to something in the fall after the King's summer campaigns were over and the harvest was in. Luveday thought it made sense to wait until the castle's stores were at their fullest, but the day was swiftly approaching. She could only guess at how many people would want to be present for the wedding of the King's Champion. "Lady Christabel's family will arrive sometime before the ceremony, should I expect anything?"

"Only trouble." He stated more to himself than to her. Father Quinn's gaze sharpened as he realized his slip. "Not to worry, Lady. De Lane will have everything in hand." The priest paused a moment as if he debated whether to tell her more. Sighing he said, "It is just that Lord Henric Sumerland is an ambitious man, and he keeps a good many friends. Some of which are not on good terms with De Lane or the King." The way Father Quinn phrased his last statement gave Luveday the feeling that there was some strong unrest towards the King. She had heard some rumors, but she knew too little about it to know who was a threat and who wasn't.

"Are there any special friends I should pay attention too?" If Father Quinn wasn't going to talk about it directly then neither would she.

"Lord Albin of Sterling. He is a cousin to Duke Ladislaus of Sterling who is currently harassing the crown. Ladislaus is said to be making plans against the King and Albin is his right ear, though not officially tied to his kinsman." Quinn turned to the door where a sound had caught their attention. "'Tis best to keep an eye on him and his men."

Luveday got up and thanked the Father. "Food will be served shortly, Father. Thank you for telling me what to expect." Luveday had more questions now than she had answers; questions she had not even thought of until talking to Father Quinn.

"Oh, Lady Luveday!" She turned back to see the father at the door. "Lady Emmalyn mentioned you might be willing to accompany me on the morrow. I may be in need of your healer's skill, and the lady thought you might like the outing. Sir Chadric is feeling ill, and I was asked to visit the Parish. Will you be able to accompany me?"

Luveday had heard of the Parish, a manor house nestled inside the wood, but she had never had the opportunity to venture that far. The prospect sounded like fun. "Yes, thank you. I will inform Emmalyn that I will be going with you. Perhaps she can suggest what to bring."

"Thank you, lady, I don't mean to take you away from your duties." The Father looked out at the busy hall. "I'm sorry to keep you so long." He looked as if he had enjoyed having someone to talk to.

Luveday smiled her farewell and couldn't help laughing. "I don't mind the escape from this place every once and a while." She looked over her shoulder at the men gathering for the meal and turned back to the Priest who watched the crowd intently. Her parting words were said with a smile, "Tempus Fugit."

As she rushed off, she couldn't see the strange look the priest gave her as he watched her cross the hall.

That night a new face joined the group around the fire. Sir Patrick Fuller had returned from abroad with a cart full of sheep and one of goats, half a dozen oxen, a milk cow and a sow who had given birth to almost a dozen piglets on the journey home. Sir Fuller was a large man with salt and pepper hair, a deep voice, and a painful gait. He was elderly by many standards, too old to take up arms and had been relegated to animal husbandry after his last battle had nearly taken his sword arm and his life. The men joked that he had settled into castle life well, but even Luveday could see the thirst for battle as the knights talked about old times. It seemed that Sir Fuller had put many a young lad through his paces, and old age did not entirely agree with him.

As the night deepened, Luveday was hesitant to interrupt Lady Emmalyn when she was deep in conversation with the returned knight. If she wasn't mistaken there was some history there, but Luveday wished to collect the items for her outing the next day, so she moved closer to the couple. "Lady Emmalyn?"

Both looked up startled. Emmalyn blushed prettily, and Luveday was sure there was something between her and Fuller. "Yes, Lady Luveday?" She asked as the knight excused himself.

Luveday was sorry to see him go. "I am accompanying Father Quinn tomorrow and was hoping you could suggest what to take with me?" It wasn't really a statement, yet wasn't really a question, but Emmalyn was happy to help.

While she suggested salves and lotions for painful joints and gout, Emmalyn filled in some of the gaps in Luveday's knowledge of the area. "Sir Chadric is the last of the Lander's line. His family owned the land and built the foundations of the castle."

"Why is he not lord of Lander's Keep and Iain is?" She asked in all seriousness.

Emmalyn didn't take offense and had grown used to Luveday's many questions. "The land was gifted to Iain's grandfather as part of his lands when he became Lord De Lane. It was he who finished the castle's construction and let the Lander's family keep the manor house in the woods. Sir Chadric was a young lad then. He is an old man now, and he and his wife are all that live in the house." Emmalyn looked across the hall. "Young Paige was betrothed to their grandson, but the boy died of a fever shortly after the wedding. She takes care of them and works here at the keep. The Landers have no title, but for Sir Chadric's knighthood, though they own a bit of land, they don't have the strength to work it." Luveday was beginning to see the problem. "It is sad when a good bloodline ends."

Luveday didn't ask what happened to the children of Sir Chadric as it was clear they had passed on. She wondered how old the couple must be, and if they ventured far from their manor. It also explained Paige's air of solitude that had only begun to be lifted by young Sir Perivale. Luveday would have never guessed that such sorrow had touched the young woman's life. She was now eager to see the Manor, remembering how the masons had talked about the house. Tomorrow would be full of new things, and Luveday was eager to get going.

The Manor was not a disappointment. It was a large two-story building that was surrounded by trees adding a foreboding quality to the gothic atmosphere. There was no lawn or open space that separated the structure from the woods. One moment they were walking down a dwindling road through the wood and the next the front door appeared out of the morning shadows. There were clear signs of neglect that were far worse than the state the castle had been in before Luveday arrived. It was clear that it had been an awfully long time since the house was properly cared for. It was sad, to say the least. Luveday longed for the funds and the help to rebuild such a magnificent old home, but she knew that it would never be possible. The masons had repaired enough that the house would last a few more years, but even they had said the manor would soon be uninhabitable. It would last long enough for Sir Chadric and his wife, but no longer.

The great door was carved with magnificent detail, and Luveday strained to take it all in, but the light of mid-morning was not enough to penetrate the thick canopy overhead. She was surprised when the door swung open silently, and an old man with ghost white hair stood before them with a single candle in hand.

The burning wax candle gave off a strange odor that was slightly unpleasant, though she thought its maker had tried to cover the smell with sage and other herbs. The mix would take some getting used to.

"Sir Chadric, my friend!" Father Quinn was happy to see the old knight, and it was clear that the feelings were reciprocated. "How have you faired this spring?"

"Father Quinn, good lad." They embraced in a manly hug that Luveday found endearing. "The spring rain pains these old bones, but what's a man to do?" He ushered them in, and Luveday noticed his awkward gait. "And who is this pretty lass?" He asked while smacking his lips on the back of her offered hand.

"Behave yourself, old man." Both men chuckled causing Luveday to smile at their antics. Sir Chadric was charming. "Sir Chadric, may I introduce, Lady Luveday. Lady, my old friend, Sir Chadric Lander."

"A pleasure lady." He replied.

Smiling at him, "The pleasure is mine, Sir Chadric." Luveday noticed he stood a little straighter in her presence. The knight wore a tunic that was baggy on his slim frame and had seen better days, though it looked well cared for. His hose were also several sizes too large, they wrinkled around his knees before pooling at his boots. The leather boots shined, reflecting the candlelight and Luveday got the idea that Sir Chadric shined them himself.

"Lady Luveday?" Sir Chadric looked at her curiously. She could tell he was trying to place the name. The light that came into his eyes made them twinkle madly. "Lady Luveday!" He chuckled. "You are the lady who sent the masons! The Lady who restored Lander's Keep." He laughed.

There was a gasp as they turned to see a little woman enter through a side door. "What a pleasure you should come to visit us, Lady."

"Lady, this is Mistress Catherine, Sir Chadric's wife of almost sixty annums."

The woman shook hands, while Catherine continued to tell her how nice it was to see her. Luveday was just as enchanted with Catherine as she was with Sir Chadric and said so. "As I said before, the pleasure is mine Mistress Catherine."

"Call me Cathy, My Lady."

"Only if you will call me Luveday."

"Luveday." She smiled. "Such a lovely name, don't you think, Chad? So lovely..." Her husband made a noise of agreement as the men began talking of news from the keep and farther abroad. Cathy ushered her guest through a series of rooms until they came to the back corner of the house where the kitchen was located. The kitchen had all the usual trappings but didn't look as if it were what the room had originally been intended for. A house of this size surely had a larger area to cook in, probably outdoors somewhere judging by the age of the house.

Luveday looked around at the dark wood walls, at the sunlight streaming through the diamonds of the glass pained windows and wondered at it all. Clearly, the room had been repurposed for the couple's needs, but why did it look as if they lived in only a few rooms. Were they too old to climb the grand staircase? She had only gotten a glimpse of it in the gloomy darkness that seemed to surround the estate. Or was there another reason?

Cathy bustled around the kitchen chatting to Luveday who only half understood of whom she was talking about. Cathy had much to say about the masons and praised Lady Emmalyn no end. Luveday mostly sat and listened.

When it looked as if the woman had finally run out of things to say, Luveday brought up the basket she had sat at her feet and began fishing out the items she had brought. It was a large and heavy basket, but she was now glad she had decided to sneak in some extras for the elderly couple.

"I've brought some ointments, and a few other things for you, Cathy."

"Oh, you shouldn't have, Luveday." But her tone was more excited than reprimanding.

While Luveday had no doubt that Cathy had a stubborn streak that kept the woman going, she could see that her new friend was grateful for any help she received. Luveday could only imagine how hard it was for them with no one to help. Paige, the quiet mouse of a girl that worked in the castle, divided her evenings between the keep and the manor house. She was the only person who saw the couple regularly, and from all accounts, Cathy treated the girl as her own granddaughter, though the tragic marriage had lasted only a few short months.

Setting out the items she had acquired, there was a noise of appreciation and delight as the table became crowded with her bounty. Luveday had grabbed a fresh loaf of bread, a pot of honey, and one of the preserves. There was some salted pork and some fresh herbs from the kitchen. In the bottom of the basket were a few jars of ointments that the woman recognized and used immediately on her hands and knees. Luveday only smiled as Cathy pulled up her skirts to rub the ointment in without so much as a by your leave. Clearly, the woman had been in some pain.

While Cathy thanked her profusely, Luveday hung the herbs up to dry in a spot in the kitchen. She set the meat and loaf on a worktable that looked as old as the house.

Once the items were put away, Luveday explained the use of some of the things she had brought that Cathy didn't recognize. Holding out a small pouch of herbs she explained that it was meant to be brewed like tea. "This is for aches and pains, especially when it is cold or rainy. I heard Sir Chadric had trouble with his joints in that weather." She cautioned. "You want to brew this in water and remove the herbs before you drink it. Don't drink more than a small pot a day, between you. It can have some unpleasant effects if you have too much of it for too long."

"How wonderful. You said it will help with his knees then?" Cathy examined the herb more closely.

"Yes, it will do better than the ointment, but only in small amounts. Too much can be a bad thing."

"Everything in moderation, dear." Cathy smiled at herself as she rearranged some items on the tabletop they now set around.

Luveday was startled by so modern an attitude, and for a moment heard the echo of her mother's voice who often used the sentiment. It was a bittersweet moment that caused her to smile sadly. "Yes, just so, Cathy."

A moment later the men joined them from another part of the house and Cathy was happy to show her husband the gifts they had received. He was more eager to hear about the ointments then the honey and bread, though clearly grateful for everything.

While the little couple chatted back and forth, Luveday caught Father Quinn giving her a smile. When she turned to look at him, he merely nodded his head, as if he approved and turned back to the couple.

There was a door that led out to the back of the house which had a space behind it that was cleared of trees and a small garden that Cathy and Chadric tended daily. The knight asked Father Quinn something that Luveday didn't quite catch, and the two moved out the door while she and Cathy followed behind.

The lady could tell that Cathy moved better since applying the ointment, but Luveday offered her arm as it looked as if the older woman could use some assistance.

They walked around the raised beds, and Luveday recognized Father Quinn's handiwork in almost every aspect of the garden. Cathy moved them away from the men to show her something, and they spent some time chatting about nothing in particular and working in the garden.

The women later retired to the kitchen where Luveday helped with the mid-day meal and prepared a stew Mistress Agnes had taught her to which Cathy exclaimed in delight. The group had a small lunch and said their farewells while promising to visit each other again soon. Father Quinn didn't speak much on the walk back to the castle, but Luveday told him she had not had so pleasant a morning for some time. The priest was secretly pleased with Luveday and thought he might have just found another protector for the old couple. Both were happy they had made the journey, very happy indeed.

Chapter 6

Experience, like a pale musician, holds a dulcimer of patience in his hand.
~Elizabeth Barrett Browning

Summer had settled in, and the warm weather was not too hot, though at times, Luveday longed for a fan or air-conditioner, but not more than she longed for running hot water and a shower. Using the common bath wasn't something she was interested in and a lot of work. Life was routine, hard work, and yet so much more fulfilling than she remembered her previous life being. Luveday often thought of her family and friends, the life she had worked hard to build and been pulled so suddenly from. She was not sure if she hoped or dreaded the thought of her return. She was not that woman anymore and often pondered just how unsuited to her old life she had become. Would she go home if the opportunity arose? What if this was some cosmic second chance, and her other life gone forever? Was that such a bad thing?

As she worked beside Cassandra and Lady Emmalyn, she thought that it was not such a terrible thing. She had been blessed every step of this odd journey, and she realized with sudden clarity that she could live the rest of her life here and be happy.

The only dark spot in her life, Luveday was slow to admit, was Lady Christabel, but the young woman was an unfortunate obstruction in the life of the castle. Luveday could see that the Lady was more miserable the closer the wedding date approached and while she could, in some ways, empathize with the girl, Luveday saw no reason why Christabel would want to make other people's lives as miserable as her own. Yet, every day proved another challenge for the bride to be.

The castle only breathed a sigh of relief on the occasions that the Lady chose to spend a day or two at the Abbey. Though there were no repeats of the previous entrenchment, a few thought the lady might never return, and many were disappointed when that did not prove so.

Luveday thought that at this point even Lord Iain was happy to see her go, though he occupied most of his time out of doors to see to the repair of his lands, with the added benefit that it let him escape the women in his life. There was nothing he could do to fix the rift in his household, short of sending the girl away, and everyone knew that that would not happen otherwise he would have done so already.

Luckily, the bride-to-be was currently at the Abbey for a few days, accompanied by her maid and astonishingly, by Lady Emmalyn. An invitation had arrived from the Mother Superior on behalf of her guests, that invited the women for a visit of several days. While Luveday missed her mentor and friend, she was sure the lady would have fun visiting an old friend, a border lord of some renown. Father Quinn had accompanied them, expecting some traveler to the inn who carried something from town at the priest's behest. The castle was strangely empty without them.

All in all, it was rather quiet, at least that was what everyone thought until Sir Warin and Gus arrived frantic at the keep's door.

Benedict, Iain, Gregori, Luveday, and Elysant sat before the fire. Benedict had just commented on the blessed quiet when the great doors had flown open. It was on the tip of Luveday's tongue to reprimand the Lordling for saying such a thing, but obviously, she was too late.

The stable boy looked white as a ghost, and the knight had trouble catching his breath as they approached the group. The men were on their feet and one look at Warin whose eyes never left Luveday, were enough to tell her that something serious had happened. Gus had brought word earlier in the evening that Cassandra was helping Archer's wife, Clair, deliver her first child. Childbirth was part miracle, part death sentence in this time-period. Cassandra had been with the young woman most of the day, and Warin had been happy that his wife was free enough to send the missive. It looked like the situation had changed.

Luveday turned to Elli and the serving women issuing orders before she even realized what she was saying. Women rushed off in several directions as Luveday ran from the hall to grab the needed items from the healing shack.

This was the third 'natural' birth Luveday would attend, the first being the birth of her second niece, Seraphina. Her sister, Annalisa was set on having a natural, at home birth. It had been an eye-opening experience for all of them, especially Annalisa who learned that she wasn't ready to go all natural in every sense of the word. Luveday could still hear her curse Mark and swear she was going to a hospital and getting drugs if she had to walk there herself. Yep, it was quite a memorable experience for everyone, even Luveday who was guilted into being present by the fact that she had been by her sister's side for her first birth. The second delivery was more recent; a woman at the Abbey who had given birth while traveling home to her mother's family. Luveday had watched her mentors at the Abbey and listened carefully as Cassandra and Emmalyn explained why each step was necessary. The Abbey had called on the local women to help with the delivery as most of the cloister could not stand to watch the woman's pain nor handle the body's process of giving birth. Luveday had always been fascinated by the way the body changed to make another life. She was not surprised that the blood and other nastiness didn't really faze her, it was just something that happened for the baby to be born.

As she ran, she mentally reviewed everything that she had been taught and prayed that Cassandra would be alright until she arrived. She prayed that she could be of some help, though she knew the situation was out of her hands.

Elli met her as she returned to the hall and handed over her cloak and some more linens to Gregori who looked like he would be accompanying them. "Here, put this on, there's a chill out. Lord Iain's horse is already saddled and will be carrying you to Archer's cottage. They are readying, Sir Gregori's horse and he will follow." They talked as they walked until they came to Lord Iain who was already mounted on his steed. Gregori handed her up with no more than a nod to Luveday, but the overall atmosphere fit with this brisk mood.

Elli was staying behind, Luveday barely caught her wishes of good luck as De Lane spurred his mount forward. Luveday clutched her bag and the arm Iain had wrapped around her middle as she rode sideways. She didn't have time to complain, as all her thoughts were on what lay ahead.

The night was quiet and the moon bright enough to see by, though she thought that Iain would know the way blindfolded. They came to the cottage swiftly though it felt like forever since Warin and Gus had arrived to ask for aid.

Luveday slid to the ground with Iain's assistance and didn't stop moving but ran for the door of the little house. She paused less than a heartbeat as a scream rent the air. The door to the cottage was thrown open as Archer looked out at her with haunted eyes. He didn't say anything, just looked at her and moved out of the way. Luveday entered, and the man-at-arms stepped outside to talk a moment with his lord, and perhaps to distance himself for only a few minutes.

Cass looked at her with concern and relief. Luveday dropped her cloak, she knew not where, as she rushed to the side of the large bed and opened her satchel.

The popular practice was to run poultices and ointments over the pregnant woman to help ease the pain, but rose oil was not extremely helpful, though extremely popular a practice. Cassandra and Emmalyn had their own ideas for what worked and what didn't. There was no one thing that any healer agreed upon except prayer and that they were doing in abundance. Cass poured out a drop of willow bark to help ease Clair, but they both looked at each other, hesitating to give it to her. It was clear that the girl was exhausted. Modern medicine would have cut the womb to get the baby out, but here that was a death sentence for the woman. The practice of cesarean section was occasionally practiced on horses. Luveday had asked at the Abbey, and neither of her mentors had ever heard of it attempted on a woman.

Luveday washed her hands and donned a linen apron as she looked to Clair. Both women spoke soft, encouraging words to her though neither was fully aware of exactly what they said. They worked for a long time turning her, encouraging her, and using oil in intimate areas to help smooth the delivery, as Luveday remembered the midwife doing for her own sister. The screams lessened after the tincture of willow bark was administered, but so did the force of Clair's pushes. Both women were worried for their patients and urged Clair to push hard just a few more times. Cassandra thought the baby had turned back into position and a few moments later the head appeared. Cassandra let loose a large sigh at the sight of the crowning head, but neither knew if they had been quick enough. A few more moments and the babe was free of his mother. They tied and cut the cord and looked from mother to child as the baby had yet to make a noise.

Archer and several men stood just inside the door looking anxious as not a sound came from the infant. Clair began to weep, Cassandra looked at the men and shook her head. Luveday was helping to clean up the afterbirth, so focused that she had yet to realize something was wrong. Archer hit his knees and began to cry silently. Gregori began a prayer in a language that sounded like Latin and Iain helped the young man-at-arms out into the night.

Luveday finished her task to find unnatural quiet and was confused. She turned to Cassandra who lay the baby to rest in a small cradle near the hearth. It was customary to wash and swaddle the babe before returning him to the mother, but Luveday watched Cassandra lay down the newborn and walk away. She sat a moment at the end of the bed, where she had been working, and looked to find Gregori, rosary in hand and lips moving in a prayer she could barely hear. She glimpsed movement outside the open door and men seemed to look out at the figures of two men, one she immediately recognized as Lord De Lane. The other took a moment to register, it was Archer.

Cassandra moved to the bed in slow motion as Luveday gained her feet. A moment later she found the baby in her arms and unwrapped the linen that covered him. He was a mess of blood and fluids, and pink, though losing color. He was not breathing. Luveday watched him for a heartbeat, not thinking of anything. There was a great emptiness inside as if the world had stopped. She acted without really knowing what she was doing.

Luveday used an edge of the linen swaddling to clean off the infant's face. She cleared out the baby's mouth with her forefinger, pulling out a gob of something dark. Holding the baby as she stood before the fire, she covered his nose and mouth with her lips and blew a large breath in. Nothing happened. She heard voices behind her, someone was angry, but nothing really registered beyond her and the child. Flipping the child over she held onto the neck and chest with one hand as she tapped his back with the other. Increasing the force of the movement, she pounded in the little back two more times before something dislodged from the little mouth and hit the floor.

There were footsteps behind her, movement drew close out of her peripheral vision, but she flipped the baby over again to cradle him in her arms, and the infant let out a cry that stilled the room. Luveday quickly looked the baby over and turned with a radiant smile to look at Cassandra and back toward the door.

Iain stood at her elbow, behind him, Warin and Gregori held Archer by the arms to keep him from advancing on her, though, at the moment, he no longer struggled to break free.

Luveday turned to Cassandra and Clair. The midwife stood at the foot of the bed, looking confused and a little lost, but no more than Clair whose expression also held a hint of hope. The baby cried again and began to wiggle in

Luveday's grasp ending the spell he had put over the room.

Cassandra took the babe as Luveday offered him to the older woman and began to clean up the baby boy as was a tradition. Archer ran to his wife's side, cuddling and whispering together, they both watched the midwife perform her duties. Luveday watched until Clair cradled her son in her arms and suddenly Luveday needed air.

People moved out of her way as she walked out of the cottage. Luveday didn't stop until she was free of the crowd and underneath a great oak tree several yards from anyone else. The moon shown brightly as she leaned against the trunk and closed her eyes to just breathe. She didn't know how long she stood there until the world righted itself, her head stopped spinning, and her stomach settled. She heard something move closer and opened her eyes to find the familiar shape of Lord Iain and wondered how she could recognize his form so easily even in the dark.

"Lady Luveday," he began, but hesitated and held something out to her. She took it without thought and realized he had brought her cloak. For the first time, Luveday felt the cold though she had the feeling she'd been shivering for a while, it had nothing to do with the temperature. "Luveday... I do not know what you did, but you have worked a miracle tonight."

She shook her head. "I..." It was barely a whisper; her voice didn't want to work. Her body trembled so much she had trouble putting on her cloak. Iain moved to help, and in the moonlight, she could see the concern on his face.

"Are you alright, lady?" He looked at her, placed a hand on her cheek, and turned her face into the light. If he could not see her trembling, he could surely feel it.

Luveday thought her teeth might chatter if she tried to speak, so she stepped away, taking great gulps of air. It seemed to help, but Iain wouldn't let her escape and turned her back towards him. It took a moment for her to realize that heat that was spreading through her limbs came from Iain as he moved his hands vigorously up and down her arms. His nearness lent a warmth of its own.

There was a moment that stretched out as their eyes met. The nearness was startling, as something pulled them closer as if gravity had suddenly shifted to draw their bodies together. They leaned in, but some noise stopped either from taking a step as they turned in unison to see Warin approaching. Torches were lit around the house as merriment broke out despite the late hour.

Warin cleared his throat before he got too near, not able to see them clearly in the dance of light and dark. "Archer and Clair wish to see you, Lady Luveday. To thank you. Cass wants to speak to you as well, though she says at your convenience, lady." He looked concerned, though Luveday couldn't guess exactly what troubled him. "She's a bit of work to do, and then she's heading to bed. 'Tis been a long night."

"Twill be a longer one for these fools." Iain laughed at the songs and merry-making, though he could understand their mood having come so close to tragedy. His attention turned to the lady at his side, and he wrapped an arm around her still able to feel the tremors that racked her body. "Thank you,

Warin. We will head back in a moment." His eyes never left her, so he saw the vigorous nod she gave the man-at-arms. Warin left without further ado, and Iain was glad he was gone. The concern he felt for this lady was eating up his gut, and he didn't know why. He had never seen her act this way before and wondered if bringing the child back from the dead had weakened her somehow. "Are you well, Luveday?" He asked though he was not entirely sure he wished to know the answer or what had really transpired in the cottage.

She looked up at him, and he could see the startled look in her eyes as if she had for a moment forgotten he was there. Instinctively, Iain tightened his hold on her. "Luveday?"

She smiled at the concern in his voice and let loose a breath as if she had been holding it. "I think I am in shock."

Iain watched her for a moment not understanding what she meant. It was a shock, the events of this night, but that was not what she had said, so he waited for the usual explanation that followed when she said something he did not understand. Silence descended around them as he waited until he could wait no more. "How can one be *in* shock?"

Again, she looked startled and smiled at him, but he also noticed that the shivering had subsided a bit.

"After an accident or a fight, after instinct and action are over, a person can experience a feeling of... of being disconnected from what is around them. It is their mind and body trying to understand what has happened to them. People can look dazed, be unaware of others around them. It's hard to focus, and they can tremble and shake," she held out her hand before them, and both could see the fine shaking of her hand, "and feel as if they might be ill." She looked out at the house as the noise of the celebration rolled across the distance to them.

"I believe you are right, though I have seen this before, I have never heard it named such." She looked to him, and he ushered her toward the cottage. "After a skirmish or a battle that we were not expecting, some of my men would have a similar look. They couldn't hear us as we spoke to them and later they could not say what happened, but they would suddenly come to themselves not realizing how they got from one place to another, though they did so under their own power. Is this what you would call being in shock?"

"Yes. Exactly." She sounded relieved, and he was happy that she seemed more herself.

They were greeted by many people as they entered the light of the torches. Iain watched over Luveday and cut their visit short when she started to pale. If she could not look after herself, then he would.

Luveday remembered the previous night, but most of it was as if it had happened to someone else. She remembered feeling something similar after working on Benedict's leg, but it was nothing so powerful and disconcerting. She remembered the awed looks she received while Archer and Clair thanked her again and again for what she had done. The group that surrounded the couple parted like the red sea as she'd come and gone. A part of her brain thought that something was wrong with their reactions, but she was still too far gone to do anything about it. Cassandra had already left by the time they entered the cottage, and she hoped to meet up with the midwife later today to explain and stop some of the gossip that had started.

A messenger had been sent to the Abbey to see if Lady Emmalyn might return, but it was learned that the Lady and the Abbey's guest had left that afternoon to visit another friend not too far off. Luveday was glad as she doubted Emmalyn would have arrived in time to be of any help anyway, and the older Lady certainly didn't need the stress.

Try as she might, Luveday couldn't clearly recall how she had gotten back to the castle and into bed. She remembered a large presence that must have been Lord Iain. She remembered mounting his horse and started for the castle, but his warmth and the slow rocking of the horse had added to the sudden exhaustion, and the particulars of the rest of the journey were missing. Had he carried her up the stairs to her room? Was it he or Elli that had helped her undress? Luveday was sure her face was bright red as she wiped off the head table as she gave way to her thoughts. Luckily, Elli, who worked beside her, had yet to notice.

She thought she remembered the girl helping her with her undergarments and exclaiming as she opened the chest to retrieve her night clothes, but she couldn't remember if Iain had been present at the time. Surely not!

Luveday tried to focus on the task at hand as she pushed away thoughts of last night. And when had she started to leave off the honorific and started to refer to him as Iain and not Lord Iain, or Lord De Lane. Thinking about it she could not ever remember using the latter address. Her thoughts turned over again, but she was saved as Cassandra made her presence known and caught the young lady's attention.

Elli waved her away before Luveday could excuse herself. It was clear to Elli that Cassandra wanted to talk to the lady alone.

Cassandra did not stop until they were secured inside the healing hut with a glass lamp lit to overcome the shadow of the great castle wall. She looked at her student with a hard eye but noticed nothing different about her, save for the exhaustion that Cass was sure was mirrored in her own face. Cassandra had seen a lot in her life. The superstitions and practices of many women sometimes bordered on some things that were truly of the dark, not that such practices had ever helped heal a woman or save a child. The midwife was sure she'd be able to spot any darkness in the girl if there was any to find. After a long look, she could perceive nothing, but the Luveday she had come to know. She was satisfied that the girl held no evil within and now wanted only an explanation of how her pupil had saved the child she could not.

"What have you done, child?" Luveday had never heard such a stony tone from her friend before. Then again, she could not fathom what the woman must think of her.

Luveday was not unaware of superstitions and the dawning horror of what trouble this act could cause her. Was she to pay for saving the child with her life? She prayed not. So, she thought of how to explain, not sure if she could do a creditable job. Her mother had explained CPR to her and had helped her get her certificate before becoming a babysitter in her teens. She remembered her mother's instructions and wondered what they would only be used now when she was a world away. "My mother taught me the technique. Sometimes, when a person stops breathing, you can use it to help restart their breath. The baby looked fine except for the fact he wasn't breathing. I don't know what I was thinking," she looked to Cass as she leaned against the workbench. "I don't think I was thinking anything at all, I just acted." She saw the mid-wife smile and thought her friend was taking pity on her and could understand that sentiment readily enough. "The practice is a little different with infants than with grown men. Babies are much easier to injure, so one has to be careful, but still apply enough force to get the breath moving through the chest." Luveday explained the technique of CPR, both to breathe for the injured party and how to help restart the heart. Cassandra had many questions and was not completely satisfied until Elli arrived to tell them a message had come, and they were able to 'practice' on the girl. Luveday stressed that only in certain circumstances would CPR be useful and that the technique did not always work. People would still die.

Elli, on the other hand, was fascinated by what she heard. Rumors were running around the castle of how Luveday had brought the baby back from the dead, but she and Cass promised to explain it to anyone who would listen, that it was just a bit of healing that the Lady had learned from her homeland. That the true miracle was that it had worked, and not some form of magic the lady had practiced.

The awaiting message was from Lady Emmalyn saying that a large party would be arriving with her, and while she could not name their guest outright, she said he was a great friend of Lord Iain's and to make haste, while making the best preparations for their guest's extended stay. The women bustled about in a flurry of activity, speculating about who such a guest could be and why the lady could not name him in her missive. Warin was sent out to find his lord, who once again was overseeing some aspect of his estate.

By the time the travelers were spotted by the watch at the gate, the best rooms were ready, the evening meal was added to, and refreshments were just being finished. Luveday was happy with the progress, though nervous about who could be visiting. Elli was beside herself with excitement and nearly jumping up and down beside Luveday, while Iain descended the stairs for the solar where he had washed after returning with Warin.

The noise in the bailey reached the hall first, as they exited to greet their guests. Luveday had never seen so many people. She spotted Lady Emmalyn and Father Quinn among the newcomers, but couldn't reach them, though she could clearly see their smiling visages. Iain went to greet a man who looked to be in his late thirties, while the women held back. Elli clutched her arm like a vice and had stopped running around like a giddy schoolgirl. Luveday took the change as a sign and tried to act accordingly. Obviously, the girl recognized their guest, but Luveday couldn't get her to speak and feared her friend was in shock.

Another Lady, dressed in a gown Christabel would envy, dismounted with the help of several men. Iain kissed her hand as he bowed over it. Lord only knew who she was, though Luveday could see affectionate glances pass between her, and the man whom Iain had greeted first. Both of their guests had sable hair, were fair skinned, and had a pleasant air about them that Luveday could not explain. They were clearly happy to see Iain or was it happy to have reached their destination?

The rest of the party appeared to be mostly knights and servants. There were a few stern-looking gentlemen, but they seemed to cave under the lady's smile. As the group approached the stairs, Elli sank into a deep curtsy, and Luveday quickly followed. She heard Iain's voice above her, introducing her, to King Edward and Queen Augusta and Luveday thought her heart might stop.

"Your Majesties, may I present Lady Luveday, recently of Lander's Keep. Lady this is King Edward and Queen Augusta." Iain sounded pleased to make the introductions.

The Queen spoke first. "A pleasure to meet you, Lady Luveday. What a lovely and unusual name. Is that not so, my dear?"

The King seemed to agree, as he looked between the women and Lord De Lane.

Luveday rose to find the couple looking at her curiously, though their smiles were kind. Before she could say something in return, she was nearly knocked over as a small body collided with her, followed by another impact after that. Luveday was able to brace herself before all three of them went down. She looked down to find two boys, one looking to be about eight, and the other a little younger, were clutching her skirts and looked up at her as startled to see her as she was to see them. The boys were unfamiliar to her and dressed in clothes so fine she knew these must be the young princes accompanying their parents on their journey.

The King laughed and ushered the boys inside the keep. "John, Henry, why do you not escort your mother to the fireside." The boys looked pleased to be given some task, though the little one looked at Luveday as if he wished to stay with her a bit longer. Both boys took their mother's hand, one on each side, and tried to drag her through the great doors. She laughed and walked inside.

Luveday thought she heard herself say, there were refreshments prepared inside, but she wasn't really sure if she had said the words aloud or not. Elysant still had a hold of her elbow, and the two turned as one as they bowed to the King as he passed.

King Edward called over his shoulder, "Benjamin?" but was swiftly informed that the boy was occupied unloading the horses and helping the men. He seemed pleased by this and continued on.

Luveday and her new appendage waited until their guests had passed inside, before entering with Lady Emmalyn who took Luveday's free arm and patted it reassuringly.

The older lady looked wary, but happy and explained how she had come to be among the royal party. "What an honor for the King to visit. Then again, Iain is his Champion." Luveday had forgotten over the ensuring months, that up until recently, Lord Iain had lived in the saddle and on the battlefield. "You may not have known, but I left the Abbey with Lord Frazier and traveled to Olean, a castle about a day's ride from the Cloister."

Elli finally spoke, "We did know of your departure, Lady Emma. A messenger was sent to fetch you, but you were already gone."

"Fetch me? Whatever for, child?" She looked to Luveday and not Elli for her answer.

Luveday nodded to the reluctant women across the room to signal that the trays and wine should be served. "Young Clair went into labor the day after you left. Cassandra called for aid."

"Oh, no!" Emmalyn knew it must have been serious for the seasoned healer to call for help.

"The babe is fine, and the mother is recovering nicely or, so I am told." Luveday gave her hand a reassuring squeeze.

Elli could not keep quiet on the subject and blurted out that Luveday had brought the child back from the dead using a healing technique from her homeland.

Emmalyn looked at her curiously.

"I will explain it to you later." She said as Emmalyn steered them closer to the royals and their entourage. The boys looked happy as they munched on cold meats, cheeses, and some flatbread. Luveday suggested one of the women get some of the juice she had made for her own breakfast for the boys if any remained. Elli ran off saying she'd do it as Iain's knights presented themselves to the King and his Queen.

The two women drifted closer yet remained a little outside of the crowd surrounding the fireplace. Luveday was happy they had made new cushions for the wooden chairs and benches their group occupied each night. Perhaps they were not up to royal standards, but the cushions were extremely comfortable, nevertheless.

As the men started to depart and head back to their duties or up to the chambers Luveday and Emmalyn had quickly assigned to them, the two women settled beside the royal couple. The two young princes were joined by a third, Benjamin who looked to be in his early teens and was taking on the role of squire for his father, though the King already had two.

Luveday didn't know what she expected, but the royal couple was very down to earth and friendly people though they carried the mantle of authority and the fate of a nation in their hands.

Queen Augusta was clearly affectionate with her children and had a hand in their day to day lives which still shocked many of her court. Lady Emmalyn seemed on more than friendly terms with the Queen, and so Luveday was also drawn into the conversation. "We were traveling north to see you, Iain, and to visit Olean and Frazier. We are thinking of Fostering John with him this winter, though I will be sad to see him go."

Emmalyn nodded in understanding. "At least you will have little Henry with you."

"Yes." She looked at the boys as they sat before the fire playing with something Luveday couldn't see. The dogs would come by every so often for attention but mostly left the children to themselves. "They grow up so fast."

"Indeed, they do." Luveday noticed the wistful note in her friend's voice and felt a longing of her own. Children had always been in Luveday's future, but she had never really found a man that she felt any connection too; certainly not enough to marry. She shook herself and noticed that Iain was looking at her strangely. *Had he interpreted her thoughts? Had her expression given her away?*

The conversation shifted to Luveday as the King's attention fell on her. "We hear you are responsible for the keep's transformation, Lady Luveday." He sipped his goblet of wine and Luveday felt his perusal of her was anything, but ordinary. She feared he could see more than she was willing to reveal.

"I was not alone in the endeavor. Lady Emmalyn and I may have overseen the project, but it was the people of Lander's Keep that did the hard labor."

"I hear you were working beside them, Lady." The Queen chimed in.

Emmalyn smiled at Luveday's humility. "Indeed, she was." She was willing to see her friend get the credit she deserved.

"I could hardly ask someone else to do something I, myself, was unwilling to do." Luveday countered.

The King laughed. "My thoughts exactly, Lady." He leaned forward, suddenly engaged in the conversation. "I hold the same sentiments were my Lords are concerned."

Augusta patted his knee, and the King turned to smile at her and held her hand. "That is why he insists on visiting the north and see these restless lord-lings for himself. Always looking for trouble, my love."

To Luveday's surprise, the King did not shrug off his wife's concerns. "My dear, how else am I to know what is going on up here? I must judge for myself." He looked at Iain. "Not that I do not trust your opinions, Champion, but things are not always what they seem."

"Just so, your majesty." Iain nodded as something seemed to pass unspoken between the two men.

Benedict arrived after showing some of the King's men around the castle. He jumped into the conversation and had everyone laughing within moments of setting down. The group conversed for some time, topics wavering between the humor and antics of court politics to the unrest in the north.

Luveday was able to sidestep most of the questions about herself, but answered as truthfully as she could, using the story she had concocted soon after coming to the castle. It was not long until she found a little hand, and then a little body snuggled up next to her.

"How extraordinary, Lady Luveday." The Queen commented as little Henry quickly fell asleep in the lady's arms. "Henry is not one to open up to strangers."

The King looked her over again. "The boy has a way about him, a good judge of character. He seems to like you." Luveday only smiled and looked down at the dark head nestled against her breast.

It was not long after that their guests retired for a while before dinner. Luveday helped carry up the young prince to the room he would share with his brothers and their servant. Laying the little boy in bed and helping to settle the others, the longing that Luveday had felt earlier hit her like a sucker punch. She had no idea what the future could bring and saved off dreaming about things that might never be.

The royal visitors stayed for several days, meaning only to check up on the lord of Lander's Keep before moving on to visit other northern lords before finally reaching their target of Lord Ladislaus of Sterling, the man behind the trouble in the north. There was yet to be outright defiance of the King, but the talk around the fire at night inevitably turned toward the topic. There were some rumors that Lord Sterling was gathering supporters and would soon rise against the King. There was no love lost between the two men, or even Sterling and De Lane. There was a long-standing grudge between them, and Iain was the first to declare that Ladislaus had a conniving and ambitious nature that lent itself to the rumors of his rebellion against the crown. The men spent many hours sequestered in the solar making plans outside of the women's hearing.

The days were filled with laughter, and children and touring the estate. The King was impressed with the improvements and liked to watch Luveday blush and try to deflect his compliments. It came to light that the King had visited once with his champion right after coming home from his battles abroad. It had been before Lady Emmalyn had been installed at the keep, and she could only imagine the sorry state of the castle then.

Lady Christabel did not return, though a message was sent to the Abbey asking her to come and meet their guests. Queen Augusta did not seem insulted by her absence, but in fact, relieved by it. It seemed that rumors of the girl's behavior had reached even her ears, and she was not pleased. She hoped her words of displeasure would have some effect on the girl, but even the Queen kept from commenting openly on the situation. The general consensus was that Lady Christabel should make the best of the situation, and change her attitude to one of polite resignation, but many thought that was impossible.

When the party finally departed it was to gracious farewells and a reminder that the royals would be back for Iain's wedding in the fall.

As the castle's inhabitance dispersed, Iain took Luveday aside. "I have to thank you Lady Luveday. Your work and diligence have impressed even the King. Without you," he looked into her eyes and cleared his throat. "Without you, I cannot imagine in what state Lander's Keep might still reside."

Luveday blushed, and for once didn't try to deflect the compliment. She simply said, "You're welcome, My Lord. It has been my pleasure." They smiled at each other for a moment before Iain nodded and walked swiftly away. She watched him for a moment before returning to the keep helping tidy up after their guests' departure.

Luveday smiled the rest of the day remembering Iain's words.

Chapter 7

Since when was genius found respectable?
~Elizabeth Barrett Browning

In Luveday's mind, summer lingered as if it would stretch on forever. Yet, guests began arriving, not for the wedding itself, that was still a way off, but to see Lord Iain, and more importantly, the transformation of Lander's Keep. They also came to hear of the trouble Sterling was causing farther north. Many came to hear Iain's opinion on the matter and offer their support should things continue to build.

With a rather steady stream of visitors, Lady Emmalyn and the women of the castle were making more of an effort to be presentable. Colorful scarves and ribbons were often seen on the women as they worked. It was with some surprise that Emmalyn and Elli invited Luveday into their room on an almost quite afternoon.

Luveday couldn't help but laugh at their sneaky smile as they ushered her into the room. "What is all this now? What are you two up too?" She looked to see Henna looking over a pile of fine gowns. "Henna?" She greeted and questioned the girl at the same time. Henna nodded back and continued to contemplate the six or so gowns laying on the large four-poster bed.

Some of the gowns were velvet and some wool, several were colors that called to Luveday; they wanted to be touched, but she hung back, still not understanding.

Lady Emmalyn was the first to break the silence. "Well, what do you think child? Will they do?"

Luveday turned to look at the lady and asked, "Do for what, Emmalyn?"

Elli huffed. "For you, silly, to wear."

Luveday was already shaking her head. "These are too fine for me." Though she fingered the trim on a lovely dark blue gown. "Won't you miss them, Emma?"

"No, no, Luveday." She laughed. "These are not my gowns. They belonged to Gwendolyn, My sister-in-law, Iain's mother." She came closer to the bed and stood beside the hesitant young woman. "Well, Henna, dear. Do you think we can salvage some of these? The style is over a decade gone, but the material looks almost new."

Henna was still looking at the gowns. "They should do nicely, My Lady. They are a little large in certain areas, but I should be able to re-work the garments into a more suitable style."

"Lovely." The older woman sighed.

"I don't need all of these gowns, surely." She could not say that some of the colors would look poorly on her, and so suggested an alternative. "One or two simple styles would be nice, especially for the wedding." Frowns crossed the women's faces at the thought of the impending nuptials, but Luveday suggested her idea. "Perhaps you can make a gown for Elysant as well. One of these colors would look very striking on her."

Elysant who had moved to the far side of the bed looked shocked. Her eyes look about the size of saucers as she waited for Lady Emmalyn to answer.

The lady laughed. "I told you, Henna." The women looked at each other.

"That you did, My Lady." Henna pulled out a burgundy gown and looked at the color and back to Elli. "This one should do nicely." Elli ran around the bed with a squeak of happiness and hugged each woman in turn.

"I knew your kind nature, we guessed you would suggest such a thing." She spoke to Luveday before turning to the younger girl. "Henna said she could make a gown for you, Elli."

The redhead seamstress handed the garment to Elli who held it up to her chest. "Plenty of fabric, the garment is in good condition, and I can rework the piece nicely." Henna smiled at her friend. "You'll be fit for a prince, Elli!"

Emmalyn and Luveday shared a look, having the same thought. *She'll be fit for a warrior monk!* Both women had commented on how much time Gregori and Elysant were spending together, and they hoped that this would lead to another wedding in the near future. Both women could not be happier with the idea, though they were unsure if Iain knew of the situation and worried about how he might react.

"Oh, Luveday!" Elli twirled with her gown, "this is the best gift I have ever received! Thank you, Lady Emmalyn!"

Everyone was smiling at the girl's enthusiasm. "Yes," Luveday turned to her friend and wrapped her left arm around the woman in a half hug. "Thank you, Emmalyn. And you as well, Henna." Luveday pulled out the gowns she liked best, a deep blue velvet garment that reminded her of the outfit she wore the day she arrived there, a coal gray wool, and pale green mint gown that looked to be silk or some other thin material. The gowns looked to be about the right height, perhaps an inch or two long, but the busts were much too large by the looks of them. Luveday was not ashamed of her figure, but she guessed that Iain's mother had been very well endowed in that area.

Henna wrapped the gowns in a large piece of material that would protect them, then placed the bundle back in the small trunk from which they had come. Luveday helped the girl carry the trunk into the sewing room and asked how long it would take her to rework the garments.

"I can't say, Lady. I have other duties, and the castle has been rather busy of late." Henna had them place the trunk in the corner of the sewing gallery where she usually sat.

Luveday looked at the spools of thick thread in dozens of different colors. "I know my sewing is not as fine as yours, but if you think I can be of help, don't hesitate to give me something to do."

The seamstress laughed. "I will, My Lady. It may take both of us to get something done before the wedding."

Luveday nodded, and both women headed down to the hall.

Another party that had arrived that afternoon had only been in residence for a few hours, but Luveday was ready to see them gone. Unfortunately, that was not going to happen any time soon. Christabel was home from her extended visit to the Abbey. She talked non-stop about the generosity of Mother Mary Odilia, that was until their visitors arrived. When her father walked into the room unannounced, the mood changed abruptly.

There was a strained moment where father and daughter were reunited. Lord Iain was more formal than Luveday had ever seen him. It seemed that every time she looked up that evening, Iain was surrounded by his knights. There was clearly some tension between the two groups, and though she had been very polite to their guests, Luveday had the feeling that Lord Henric Sumerland was watching her.

Sumerland's men were given rooms, though several stayed in the barracks. Some of Iain's men moved into the back hall, now called the under-gallery, a long and narrow corridor at the back of the keep that was more of a grander hallway leading downstairs to the kitchen than a true room. The under-gallery was usually used to store things, as the castle had not had enough visitors to fill its many rooms for over a decade. Now it would house the fiercest of Iain's knights, leaving the servants and other guests to the great hall.

It seemed with every passing day more people arrived; most having heard that someone they knew was at Lander's Keep. The women were overtaxed and grateful that some of their guests traveled with their own servants. Many thought that the servants were much more tolerable than their masters.

Luveday and Emmalyn were pulling out the stops for dinner a few days later, while many of the guests looked to Christabel for details about daily life in Lander's Keep. They asked simple questions like what would be served for dinner or where the items came from that decorated the hall, or even details about the coming nuptials. Each time Christabel would shrug, too delighted to be the center of everyone's attention to see the disapproving glances of men like her father as she turned to Luveday or Emmalyn for the answer to those questions.

It was clear that Lord Sumerland thought that Luveday was overstepping her boundaries. Word had traveled through the castle about a rather loud argument between father and daughter that had brought up Luveday on more than one occasion. He had even gone so far as to subtlety suggest Lord Iain might be keeping her as a mistress. Lady Emmalyn had taken her sharp wit to the man before Luveday could even form a reply. Luveday hated to think that she might be one of the reasons why tension was thick in the air.

The other was Lord Sumerland's companion, Lord Albin Sterling, cousin to Ladislaus, Earl of Sterling and a man known to be the Earl's ears and eyes at court, though he had been scarce as of late, all things considered. Rumors continued to spread, and all pointed to trouble brewing in the North, and the elder Sterling was stirring the pot.

Luveday watched the man, having overheard a bit of conversation as she brought up wine to the solar one evening. "He's not to be trusted, Iain." Benedict had just returned from a visit to his mother, and though the journey had taken a lot out of him, he was adamant about Albin. "Sumerland is a fool to trust anything that dog says."

Gregori agreed. "We know Albin carries news back to his cousin. Word has it that he is trying to see what men would be willing to rebel against the King. Ladislaus has something up his sleeve and thinks he can coerce or bribe the lords into following him."

The conversation had stopped as they heard her open the door. Luveday left the wine and goblets but kept what she had heard to herself.

Tonight, the hall was packed with guests, some stayed at the keep, some at the inn and some journeyed from the Abbey. Minstrels provided music and wine improved the humors of their guests. Dinner had been a stretched affair as no one had anticipated such a turnout, but no one complained as long as their cups were full and so Luveday helped to make sure that none went dry.

Christabel held court by the fire surrounded by a handful of men who adored her. Some even wrote her poems, though not particularly good ones. At least the handful in her pocket were rather contrived though the gentleman's handwriting was rather pretty. Luveday was sick of men being too shy, or perhaps they thought themselves cunning as they slipped her missives to give to the bride-to-be. Declarations of undying love abounded, brought on by the looming wedding. No one else was embarrassed by grown men groveling at the betrothed's feet, and so Luveday clenched her jaw and helped pass notes like she was in grammar school.

She saw more paper passed around the hall than she thought were in the steward's books. Luveday could only hope they had purchased the material themselves and had not raided the keeps small store.

As she continued to fill drinks and tried to ignore the spectacle Lord Sumerland was making at the high table, Luveday was pulled suddenly to one side. It was not the first time that night that someone had drunk too much and thought to get frisky, but Luveday was surprised to see that it was someone who had not been overindulging that night. At that moment she could not remember his name, though she knew his older brother was a rather powerful man whose lands lay north and farther east. He had been pointed out in reference to his brother, who was a good friend of Iain's.

He pulled her down so that he could speak to her over the merry noise of the hall. "Lady, could you see that Lord Albin gets this. I hate to have to wade through all of the bride's admirers. They look as if they might duel each other over her attentions at any moment." He shoved something into her hand and laughed as he looked to the fools that surrounded Christabel. Luveday agreed with him, they looked as if they might kill the next man that tried to join their number.

Luveday only glanced at the folded paper but noticed the seal on it. "As you wish, Sir. Though it may be a while for me to make my way over."

He nodded, as almost two dozen people stood between her and her goal. "At your earliest convenience, My Lady." He held up his drink for it to be refilled, the first time that night and Luveday noticed he downed the cup as she walked away.

It was some time later that she remembered the letter, taking it out of her pocket for a moment to fish out the pile of poems there. That was when she saw the writing on the letter's face and the intricate seal on the back. The seal was cut in a jagged line across a portion of its face, giving Luveday the idea that someone already knew its contents, someone the letter had not been intended for. It looked as if the seal had been broken, but someone had tried to make it seem as if the letter had not been opened.

Luveday had to set down the pitcher she had carried around all night. She moved into an empty nook out of the flow of the hall, and though the light was dim here, she studied the letter. The paper was course, nothing like she was used to, it was folded many times making it a small but rather thick rectangle. Luveday thought it would be easy for someone to carry it in a pocket or against their breast. The most startling thing about the letter was not the neat block handwriting or the intricacy of the seal, but that it was addressed, not to Lord Albin, but to Lord Iain De Lane of Lander's Keep from Lord Grayson Stern of Havenwood. Luveday thought quickly. The knight still watched her as she moved around the hall, and while he had had several more cups in the hour since she had been charged with the note, he had watched her intently for that length of time.

She had to figure out what to do. As Luveday saw it, she had a few choices. She could read the letter, give it over to Albin and rely its contents to Iain. Or she could not give the letter over and draw some suspicions. She could take the thing straight to Iain and let him deal with it, but all of those options had their flaws, mostly letting the knight know that they were on to him, and not knowing why Albin was intercepting missives meant for De Lane. There was another option, but Luveday didn't know if it would work.

Taking out the papers in her apron pocket she folded them to resemble the letter as best she could. Going to the kitchen, she took some wax and used a bit of red spices mixed with the wax to seal the decoy letter. The new seal was remarkably close in color to the crimson of its brother. From a distance, the two looked identical. Luveday put the real letter in her gown, stuffed between her bodice and her kirtle. The other she returned to her pocket. No one paid her any attention, though the kitchen was full. She picked up the pitcher where she had left it in the hall and continued filling cups until she finally made her way over to Christabel and Lord Albin who was installed by her side.

She filled cups, laughed at jests she found in no way amusing and slipped the lordling the letter. He only glanced at her a moment as he put the missive aside. Luveday somehow resisted the urge to look to Iain or to the knight that had given her the letter. The night progressed, and finally, people began to find their beds. She took a tray of goblets and wine up to the solar after she had stayed in the hall long enough to see Iain, Benedict, Gregori and Sir Fuller enter the room.

The men stopped their conversation as Luveday entered. It was the third night in a row that she had brought up the wine, though Iain had expected her to be in bed hours ago. He had not been happy that she had been commanded around the keep like some serving wench. Sumerland's veiled comments about her made his blood boil, and he had nearly thrown father, and daughter, out of his keep. Luveday hesitated at the door, and all eyes turned to her. The expression he saw on her face had all of them troubled.

Luveday stopped just inside the door, suddenly aware that her actions tonight could have much greater consequences than she had at first thought. Perhaps they would not be happy that she had taken matters into her own hands. Maybe they would even punish her for it, but it was too late to take it back now, and something said that what had almost transpired tonight been very important.

"Lady Luveday?" Iain's voice jolted her out of her thoughts, and she moved to set the tray down on the table before the fire. Everyone was looking at her. "Luveday?" He asked again, and their eyes met.

She had taken the letter out of her bodice and returned it to her pocket when no one was around to see. Now she pulled it out and handed it to Iain who handed it to Gregori who was better with letters. Luveday didn't say a word.

"Where did you get this lady?" The monk asked.

"That is a bit of a story, Sir Gregori." She looked at Iain as she spoke and only glanced at the others around the table. Gregori examined the letter and seemed to notice what she had, and let Benedict see it before they continued.

Benedict confirmed her findings. "This letter has been opened." They looked to her. "Someone had resealed it, and done a credible job, though it's not perfect."

"Who is if for?" Iain asked, still watching Luveday and was surprised when she answered.

"It's addressed to you. From Lord Grayson Stern of Havenwood." She said quietly. The men looked even more curious.

"How would you know that?" Benedict asked.

Gregori answered Benedict by simply saying, "Because the lady can read." He had heard such from Father Quinn, but many ladies said they could read when, in fact, they could make out only a few words and letters.

Fuller had remained silent until now. "How did you come by the missive, Lady?"

Benedict frowned though his tone held a bit of his usual mirth. "And don't say 'tis a long story."

Luveday smiled. "I was serving wine in the hall," the men looked as if they did not like that, but she continued, "when a man stopped me and gave me this letter to be handed over to Lord Albin." Their expressions turned darker. "I glanced at the letter and put it in my pocket and forgot about it for over an hour. I had just refilled my pitcher when the crunch of papers in my apron distracted me." She watched them as they watched her intently. "I had a handful of poems for Lady Christabel," they scoffed and snorted at the mention of the love poems. She guessed the men were not as unconcerned about them as she had thought. "When I pulled them out of my pocket, I saw the letter, and clearly read for whom it was intended."

Iain looked at her. "Why did you not deliver the letter?" The men looked at him with degrees of impatience and a little anger.

"Why would I deliver a letter addressed to you, to someone else, let alone Sir Albin of Sterling." She crossed her arms in front of her, clearly showing her anger at being asked such a question, as if he questioned her loyalty.

"So now either Albin or this knight will know that you have not delivered the letter." He stated as Gregori finally opened the missive.

"Not necessarily." She said, and their eyes moved back to her. "I may have delivered something to Lord Albin that looks strikingly similar to that letter, at least similar enough if one was at a distance."

"You switched the letters?" Benedict had a bit of awe in his voice before he laughed at her cunning. "I knew you were too good, Lady."

Iain glared at her. "I told you she had overheard our conversation."

Gregori countered, "And I told you that Luveday could be trusted with whatever information she had gleaned."

Before she could become angrier, Iain redeemed himself, if only a little. "I have no doubt about that, but it is not something a woman should have to undertake."

"And yet I have." She countered.

"Where did you get the other letter, Lady?" The older knight asked.

"There was no other letter." She couldn't help the smirk that rose to her lips. "I used the poems and made them look like the letter. A bit of candle wax with some red spices and it would be hard to tell the difference."

"Hard to tell the difference if one could not read?" Benedict asked.

"Even if they could. Though the trouble will be if Albin was expecting the letter or not." Luveday looked at the letter as it sat before Gregori who frowned at it and rubbed his eyes.

Iain's concerned gaze turned to his friend. "What is the matter, Brother?"

Gregori sighed. "I am afraid I've had too many cups tonight, the words swim before my eyes."

Iain's eyes move to rest on Luveday, who picked up the letter and turned slightly towards the fireplace to take advantage of its light.

"To Lord Iain De Lane of Lander's Keep, Loyal Knight, and Champion to King Edward the third of Anora. From your friend and distant relative, Lord Grayson Stern of Havenwood in the High North. I hope this letter finds you and your household well, and that you have settled into your estate since last, we spoke. Word has reached the North that Lander's Keep has returned to its former glory and I know of no one more deserving of such a gem than you, De Lane. I also wish to renew the promises I made before you and our King. Should trouble start in the North, you and his majesty will have my sword and my men at your immediate disposal. Long live the King." Luveday shuffled the papers to read the next page. "Rumors abound, and one cannot gauge how true their content, and I ask that you return any news so that Havenwood might be of service when the time comes. Sterling grows bolder every day, and there are more rumors of men joining his cause. Money has changed hands, and I fear this bodes ill for the King." She looked at figures and names on the bottom of page, reading them aloud though they meant nothing to her. "I am unsure about the loyalty of my neighbors, all except Lord Frazier have publicly voiced their displeasure with the King at one time or another. Please send word for any you may vouch for, I gather our enemy will move as the days turn colder, hopefully not before the harvests are in. I hate to say such a thing, but I fear your wedding may have to be postponed until this matter is settled. There is word that the King travels north. Should he rest at your house, please convey these words and warnings. We would not want a repeat of Jasper's Woods. I pray my troubles prove fruitless, for all our sakes. Give my sincere affections to Lady Emmalyn and Elysant. And I hope to visit you after the wedding, at least to meet..." Luveday paused and looked to Iain, and back to the paper before continuing, "at least to meet Lady Luveday, whom I have heard so much about. You have all the luck when it comes to women, my friend." She almost laughed at that. "God Bless, your faithful friend, Lord Grayson Stern. dated: The sixth day after the summer solstice, the merry month of Tem." Luveday handed over the letter.

"So, the letter is rather recent." Benedict was the first to speak. "You read very well, Lady."

"Lord Grayson has very nice handwriting," was all she said.

Iain had not stopped watching her since she began the letter. "Do you remember who gave it to you?"

"Do you have someone in mind, Iain?" Benedict inquired.

Luveday could point him out, but could not remember his name, and said as much. "I know what he looks like, but I cannot recall his name, though I remember being introduced to him." She looked away, trying to jog her memory. "There was something about his demeanor that I thought was ironic, as it so reflected his manner." She shook her head, not believing the bit of information that sprung to mind. "I am not sure," she hesitated. "I cannot be sure but is there a knight from Havenwood here. Could he be related to Stern?" Iain nodded. "I remember thinking that his expression was very dower and too serious compared to his companions, and how appropriate it was to his last name, how could I have forgotten Sir Stern?" She thought harder. "Was it, Patrick? Or was his name... I know it started with a P. Patrick, Piers, maybe Peter?" Fuller growled as the men exchanged looks that spoke volumes as if they hesitated to speak of anything in her presence, which only irritated her more.

"Sir Peter Stern is currently under our roof, I believe he is staying in the under-gallery with Sir John Templeton. They are old friends. The boy trained under him."

Gregori looked at Iain. "Are we suggesting that Peter Stern is betraying the King and his lord, his own brother?" No one spoke to deny the accusations.

Luveday asked what was on her mind, determined to be part of the conversation. "Why would he not hand over the letter to you? I am assuming his brother sent it with him." Luveday looked at each man in turn. "What would he have to gain by joining Sterling?"

Fuller spoke as the other's contemplated this latest betrayal. "Sir Peter is Grayson's younger brother, though more than a decade separates them." The knight poured the wine and took a drink. "Should his brother die, the title and all the lands would fall to him."

Luveday nodded. "So, if there is a skirmish or battle in the North, and Sterling can somehow guarantee Lord Grayson's death, then Sir Peter inherits the lands and Sterling has a loyal follower that appears to be on the King's side. Or should Sterling prevail..."

Iain finished the thought for her, though he had almost as much trouble voicing it as she did. "Then Sir Peter would have proved his loyalty to the new King and secured his positions, with or without his brother's death."

Fuller gulped down more wine. "This is a nasty business, this is."

"Aye," Gregori seconded.

Benedict rang in, with his thoughts. "Grayson mentioned money and Jasper's Woods."

"Aye," Iain said. "I caught that."

"You know what that means." Luveday had never seen such a dark look cross Benedict's golden features.

Gregori shuddered. "Jasper's Wood. Mercenaries."

Luveday gasp. The air in the room turned bleak. "Mercenaries?"

Fuller growled and a dog stirred by the fire. "'Tis not a tale to be repeating to a lady." Luveday watched Gregori take a long drink. The monk was clearly upset.

Iain looked from his friend to the lady. "There was an ambush."

"De Lane!" Benedict said his name in warning, agreeing with Fuller. It was not a story to be repeated in front of a lady, especially not soft-hearted Luveday.

Luveday understood. They had lost too much at Jasper's Wood. "Is he warning you about the mercenaries or the ambush, or maybe both?"

They turned to her, once again surprised by her insight. Benedict rubbed his chin. "'Tis best to think it's both." Gregori only nodded.

Iain looked up at her. "'Tis past time you went to bed, Lady." He cut off her protests. "Dawn is almost here, get what rest you can. Tomorrow we watch and wait for our enemy's next move."

Luveday couldn't argue. A new day would bring a world of work, and watching this new foe was one more task she would undertake. She wished them a good night and sought her bed. Despite her worries, she was asleep soon after.

The next day proved uneventful though Luveday kept a watchful eye on Lord Albin and Sir Peter Stern whenever she could. The two kept their distance from each other, barely exchanging more than a few words all day. It wasn't until night had fallen, and the castle was quiet that something happened.

Luveday was abed, but not asleep. She used her small wind up flashlight to read a few pages in her books. Though she had read the herbal from cover to cover, she still studied its pages, willing herself to commit it to memory. She spent about half an hour learning its secrets before turning to her favorite book, the Poetry of Elizabeth Barrett Browning. The romantic poet was her one indulgence.

Browning's life and poetry touched her heart, "How do I love thee? Let me count the ways. I love thee to the depth and breadth and height My soul can reach..."

It was only because she had gotten lost in the words, and had yet to go to sleep, that she heard the noise coming down the hall. Thinking Emmalyn might need her, she rose and made it to the door before the person on the other side. There was something odd about it. And Luveday stood looking at the latch as her mind registered that it was not Emmalyn or one of the other ladies who had sought her out. The presence in the hall seemed large, its footfalls too heavy to be a woman. When the latch moved, Luveday threw her weight against the door holding it closed. The man on the other side didn't push through or she would never have been able to hold her ground. The voice she heard muttering in the hall was one she recognized.

Lord Albin was a talkative fellow, who believed his position was more important than any other at Lander's Keep. He had made a small speech that night at dinner, that Luveday felt, was full of innuendos and metaphors that she didn't' fully understand, but the result was far from subtle.

He cursed as the door refused to give way, and a few moments later he moved back down the hall. Luveday waited for a door to sound but heard none. She made a fast decision. Grabbing her belongings, she hid them back in their cubbies, wrapped herself in the purple fleece blanket and headed for the solar.

She cracked open the door, listening down the hall. Opening it a bit wider, she stuck her head through. There was no sign of anyone, though she wouldn't put it past Albin to check her door again tonight. She closed the door as quietly as she could and raced for the solar.

Luveday let herself in, and closed the door behind her, leaning back on it to catch her breath. Coll was stretched out on the bench under the glass windows. A lantern burned in the small space while more light shown around the bedroom door. Luveday sat down, taking one of the cushions on the floor that had belonged to the bench and leaning back against the wall. No one would look for her here, she just needed to rise before the rest of the castle and head back to her room before anyone was the wiser. Settling in, she looked up as Coll rolled over and looked at her. He was still mostly asleep and settled back in when she whispered that everything was alright and that he could go back to sleep. Luveday curled up on the cushion leaning against the built-in cabinet that flanked the bench. With the cold stone wall at her back, she tried to get comfortable and didn't realize how quickly she drifted into sleep.

A hand touched her shoulder, and Luveday leaned into the warmth still somewhere between slumber and wakefulness. Her name was whispered as she was pulled to her feet and ushered into the bedroom. There was a heated exchange between several familiar voices, but Luveday was having trouble focusing, and could barely open her eyes. There wasn't much she understood other than their angry tones as she listened from her perch. She ran her hand over a fur and looked down to find herself sitting on the large trunk at the end of Iain's bed.

Blinking a few times, the room swam in and out of focus. She just couldn't get her eyes to stay open.

A moment later large hands tilted her head up as they framed her face then slid down to where her skull met the column of her neck. There was her name again, in that deep whisper she liked. A thumb stroked her right cheek as she leaned a little to her left. She felt warm and safe and smiled sleepily to herself.

"Luveday. Wake up, Lady." Iain's voice sounded directly in front of her, it's timber a bit louder and more insistent.

Though exhausted, she opened her eyes to see him standing too close. He still held her head up, she feared without his support she might just tumble over into a useless heap on the hardwood floor.

Another voice, from her left, sounded. Fuller asked something that she didn't catch, though Luveday could just see him turn towards the door out of the corner of her eye.

Sir Gregori entered with a sleepy Coll who looked on in confusion and continued to shake his head at whatever the knight was asking him.

"What happened, Luveday?" Her gaze moved only a fraction to center on Iain once more. She smiled at him; he really was too handsome, but that frown on his face was troublesome. "Why were you sleeping at my door?"

"The door." She repeated as a way of explanation. Her wits were starting to trickle back into her head, and she frowned in return. Something was wrong with this situation. She had fled her room. "Door doesn't lock." She tried again.

Gregori looked at them as Coll went back to bed. Fuller growled a warning, much like the hounds that he cared for.

Iain still held her head up. "What door?"

Fuller answered as she licked her lips. "The lady's door doesn't have a bolt on it. She mentioned it to me a few days ago, with the many guests and all." Gregori turned and left the room. Fuller stationed himself before the door, and Iain stared at the lady trying to control the growing fury that turned his stomach to fire.

"Did someone try to enter your room tonight, Luveday?" She nodded moving his hands along with her head.

She was relieved he understood because she was having trouble communicating. She felt the anxiety and the hard work of the last week had finally caught up with her. All she wanted was to lay down and get some rest.

Gregori returned, and words were exchanged between him and Fuller. Iain didn't seem to be paying attention to the conversation, but Luveday saw his pupils dilate as his nostrils flared; she was so close.

Gregori stepped closer, standing just behind Iain's left shoulder and in Luveday's line of sight. "Albin was in the hall a moment ago. It looked like he might have been coming from her room."

The muscles in Iain's jaw clenched and moved as Luveday realized he was grinding his teeth.

"I will see to a sturdy latch and bolt on the morrow." Fuller offered.

"Call the blacksmith. I want his strongest bolt on that door by tomorrow evening." Iain never so much as glanced away from her. "Was it Albin?"

She nodded slightly. Gregori left to make sure the lordling returned to his room, while mentally plotting the man's demise. They knew they could not throw him out of the castle, or better yet, throw him in the dungeons, as they needed to learn more of his cousin's plans and what part the slimy young man played in them.

"She'll stay here the rest of the night." Fuller didn't argue as Iain began making a palette before the fire. A few moments later, she was nestled between the soft furs and sound asleep, unaware of the fury that churned in the heart of the man who watched over her.

It was a bit awkward as Iain woke her a few hours later, just before dawn and escorted her back to her room. He stood guard outside as she washed and dressed for the day. She thanked him as they stood in the hall. Luveday looked at everything but him, while she felt his gaze like a weight on her body. He merely nodded and headed back to the solar for a moment. Luveday went about her usual duties, though she was up a little earlier than normal. The Blacksmith, Barth, was called in and began the work of fashioning a bolt to lock Luveday's door. The activity around her room did not go unnoticed, and while no one spoke of it directly, Emmalyn inquired if she was alright while the rest of the women kept a watchful eye over her. Luveday didn't mind that they kept her close, it made her feel like one of them, like family.

The men were out most of the day, Iain had somehow gotten the majority of them out of the castle, Albin and some of the floppy court men included.

Luveday did not worry about her safety, though she kept a wary eye out anyway. She had given the lordling the poetry, and perhaps he had taken that as some sort of invitation, but she would make it clear that it was no such thing.

By nightfall, the men were more subdued, though tensions were at a peak. Henric and Iain had had an argument while hunting and touring the estate. No one seemed to know exactly what they talked about, but the castle ran rampant with speculations. Though the men sat next to each other at dinner, they were still very brisk, and every other comment from Sumerland's mouth was a thinly veiled insult. Lord Albin Sterling had returned with the men and was acting like a spoiled brat, complaining about everything in sight while Christabel agreed with him and begin pointing out items he might have missed.

Angry words were exchanged as dinner came to an end, and several knights at the long tables began shouting. As punches were thrown, the women scurried out of the way. Christabel screamed and became hysterical, the men at the high table began shouting. Albin said something he shouldn't have, and Iain and Gregori both turned to him with thunderous looks. Iain grabbed Sterling by the front of the shirt and hauled him out of his chair. Lord Henric took offense at how his companion was being treated and stepped in, threatening De Lane.

Luveday watched from the fireside, having just refilled the cups of the minstrels who were more than happy with her hospitality. She had been barred from the high table for the last two nights but didn't mind as she found the company not to her liking anyway. Elli flew to her side as more chaos erupted. Luveday watched only a moment longer before she set her pitcher down, took up an iron pole used to stir the fire and quickly wrapped the end in her discarded apron before standing atop Elli's stool and hit the large silver dish over the mantel like a giant gong. The resounding peal echoed through the hall, and everyone froze, turning to the source of the noise.

Luveday stared hard at Iain, who looked at her, stunned for a moment, before gathering his wits and issuing orders. The minstrels looked at her with expressions of amusement and respect as the hall immediately settled back into place. Apologies were made, but several guests left their seats declaring they would be leaving in the morning, before marching off to their rooms, Lord Albin among them.

"Luveday," Elli whispered in awe as she stepped off the stool.

The lady turned to her friend as Emmalyn quickly joined them beside the hearth. Emmalyn's smile was ear to ear as Christabel and Adela swept passed them. The young lady's nose was in the air, and she spared not even a glance to anyone as she passed, while Adela looked Luveday in the eye for only a heartbeat and nodded as she followed after her mistress.

Emmalyn beamed at her. "I do not know where you get some of these ideas, child, but that was one of the most brilliant things I have ever seen." The women moved away from the minstrels who were collecting their things and heading out to the stables where they slept comfortably in the hayloft. "Swords were almost drawn and with one move you quelled the trouble." The lady almost laughed; she was so delighted.

Lord Henric walked by, he stopped a moment to wish Lady Emmalyn a good night, but the entirety of the short conversation he spent glaring at Luveday. The serving women began clearing the tables as men quickly departed. They chatted amongst themselves and sent grateful looks toward Luveday who nodded in acknowledgment of their praise.

It seemed like it took only moments for the hall to empty. Iain and a group of men still crowded around the high table as the ladies watched from their spot by the fire.

Emmalyn rested her hand on one of Luveday's arms as the young lady stood with them crossed protectively over her chest. "You did well, Luveday. Very well." Emmalyn looked at her meaningfully before moving off to talk to another guest who lingered near the stairs. Elli only looked at her with a grin before running off to the kitchens, where Luveday imagined the girl would replay tonight's events to anyone who would listen.

Luveday sighed, partly in relief and partly from exhaustion. She began collecting forgotten cups and plates around the fire. She wiped down the sitting area as the women readied the rest of the hall. Iain stopped at the bench and leaned over its back to watch her work for a moment. She glanced up to see him there and paused. Straightening, she gave him a quizzical look, curious that he hadn't immediately gotten her attention. Was she in trouble? Luveday doubted it.

They stood for a moment just watching each other, Luveday unconsciously tilted her head slightly to the right when she was curious about something and couldn't know that Iain found the gesture endearing.

"Thank you," was all he said.

Luveday nodded. "You're welcome." He left as Gregori came by to join him before they both went outside, and she went back to her duties.

The next morning proved to be a mass exodus. Lord Albin and more than half their guests, left. Some had planned to move on soon and took the scene the night before as their cue to exit. Some wanted to carry the news of what had transpired to ears waiting to hear of Lord De Lane and the upcoming wedding. Some promised to return for the ceremony. Only a few were truly angered by what had happened, Lord Albin and his men most acutely felt they had been insulted. Lord Henric stayed a bit longer, long enough to have a talk with Iain in the solar and then leave, but not before stationing two of his men at Lander's Keep, supposedly for Christabel's convenience. Many took the gesture at face value, but Iain knew what Henric intended. It was a warning. Sumerland now had eyes and ears inside his keep, and Iain didn't doubt the men would report back to their master at the slightest provocation. De Lane almost wished something would happen to bring Henric back to collect his daughter and call this whole mess off. That was wishful thinking. Henric would see this through, no matter what; De Lane was too big of a catch to surrender.

Several days passed in quiet solitude. The last wave of summer crops was being picked. Luveday's band of trees were heavy with fruit. The men continued to tend the orchard, though the rest were not doing nearly as well. Archer came to congratulate her and said he would see to the rest of the trees himself come spring. Overall, the land flourished.

It was with some surprise that Luveday came across a hidden garden. Benedict helped her force open the iron gate that was overgrown with climbing vines. The garden was visible from the room Emmalyn and Elysant shared, but Luveday had never known of its existence. It was a secret garden, and from the looks of it, no one had cared for it in some time. The walls that enclosed the space were of the same stone as the castle and outer wall, though much shorter and thinner than their protective big brothers. Like the rest of the castle, there were hidden gems among the green chaos. There was a stone path under the weeds that blanketed the garden. There was a nook with a stone bench, and nearby a small stone basin tucked up against a wall that had a simple fountain though its water had run dry long ago. In the center of the garden was a large tiered fountain like one might expect in an Italian garden, though it was also empty of water, but full of debris.

The garden became Luveday's newest project, what free time she could claim she spent dividing between working in this garden, riding lessons and helping Henna with the dresses. She spent most of her free time there, which she had more of since their guests had departed. Helpers rotated in and out. It seemed as if she never had the same helper twice. It took a week for the garden to be cleaned up and trimmed down to its bare bones. Once the vines and roses were shaped into a manageable order, she began to think of ways to improve the space, to build back layers to create a special oasis. Iain had given her permission to do as she pleased, not seeming to care about the space one way or another though Emmalyn said his mother would spend most of her time there, especially when he was a child.

It was another surprise when Sir Chadric and Catherine made their way to the castle and sought her out in her new sanctuary.

"Here she is, Cathy!" Sir Chadric moved into the garden, his wife not far behind him. Coll held the old woman's hand as they walked through the stone arch. "Hard at work, as usual, Lady Luveday."

Luveday got to her feet and wiped off the dirt from her apron. She had been planting some flowers from the castle's vegetable garden. They had been doing poorly, too crowded in their beds, so Luveday had taken a few to add some color to a raised stone bed.

Coll dropped off a large basket at the bench in the nook and helped Cathy walk the paved paths. Luveday was overjoyed to see the little couple as she had not been able to visit them as frequently as she had planned.

Sir Chadric looked at the fountain in wonder as the sunlight turned the three-tiered waterfall into prisms of shining rainbows of color. His wife made her way to the far side of the garden where only a few days before, Luveday had found a remarkable sight. In another nook that mirrored the archway over the gate, stood an almost life-sized statue of a woman. She was dressed in a flowing gown that was all one piece with only a belt at her waist to give the garment some definition. She wore a covering on her head that hid her features in shadow though a curling length of hair rested on one shoulder. The statue's pose was relaxed, but there was something a little sad about her as she rested her right hand over her right collarbone. Her head was tilted down ever so slightly, and there was almost a smile on her face, just the corners of her mouth hinted at something.

Cathy headed straight for her, and Luveday watched as the woman raised a hand to touch the hem of the stone dress. Luveday was hesitant to interrupt what she felt was a personal moment, so she greeted Sir Chadric as he stood beside the fountain.

"Sir Chadric, it is good to see you again." She hugged the old knight.

"My dear, this place is looking wonderful. I have not been here for many years." Luveday thought his eyes looked a little misty as he spoke, but it could have been the bright sunshine.

"She is looking better. The garden was in sad shape when I found her." Cathy moved towards them, Coll once again taking up his place as her escort though the boy was a few heads shorter than she. "Unfortunately, not much was left, but weeds and vines. Some of the roses have survived, but the place is rather bare."

Cathy patted the boy's arm as they stopped before the fountain as well. "Perhaps we might help with that." She motioned for the basket and Coll retrieved it from the shaded nook. "Father Quinn spoke so much of your garden on the last visit that we decided to come and see for ourselves. Paige said that you were working hard to transform the Lady's sanctuary." Cathy handed over the basket. Luveday held it as she pulled back a cloth to reveal several plants whose roots were wrapped in pieces of old cloth. "Do you think these will do?"

Luveday laughed. Catherine had collected the best of her own garden to transfer into this new one. "These are perfect, Cathy. Thank you." She gave the cunning old woman a peck on the cheek. Cathy waved her away. Luveday moved aside. "Come, sit down out of the sun." The couple moved to the stone bench in the nearby nook and rested in the shadow of the garden wall, which was about twelve feet high, about half the height of the outer walls. The garden had three trees, one in each back corner and one along the side wall away from the castle structure.

There were trellises that had somehow survived the neglect over the years though the plants they had supported had died long ago. Wide stone paths bisected the garden and quartered it into four sections like a giant cross with the three-tiered fountain in the middle. The fountain was large, though rather plain, with circular basins, though Father Quinn had said square was the usual design. Clear water circulated through the fountain that was somehow connected to a nearby well. Once the fountain had been unclogged and filled with fresh water, it began to function again, and they no longer needed to fill it by hand. Luveday was glad, as it provided a way to irrigate the garden without having to carry water from the kitchen well or the well in the outer bailey.

The four main planting beds were cut into smaller raised beds. They were the average wicker basket weave like the kitchen garden and had needed some repair before they were ready for planting. A few stone beds lay nestled against the garden's stone walls. These needed scrubbing but the capstones atop the small walls of the raised beds shone a craftsman's care in their beveled edges and solid seating. Luveday had begun to replant them once they had been cleared. They now held an array of plants, from mint and rosemary to strawberries and dandelions. A few shrubs and other plants had survived around the border of the garden somehow aided by the walls. Two rosemary bushes looked as if they might have been formed into topiaries, but Luveday could not discern their original shape. There was a vine along the inner wall. The trellis was rather bare, but the plant had survived, what it was she couldn't be sure, but it looked like a grapevine; only time would tell if she was right. The only things that seemed to grow in abandon were weeds and the ivy vines that had sealed the gate shut. Luveday and an army of helpers had trimmed and pulled until the ivy was a more manageable size, with some maintenance the vines would make a lovely wall of green to welcome visitors. Between the beds were paths of gravel, the same tan color as the stone walls. Overall, the garden was still rather bare.

Luveday looked at the plants in the basket as her visitors sat in the shade and enjoyed the tranquility. Catherine had brought three violets, two marigolds, an Iris and a vine of her sweet peas. Luveday had exclaimed at the beauty of the flowering vine. Sweet peas were one of her favorite scents, and now the garden would have a vine to grace its walls. "This is wonderful, Cathy. Thank you so much."

The older woman padded her knee as Sir Chadric excused himself to visit the hall.

"Coll!" Luveday got the boy's attention as he played in the water of the fountain. "Can you escort Sir Chadric to the hall to find Lord Iain. I will make sure Catherine gets back when we are ready." The boy nodded and rushed off after the old knight.

Cathy smiled to see the boy's enthusiasm. "Is there anything else you need, child?" She looked about. "I could bring some more clippings, foxglove, poppy, some sweet mint if you'd like." For a moment, the old woman saw the garden as it once was, filled with the lady and her two small sons playing and laughing in the golden sunshine; it brought tears to her eyes.

Luveday pretended that she didn't notice. "Thank you, Cathy. I would like that." She looked out at the garden, and her mind conjured up a vision of what it used to be which was remarkably close to the one in Catherine's memory. "The hard work is done, and now we wait for nature to do the rest."

"All in good time, my dear." Luveday looked to her companion and thought there was some hidden meaning to her words but didn't ask Cathy what she meant beyond the obvious. Luveday picked out spots for the new editions and planted them as her friend watched from the bench. Cathy commented about this or that, but Luveday didn't really need to answer her, so she worked and watered the plants before the two women headed into the castle for the mid-day meal.

Sir Chadric and Catherine were on their way home in a village cart when the first messenger arrived that afternoon. The man was pale, dirtier than usual, and dread filled his eyes as the ladies met him in the courtyard. Someone ran to find Iain. Just as the lord entered the courtyard a bell tolled at the Abbey and continued to ring.

"Five bells," Emmalyn whispered and looked to Iain and then the women. Elli grabbed hold of Luveday, once again hanging off her friend.

Gregori ran out of the chapel heading straight for his lord and the messenger. "Five Bells, De Lane."

Benedict ran from the Hall, nearly running into Luveday and Elli. "Was it five? Five bells?" He asked.

Luveday nodded, not comprehending the significance, but

understanding the quiet dread around her. "Why five bells?" She asked.

Emmalyn looked to her and recognized the confusion in her friend's gaze. Sometimes the older woman forgot that Luveday had not been born on the shores of Anora. "Five Bells sound when the King calls his men to arms. The King is under attack, and his men must rally to him."

The woman watched as the men talked heatedly with the messenger. Luveday asked one of the women at her elbow to go and get some provisions for the man, as it was clear he would not be staying long. No one moved, so Luveday went and retrieved the items herself. Agnes looked at her with worried eyes, but no one asked what the commotion was about. The castle held its breath for news. When Luveday returned to the courtyard the King's man was mounted on a fresh horse, and Luveday handed up her bounty. She could see the gratitude in his eyes as he accepted her bundle and the cup of cold ale, she offered him. He downed it quickly, nodded to the men who still crowded him and turned the mount towards the gate. He was gone as quickly as he had come.

"You needn't have done that yourself, Lady." Iain turned to her as they watched the King's man disappear down the road.

She looked at him and noticed the tightness around his eyes and jaw. She could guess that the news was not good, but how could it be anything but bad when the King had sounded the call. Luveday shrugged and turned to him. "No one else was inclined to go, and I didn't mind."

Iain nodded and brushed a hair out of his eyes. He looked at her for a moment without speaking, and Luveday wondered if he saw her at all. More than likely he was planning for what was to come, so she didn't interrupt him, just waited for the orders she knew would follow. "The messenger said that wounded will be arriving shortly. My men and I will be heading out tomorrow morning. Our neighbor, Lord Frasier is mustering men, we will wait to accompany him and join Lord Stern in the North."

"Is the King in immediate danger?" She asked, remembering the cheerful young King and his family.

Iain smiled at her concern. "He is well defended, Lady."

Luveday only nodded. "We had better prepare. Do you know how many will be arriving?"

"No, but I expect it to be a fair number, mostly those who can no longer fight yet were able to travel."

"The King must have thought this a safe place for his men." Luveday said more to herself than to anyone.

"Aye, Lady." Their gazes locked and held for several heartbeats, each lost in their own thoughts. Voices called for their attention, and soon the two were parted.

Luveday relayed what information she had, and the women got to work, while the men began to ready for battle. The castle buzzed with activity, as healing supplies were collected. Luveday called for Cassandra and more help from the village. Even Lady Christabel and Adela were put to work making bandages. Large cauldrons of willow bark and fever's foe were brewing in the hearth. Cassandra brought her own supplies to add to the castle's stocks. By the time the first men came pouring through the gate, they were as prepared as anyone could be.

Iain spared a few men to help unload and settle the wounded. The main hall was kept clear and the under-gallery lined with cots and palettes as his men had evacuated the area. Torches burned in sconces and candles abounded in the once dark space.

Luveday quickly evaluated the injured and moved them on to designated areas. The severely wounded were seen to by Emmalyn and Cassandra, the rest were cleaned up and bandaged by the women. By the time the last man entered the castle, the number of injured had reached twenty-three. Luveday joined her mentors to work on some of the men who hadn't fared so well during the trip. Several wagons had been full of men, and Luveday secretly wondered how they had survived the journey.

The women worked with quiet efficiency. Luveday had had a taste of what battle might bring thanks to the ambush that had wounded Benedict and the constant drills the knights practiced, but nothing could have prepared her for the damage these men had suffered. Lacerations were easy to clean and stitch back together, but what did one do when the flesh was ripped and torn, when there was no clue of how to return a limb to resemble what it once was. Luveday dreaded the idea of having to amputate and prayed fervently for each man. The infection had already set in on many, and some of the women feared that they were already fighting a losing battle.

Logically, Luveday knew that she couldn't save everyone. People died, and in this age, they died badly, but that didn't stop her from becoming emotionally involved with each man that she cared for. Some had good humors, some cursed their fate, some were quiet, waiting for death to take away the pain, and others were so far gone they barely woke up as they were stitched back together.

By late evening, the controlled chaos had settled into a routine. The wagons that had held the wounded were repurposed to carry arms and supplies for the departing troops. Lord Iain was seen about the castle and Luveday finally cornered him in the solar after a hasty dinner.

He met her eyes with a resigned look as he sat in his chair before the full hearth drinking wine out of a silver goblet. Clearly, he was expecting her, perhaps he was waiting for an update on the wounded, but she was there for another reason.

"My Lord, I wish to accompany you to the North." She didn't hesitate or make small talk. Her mind was made up.

Iain stopped the cup before it reached his lips. He swallowed and glared a moment at the fire before setting the goblet down on the table at his elbow and turned to her. "No."

Luveday should have expected the weight that dropped into the pit of her stomach but didn't. The logical part of her knew that he would say no, even knew why he would say it, but it still didn't soften the blow of his firm refusal. She wouldn't give up. "I know what you're thinking."

121

He interrupted her with a low growl. "I doubt that very much, Luveday."

"A battlefield is no place for a woman." She started to counter the arguments she had devised in her head. "It's dangerous, hard, and people die." She took a step further with each word until only the table's width separated them. "I know I have never seen battle, and a part of me hoped there would never be a need," he looked as if he was about to say something, but she pushed on, gripping the back of one of the chairs around the table for support. "The truth is you need me."

Luveday was unprepared for the hollow laughter that rang through the room. "And what need could you fulfill, Luveday? We are on the brink of war with Sterling. You are no camp follower."

She straightened her backbone. She would not let him reduce her offer to something tawdry. "No, I am not a camp follower, I am a healer." She cut him off as he opened his mouth. "I have spent hours tending to the men downstairs, and I know that you need me to come with you because some of those men down there will not last the night. If they had been seen to, properly seen to, on the field then perhaps they would have had a fighting chance, but..." her voice faltered, "but all we can do now is make them comfortable."

"Luveday..." He rose to his feet and rounded the table, but she would not let him comfort her.

"I can handle the blood and broken bones; Emmalyn and Cassandra have taught me well." She looked up at him with stubborn determination in her watery eyes. "I promise to follow orders, to not put myself in undue danger, and to leave when you tell me to, but if I can save lives, wouldn't it be worth it?"

The look he gave her was unreadable, but the sigh that followed brought a mixture of triumph and fear. "You will go when I give the word." She nodded solemnly. "I cannot spare many men to look after you, so you will have to look after yourself. Don't get into any trouble!" A small smile turned the corner of her mouth at his concern.

"I swear I will be on guard and vigilant. You can count on me, My Lord De Lane."

His smile mirrored hers from a moment ago. "I know I can, Lady. Pack what you need. We leave at daybreak." Luveday left to check on things below, and the plans she had already put into motion. As he finished his wine, Iain wondered if he hadn't just invited the fair lady to her death.

Chapter 8

'Guess now who holds thee?'—'Death,' I said. But, there,
The silver answer rang, . . . 'Not Death, but Love.'
~ Elizabeth Barrett Browning

The journey North started out a solemn affair, but soon the men were chatting amicably to entertain the women. Luveday and her reluctant companions were near the front of the line; only a few dozen men separated her from Lord Iain and Lord James Frasier. She felt a sense of security each time she glimpsed one of their broad backs.

The women chatted, mostly with Sir Gregori or Lord Benedict, but a few of Frasier's knights stopped to charm the ladies. Luveday had been surprised when Lady Christabel, with Mistress Adela in tow, was preparing to leave with the troops at dawn. Elysant had joined their number, though Luveday suspected that Emmalyn had something to do with that. Luveday didn't know if the girl was meant to be of aid or to protect her virtue, but she was glad for the company just the same.

The procession moved by at a snail's pace. She thought there would be more speed, but though there was not an exceptionally long way to their destination, the troops moved on at a singular pace. Men on horseback moved as fast as the men on foot, and they all kept pace with the wagons weighted down with supplies and weapons. The knights wore light leather armor, saving their metal suits for the battlefield proper.

Three days passed before they were in sight of Havenwood. Lord Grayson met them on the road, and together they journeyed another two days to find themselves amongst the King's men.

"My word." Christabel's gasp could be heard from her position beside Luveday. Ellie had decided to ride double with her friend and was happy that she got a look at the scene before her from such a height, rather than waiting with Adela in the wagons. Before them stretched a maze of tents, large enough to be called a city. Luveday was sure their numbers quadrupled the people of Lander's Keep. Most of the tents were a cream-colored canvas with brightly colored flags and banners declaring their noble occupants. The more powerful lords were situated nearest the King's tent which bore his banner.

"Lord Grayson said he had sent men ahead to prepare a space, but where shall we be able to set up camp in this mess," Ellie spoke into her ear as the girl leaned out to get a better look. Luveday was ready to catch the girl before her friend went too far and tumbled off the horse.

"We should ask were the healing tents are. I know Lord Frasier offered us one of his own, but surely they have some set up already." Luveday looked around, there was some design to the camp as large thoroughfares sectioned off the tents. No one seemed in a hurry, nor were there any sights of the battle she knew was fought here so recently. "We should drop off the supplies as soon as possible." At that moment, Gregori separated from the group and rode for the head of the line. He gave Luveday and Ellie a nod as he passed, and she wondered if he would relay her concerns to the men in charge.

"Do you think we are in any danger?" Christabel asked, looking around at the men with a mixture of fear and disgust. Luveday knew why the Lady had insisted on coming, she was jealous and would not be outdone, but wondered how long a court lady would last out here. Secretly, Luveday wished she had turned back the first day, or taken up the offer Stern had extended for her to stay at Havenwood, but the stubborn girl would not listen though the tales the men told turned her fair skin an unusual shade of green.

Luveday noticed women moving around the camp, most dressed in bright colors with secret smiles, and she knew that they must be the camp followers that Iain had talked about. The few who met her gaze looked back at her with equal interest. "There are women about, so I doubt we will be in any real danger."

Gregori and a few men came back down the line and escorted the women to an opening in the left wing of the camp. There was a large grouping of trees, too small to be called a forest, which lined a wide but shallow stream that was supplying the healing tent with fresh water. Iain had his men set up camp nearby. They would also keep an eye on the small wood as they shored up the defenses of the left wing of the camp.

Ellie chatted almost none stop as she followed Luveday around the healing tent. It was chilly outside, but the number of bodies in such a small space made the tent exceedingly warm. Christabel and Adela were somewhere outside. The old woman had started ordering more hot water, knowing that Luveday would need it soon enough. The healer in the tent was watching the women with veiled hostility. The master healer was currently absent. From what anyone could gather, he was out seeing to the wounded in their tents, as most knights tended to take care of their own injuries. Luveday had been tuning the girl out for a while as she methodically looked over each man. Right now, there were over a dozen men in cots and palettes that lined the tent walls. They worked on the seriously injured in a small room at the back. With the flaps down, and the lamps lit, it was stuffy and smelly work, and Luveday wondered how anyone could see what they were doing in such an uncomfortable state.

"Elysant." Luveday's voice seemed to catch her off guard, and her friend was suddenly silent, "help Mistress Adela start brewing some feverfoe and sorting out the bandages. We will need more cooking pots than the two we brought and what I saw out front." Luveday had seen enough and decided it was time to really get to work. "I will start cleaning the more serious wounds, and we will move anyone we can out of this tent." The young healer who had been watching her with a keen eye, stepped forward as if to say something, but Luveday purposefully ignored him. "Lord Frasier offered another tent, we will need it. I imagine there will be more wounded on the morrow. Have them set it up behind this tent and have them open one of the sides on the back room. No need to carry the injured through this lot to reach the table."

Ellie nodded and ran out of the tent. Luveday rose from her position beside one of the cots and looked at the healer. "I know you do not want me here, but I am not leaving." He was taken aback by her hard eyes and determination. "I swore I would see to the injured and I mean to be of whatever help I can. You are either with me, or you can leave. I have permission from Lord De Lane and Lord Frasier to care for the injured here, and I don't need someone in my way." At the mention of the two lords' names, he seemed to start.

"I am Thomas Moore, apprentice healer to Master Liam Pope. My master is one of the finest healers of the King." The young man finally introduced himself, showing the first signs of cooperation.

"I am Lady Luveday of Lander's Keep. Lady Christabel of Rindstaff, Lord De Lane's betrothed, her servant, Mistress Adela, and my aid, young Elysant of Lander's Keep are here to see to the wounded. We have brought healing supplies, and some remedies with us." Thomas looked around as they heard men rolling up the tent's side flap in the back room. Thomas seemed to be resigned to the lady's interference, and Luveday looked at him seriously. "I have not been trained as you have, though Lady Emmalyn has taken great care with me. If I am doing something wrong, then tell me. If you have suggestions, then show me. I am here to help."

"Aye, My Lady." She could tell that it would take time from him to truly see her skill and sincerity. She could have been nicer, but she was about to step on his toes, and she didn't have time to play nice with lives hanging in the balance.

"Where are your healing supplies?" She asked.

He glanced over his shoulder. "You have seen them."

Luveday was momentarily dumbfounded. "All you have is in the back room?"

"My master has a case with him as well," Thomas said gruffly.

"A healing case? A few jars of salves and you expect to treat an army?"

He frowned at her censure. "We treat those who can afford our services."

"That stops now. We will treat the injured, regardless of coin." Luveday left the tent, suddenly ill. She spotted Mistress Adela and Ellie as they worked by the fire. Men were raising the second tent. A few young women looked on. Looking back into camp, she could see familiar silhouettes putting up their own tents in the growing darkness. Some of the men had started cooking the evening meal.

Iain looked over and spotted her. He appeared out of the shadows. "You do not look so well, Lady Luveday."

"I am fine." She said a little too clipped. "I need the healing supplies unloaded as soon as possible. I plan to see to the men here tonight."

"You should rest. It was a long journey." He watched her intently.

"I am not tired." The sigh that left her was loud and heavy and carried with it all of her pent-up frustration. A hand came to rest on her shoulder, and she looked up into Iain's face and smiled hesitantly. "The situation is both better and worse than I imagined." He didn't say anything, just looked at her. "The men have been seen to, but they are not being cared for as they should. One healer and his apprentice are hardly enough to care for an army."

She looked at Gregori as his voice rang across the area. She noted that the tent was nearly up. "We will need more help, men or women, I do not care." She turned back to Iain, his hand on her shoulder a comfort. "They have barely any healing ointments, I will start preparing the raw ingredients we brought with us. I will need men to help move some of the injured into the new tent." Looking up into his eyes she hesitated to involve him, but perhaps he could think of some better way. "Apprentice Moore has informed me that they only see to those who can pay."

Iain nodded. "'Tis a common practice." He wasn't at all surprised by the fact.

"Can you spread the word that that is about to change. We will see anyone who is injured, no matter how small. Do you know how to get the word out quickly?" She looked at him hopefully.

The small smile that moved his lips was heartening. "I can think of something." He looked to Benedict who only nodded before heading out again.

"Thank you." She was about to say more, but Ellie appeared at her shoulder looking at her expectantly. "Elysant, see if Lady Christabel can help you unpack the supplies into the back room of the tent. Perhaps the men can devise something to hold everything, a shelf of some sort. Make sure to keep the bandages and linens clean. Perhaps we should set up a drying line between the two tents. We will need an area for washing."

Ellie nodded solemnly or was it that the girl was only tired. "The hot water is almost ready. Mistress Adela is watching it now." Some women were talking to the old nurse, and Luveday wondered if they could be able to persuade them to help in the healing tent. They could feed any who would help as a form of compensation.

"Good. See if those women wouldn't come to help in the tent, or perhaps they would know someone who can. We need hands that will not get sick at the sight of blood. Spread the word if you can. We will feed any who come to help." Luveday thought she saw some of the women perk up as they overheard her words.

She headed back into the tent, as Iain issued orders to the men, and Elysant ushered Lady Christabel over to the crates and baskets of healing supplies. Luveday had faith that Ellie would set up the workroom as neatly as the one at Lander's Keep, so she focused on the men before her.

When she looked up from the last cot, it was to see Iain standing in the middle of the tent, watching her with a furrowed brow. Healer Thomas was opposite her, on their patient's other side, as they cleaned and bandaged a nasty gash that was starting to fester. Thomas had begrudgingly admitted that with more injured coming to them each day, he didn't have time to change all of the bandages as often as he should. Luveday hoped that with some extra help, they could delegate such tasks to others.

Iain watched as she applied the salve and placed the clean strip of linen over the wound. Thomas kept glancing up to see the large knight and shuddered a time or two. Luveday didn't have time to think about the apprentice's reactions, she was glad that he had settled in to help her. She thought they might be able to get along after all.

A deep voice scattered Luveday's thoughts as she put away her supplies. "It is late, My Lady. We've prepared a palate for you in my tent."

In his tent? She thought. The other women must be there as well, and so Luveday finished her tasks for the night and wished Thomas a good rest as she left. It was not far to the Lord's tent, though she didn't know how she would have made it if he hadn't kept a steady hand at the small of her back. His presence seemed to give her energy, though she didn't know were hers' had gone since stepping into the chilly night air.

She was given a mug of something which she ate with relish before being shoved into the tent. Iain held the flap back as she stepped inside. A small lamp illuminated the space, which wasn't anything like the elaborate tents that the King and his lord inhabited. The space was practical. Pallets lined the walls, a small table was spread with parchment, a few crates and a chest held their belongings. Coll was already asleep near the front tent flap, as was Ellie, who was curled up in a pallet made for two. On the opposite side of the narrow space was another palette, which Luveday assumed was for Iain as it was covered with fur and one of his wool cloaks. She was too tired to wonder were Christabel and Adela were sleeping. Iain excused himself for a moment, and Luveday undressed, putting on a tunic and slipping in beside her friend. The lady was asleep before Iain returned a few moments later.

He watched the sleeping figures for a moment and couldn't help the sense of pride he felt when he looked at her. He blew out the light, not because it was an expensive luxury, but because he feared that if he looked on her for too much longer, his thoughts would get away from him again, and that was something he needed to avoid at all costs.

Dawn came too quickly. Iain was in the King's tent a few moments later, though it was clear that many of the nobles were unhappy to be there so early in the morning. De Lane was informed that he and his men were leading the charge that morning, a fact that he had already been aware of, the announcement was more for morale than anything. Benedict, who had a keen sense for strategy, was given charge of a group of men who would scout the surrounding areas and hinder Sterling's spies and supply lines when able. He was happy to harry their enemy any way he could but didn't relish the fact that he would be separated from his friends, though a special mission from the King was nothing to sneeze at. Iain and Benedict only had time to exchange a brief farewell and wish each other health and victory, before the young lordling left to lead his own group of men, wondering when he would be back again.

De Lane and Frasier had talked briefly with the King after their arrival. Edward wanted his champion front and center so that Sterling knew just who he would be dealing with. Iain agreed that a show of strength was what was needed. Sterling had been beating them back too easily, but with De Lane's arrival the majority of the King's forces were assembled, and the fighting would begin in earnest.

When Iain returned to his tent, Coll was already arranging his armor, and he was about to scold the boy for making so much noise when the women were still sleeping, only to be informed that they were already up.

"Lady Luveday readied herself not long after you left," Gregori said from over his shoulder.

"Aye, My Lord." Coll set down the knight's helmet that he had been polishing, although the item already shined even in the dim morning light. "Ellie followed her over to the healing tent after a quick breakfast, though she didn't look happy about it."

"Lady Luveday is already at the tent?" Iain looked over to see the healing tent surrounded by the swirling mist of the morning fog and wondered at the chill that went down his spine.

Gregori, grunted as he sat down on a log to put on his boots. They were preparing the armor now, and it would take some time to get into the heavy chainmail. Men moved to ready horses, and already caldrons boiled before the healing tent. The men said nothing while they readied themselves, but prayed they'd carry the field, and not end up on Lady Luveday's table, but would return to have a warm supper with her later that night.

Luveday worked on ointments and potions to ease pain and fever. The supply she had brought might last a few days if the fighting were light, but she knew that Frasier and De Lane's arrival meant that the battle would really begin. A few women arrived after word had spread that they asked for aid. Luveday set them to checking and cleaning wounds and several left within the hour, but that was as she had planned. They needed women who could stomach what was to come, because sure as day, the worst was not yet upon them. Out of the three that remained, two shown some skill. An older woman called Margaret and one about Ellie's age called Clair. Clair had the same dark coloring as Christabel, ar ut of the corner of her eye, Luveday had almost mistaken the two, except
l, was nowhere to be found.
e women worked, and when men walked in with cuts and bruises,
best they could. Margaret had some cooking skill and arranged
nade for the men in the tents. Sir Templeton was seen eating
day meal, but the rest of the men had yet to return. Every

once in a while, some noise would travel far afield and reach the women. Many would stop and cross themselves, Luveday would take a deep breath, send off a silent prayer, and focus once more on the task in front of her.

When the stretchers arrived, and men screamed in pain and fear, she would not even flinch. Every fiber of her being was wound tight, and it was as if she had been doing the work all her life. Luveday willed life into each man she touched. Her prayers were a never-ending litany in the back of her mind as she methodically treated each man. The smaller injuries she left to the skilled women while she and Thomas took care of those whose life hung by a few bits of sinew. She did not let even one doubt enter her mind as she stitched together muscles and set bones. She issued orders like a general and never glanced to see how quickly they were obeyed but knew that what she needed would be at hand.

By evening, groans filled the tent, and men came to visit their comrades and share the news of their victories, however small. Voices filled the dusk, and despite the devastation she had just witnessed, there was a lighter air around the camp that let Luveday breathe a little easier.

Thomas stretched as they exited the back room and looked to the Lady. His Master had not returned, and Thomas suspected he was catering to some Lord on the other side of camp. Several had come to battle with wagons of provisions fit for the King's high table, and he knew Pope had a weakness for good wine. He was not perturbed by his master's absence, but rather grateful that they did not need to deal with the stubborn old man.

The lady washed her hands in water so hot he could barely stand it. Over the hours they had spent together he had witnessed something extraordinary in her. Not even Master Pope would have performed the miracles that she had. Men he thought could not be saved had lived through the day. The Lady refused to let even one life slip through her grasp, though he knew she had no illusions about who truly had the power here, and it was neither of them.

As she turned towards the other tent removing her soiled apron and tying on a clean one, he grabbed her elbow. The clothes she wore were covered in blood and sweat soaked the collar of her gown. The simple material would never come clean, but she was unaware or uncaring of her appearance. "Leave it." He pulled her towards the fire and Margaret who was scooping out large bowls of stew. Their patients already had their meal, and he looked at the simple fair with ravenous eyes. The lady didn't budge, and he had to pull her away from the tent and set her down on a crate.

Thomas accepted two bowls and turned back to his companion. Somewhere among the blood and pain he had looked up and found a compatriot in this bossy, demanding woman. They had worked side by side all day, and he had become aware of her skill, and her knowledge of the body rivaled his own, perhaps even excelled what he had spent nearly his whole life studying. He turned back to her and found a lost lady. She looked around as if nothing were familiar. "Here, eat." Shoving a bowl into her hands, he took a perch nearby and ate as if he had not had a meal in days. Perhaps he hadn't, not a decent one, he mused. His Master was not one to spare coin on comforts for anyone but himself. What food he consumed was usually tasteless or burnt as neither of the two men spent time on such a skill if it did not earn them coin or further their profession. Some of the camp followers brought goods in exchange for medicines. Thomas was not shy and knew his reasonably good looks had gained him more than one meal from the women, though his Master looked down on helping such creatures.

A shadow seemed to fall over them, and he looked up to see a large figure before them blocking out the light of the fire. Dirt was caked on the side of the knight's face, and a dark scowl made his hard features fearsome in the night. Thomas sat back and reached out for Lady Luveday as the instinct to protect her kicked in. The Wolf's expression darkened as he reached for the lady as well and brought her to her feet before Thomas could do more than blink.

"My Lord." The Lady protested as the two moved off.

Thomas watched as they talked, but he could only hear a few words. It looked as if the knight were berating her and his hackles rose, but at heart, Thomas knew he was a coward. He had once seen what the King's Champion could do to a man. They had tried to save the knight's arm, but the damage had been too much, even for the knight to take. They had found the man dead from a dose of painkiller. He had downed the bottle rather than face a life without his lost limb. Thomas had cursed the knight, cursed a man who could take everything from another without so much as a hint of regret. Though word had later reached his ears that De Lane had offered some aid to the knight's family, what kind of compensation could he provide for a man's life? No, men like De Lane, the Wolf, dealt death wherever they went. It was Thomas's task in life to try to repair the damage such men meted out.

Though he wished to defend the lady, he knew that he would never step in front of the Wolf willingly.

It looked as if the lady didn't need his help anyway. She scolded the lord in return and left to enter the far tent. Thomas gulped down what little was left of his meal and followed her. He felt the Wolf's eyes on him as he let the tent flap fall back into place.

Luveday replayed the conversation with Lord Iain as she checked the men one final time. Ellie had already gone to bed, as had the other women. She was left to herself, except for Thomas, who worked on something in the opposite corner of the tent. She had the feeling he would not go to bed until she did, though she knew he was as exhausted as she was.

That Iain had tried to bully her into going to bed, like she was some disobedient child, had rankled her tired nerves.

"All fine ladies are abed, Luveday." He took in the smudges under her eyes, the stains on the old gown that she wore, and the harsh sent of soap that seemed to cling to her.

"I have a bit more work to do tonight, My Lord." She searched him for wounds, but while he looked rough, he was whole. The sigh that escaped her was one of relief. She had not let herself think of him out on the battlefield. Fear for the men of Lander's Keep was enough to stop her dead in her tracks if she let it get even a foothold in her head. She tried to focus again, though ignoring the danger to her friends was the hardest thing she had ever done. "I hear you carried the field today."

"There was never any doubt." He said offhandedly, and she had the sudden urge to kick him.

Luveday closed her eyes for a moment and took a breath.

His harsh words met her unforgiving ears. "You should be in bed. 'Tis not proper for you to work through the night."

"Proper?" She choked. "Death doesn't care what the hour is. I will work until the work is done."

"Luveday!" he growled. "It is not safe among these men. A young Lady must think..."

"I am thinking, not as a Lady but as a woman. If these were my men, if these were my people, I would want the best for them, someone to care whether they lived or died, not how much they will pay to live. I am here to heal, Iain. I am here to work, and I will not go to bed until I have done my best to make sure these men survive the night." He didn't look chastised, he looked angry. "If you will excuse me, My Lord."

She had turned and left to return to the tents. It had been some time since that argument if that were what anyone would call it. She had finished up, checking the men and medicating many for the night. She cleaned the workroom with harsh soap and a stiff brush, before using what remained of the hot water to take care of herself.

After wishing Thomas a brief goodnight, she made her way back to the tent. Iain sat on his pallet in the dark, waiting. The moon illuminated the sides of the tent and she could easily make out his outline as he watched her duck behind the partition, they had set up so that the women could change. There was a bowl of water that had gone cold, but the liquid was refreshing on her skin. She washed down as quickly as she could and donned the tunic and shorts, she wore to sleep in.

Ellie snored softly as Luveday slipped into bed beside her. She didn't look at Iain, though she knew he didn't lay down for some time. She listened to him settle down before letting sleep overtake her.

Days passed, and the two armies seemed to be evenly matched. Though casualties were fewer than she had imagined, there were still dozens of men flocking to the healing tents each day. Fortunately, most of the injuries were minor enough to send the men back to their tents, with the promise that they would return to have their bandages changed or if their situation worsened. Several men were released from her care and returned to their tents and their comrades. Some even took up their swords to join in the fray after word had gone out that the Wolf De Lane had arrived. Men talked of making history, Luveday listened half-heartedly. She had lost only two men thus far, and she prayed with fervor as she worked that the Lord would grant her the wisdom and the strength to see this through.

It was no surprise when Mistress Adela appeared, bundled against the cold, to inform her that she and Lady Christabel would be returning home to Lander's Keep. They had seen enough of battle and were too grieved for the men. The mistress looked bone wary, and she could see Christabel's complexion was too pale with tints of green as she watched the men being carried into the tent with a look of disgust mixed with horror. She used her cloak to hide her face, or perhaps it was to guard against the gut-wrenching smell of blood and death.

"You will inform Lord De Lane, Lady?" Adela looked on her with pity. Luveday knew the sight of her must be distressing as she was elbow deep in blood, with unmentionable stains on the apron that barely protected her garments. She returned Adela's weak smile with one of her own. Luveday knew the pity was not directed at her, but at the men, she was trying to save. The look in her eyes said the mistress knew all too well the cost of war.

"I will as soon as I see him. Good journey, Mistress Adela, and please extend my well wishes to your lady." She nodded to Christabel who refused to come any closer.

"I will, Lady. Bless you." The old nurse turned to go.

Luveday found herself calling out. "Wait, Mistress." Adela turned back in concern. "How soon do you leave?"

A brief glance over her shoulder, confirm her lady's impatience. "As soon as possible, within the hour I should think. Lord Frasier is sending men home, and they shall see us part of the way. A few of Lord Sumerland's men are here, though My Lady's father was kept away. The men shall see us to Lander's Keep as all of Lord De Lane's men are on the field."

She was thinking quickly, though why the urge came upon her, she didn't know, but she knew with a certainty she couldn't explain, that it was the right thing to do. "Can you take one more with you? I would like to send young Elysant home."

Adela placed a comforting hand on the young woman's shoulder. Luveday smiled to thank the old nurse for her understanding. Ellie had cried herself to sleep two nights in a row, the girl looked haggard, even more so than Luveday who had seemed to hit her stride. The girl was miserable and frankly, Luveday didn't like the way some of the men were looking at her friend. "I will have her ready in a half hour. Coll can escort her to you."

"We can wait for her, Lady." Adela didn't repeat her farewells but left with her lady and the man who had escorted them across the camp. Luveday cleaned herself up and washed her hands as she thought quickly.

"Coll!" She called out. The boy had been there, but a moment ago. "Coll of Norhthelm Keep."

A voice rang out from a way away. "Here! I am here, Lady Luveday!" A moment later the boy appeared running for her as if the hounds of hell were chasing him.

Luveday stepped aside, or he would have run right into her. She caught his shoulders as he almost tumbled over, trying to stop himself. He panted and grinned at her like the young boy he was. "You called, My Lady?"

Coll had been running errands for her as his lord had kept him off the field. She imagined the squire was Iain's eyes and ears, and happily repeated everything that happened to his master.

"I need you to pack Elysant's belongings as quickly and neatly as you can. She will be returning home with Lady Christabel and Mistress Adela." She looked at the boy, he looked saddened at the news but nodded as if he understood. She guessed she wasn't the only one who saw how miserable Ellie was. "Do you know Lord Frasier's tent?" At his affirmative Luveday continued issuing orders. "When you are done packing, escort Ellie there, the party is leaving within the hour, so you will need to be quick. They will be waiting for her." The boy straightened as if he felt the burden of responsibility. "Understood?"

"Yes, My Lady! You can count on me!" Like a flash, the boy was gone again.

Luveday spotted Ellie helping Clair, a camp follower about her own age. The two had become friends as Ellie had taught the girl what little healing she knew. Clair had returned the favor, showing some skill with herbs and ointments that even Luveday did not know. The girl had a sensible head on her shoulders and eyes that said she had seen too much, but she was a constant help and would be a fine replacement in Ellie's absence.

Luveday cleaned herself up as quickly as she could and walked over to the girls, giving Thomas a look as he stuck his head out of the tent in search of her. "Ellie." She called. Both girls turned to her, Ellie paled a bit. Luveday suddenly realized the strain she had unknowingly placed on her friend. Healing was a burden, one that Ellie had taken up for a friend, not because the girl had a calling or aptitude for it. Ellie was willing to help any way she could, and Luveday felt she had taken advantage of that, not fully realizing the toll it was taking on the girl.

"Ellie, I need you to get cleaned up. Take some of the bread and cheese with you. I am sending you home with Lady Christabel and Mistress Adela." The girl looked at her for a moment, and tears filled her eyes. Without warning, she wrapped herself around Luveday who hugged her friend back as fiercely as Ellie was holding on to her.

The whispers that reached Luveday's ears weren't words protesting against abandoning her but of gratitude. "Thank you, Luveday." Tears filled the lady's eyes as she realized that Ellie's tears were a sign of her relief.

"I'm so sorry, Ellie." She whispered back. "If I had known..."

Elysant let go and sniffed as she shook her head. "No, I wanted to come, I wanted to help, but..." the girl couldn't finish.

"I know. I know." She said around the lump in her own throat. "Coll is packing your things, Frasier's caravan leaves shortly. Coll will escort you to the tent."

Elysant looked at the plain tent that had sheltered them during the cold nights. She would not miss it, though she longed to ask Luveday to come with her, she knew that her friend was doing good. Luveday was truly saving lives, and Ellie would not selfishly ask her to leave. She knew that Luveday would not come anyway.

"You will be safe?" She asked Luveday.

"I will take precautions. You be safe; it is a long journey home." They hugged again. "I will miss you. Keep Lady Emmalyn from getting into trouble while I am gone."

Ellie laughed. "Someone will have to." She couldn't quite make herself let go of Luveday's hand and gave it another squeeze. "I will miss you." She turned to Clair whose sad smile reflected their own. "I will miss you too, Clair. It was good to meet you."

Clair looked as if she too might cry, as she pushed a strand of dark hair behind her left ear. "It was good to work beside you, Elysant. Perhaps we will meet again."

"Yes, perhaps. Be safe." She said, and Elysant ran to the tent. She and Coll were seen a moment later, moving quickly through the tents towards the center of camp.

Luveday didn't wait to see her friend off, more injured were arriving, and Thomas needed her help. She hoped that he would ignore her puffy eyes and focus on their work as that was exactly what she planned to do.

Blood dripped onto the ground in a steady rhythm. The sound was like the ticking of a clock in the silent tent. Luveday was breathing hard as she whipped her brow, trying to ignore the blood that coated her hands and made it hard to hold the needle she was using to stitch up the abdomen of the faceless man on her worktable.

The figure beside her, who she vaguely recognized as Thomas, was saying something that she didn't quite catch. She was annoyed with him for breaking her concentration but couldn't stop to tell him so.

No, she was running out of time. The body before her was moved, carried away as a hand came to rest on her shoulders. She was too hot and couldn't take a breath; it felt as if she were smothered yet she still felt the bite of cold air across her cheeks.

Noises at the tent flap drew her attention. Another man was being carried in. The voices of the men were rough and urgent, though they fell on deaf ears. Luveday immediately recognized the injured man. As he was put on the table, she saw that his armor had been removed and what clothes remained were shredded. Deep wounds marred his broad chest and blood flowed freely in rivers over his sides. Luveday froze as tears clogged her throat and blurred her vision. Thomas urged her forward, to look, to work, but she felt like someone had taken a knife to her heart. A stone dropped to the pit of her stomach as she nearly doubled over with the emotions she was feeling. The pain was unbelievable. Tears ran down her face unchecked as she moved closer and tried to focus. She played the mantra again in her head, the words that helped her concentrate and shut out the world around her, but he chose that moment to look at her. Suddenly conscious and asking for her help, she placed her hands over his wounds as if she could hold back the flow of blood as if her touch alone could heal him. His wounds were great gashes of ripped flesh, and they were too many. There was nothing she could do. There was no way to save him.

With his last breath, Iain De Lane said only one word; one word that tore her very soul to pieces. "Luveday."

Luveday opened her eyes as pain radiated through her. She couldn't tell where she was or what was going on in the darkness that engulfed her. Iain's voice echoed in her head until she realized that the urgent whisper wasn't a figment of her imagination. Still caught in the dream, she didn't think before she acted. She tore the furs and linens from her body and moved the short distance that separated them until she was at Iain's side.

He was up, leaning on an elbow as he looked over at her palette. Her distress had awoken him, and he was a moment away from getting up to come to her. Her sudden movement startled him, especially as she reached him, pushing him onto his back and began ripping off his coverings to run her warm hands over his body. She mumbled to herself, her words not making any sense to him. He tried not to react as he let her finish the examination. In the dim light he could make out the shine of tears on her cheeks, but couldn't bring himself to stop her, or even to speak.

She collapsed on top of him with a suddenness that alarmed him, and it took a moment to realize that she was embracing him. Her tears continued to fall; he felt the wetness as it hit his bare shoulder. Gathering her close he tried to comfort her. Her head was nestled in the crook of his neck, her hair caressed the side of his face and only then did he hear her clearly.

"You are alright. You're alright. It was just a dream." Luveday seemed to be getting a hold of her emotions. "It was just a nightmare. You're not hurt. Just a dream."

Iain was stunned by the implications of her words. As she pulled back, he tried to look her in the eye while he brushed the tears from her soft cheek. "Are these tears for me, Love?"

His voice jolted her from the remnants of her nightmare. Was it his tone or the use of her childhood nickname? Either way, reality came rushing back. Luveday was suddenly aware that she was draped over Lord Iain De Lane, who she knew preferred sleeping in the nude, or in as little clothing as possible, even in the frigid fall air. In fact, her mind took a moment to point out, she hadn't felt any clothing whilst she had examined him for injuries. She berated herself for her foolishness as she thanked the Lord that it was too dark to see the blush that was turning the upper half of her body a flaming pink.

She tried to pull away, but Iain was having none of it. The lady was finally in his arms, and he wasn't going to let this opportunity pass him by. If he had been fully awake, his mind would have let loose a bevy of reasons why his current plan of action was a foolish idea that would only lead to catastrophe. He wasn't quite there and whatever protests his better half offered up, where easily ignored as he focused on the feel of the soft curves that encased the willful woman in his arms.

Luveday had continued to argue with him over the ten days since their arrival. He spent his days locked in a contest of wills on the battlefield and came back to spar words with her in the evenings. He had never met a woman so stubborn, and so driven to do good. She had seen to half the camp by the end of the first week. Those who doubted a woman's skill had begrudgingly come to her once they found out that her services didn't require coin, and Iain had made sure that the men weren't confused about what other services she offered. Whispers of miracles ran through the camp. Luveday had seen the worst this battle had to offer, and she hadn't given up; she had helped the men pull through though he didn't know how some of the wounded had survived. Luveday wouldn't stop her ministrations until she was sure the work was done for the day, and no amount of badgering or persuasion on his part would make her find her rest a moment earlier.

Iain marveled at how such an iron-willed woman could be so soft, but he knew Luveday's heart bled with the pain she witnessed, and it was her will and determination alone that saw her through. How he longed to help and comfort her, especially when her efforts proved in vain, but he was her Lord and Luveday, like himself, had set the boundaries of their relationship months ago. Neither had dared to cross the line in the sand, but he no longer cared. *She had wept for him.*

Pulling her closer, he wrapped the linens and furs around them to fight off the chill. "Shhh, easy lass." He whispered into the darkness. Luveday's breathing had settled, but still ran a little fast, from the remnants of her dream or from his nearness, he could not say. Their warm breaths mixed as she tried to pull away again. She reminded him of a skittish colt, curious but ready to run. Shivers raced down her frame as she lay down, the cold was fierce tonight, no doubt another layer of snow would greet them in the morning, and he thanked it for the excuse it afforded him.

"Easy, love." He helped her settle next to him, turned her into his side, into his heat and he could barely stop himself from running his hands over her. Her legs were bare under the tunic she wore to bed. He had gotten a glimpse of her attire one night when an alarm was raised, and she rushed back to the healing tent to aid Thomas Moore. He growled to think of the way the healer looked at her, but she was in his arms now, and nothing could take her from him.

"Iain." She spoke into his shoulder, another shiver vibrated through her, rubbing her against his skin. "I..."

"Easy Lass," he knew she would retreat at the first opportunity and whispered to her to stall her as long as he could. "'Tis too cold to sleep alone." She sighed and rolled over onto her back, he moved with her until their positions were switched. He lay on his left side and enjoyed her warmth and the access this new position offered him.

"Iain." She sighed again, and he knew she was as reluctant to leave him as he was to let her go. They had been dancing around each other, pretending they didn't feel whatever was growing between them, pretending they didn't care for each other any more than was appropriate between a Lord and a Lady under his protection. The future was set, and as much as Iain grew to hate it, he could not turn from the course now. Too much was at stake, and Luveday's heart could not compensate for the stability Christabel's dowry would bring him and his people. He moved in closer, trying to dispel his unpleasant thoughts. He was fully awake now and knew better than to keep her here, but every fiber of his being wanted her close, if only for a night. He promised himself he would not do the lady any harm, but to feel her near him was more intoxicating than the King's finest wine.

Almost of its own accord, his right arm reached out to run his fingers down her arm. He had to reach over her and felt the brush of her tunic against his forearm as her breasts rose suddenly while she drew air into her lungs. He didn't stop but skimmed down her left hip to the end of her tunic. The material was a little rough, especially in contrast to the strange garment she wore under them. The thin fabric was soft and lose around her hips. He found that it didn't quite reach her knees. Luveday was so much smaller than him, the top of her head didn't reach his shoulder unless she had her hair piled atop it. As they lay there, Iain could easily reach from the top of her head to well past her knees. He was surprised at how smooth and hairless her legs were and took a moment to rub the area of her inner thigh just above the bend of her right knee. A whoosh of air left her, and he grinned wickedly into the darkness.

Iain could feel her muscles tighten as she tried to keep from moving as he let his hand rest there a moment. He leaned down and caught the fragrant scent of her hair, some flower he could not place. It made his staff twitch, and his own muscles coil tighter. Iain could just make out the flutter of her lashes as she closed her eyes. He was transfixed.

Why could she not flee? Why did she linger, tormenting herself? Luveday knew that if she made a move, Iain would let her go, but with every fiber of her being she willed herself deeper into the palette longing to be still and let whatever this was run its course. Her eyes were closed, but could feel his warm breath across her cheeks making her insides clench at his nearness. Madness, this was utter madness, and she prayed that the dark would somehow keep this moment from reality, for surely, dawn would change everything, and she wasn't ready.

Lips brushed her cheek, but she refused to open her eyes. The large hand that nearly encased her upper thigh began to ascend what remained of her leg, and Luveday's modesty demanded that she stop it. Her own hand flew to halt his progress as she uttered a sound that had a decidedly negative quality to it, if not actual words. His name wouldn't move past her lips, and her small protest arrested his movements for only a breath.

She knew what was happening, his destination was clear, but she could count on one hand the number of times she had been intimate with someone. Her past experiences were brief and none of which had ever resulted in her going all the way. It wasn't that she had never wanted to, only that the guys who had been interested in her had never really been interested in *her*, but had thought that since she was curvy and nerdy that she would be easy, and that had never been the case. Luveday had always waited, for what she didn't really know, but none of the guys that had tried to date her and get in her pants had ever fulfilled that nameless requirement. Iain's presence didn't set off any of the alarms that automatically activated her sense of self-preservation. It was reason that kept trying to intrude, and he was doing a particularly good job of silencing all of the thoughts that kept popping up.

When the hand under her tunic finally reached the flesh above her waistband Luveday's eyes flew open of their own accord. In the dim light of the tent, she could make out his intense stare as he was only a few inches away from her and looking directly into her own eyes. She had only ever seen that look in movies, and it stole her breath away.

Their lips collided, and both groaned. A moment later the waistband of her boxer shorts was lowered past her hips making Luveday both pleased and disappointed that she had washed her underwear that night and left them to dry over on her side of the tent. There was no defense. Without the additional garment his warm hand met her sensitive skin causing her back to arch off the pallet. Iain kissed her, soundlessly catching the moan that was torn from her lips. His hand cupped her, applying pressure as he seemed to wait for something. It was a maddening sensation that she could only stand for a moment until she had to move. Fingers ran lightly along her outer folds causing Luveday to realize the difference in their temperatures, his warm hands felt cold compared to the heat radiating from her core. When the first digit pushed into her folds her back arched again, and a silent, gasp of wonder, contorted her features. A groan rumbled out of the depths of Iain's chest as he shifted to bring his body closer to her. She could feel the evidence of his arousal but couldn't focus on anything but what he was doing to her.

Their breaths mingled while they lock gazes. Sensations neither had ever experienced so fully, rolled over them.

Her name was a harsh whisper as he pushed deeper to find what he had been searching for. Her mind splintered for a moment, suddenly overcome with what was happening. Instead of shutting down with the ecstasy of what she was feeling, her mind jumped to light speed as logic played this out to its conclusion and the ending didn't look good for her. She struggled, her mental state producing a physical reaction. Iain countered by moving to stroke her, and she knew why they called the spot a hidden bud. The gentle pressure against her clitoris sent waves through her, but the euphoria wasn't enough to cloud her mind completely. The passion was still present, but in the background, was building a horror she couldn't contain.

"Wait," She moved against him, and every muscle in his frame seemed to coil over her. "Iain." She wasn't sure exactly what she was pleading for, for him to stop or for him to give her a reason to stay in his arms. Maybe it wasn't either of those things, perhaps it was really a plea that fate would be kinder because at that moment, locked in this sensual intimacy Luveday felt more keenly than ever the gap that lay between them. If fate would be kinder... but no.

"Luveday," he began, but she knew there was no way she could listen to what he was about to say so she tried to gently push him away shaking her head. Trying to move Iain was like an ant trying to move a mountain. The growl that echoed in her ear was worthy of one of his hounds, or the wolf he took as his emblem. The hand between her legs grew insistent, but not rough. Words issued from his mouth, but they tumbled in the space between them so that all she really heard was the tone of his voice. Had she ever heard him beg before? Surely this was as close as a man like him would come, and the thought shocked and troubled her. What should she do? What did she want? And could she live with it?

She began to struggle, holding on to him as much as pushing him away. Words poured from his lips to reassure, and comfort, to plead and to persuade if only to keep her for a few more moments. He was so close to what he desperately wanted, and he could not remember wanting anything more, not just for himself, but for her. Her pleasure made his sharper.

"Luveday," he repeated her name a few times before the words he was desperately searching for could be formed. "Easy, lass, easy. I will not hurt you, Luveday. Never, just let me..." and he moved to stroke her hoping the pleasure would push out all else. He was not sure at that moment, that if she began to struggle in earnest, he would be able to let her go. "Easy, let me give you this, Luveday. Let me..." and found her opening and carefully inserted a finger into her heat trying not to scare her. She moaned as she moved, but instead of pushing him away again she grabbed hold of his wrist. He marveled at the strength of her grip and rejoiced as she stilled. But his joy was short-lived as the word he had come to loathe was repeated. "Wait."

Iain had never been so tested, but this seemed to wrap around his will and pull him apart. He was speaking again, repeating his earlier admissions and pleading, until what he wanted came to hang in the air between them. "I'll not take you this night, Love. Not against your will but let me pleasure you. Let me do this." His plea turned into a command, not sure if he would survive another denial. "I need to make you come, Luv."

He moved deeper feeling her heat embracing his digit. When the grip on his wrist loosened, and he saw a look in her eyes and a barest of nods; there was no more hesitation. Another finger joined the first, and he stroked with purpose, angling so that she would get the most pleasure and stroking her nub with each penetration. A few more strokes and her back arched from the ground again. He had never seen such a beautiful sight as her eyes glazing over and her mouth opened wide. Her gasps were nearly more than he could stand. Luveday didn't let go of him, and he felt her touch as it slid further up his arm as if it were sliding up his staff.

Another finger joined the fray and when the first spasm hit, he thought he might lose himself, but he kept up a steady rhythm though it took only a half-dozen strokes before she came apart in his arms. Even the dim light could not hide her pleasure from him. His mouth drank up the cry that was torn from her, and he held onto his control by a thread.

Her breathing slowed to a steady pace before he fully removed himself from her. The feel of his fingers sliding free from her slick folds nearly made him come, but he gritted his teeth and breathed slowly. He prided himself on his control and reminded himself that Iain De Lane was no green young man. He had patience, he had Luveday, and he would wait to see how fruitful either would be.

When her eyes fluttered open and met him unerringly, he knew he was lost. The look in her eyes was part panic, part shame and he had never wanted to see that look on her face. It hit him in the gut, and somewhere right behind his ribs so that when she moved away from him, he was still reeling from the unexpected pain.

He reached out to her. "Luveday," he called, but he was too late. She dove into her side of the tent and huddled into her palate, wrapping the furs around her as if she were hiding from the world. He imagined she was crying, or perhaps she was too strong to let a single tear fall. That thought hurt him even more. He cursed himself a thousand times for a fool, a damned fool. He knew deep down he had hurt them both, though he had sworn he wouldn't. He cursed again but could not bring himself to be repulsed by what he had done, though logic told him it would have been better if he had let her go in those first moments. After all, how could a man miss what he had never known?

Chapter 9

Whatever's lost, it first was won.
~ Elizabeth Barrett Browning

Luveday didn't cry. She stayed curled up against the cold and the bombardment of her thoughts, though she found respite from neither. She couldn't bring herself to hate De Lane, though she tried to distance herself from him if only mentally. He hadn't hurt her or mistreated her, he hadn't taken anything she truly didn't want to give, but she knew in the depths of her soul that he was not hers, and she couldn't stomach what that meant. The endless circling of her thoughts made sleep impossible as she tried to reason out her changed situation and what options lay before her.

Logic had always been her saving grace. She might be a closet daydreamer, but in everyday life, she was practical, fact-oriented, and goal driven. Yes, she overthought things, but she also rarely experienced the regret of an impulse decision. It wasn't guilt and shame that haunted her, but that glimpse of that elusive something that Iain had shown her. It was unattainable, at least with him, but that did not stop her from wanting it. It took her a great deal of effort to put that train of thought aside and focus on tomorrow. The fact that Iain wanted her was world changing, at least for her, but how much was her world going to change come dawn? That was the real question.

She could go home, back to Lander's Keep that is, but a part of her thought that she was just running away, and she couldn't stomach that. She wanted to stay, this battle was far from over, and she had done a great deal of good. What if Iain asked her to go? Could she brave the look in his eyes and argue with him to let her stay? Pity would be intolerable, though disappointment or hatred would be worse, but only marginally.

The shivers that raked her body did no good. Becoming aware of her physical state only made her think of Iain's warm body not twenty feet away. Thinking of his warmth drew her focus to him, and she moved enough to uncover her head and listen. She could not guess how much time had passed since she fled, but she knew it had been a while, perhaps he was asleep. He hadn't come after her, and for that she was grateful. She told herself she was grateful.

There was a noise, she had been vaguely aware of for several minutes.

It was a quiet rhythm that reminded her of something, but a low groan pierced the air, and Luveday suddenly had no doubt of what she was hearing. Iain was finishing what she did not and bringing himself to release. Hiding in her blankets and trying to drown him out was not the adult thing to do, but she didn't know if she could handle all of this. If she were like one of the heroines in her novels, she would muster her courage and replace his hand with her own, but the thought made her curl in on herself even more.

Her mind screamed no, but her body went liquid with the images her mind was conjuring. She was tormenting herself, and try as she might, she could not place all of the blame on De Lane. She listed off the reasons why a man like him would be interested in her. De Lane was a warrior in a high-stress environment, and he needed something to relieve that stress. She just happened to be the woman in closest proximity. Or perhaps De Lane thought that she needed comfort and their budding friendship, or attraction had taken a turn toward the intimate. Maybe De Lane was just lonely. Maybe it was just his needs, yes, men had needs, and De Lane was known to be a lusty man. It was De Lane this and De Lane that, but the mental distance wasn't helping. Few of the reasons were worthy of him; they were more suited to her two exes' if she could call them that. Truthfully, she could not gage his reasons. That he wanted her was a fact, but to what degree and for how long was a mystery. His actions spoke of tenderness and selflessness, but he had offered no lasting promises, not that she should have expected any. Still, a part of her had longed to hear something more that might offer hope.

Chastising herself yet again for ignoring the facts didn't really help. Again, she pushed the images aside, calling them delusions and hoping the negative connotations would somehow keep them in their place. She moved to her side, as the position on her stomach was becoming uncomfortable, though she was still subconsciously in a fetal position.

Her mind resumed its course and could not deny the facts. Iain was a lord with people who depended on him. He was honor bound and tied to Christabel and desperately needed the coin this union would bring. Luveday was a lady, at least everyone believed that was so, but a poor one was little better than a peasant. She had no coin, no way to make coin other than her healing skills in a time when women had no rights and ladies had no profession. Luveday didn't dare leave on her own, and unless she was thrown out could not see herself leaving willingly. She depended on De Lane's charity. She knew him to be noble and honorable, and saw no hope for herself, though a pearl of it seemed to shine in her soul; it was a small and cruel hope. Anyway she looked at it, her future pivoted on Iain, and more importantly, his actions come dawn. She would gage her reactions accordingly. Her tired brain attempted to loop back around again to gnaw on her worries, when her heart decided it had had enough of this round robin and gave her a way out, for both of them when it pulled out a piece of information from her past.

Perhaps this was merely a case of disaster sex. Luveday had heard of the term after 9/11 on some news station. At the time many had snickered at the thought, but it made sense to her. After a disaster or near-death experience, humans want to reaffirm their life, their vitality, and what better outlet than sex. Both of them had been under tremendous pressure, Iain fighting for his life and she was fighting for the lives of others. There were no other women as close to him as she was. When brought together by the remnants of her nightmare, was this not a logical conclusion? For some reason, these thoughts seemed to settle her. She had a reason, one that made sense to her and one that she could deal with. The responsibility for their actions was laid at both their feet equally, and her mind could finally find a measure of rest.

Luveday fell back into her routine. The past few days since her night with Iain were so similar to before the incident that she was almost convinced it had all been a dream, that is except for the awkward silence that now fell between De Lane and herself. Luveday had taken her cue from him and acted like nothing had happened. On more than one occasion she had felt the unrelenting weight of his stare and tried not to become angry, especially at him. Each day Iain left to fight, except on the occasional rest day. Battle was hard, and Luveday wondered who decided when and where to rotate the men. Rest days made sense though this battle seemed more ridiculous to her the longer she worked.

Now she stood before the King, Iain at her side and a number of lords eyeing her curiously. King Edward was as charming as she remembered, but not as lively. She could only imagine how lonely the man must be, and how the weight of his responsibilities must burden him. What was it like to be in charge of so many lives, to be responsible for their deaths? Shuddering at the thought, Luveday had no wish to carry that sort of power. It was terrifying to her.

"You remember my son, Benjamin, do you not Lady Luveday?" The King pointed out the young prince.

"Your Highness." She bowed slightly and smiled at the boy. He was shy for the most part, but Luveday remembered that he and Coll had gotten on well. She thought she saw the prince smile back at her, but it was hard to tell with his chin tucked into his chest, and his brown hair hanging in his face. Dressed like any of the royal squires and pages she had trouble recognizing him.

"His eldest brother is still in town with his mother." Luveday nodded. Did the King's comment have some other meaning? Was she supposed to comment?

Luckily, Iain saved her from being too awkward. "Prince Archibald has just returned from the south and the skirmishes with our neighbors there. He handled himself well by all accounts."

"Indeed." Lord Frasier nodded, but he watched the other lords as they watched her. Frasier was an older noble, battle-hardened with salt and pepper hair. He was a bear of a man, with a sharp wit and a gruff manner, but he was also apt to tease a lass, and over the few times that they had been thrown together Luveday found him extremely likable. James Frasier flashed her a mischievous smile that more than one man puzzled over, then again, many did not as they had met her earlier having sought her out for her healing skills or to thank her for seeing to their men. Those that remained aloft were the nobles from court and were often heard complaining of the prolonged battle, though never in the King's hearing of course.

"Aye, he's done well, and thank God he was away when all of this started." There was a moment of silence at Edward's words, and then a roar of noise as men started to talk over each other. Many remained silent and watched as their brothers tried to persuade the King to come to terms with Sterling or to crush him. Defeat didn't cross anyone's mind, but the length of the battle was wearing thin on the court followers, and it showed.

Edward held aloft his right hand and silence fell. "I'll have no more talk of meeting that bastard's demands." He looked to several men in particular while Frasier, De Lane, and a few others smirked. "Sterling will learn what it means to contend with the crown, and I mean to end him and his line." There were a few gasps, but no one spoke out. "De Lane. Are you and your men ready for another round?"

Luveday looked at him startled. She had never seen such a wicked expression on his handsome face.

He bowed in an almost mocking fashion. "Give the word, my King."

The King didn't seem to take offense, but rather shared Iain's dark humor. Soon a few others wore similar expressions, and Luveday sent up a silent prayer that whatever they were planning, she would not see the aftermath of their endeavor. "The word is given." Edward nodded, and the men scattered.

Luveday was escorted back to the tents, while the men of Lander's Keep geared up for the day. It was hard to believe it was still so early in the morning as the mists and frost still clung to the ground. The last few days had taken a turn for slightly warmer weather, though winter was now nearing full swing. As she watched the men ride out, Luveday couldn't help but wonder at man's proclivity for war.

The day passed like any other. The camp followers that had joined their group were now a regular sight. Clair had a hand for herbs and Margret a skill for cooking that amazed Luveday when she had the opportunity to contemplate them. Clair had been shy at first but quickly opened up to her, though that had been Ellie's doing more than her own. Luveday missed her young friend and Lady Emmalyn fiercely. They were a comfort she hadn't known she needed, and she looked forward to the day they would be returning home.

Later that morning, when Clair approached her with that same shy look that Luveday had not seen for days, the lady was concerned.

Luveday sat down her meal giving the girl her full attention and waited. Clair sat down, fiddling with the edge of her apron and glanced at Luveday every so often, but it took a while for her to speak. "Lady, I've been told to ask a favor of you, but I... I don't want to lose your good opinion of me."

She couldn't help smiling at Clair. Perhaps the situation wasn't as dire as her apprentice's expression suggested. "You can ask me anything, Clair."

The slight smile that flashed across Clair's features was slightly pained, and a little embarrassed, but there. "My mistress, she... some of the other women they..."

Margaret stood not ten feet off and easily eavesdropped on the conversation. The woman harrumphed at how hard the girl was making this and finally blurted out her impatience. "Get on with it, girl. Ask her straight. The worse she could say is no, and we'd be in the same shape we're in now, ya keen?" The cook went back to stirring the pot over the fire with vigor.

"Lady, the camp women like myself, some of us have run out of the herbs that keep us from bearing children, and some of the women have taken ill from the cold. My mistress asks for your help; I ask for your help."

Clair seemed especially young at that moment; her eyes had a shine to them that spoke of unshed tears. Luveday's heart went out to her. "Of course, I shall help." Luveday mentally checked her supplies. She has enough of the root the women used as a contraceptive for a batch or two. She didn't know who had included it among her supplies, but she was now grateful. "I have the lover's root but not enough for very many women, we can start the potion today. As for those who are ill, take some of the willow bark, the syrups, and see how they fair. I will write to Lady Emmalyn and ask for her help with supplies."

"Oh, thank you, Lady." Luveday was hugged fiercely and then left alone to finish her meal. Margaret took her bowl and gave her a second helping, only nodding to her as the cook returned the bowl. It seems she had gained the woman's respect, she only hoped that Iain would see the deed in such a light.

The lover's root potion took a bit of the morning, but Clair was eager to dispense it throughout her camp sisters. Though the fighting could be heard in the distance, Luveday's work was lighter than it had been to date. Some supplies had arrived with a group of men. Luveday penned a missive to Lady Emmalyn asking for a number of herbs by name and any linens or blankets that could be spared. She told Emmalyn of the camp women, and how helpful young Clair was. She tried to keep her letter concise and not let any of the loneliness she was feeling slip in. Once penned, she had nothing serious to occupy her time, until a page came rushing into the area before their tent.

"You are needed, lady!" The boy looked to be about sixteen as he leaned on his thighs trying to catch his breath. "Please hurry!" Luveday had a pack ready for the call and grabbed it without hesitation to follow the page. Thomas stayed with the tents, John Templeton had returned with an injury to his arm, and while it kept him from fighting, it didn't keep him from accompanying her to the front of the camp.

The first thing she noticed was the noise. It was hard to believe, but the tents had dampened the sound of battle, so that little reached the healing tent, or perhaps it was that the battle was much closer than she had at first realized. They were on the higher ground with a valley of sorts between the two camps. It was not really a valley, just a soft downward slope that meandered some ways before meeting the next hill. The fringe of battle lay about a hundred yards off, with men struggling in combat. Centuries manned a line between her and the battle, a last line of defense. As she watched, more men came to stand at the mark, whether to watch or to defend she couldn't say.

Luveday's attention returned to the page, who had also been arrested by the scene in front of them. John was in her peripheral vision, but she recognized the movement before her mind could completely register the fact that he had drawn his sword. Luveday turned back to face whatever was coming, but by that time she had realized her mistake. She should have moved to safety, not turned to see the threat bearing down on them. John moved to defend her, calling a warning, but the rider who had broken through the line kicked him in the shoulder sending him to the ground, where he stayed.

The knight's armor didn't shine in the cold winter light, and Luveday had only a heartbeat to think how strange that was before she was swept off her feet and thrown over the horn of his saddle. As the air left her lungs in a painful rush, she could hear her name on the wind. They rode hard for the far camp, but Luveday was able to look back, past her kidnapper's thigh to see John gain his feet, and she felt a little rush of relief that he was safe, but it was short-lived.

Luveday covered her head with her hands as best she could while the mount's strides beat her against the saddle. It was the most uncomfortable position she had ever been in. The knight used the pack on her back to hold her in place as they rode straight through the battlefield. She wondered if Iain could see her if he'd be distracted by the sight of a woman thrown over the lap of an enemy knight, but only one question resounded in her head. *What did they want with her?*

About twenty minutes later that question was answered for her. Luveday stood in the middle of a tent that was larger than those the King occupied. The ground was carpeted in soft wools, while gold and silver gleamed from open trunks in the light of a dozen wax candles. Sterling was putting on a show, though not for her benefit. No, it was for the men who sat in equally uncomfortable positions around the perimeter of the tent. His guests had been plucked off the battlefield, most that very day. These were Sterling's prisoners, the King's noble knights.

"Ah, the little healer!" A deep voice crooned. The man who sat on the throne-like chair at the back of the tent was handsome in a dark and sinister kind of way. He wore full armor except for his helmet. Long black hair ran in straight rivers over his shoulders which accented his sculpted face that reminded her of some dark fey from a novel; his beauty spoke of vanity and cruelty. The color of his eyes was an ice blue so light and cold that they had barely any color at all. Luveday tried to find some resemblance between him and his cousin, Lord Albin but was hard pressed to find a familial connection. There was something about the aura that surrounded him that was similar to the slimy feeling his cousin had exuded, only with this sensation was also something powerful and deadly that made the pit of her stomach drop. "Welcome!" He gestured to her, and Luveday realized he expected her to bow or beg or plead for her freedom, but the thought of doing any of those things left an acidic taste in the back of her mouth.

She nodded and kept her lips tightly shut as she gritted her teeth. She looked at the men around her and noticed quite a few from that morning. It was with no small amount of horror that she saw James Frasier seated among

Sterling's prizes, but she tried to school her expression. Luckily, only a frown marred her countenance.

Ladislaus Sterling seemed to find this extremely amusing. "You must be wondering why I asked my men to bring you here." He swept a hand in front of him, bringing attention to the mass of wealth before him as if she might have missed it. The atmosphere was thick with tension, but his theatrical attitude made her want to laugh in his face. She knew that would be terribly unwise and stomped down the sensation as he began to explain his motives to the room at large. "We have heard of your healing skills or the miracles you have worked for Edward." Luveday thought to protest but then thought better of it. "You see, I have no one with such skill in my camp, and while I may doubt that a woman can out-wit a man in any capacity, the whispers about you have intrigued me." He leaned forward as if trying to see something more than was visible with the naked eye. Luveday imagined her mind was protected by battlements and she had just slammed shut her gates and lowered the portcullis. Archers were at the ready, and she was girdled for war. She stared back at him, unblinking.

Once again, that sickly sweet smile crossed his lips. Luveday refused to flinch.

"Time to test your skills, Lady Luveday." Luveday fought the urge to swallow, the fact that he knew her name sent a chill down her spine. It was as if the devil himself had just called her by name. "Let us see how well you can do. I don't yet trust you to see to my own men, but with time you might be able to earn your freedom if that is what you wish." Luveday couldn't believe he'd think she would ever have a desire to stay. "My guests," the word seemed to roll off his tongue, protracted in a way that reminded her of a serpent, "have been reluctant to receive care from my own healer, though I suppose they cannot be blamed for that. You will see to them." He got up, moved to the back of the tent, Luveday noticed another opening there. "Do not try to escape, or plot anything against me, my dear lady. You will not be spared my wrath though you are of noble birth." He looked at her in such a way that a stone settled in the pit of her stomach. "Prove yourself and prove me wrong, but if my efforts have been wasted, you and my guests will pay the price."

He swept from the tent followed by the two guards that flanked him. Obviously, he didn't consider her a threat as he left her alone with his captives.

Luveday let loose a sigh and felt as if her knees would suddenly give way. She took the pack from her back and began looking at the men around her. Four men sat on her right and four men on her left. From what she could tell they were all important noblemen, perhaps the most important men on the battlefield save De Lane and the King himself. Luveday realized that Sterling had collected these men on purpose, effectively cutting down the King's army at the knee. Only a few men of rank would be left to lead the armed forces. Luckily, De Lane was yet free, for Luveday feared that without him this battle would be over.

"What happened, Lady?" Frasier's gruff demeanor was hardened by pain. It was clear he was injured in some way, but with his armor still in place, Luveday wondered how she was going to be of any help for him or his brothers-in-arms.

"A page came, and we moved to the front of the camp. The fighting is nearly on our doorstep. I admit I froze at the sight. A knight on horseback broke through the line before the camp and came straight at me. I didn't have time to flee."

"Were you not protected, lass?" He looked concerned though still in pain, and Luveday smiled faintly at him.

"Aye, I was. Sir Templeton was with me, though he'd received a nasty shoulder wound this morning. He drew his sword, but the rider knocked him off his feet and threw me across his saddle to ride straight here."

A voice across the tent grumbled. "That's no way to treat a lady."

"I don't think they much cared about that." Luveday countered.

"Nay, Sterling is a rough bastard." Frasier looked suddenly at her as she checked a wound in his side. "Excuse the language, Lady Luveday."

"You are forgiven, Lord Frasier." She smiled and then grimaced at the wound. It did not look too good, and without removing his armor, she didn't see a way to close the wound, let alone a way to clean it properly. It was only as she examined Frasier for other injuries that she noticed each man sat with his hands bound behind him. Some wore manacles, others were bound with rope, but either way, she didn't have the means to free them, and some looked as if they wouldn't get far if the chance to escape presented itself. "I am not sure about this wound, Frasier."

"James, lass, call me James." He grunted.

She pulled some items from her pack. "How do the rest of you fair?" She asked the room. "I'll see to the worse injuries first, and then the others." No one spoke though several grunted. She shook her head at them. "Pride will do you little good when your wounds sour." There was more noise from the far side of the tent.

A man she could not identify spoke up, "His Grace, Duke Orland took a mighty blow to the head."

"I wouldn't call it mighty, Henry. Backhanded, cowardly, conniving, perhaps, but not mighty." The man in question was railed.

There was a bit of laughter, as Lord Henry smirked. "I am corrected, your grace."

Luveday removed the bit of cloth that covered Frasier's wound. She was used to this gallows humor that seemed to infect the men at times. Disgruntled, she mumbled under her breath.

"Is it so bad, lass," Frasier asked quietly. She had not realized how much her attitude was affecting him.

"Nay, James." She sat back and looked at him. "'Tis just that I am not as prepared as I would like. I'd ask these men for hot water, but I'd not trust them enough to use it."

The Duke laughed a little pained. "Smart lass."

Looking around at the wary expression of her fellow captives, Luveday found more similarities among the group than differences. All had darker hair ranging in color from deep auburn to black. Their grim expressions mirrored each other; each had a suspicious gleam in their eyes that Luveday belatedly realized was banked fury. "De Lane speaks highly of you, Lady." Henry's words turned their attention back to her.

"I have some skill, but the healing is not really in my hands." She opened a skin of water she kept in the pack and proceeded to clean the wound as best she could.

"To be able to admit that shows wisdom indeed." Orland seemed a little impressed, as others nodded their agreement.

She applied a foul concoction that both protected and sterilized the wound. James hissed in pain, as the syrupy potion burned as a mild antiseptic. She used a bit of clean cloth and more of the gooey liquid to hold the dressing in place.

The Duke was next. She was surprised by how young he looked, though there were lines of fatigue around his mouth there were also laugh lines at the corner of his eyes. He gave her an appraising look as she moved to examine his head wound. It was on the left side of his head and near the back of his neck. Blood had dried as it ran down into his collar. The blow had folded back a layer of his scalp so that she could see the bone beneath. Even with his thick hair to cover most of it, the area around the wound was deep shades of purple and red.

She cleaned the wound while asking him some questions. "Do you feel like you need to sleep, your grace?"

He laughed. "No more so than usual. Why do you ask?"

She didn't answer him but continued to clean the wound. "Have you noticed any changes in your vision?"

"I saw spots for a while after I woke up, but they've disappeared." He answered seriously.

Luveday was concerned that he had lost consciousness, but the fact that he had awoken from it, and was alert now was a good sign. "How long were you unconscious?"

"Unconscious?" He asked not recognizing the word.

"Asleep. Knock out, unaware." She tried to rephrase her question, not knowing how to say it better.

"He was down for a good hour at least," James answered. A few others agreed with that estimate.

Luveday hummed to herself. "Do you feel as if your thinking is slowed, or different in any way."

"You mean other than the pain that is radiating down my spine? No, not really." He was confused by her questions, but very aware of her concern for him.

The salve she put on was a numbing agent. And he immediately noticed the difference. "What have you done, lass? My head hurts a bit less than a moment ago."

"It is an ointment to lessen the pain, it will last for a bit while I clean and stitch up this wound."

"I hope your needlework is as good as my wife's, lady." He jested.

Luveday smiled though he could not see her. "I'll be sure to make it look pretty, your grace." The stitches were quick and neat, and with any luck, the scar would be lost in his hairline. "All done."

It looked as if he wished to touch her handiwork but could only raise his shoulders in a useless shrug. "I have to say that was as good a job as anyone could ask for."

"Your welcome, your grace." She looked at the men. "Who's next?"

By the time Sterling returned it was getting on towards evening. The men were all seen too, their care as good as she could provide given her restrictions. She had come across some healing ointments left in the tent but didn't even think of using them though she could identify a few by sight and smell.

Their captor didn't look impressed, though he swept a sharp eye around the room. Luveday hoped Iain got the opportunity to take that smirk off his face, she'd settle for taking his head with it.

"Well, you have not killed any of them, so I believe that's a start." Luveday glared at him. "You will be taken to our healing tent and begin work on my men. If one of these lordlings perished during the night, you will meet a similar fate come dawn." The men began to protest, but Sterling held up a hand to silence them.

"If I think you have harmed my people in any way, or do not care for them to the fullest extent the outcome is the same... but first I will let them have their way with you, and if you somehow survive their ministrations then I will kill you myself." His expression turned serious. "Are we understood?"

She uttered her first words in his presence. "Crystal clear."

And so, it went. Two days she worked in the enemy's tents, and at night she was brought back to sleep under the watchful eyes of her fellow captives. The men were unbound only long enough to relieve themselves every few hours. They rotated through the tent. Luveday visited them at mid-day to check on them and give them water. They ate little to nothing. Sterling would not free them and so if they wished to eat it would be like dogs, bent over scraps on the floor. Luveday used a few herbs she knew would give them strength, but even that would not last long if this situation continued.

Luveday was shadowed on many occasions by a large man, she learned he was the same one who had charged the line and taken her. He watched her like a hawk and hid his face though she would probably have nightmares about his dark eyes for the rest of her days.

It was on her third night in the camp that Sterling decided to play court in the prisoner's tent. He served himself a lavish meal while the rest of them looked on in hatred and longing. The smells alone were torture enough, even for Luveday who had consumed the ale and stale bread she was given, she could not imagine what the others were going through. Luveday watched the scene unfold. No one spoke, Sterling merely ate with relish surrounded by a halo of light so that none of his audience would miss a morsel of his meal.

As the pages came in and out, Luveday noticed that a few of them gave the captives covert glances. Under further inspection, she saw that a few of them wore clothes that matched Frasier, Orland and Lord Stern's own colors. Sterling had not only captured the lords but their squires as well. Usually, the lads were flag bearers for the men, staying behind the front lines so that the different groups knew where to regroup. Seething anger welled up inside her, as Luveday watched the boys, many of which were black and blue with bruises, serve the would-be king. She gritted her teeth and glared daggers at him. He looked up suddenly, met her eyes and was momentarily startled by her fiery expression. Luveday hoped he'd choke on a bit of food and perish. The irony would be delicious.

As the farce of a meal continued, and Sterling sat back to enjoy a glass of wine, the page at his shoulder caught her attention. There was something familiar about the boy, though he wore a scrap of cloth around his neck that hid a good portion of his face. It wasn't his features, but the pose that struck a chord with her. She had seen that somewhere before, and it was important.

The lad stood with his chin tucked to his chest, dirty hair hung in his eyes and dirt and bruises marred what skin she could see. He stole a glance at her, and their eyes met for a split second causing Luveday's heart to stutter. She didn't move, she didn't breathe, for several heartbeats, she was a marble caricature of herself. When the boy was dismissed and left the tent, she forced herself to breathe normally hoping that no one caught her reaction, small though it was.

When Sterling left them to what little rest the night could provide, given that the nobles were still encased in armor and sitting in their spots with hands bound behind their backs as they had been since her arrival, it was little to no rest at all. Luveday debated whether or not she should share her information with the men, James at least, would have good counsel, but if someone overheard, and there were ears everywhere, then the boy's life would be forfeit for sure.

What had happened that Prince Benjamin was captured on the battlefield? If he was with the other squires then perhaps, he had snuck away from his father's watchmen and ventured out beyond the line, beyond safety. How was she to get the boy out of here without anyone the wiser?

That question plagued her the following day, and it was only by sheer luck that she was back in the tent when Sterling and his men were quarreling.

"Vance can't be trusted. Price will be shot on sight. Granger is an idiot; I wouldn't have him clean my piss pot, let alone carry the message."

The men grew angrier as Sterling insulted their brothers. Luveday listened carefully as she checked wounds and ladled out water. "Carter is wounded, he can't even stand let alone mount a horse, My Lord. We could send one of the mercenaries to do it."

"Don't be a fool." Sterling spat in his face. "This requires finesse and intellect; besides, I wouldn't trust them to not make a deal with the King for more coin and turn against us."

"True, many are impressed with De Lane's prowess on the field. I've never seen a man so bloodthirsty as he has been these last few days." The other man said, only to be hit upside the head by his lord.

"Never praise that bastard in my presence, fool." Sterling entered their section of the tent and looked across the space as if to reassure himself that his prisoners were still there. His eyes settled for a moment on her, but the man at his side was speaking again, leaning away just enough to give evidence of his fear.

"That leaves one of us." His voice was shaky at best.

Sterling whirled to face them with such fury that Luveday feared for their lives.

Orland whispered in her ear, "They've been at this for hours. It seems they wish to make a bargain for our exchange. The mercenaries want more money, De Lane is delivering their heads to them." He laughed, but it turned into a cough. Their health was deteriorating, and nothing Luveday could do would stop it.

An idea struck, foolhardy and something one of her heroines would do, but it was more of a plan than anything else she had come up with. So, she let the arguing continue and finished giving the men water, before planting herself in the middle of the room as she had been that first day. Sterling and his men paid her no mind, though the King's men looked at her in confusion.

At the first lull in their heated argument, she put her plan in motion. "I will go."

James shook his head; she could just see the movement out of the corner of her eye.

Sterling turned to her. "You?" He looked intrigued. "Why would I let you go, little healer? You've proved yourself to be useful to me and mine."

"Useful enough to carry your missive to the King?" She countered.

He approached, eyeing her dirty garments, her smudged face, and her stony expression. If Luveday could read the look in his eyes correctly, he was giving her suggestion some serious thought, and that was the best she could have hoped for. "Brave, resilient, intelligent," he paused before adding, "for a woman." Grabbing her chin in his hand, he yanked her head up farther as he towered over her, though there was no need, she hadn't looked away from him since their eyes met as he crossed the distance between them. He lowered his head, and Luveday thought he meant to kiss her, and she was ready to bite the bastard if he tried, but he merely turned her head a little before laughing in her face and letting go of her. "You've earned your freedom. My healer tells me he has learned your tricks, and you've proven you keep your word." He looked at her as he took up his seat in the great carved chair. "If you stay you can make some handsome coin, without having to sell your other skills to my men." There was some name calling from the nobles, but neither Luveday nor Sterling gave any indication that they had heard anything. "What do you say, My Lady?"

"No." She looked at him and conceded only a little. "No, thank you." That seemed to pacify him, as the narrowing of his eye lessened a fraction before his features resumed their usual dispassion.

He laughed after a moment of thought. "I am feeling suddenly generous, little healer. Let it not be said that I am not a benevolent man. You may take what you wish from my chests for your service." The men began to protest. "But only what you can carry."

Luveday looked at him, searching his motives. "Anything I can carry?" A movie reel played in her head as she remembered the scene from one of her favorite Cinderella stories.

He smirked again. "Anything you can carry!" He rose to leave. "Prepare yourself, choose what you wish quickly for as soon as we are done discussing this matter you will be on your way."

The men left not only this room but the tent altogether.

The captive nobles looked at her with a range of emotions. Some were just wary; others wore hatred and disgust.

She did not have time to explain herself. "What can I carry back to the King that will let him know you are here?" She asked them, looking around the room. "Do you have a token on your person? A message, a word that will let him know I speak the truth?"

Henry looked at her and sneered. "Would you not rather fill your pockets with Sterling's gold?"

Luveday didn't give him a glance as she took the ointment that had been left there days ago, still unused. She chose a large and smelly pot. "I doubt any of that gold is his, Lord Henry." She looked to James first.

"There is a ring around my neck, lass. Take it with you, the King knows it well." Frasier tilted his head back as she took the chain from around his neck and dropped it into the clay pot. Orland had a worn silk handkerchief that Luveday shoved into her bodice. A few of the other men had rings that Luveday dropped into the pot, and words that she spent several minutes committing to memory. She moved quickly finishing the tasks she had set for herself and praying that this plan would not be in vain.

She heard movement around the tent and quickly shoved a few items in her pockets before she went back to James. Luveday hugged him as tightly as she dared and whispered what bits of her plan she could. When the men entered the tent, she pulled away, and her friend looked at her with a little awe. She smiled, he had given her a bit of courage, and she knew that she had given him a bit of hope to see him through.

"Well, woman, your time is up." Two of the mercenaries flanked one of the men Sterling had been arguing with. His eyes were hard, and his blonde hair hung limp and dirty in his face. His sneer told Luveday that he was not going to make this pleasant for her. Luveday had already put her belongings away in her pack and selected a few choice pieces from the horde with Orland's quick help. She presented herself to them, and as she had guessed they searched her before leaving the tent. Sterling's minion took a few of the items she had chosen, but not the ones she was determined to return to the King. They checked her pack and even her pots. "What have we here?" They opened the pots and looked inside.

"That is an ointment for fever and burns." There was barely enough to hide anything in the bottom of that jar, but the men checked anyway. They checked all the jars until they got to the last one. It was nearly full thanks to the items it contained, Luveday had topped it off with another pot and mixed the two ointments together, the smell was so horrible that the men gagged as soon as the lid was off. It smelled like a cesspit covered in decaying flowers. The smell turned her stomach though Luveday thought she had become nearly immune to such things.

They clapped the lid back on the jar and handed it to her. "What is that fowl potion? It smells like the bowels of hell." The lordling, or whoever he was, spoke from behind his sleeve, still trying to ward off the lingering fumes.

Luveday fought a smile and lied through her teeth. "Mirkwood ointment." She stated in the matter of fact tone she had used with all the other jars. "Loosens the bowels and purges the humors." They looked at her. "I've not had any use for it yet, but it works wonders."

"I'll take your word for it, lady." Luveday was returning the items to her pack when he grabbed her arm and dragged her from the tent.

Luveday tried not to show her relief. Step one was complete. They stopped a few feet outside of the tent flap and waited. It was an opportunity to look around, and she spotted what she sought heading towards her. The group of pages marched with their jailer. Sterling leading a group of lads was such a laughable sight that she wanted to smile, but she saw the smirk on his face and kept her features schooled. If he saw any relief in her visage, she hoped that he would attribute it to her coming freedom.

"You will deliver this message straight to Edward." He stepped closer to whisper in her ear, "We will be watching and if you make a move to run or turn from your path I will have an archer strike you down, and Edward can pry the letter from your cold dead fingers." His smile as he stepped away was almost genuine. "Do you have what you want? All you desire?" Luveday had a tight rein on her emotions, otherwise, she would not have survived her captivity, for at every turn she wished to do Sterling bodily harm.

"Almost." She said as Luveday stepped around her guards straight for the smallest squire.

"What more do you require?" He asked utterly confused by her reply, and curious to see what the lady was planning.

Benjamin locked eyes with her, and she hoped her expression conveyed her apologies at what was about to happen. She reenacted her movie scene to the tee. She took the boy by the arm, bent over and picked him up. He rested on her pack; she hoped the position wasn't too uncomfortable and that they might forgive her manhandling a prince.

Luckily, the boy was only twelve, and a little small for his age or Luveday would not have hoped to carry him across the field. Turning back to her jailors, she straightened as much as she dared without unseating the boy. "Now I am ready."

For a moment Sterling's face was filled with fury and Luveday thought her plan had gotten them both killed, that was until he doubled over in a fit of laughter. Even the mercenaries joined in. Once his mirth was spent the man stepped closer again, and Luveday knew another threat was pointed at her. "Do not think this will change anything, Lady Luveday." He made a show of using her title. "The rules are the same, but now, if you put down the boy before you reach the other side, I will kill you both."

"Understood." Was all she said as she took the first steps to freedom under the sharp eyes of Lord Ladislaus Sterling, his men, the mercenaries and the best archer in all the land.

A bead of sweat made slow progress down Luveday's spine as she repositioned the prince. She turned her head slightly to whisper to him. "How are you, your highness?"

A quiet voice answered in her left ear. "I'm all right." They were walking straight through the battlefield where men still fought for their lives, but as the two approached their progress was noticed, and men on both sides began to stop and stare. As they entered the area where the fight was thickest, Luveday had to step over bodies, and on one occasion she dodged the backswing of a knight, though she couldn't tell what side of the battle he was on.

She kept an eye out for Iain, and her steps light. Men stopped to help her, and she warned them off unwilling to do anything that might make those arrows fly for her and the boy. She knew that the enemy did not make idle threats. The men parted like she was Moses at the red sea and a hush fell over the battlefield that had not been heard in the light of day.

Luveday put one foot in front of the other, though the boy now felt like she was carrying Iain or Gregori on her back and not the young prince. Her shoulders drooped with the effort to keep him aloft. When the line of knights that had gathered before the tents after word spread that a woman was crossing the field came into view, she almost started to run. What little she could see with her stiff neck and slumped shoulders was hope enough to quicken her pace, but still, the threat of that arrow hung over her, and she could not risk it if she stumbled and dropped the boy. She had no idea how far an arrow could travel or how good a shot Sterling's archer was.

When men came to take him, she refused, and the prince held her tighter for he had heard Sterling's promise too. She walked until she stood before the King's tent, and it was he and not one of his servants that held the flap for her. Luveday stepped inside, took two strides, set the boy down and fell to her knees utterly spent.

Word traveled through the camp quickly. A woman was crossing the field, and every able man ran to see the sight for himself. Some recognized the little healer for she had been through the camp healing anyone who needed her skills. Those who did not know her knew of her and were reminded that she was captured some days ago by the enemy. That she carried a boy on her back did not surprise them, as many knew her passion for healing the sick and many recognized one of the missing pages, though which one it was, they could not say.

By evening everyone had heard that Luveday had carried the prince back from the enemy camp and that the King had given her his eternal gratitude, no matter that the method of his safe return was unbefitting a prince. They lauded the lady's cunning and were more determined than ever to defeat their enemy.

Someone returned with the items from Luveday's pot, and she was sorry that the task was such an odious one, but the items needed to be cleaned. Once she had delivered the messages to the King, given him the tokens and told her tale, Luveday wanted nothing more than to seek out a bath and her warm bed while the men made plans to retrieve what was taken from them, yet she was not given leave to go.

The King continued to give her looks that spoke of the depth of his love for his son. The remaining lords bickered among themselves with Iain standing guard behind her. She felt that many of the looks Edward cast her way were really meant for De Lane, but she was too tired to try to look and gage the champion's reaction, and she knew better than to ask for an explanation here.

Iain had asked her if she was hurt, with an emphasis she couldn't mistake. Her reply was as serious as his tone and a simple, "No." The breath he expelled was too powerful to be a sigh and too quiet to be a growl. For a moment she thought she had seen the sheen of moisture in his eyes, but he looked away and when he looked back again it was gone. He nodded to her, as she sat in a canvas folding chair and willed the proceedings to their conclusion.

Luveday had been unaware at the time, but Iain had been on the battlefield during her sojourn, though not close to her. He had recognized the slight figure from afar having watched her for months previous. He was frozen with fear at the sight and rode his mount to camp a moment after she crossed the line. He was forced to wait as men piled into the King's tent. By the time he entered Luveday was on her knees, holding a sobbing prince Benjamin who looked as if he were crushing the lady's neck. Only the King could pry him loose, and then the two royals embraced for a length of time. Luveday was escorted to a chair where she collapsed until someone revived her with wine. Iain stole a moment to talk to her and was sure that his unspoken question was clear in his eyes. "No." It was such a simple answer, but it lifted a burden off of his heart he could scarcely imagine. Blinking back the emotions that threatened to overwhelm him, Iain became her silent protector, her shadow, and steeped himself in patience until the facts were brought before the King.

Benedict had returned with news from inside the enemy camp that morning. Wary and concerned for the lady, Iain had never seen his friend so bleak. They exchanged a knowing look that settled his men, more than anything that was said.

After she had explained, and her messages had been delivered, after the tokens were handed over and Benjamin had hugged her a dozen more times, they looked to get the lady's opinion on the enemies' defenses only to find her sleeping deeply, curled up in the chair.

Iain gathered her to him, gave the King a nod of his head and carried her back to his tent. He stayed outside while young Clair helped her bathe, and dress for bed. By the time he entered the tent dark had fallen, but his men still lingered around the fire wary as they were. They had asked him only if the lady was well, and with each gruff affirmation, he saw the same burden lift from his men, especially John who had not stopped blaming himself for her loss since that day Iain had confronted him demanding to know what had happened.

The night wore on, but a precious candle burned in De Lane's tent. Coll slept between Luveday and his lord, unwilling to leave her side and Iain couldn't blame him. If it were up to him, Iain would be wrapped around her small frame, where he could protect her from all harm, but he knew in his current state, he'd not be able to leave the lady alone. He'd take her and destroy what he wished to cherish the most. So instead, he kept watch in the night until she was truly safe and to his thinking, that would not happen until he had Sterling's head on a silver plate.

Amelia M. Brown

Chapter 10

For 'tis not in mere death that men die most.
~ Elizabeth Barret Browning

Luveday was unaware of the plans the King was making. Many were reluctant to let her return to her previous duties, though she assured them no real harm had come to her. Iain finally gave in though it took two days of arguing back and forth. There was no thought of sending her home, once the enemy knew of her deception, Iain feared an ambush on the road to reward his lady's cunning. So, he stayed by her side when he could, or fighting hard to win the battle that had become so personal for him, thanks to her capture. Healing was healing, though she insisted on seeing to the captured soldiers as well as their own. After she saw the way Sterling had treated their men, she could not let it happen here.

It was several hard winter days after her return that Clair arrived with an invitation. Her mistress, Madame Jane, as Clair called her, had requested that Luveday join her that afternoon. While Luveday had helped to treat the camp followers, she had never truly interacted with them and was kept from their section of camp as if some association might taint her. As if she didn't know what the ladies were there for.

Iain was gone, Coll was running errands, and when the time to set out came around, there was no reason to stay at the healing tents. Luveday took with her a basket that carried a teapot and two cups, rose hip tea and a small clay jar of honey. She hoped the offering wouldn't be turned away, for she was fascinated by what little Clair had told Luveday of her life in the camp.

Clair led the way to what Luveday had termed the restricted section. The tents here were much smaller but brightly colored. Decorations seemed to hang from every flap and pole, each different from the other and Luveday wondered if they were identifications of some sort.

When she asked Clair about them, the girl confirmed her suspicion. "Aye, some of the beads tell men the price for a woman, some show her age, and some show her health. It is how the men can find a woman they like after the camp moves." The tents ranged in size, and many seemed to house a number of women. A group exited a tent as a man was pulled inside by a busty young blonde. The women looked at her curiously as they passed and Luveday nodded to them in greeting. "Not far now, Lady Luveday."

Whispers followed her. The women knew who she was. They arrived at a series of covered wagons, one with what looked to be a sort of stove, billowing smoke out of the top. She had only seen the like in the King's tents, not even De Lane possessed one. They stopped before a wagon that had all the trappings of a gypsy cart and was as luxurious as one of the tiny portable homes that had started to be so popular in her own world.

Clair knocked lightly on the wooden door which swung open a moment later. They were both greeted by name by one of the most beautiful women Luveday had ever seen. Madame Jane was younger than Luveday would have imagined, perhaps in her early thirties, perhaps a little older. She had perfect ringlets of black hair, and for a moment she reminded Luveday of Cassandra, but there was something to the woman that the healer didn't possess. "Clair, thank you for showing Lady Luveday the way." She looked Luveday in the eye as she moved out of the narrow doorway. "Come in, My Lady."

"Thank you, Clair." Luveday was about to ascend the small three-step ladder into the wagon when Clair tugged on her sleeve, and she heard the girl whisper.

"Don't worry, Luveday. Jane is a fair woman; you'll like her." Luveday was about to reply that she thought she already did, but the girl was gone.

Luveday was quick to close the door behind her, not wanting any of the wonderful heat to escape. "Thank you for inviting me, Madame Jane." The inside of the wagon was much as Luveday expected it to be. There was a bed in a loft with a small ladder, there was a table and two chairs with cushions, there were brightly colored fabrics and drapes over the canvas sides of the wagon. The wooden sides only went as far as Luveday's hip, but the space was much warmer than even her own tent.

"It is I who should be thanking you, Lady Luveday. And you may call me Jane if you wish." She smiled as she looked to Luveday's basket with curiosity.

"Please call me Luveday. I've brought tea." She offered an explanation.

"How lovely," Jane said sincerely and poured out some water into a kettle and put it on the stove. They sat around the small table as the water heated. "I must extend my gratitude for the help you have given my girls, and for all you are teaching little Clair."

"Clair has been a great help to me." Luveday watched the laugh lines around her eyes crinkle as Jane smiled. "She learns quickly and had some skill with healing before she came to me."

"Aye, Anne took care of Clair when she first came to us. Anne was old, even when I first met her as a young woman. She was a healer, and Clair learned at her knee." Her affection for the old woman was clear in her voice, but there was sadness also.

"I take it that Anne has passed away." Luveday's heart went out to her, she had become awfully familiar with loss lately.

"Aye. Over a year now. Her death has left a hole in our little group that Clair has tried to fill. A healer is something we desperately need." There was a pointed look in Jane's eyes.

Luveday got the feeling that her companion was hinting at offering such a position to her. It was an interesting thought, but she wouldn't join that world unless she had no other choice. Clair had spoken highly of Jane, making her sound more like a mother, or a benevolent ruler than a Madame of a brothel and that underlying kindness is what had Luveday so interested in these women and a fate she felt she had narrowly escaped herself.

"I imagine such skill is especially useful. Perhaps with a little more training Clair will be able to take on that role in earnest." Luveday gave her answer as politely as she could.

Jane's smile held a hint of humor, perhaps the Madame was not expecting so civil a rebuff, but she understood and let Luveday know she conceded the point. "I had not thought so up until now, but perhaps you are right." The kettle began to clink. "I think the water is ready." She got up and carefully took the hot kettle off the stove. Luveday had the teapot ready for her and watched her graceful movements. There had been rumors that Jane had once belonged to the King, and at that moment Luveday believed them to be true. Jane had a regal elegance; it was the kind of confidence any woman would long to possess.

As the tea steeped, Luveday thought they had passed the point in the discussion where they could now get down to business, and she had some questions about Jane and her women. "Clair told me that you look after the other women. You don't force them to work and make them take care of their health." She paused. "That doesn't sound like any woman in your position I have heard of."

"About that you are correct." Jane looked at her earnestly, and a game smile relaxed her features. "Clair was right about you. I will have to thank the girl for disobeying me and staying with you. I think we will be good friends." Jane seemed to have settled something for herself.

"I think so too. Now, what can I do to help?" Luveday was sure they would be seeing more of each other, and her questions could wait a little longer.

Laughing, Jane turned and pulled out a small bundle of biscuits and set them on the table. "To the point, Lady. I like it." Luveday brought out the honey and set it between them. Jane looked surprised but delighted. "You are a woman with a good heart, Luveday. There are not many in this world, to begin with, and life has a way of turning us cold and bitter if we are not careful." Jane looked at the biscuits, but Luveday knew she saw something else. A heartbeat later her eyes snapped back to Luveday and the moment had passed. "The cold is hard on us, though we have been through worse I assure you." Luveday could only imagine and tried to hide the shudder that serious tone sent down her spine. "My girls are hearty, but not all of the others are faring so well. Some think they can make it on their own, but there is strength and security in numbers." Luveday nodded her understanding. "Some of the others have asked for my help, but I have barely enough to care for my own girls let alone a few dozen more. I need your help." Luveday was surprised when Jane grabbed her hand, and by the desperation in her cultured voice.

Luveday had already decided to do what she could for these women. Perhaps it was the feminist in her, or the healer's spirit she came by so honestly thanks to her mother, but Clair and the stories of Jane and her band of sisters had moved Luveday. Yet again her mind returned to the bleak possibilities of what could have happened if Gregori had not found her. How easily their fate could have been hers. Nodding, Luveday tried to reassure her. "I will do what I can. My supplies are low, but more should be coming soon, I've sent a missive with the men. For now, we will have to make do with what is available. You may send women to the healing tent," but Luveday hesitated at the idea of mixing men and women, not that modesty was big with any of them. "I can return in a few days after Clair and I have brewed up some items and see to your women. Perhaps if there was a tent large enough to hold a few of us." Luveday was thinking quickly. Most of her healing ointments would work for men or women, but there were some things a woman would need that she had had no reason to stock when treating battle wounds.

"Lady, we will owe you a great debt. We have taken up some coin..." Jane moved to retrieve the purse, but Luveday stopped her.

"I have not asked coin from the knights, I will not ask it of you, but if you wish to help, perhaps your women might have some things I will need." Jane sat down, intrigued and grateful for the lady's generosity.

They talked for some time, drank two cups of tea and ate their biscuits. Luveday listed off the herbs and supplies she would need to treat the women, and Jane knew that among her group alone they had most of the list. When a heavy knock came to the door, both women jumped. There were male voices outside.

"I am not expecting anyone," Jane said flatly.

Luveday looked to her and blanched when someone outside called her by name. Luveday recognized that voice immediately.

Jane must have guessed what was going on for she said, "I think you have stayed too long, Luveday."

Luveday swallowed and quickly collected her things. "I think you are right." There was another knock at the door, and Luveday could have sworn the force of it rocked the wagon.

Jane opened the door for her, and the men took a step back. She turned back inside to her guest. As Luveday passed her, Jane inquired quietly, "Are you sure you will be able to return?"

"Oh, I *will* be back." Luveday lifted her head and descended the steps with an air that was worthy of Jane.

Luveday had never seen Iain so upset with her. She followed along beside him constantly aware of the hand that rested at the base of her spine. He wouldn't let her put any space between them and trying to match his long strides was wearing her out. He hadn't said more than a few words before he and the men with him circled around her and began the trek home. None of the women had called to them, no one they happened to meet stopped to have a word. Though several men seemed as if they had approached for a reason, they had quickly turned and headed in a different direction. Luveday couldn't see Iain's expression, but from the reactions of others, she gathered that it was set in stone.

By the time they reached the area between the healing tents and their own, Luveday had thought of several reasons why what she did was wrong and several reasons why she was free to go, but one look at Iain as he shoved her into the tent silenced her.

Stumbling inside, she found Coll seated in his usual spot by the door, working on a bit of leather. He looked up at her and back down at his hands without so much as a smile and Luveday realized something was very wrong. She moved deeper into the tent, making room for De Lane who seemed to take up more of the space than usual.

She waited. He stared. Neither said anything.

Iain gave in first.

"Of all the places I could have found you! What the hell were you doing there, Luveday?!" He began to pace, moving his hands through his hair in frustration. "Do you know how long we were looking for you?"

A light went on inside Luveday's head. Perhaps it wasn't where she was that had angered him so much, but that he didn't know where to find her. She had left word with Margaret and Thomas, but perhaps they had not stopped to inform De Lane. She didn't have an argument for his worry.

"You left without a word. Coll came back, and you were gone," He gestured wildly at the boy who watched them with a shocked expression. "John waited for me at the line, with news that he couldn't find you. Do you know what that did to me? To him? You can't just disappear like that! Do you understand me?" He grabbed her by the shoulders so that he could look her in the eyes, watching her answer.

He was worried about her; she had scared him, and Luveday didn't think that was an emotion he was familiar with. The guilt that assailed her was instantaneous and heavier than Iain's armor. "I'm sorry," was all she could push past the lump in her throat.

His hand slid up to cup her right cheek. "You can't run around camp like you would the village. It's not safe, Luveday." The pain in his eyes hurt her physically.

"I know. I'm sorry." She looked down, but he lifted her chin until she was forced to lock eyes with him again.

"I forbid you from going back there again." The command was given as if he were carving it in stone.

It was the wrong thing to say to her.

"No." She didn't look away.

"What?" Shock straightened him back up to his full height.

Luveday repeated, "No."

"Luveday." He growled; this was how so many of their arguments began.

"The women have asked for my help. I am going back to help them in a few days." She stated flatly.

"A proper lady..." he began, yet again the wrong thing went flying from his lips.

"Don't." She threw up her hands. "Don't finish that thought." Her anger was growing steadily.

"I am your Lord, and it is my duty to protect you." He began in an indignant fury.

"I am a healer, and I *will* see to the ill, whether they are Princes or paupers." Luveday was aware that she had just stamped her foot at him.

He was grinding his teeth, and she was close enough to see the lines at the corner of his eyes as they narrowed at her. "You will not associate with those harlots..."

"I will be helping them, not having tea." There was no reason to tell him that was all Jane and she had done. You would think the woman had leprosy from the way he was acting.

"You are a lady of good repute, there is no need to sully..." he continued, but she couldn't know that some of his anger was due to the fact that he was embarrassed by past associations with women of that nature and Jane in particular.

"How could helping a bunch of women sully my reputation? Do they sully yours or the men that visit them?" She countered, remembering their first meeting when he had insinuated that she was no better than a tramp looking to weasel her way into his house.

"I am not talking about this with you, Luveday." He turned to retreat, but she wasn't done.

"I want an answer, Iain." She stepped into his space. "Or have you forgotten how close to them I might have come?"

He looked at her with a fury that was barely contained. "You are nothing like those women!" He yelled in her face.

"I could have been!" Luveday shouted back. "Do you think that they chose that life? That they aspired to be someone's whore?" She pushed him, and he stumbled back a few steps. "Do you think they had a choice?" She pushed again. "They chose between living and starving to death, between working in the fields and breaking their backs in toil and trying to make coin enough to settle down on their own. They used their looks, their wits, and if they had had another choice you can believe, by God, they would have taken it, but all they had was their bodies and men are eager for a pretty face." She looked at him suddenly lost. "We don't have the choices you do. We can't hold anything of our own, not even our own children... It all rests in the hands of men." Luveday sighed and turned away. "I know," she looked back at him. "I know what it's like to fear for the future, with nothing to hold onto. I know how much a helping hand can mean when you have nothing else." Iain turned her back toward him.

"Luveday." He reached for her.

She sighed again as she looked deep into him. "I want to help them. You may not know it, but they are fighting too, and I may be giving them more than you think is their due but..." He embraced her. And for a little while, Luveday just let herself be held.

A throat cleared in the tent. Gregori had stuck his head inside the flap.

"If you two are done in here, the King wishes to see us, Iain." He added for her benefit. "Lady Luveday has some more injured to see to."

Iain let go of her suddenly and moved to leave. "Of course." He didn't look back.

Luveday was at a loss, suddenly missing the comfort of his big frame. Coll got up from his spot, a little shell-shocked from the look of him, but the hug he gave her made up for Iain's sudden absence if only a little.

Gregori stuck his head back in and smiled at the two of them. Luveday nodded over the boy's head, signaling that she was fine. "Back to work then." And he was gone. Coll dragged her out of the tent and ran off saying he was getting her something, but she couldn't make out exactly what he had said.

The healing tent was full of activity, Luveday squared her shoulders and walked to the open flap with determination in every step.

The camp followers were more reluctant to come to her for help than the men had ever been. With Iain's help, Clair and Luveday set up in a large tent and began treating women. There were a few with wet coughs, some with sprains and more than a few with their own share of bruises. The women were far from idle. While they did sell their bodies, they also provided other services for the camp; many washed clothes, cooked and sewed for their men. Knights paid to have garments repaired, some lonely men even paid for conversation though not many. More often than not it was a barter system rather than an exchange of coin, which told Luveday how desperate they were for her help when Jane had offered her that purse.

To her surprise, supplies arrived from tents around the camp. Extra blankets, packets of herbs, and a few skins of wine. It seemed that some of the men genuinely cared for these women after all. Jane watched with gratitude and not a fair bit of amusement. The women often joked at Luveday's expense once they learned she was a maid. Her blushes had eventually given her away, and while the women's humor could turn a little crude, they were a joy to be around. It made her miss Elli and Emmalyn even more.

In the days that followed, women would make the journey to the healing tents. Some helped change and dress wounds while other's washed linens and learned to sterilize the healing supplies. Luveday liked the banter between the injured knights and the women. It was a pleasant change in the middle of so much misery.

It was another chilly afternoon when the fighting had settled for a time. Negotiations of some sort were taking place, but men still came and went from the healing tents. Thankfully, many left on their own two feet, rather than being carried home. Many still offered their gratitude for saving the prince, and word came that the prisoners would be returned in an exchange, though Luveday hated to think of Sterling getting anything out of the deal.

Luveday walked the tent, putting away supplies, checking on the worst of her patients and chatting with others, when an unfamiliar man entered the tent. He looked around, but quickly found her, and moved to her side.

"Lady Luveday." It wasn't a question. Luveday noted the tan of his skin and the undertone of some accent to his words. "I have need of some supplies for my master." She paused a moment at the word master. Most of the men referred to the nobles by their titles or the common milord, but not master.

"What ails him?" She asked. A few men still hesitated to come to her, relying on their own remedies or Master Pope who said he cared for only the best.

"A gash to his leg and a slight fever." He stated matter-of-factly. Luveday would have offered to go with him and see to the ill herself, but something stopped her from speaking. She looked around and saw that many eyes watched them, and it seemed her guest noticed that something was odd too.

"I have something for the fever and to clean out the wound. I will give you some of each, but please return the cups when you are done." Luveday enter the back room, her operating room, now empty, which was secluded with all of the sides down to keep out the chill. She moved through the makeshift shelves to collect the ingredients, wondering about the man waiting beyond. Something wasn't sitting right with her though she could swear that she had never seen the man before. She thought that perhaps her unease was caused by the sudden quiet, but when she turned back to the table, she found that the man had followed her inside, standing right inside the flap and almost screamed in fright at his sudden nearness. He menacingly advanced on her, and she didn't stop to give him a warning to back off, because, in that moment, she knew who he was. That unwavering gaze, so intent had watched her constantly during her stay with the enemy. It was the mercenary, her kidnapper.

"You think you can make a fool of my men and me, little healer?" His voice carried only so far as her ears.

Grabbing the first thing at hand, Luveday struck him upside the head. Her attacker was caught off guard by the strength of the blow and stumbled back a bit, but Luveday gave him no quarter. He moved, and there was a sudden stinging sensation in her upper left arm, but she struck again. He stumbled through the tent flap and tried to gain his equilibrium, and that was when Luveday saw the knife he carried and the blood on it. Someone yelled for help raising the alarm, but Luveday let loose a cry of her own and pelted the man with blows to his head and shoulders. There were men calling out and movement around her, but she was so focused on him that nothing else got through to her. The mercenary went down, and Luveday continued to hit him until arms wrapped around her from behind, pulling her off him to carry her out of the tent.

Iain's voice penetrated the anger and fear in her head until she could finally hear him as she was enfolded securely in his arms. Her breath moved the hairs at the base of his neck, she spoke to his shoulder as she told him that she was alright. The violence of her emotions subsided quickly leaving behind a dread and a dark epiphany. Luveday, who had spent so much time learning to heal, who had focused her life on helping others was capable of killing someone. The realization rocked the foundations of her being. She looked up at Iain as tears filled her eyes, unable to speak at the horror of her actions.

Iain hugged her fiercely but handed her off to Gregori who moved her to the fireside and wrapped her in the edge of his cloak as she melted into his side.

Luveday watched the fire and the world around her through the blur of her tears, but not a single drop fell. She could admit to herself with utter certainty that she could have, indeed she had tried, to smash in that man's face with, she looked at her right hand and brought the metal pitcher to eye level. It was severely misshapen, having tried to conform itself to the shape of a man's head. Gregori took the pitcher from her hand, and it disappeared somewhere.

Someone handed her a hot drink, it might have been Benedict, she couldn't tell, but there was a lump in her throat that nothing, not even speech could get around, so she held it in her hands, savoring its warmth. At some point, Iain took up the space on her other side. Luveday finally found the ability and courage to ask, "Is he dead?"

"No." Iain's gruff voice resounded somewhere over her head. Both men felt the sigh that escaped her.

She fidgeted a moment later. "I think I need to go lay down."

Iain stood to help her. "That is a good idea." He untangled her from Gregori's large cloak and grabbed her upper arms to steady her.

Luveday let out a hiss of pain, closing her eyes a moment.

Iain removed his hand, and they both looked at the blood that marred his palm. For the first time, they both noticed the blood and the gash on her arm. Luveday watched as his features went blank for a moment then began to distort. She had never noticed how white and straight his teeth were, which was a silly thing to take note of at the moment. A blast of breath hit her in the face, and she blinked, the Iain that stood before her now was not the Lord of Lander's Keep, but the Wolf De Lane and she now understood why men ran in fear, though she felt no fear for herself. Iain was furious, more so than he had ever been with her. Flames seemed to burn in the depths of his eyes, as rage, the likes of which she had never seen, took over his entire being. His focus shifted from her arm to a commotion behind her as men hauled her attacker out of the healing tent. It looked as if the man needed a stretcher, but no one would offer to carry the prisoner. Iain was gone from her side in a flash. Gregori called after him, something like panic in his voice. Benedict moved from his place across the fire, where he had been questioning some men. Neither knight could stop their friend, and none got in his way.

Luveday watched still detached, noting that Iain had drawn his sword and the guards had dropped the man to his knees and stepped aside. He was conscious enough to look up as Iain approached. Men called for De Lane to halt, that the King wished to speak to the prisoner, but Iain merely raised his sword until suddenly Luveday was there, standing near them.

Her hand was raised to stop him, but how she had gotten there, and what she said to him before that moment she couldn't recall. "Stop." She looked at him, and his eyes quieted. "Please." The point of his sword dropped, and he looked at her in confusion. The man behind her groaned causing Iain to snarl at him, and grip his sword tighter, but he did not raise it again. He grabbed Luveday and moved them both back to the fire, breathing deep through his nose and mouth to regain some control.

Iain looked around at his men and saw an array of emotions ranging from understanding to wariness. They had seen the bloodlust over take him once before, no one talked of that battle in Jasper's Wood, but none who were there would ever forget. Iain couldn't focus, couldn't think. Luveday, Luveday was hurt. He turned back to see her, he still held her by the upper arm. Blood marred her other sleeve. Thomas appeared and bandaged the wound. Luveday spoke to him softly, as much for Thomas's benefit as for his own. He was hanging on to his sanity by a thread. The need to kill the bastard who had hurt her was still raging, but his concern for her was greater. The mercenary's time would come, and soon.

At the moment, all he really wished to do was hold her close. When the call came out that the healing tent was under attack, he and his men had dropped what they were doing and ran. He had never run so hard in his life. To see Luveday, his kind lady, having to defend herself, while injured men tried to gain their feet around her, to see her commit such violence, had unloosed something inside him. His first priority had been her safety. Her attacker was too injured to speak, but some of the King's men knew ways to get the words out of him. Someone had mentioned seeing him during the exchange. Frasier and his men had only just been returned to their tents. The prisoners had fared poorly through their days of captivity, and Master Pope was seeing to a few of them. Iain had been on his way to collect Luveday as Orland and Frasier had asked for her by name, refusing the old healer's aid.

The time it took for him to reach her was mere moments, but his mind had been filled with terror at what could be happening to her. He had only felt that kind of panic once, his first time at battle as a young squire when war had been revealed as the chaos and blood driven madness that it was.

Iain turned to her, once again seeing the blood that marred her sleeve and for a moment his vision was tinted in that same hue. A small hand came to rest on his forearm, and the sanity slowly returned. What would he have done if something had happened to her? Without warning, he understood his need for her and the destruction he would have rained down on Sterling and his men if she had been seriously harmed, or worse. He couldn't contemplate all that this revelation meant to him, instead, he turned her toward the tent, remembering that she had wanted to rest.

Guiding her to the tent, he watched her as they both looked around the space as if they were seeing it for the first time. Clair, the girl who assisted Luveday, came in to help and Iain was immensely grateful for it. He wanted to help, but what could he do that would not lead to her spending the night in his arms?

Luveday was being cared for, that was all he wanted. So, he left the tent to talk to his men. Benedict had returned, but the King kept him running errands of diplomacy as his brother in arms could charm the shirt off a saint. Both he and Gregori were eager to hear how the lady faired and Iain was happy to tell them that she was not grievously injured, and her spirits were as good as could be expected. He was aware of the long looks that they gave him. He answered their unspoken questions with a long look of his own, letting them know that he was sound in mind if not in heart.

Without orders, his men took up posts around the area, as he and Gregori made their way to the King's tent following the prisoner.

Luveday slept fitfully that night. After a quick nap, she had returned to her duties, even going out to see Lord Frasier and the Duke. Both men had heard of what happened in the healing tent, but though they gave her concerned looks, they treated her as if nothing had happened. It was a good thing because Benedict was treating her as if she were made of glass. Luveday was wondering what the punishment was for boxing a lordling's ears.

She exited the last tent to find Benedict and Iain talking in hushed, but fervent whispers. It was obvious that she was the topic of discussion, but Luveday's tired mind couldn't quite catch the gist of their conversation.

Both looked up at her at the same time. She noted the scowl that De Lane gave her but wondered why Benedict looked so contrite. She did not have to ask to know that she was not going to like what they had to say.

Iain didn't even greet her or ask how she was doing as he took her elbow and steered her back towards their tent. The light was growing dim as the night now outweighed the day. Winter had turned the days colder than Luveday could ever remember. In the light of multiple campfires, she could see their breath as they rushed through the camp.

She thought she should talk to him about a number of things that had happened today, but she couldn't summon the energy for what she knew would be an emotional endeavor. So, she remained quiet and let him drag her along.

Clair waited in the light of the healing tent's cooking fire and took Luveday's basket and pouch as Iain quickly divested her of the items and handed them over to the girl.

"She is done for tonight. Tell Moore he is in charge. He will have to make do without her." The girl only nodded and walked back into the tent.

Luveday saw shadowy figures watch their every movement as he escorted her beyond the last of the tents and toward the stream that supplied their water. The stream was wide, but not very deep and the water was icy cold no matter what time of day. On the pebbled bank was a blazing fire, a large wooden tub, and a stool. Large pieces of linens had been left to dry in the weak winter sun and still hung off the rope lines creating a three-sided privacy screen. In the light of a half-dozen candles, was Margaret, who finished poking the fire and looked up at their arrival. The old woman only nodded at them before taking her to leave.

Luveday looked around bemused as Iain stayed silent by her side. "What is all of this?" She finally asked, noticing that her voice carried a little across the stream.

"Clair and the women brought you a tub, some fine soap, and oil for your hair. They suggested that you might like to bathe. The fire should keep you warm for a bit. The water's hot and the tub is full. I'd hurry though, 'tis bound to grow cold in this weather." Iain grew uncomfortable for a moment as she just stood there looking at him. "The women thought you might like it. I suggested the tent, but they said you would prefer some time alone, outside of camp. It's the best I could do..." She put a hand on his arm as he crossed them in front of him in a defensive manner.

"Thank you." She looked out at the steaming bath, her clean garments and toiletries waiting, and it brought tears to her eyes. "Thank you and thank the women for me." He nodded.

De Lane moved to step beyond the screen, and she called out to him. "You won't be far?"

He looked back at her with a pinched expression. Luveday couldn't tell if it was anger or pain. "No, not far." She was unsure if he heard her whispered gratitude or not.

She stripped quickly, not knowing how long the hot water would last. Her undergarments were little protection from the cold as she decided to go to the water's edge and scrub her gown and body before using the tub. She felt unclean, more from recent events than any lack of hygiene. The water was colder than she imagined and couldn't help the startled noise that escaped her. She called out that she was fine, not sure who was out there and might come to her rescue. She heard movement around her, but no one approached.

The tub was little more than a wash bin, but it was full of steaming water, with buckets of cold and hot water in reach and a pot boiling over the fire. Luveday soaped down and washed off outside of the tub, before sinking into the blessed warmth. The fire was close enough to ward off the chill with its heat, and the screens helped to corral what warmth there was while halting the soft breeze.

This was heaven. She had not realized how much she had missed bathing. The quick wash downs in the tent were enough to placate her modern sensibilities, but those quick endeavors were not a proper bath. She used a wooden bowl to wet her hair and lathered it with a flowery soap. She rinsed it over the edge of the tub, before getting up to put in more water. Her wound was not deep though it stung under her vigorous cleaning. She was more than happy for the chance to relax, not realizing how much the stress and constant presence of others had begun to weigh on her.

She didn't know how long she rested there, but she didn't wait for the water to cool. Finished bathing, Luveday longed to linger even knowing that the cold would turn her wet body to one of ice in minutes. Luckily, the temperature had not dropped enough to produce snow again.

Luveday dried off and dressed while sitting as close to the fire as she dare. "Iain?" She called. "Lord Iain?" He appeared around the corner of the screen and looked at her with an expression she couldn't read. She smiled at him as she finished drying her hair with a piece of linen. She was fully dressed in her nightclothes with her cloak wrapped around her. Looking at his hooded gaze, she became worried. "Did I take too long?"

Stepping closer he didn't answer, only lifted a strand of hair and seemed to test it. She pulled back to get a better look at him, but the movement caused him to drop the strand. The moment was suddenly intense, and the silence deep. Luveday sat gazing up at him, and he looked down to her, but neither moved and barely drew breath until some noise from the woods beyond their little ball of light caused him to remember the time and place.

He scanned their surroundings. "If you are done, we best head back." His voice seemed too deep in the quiet.

"What about all of this?" She gestured around her.

"It will be taken care of. For now, you need to rest." He took her hand, pulling her to her feet. For a moment she thought he might sweep her up into his arms, but they stared at each other a split second before he turned to guide her back to camp. Figures brushed past them as they moved towards the ever-present rumble of the King's army. Luveday wanted to stop and thank the women, but Iain's grip on her was tight and brokered no delays.

She was deposited inside their tent where Coll waited with a hot meal and lively conversation. The boy showed his concern by not leaving her side and chatting about every bit of news and anything he thought important. Luveday laughed a good deal, amused by what a twelve-year-old boy thought was news. It was not long until the bath, and the warm food began to take its toll. Luveday fought to keep her eyes open in the lamp light, but it soon became too much.

Strong arms lifted her and settled her into her palette. Luveday roused enough to be aware of the warm presence that lingered by her side and a gentle hand that brushed across her cheek. Sleep claimed her again, and her last fleeting thought was for Iain De Lane.

Dawn was as brisk as ever, and maybe it was the long nights, but Luveday felt as if she'd rested better than she had in weeks. Men and women were already huddled around their fire as she emerged from the tent. Compassion filled eyes followed her with unwavering scrutiny. Luveday ignored what she could and took comfort in her familiar routine. Luveday met Coll beside the fire, the boy had run out of the tent a moment before her, too eager to fetch her anything she might need. Food and drink seemed like manna from heaven as she sat amongst her friends and broke a late fast.

Iain was nowhere to be seen, but Gregori or Benedict were never far from hand. The day wore on with visits from the camp women. Luveday thanked them for their kindness the night before, and saw to any issues they might have, often offering some food or a hot drink on this chilly day.

Thomas didn't ask how she faired, merely looked her up and down, nodded and got back to work. The injured grew less and less as an uneasy negotiation had started between the two groups. Luveday wondered how the incident in her tent would impact the cease-fire.

Luveday had reassured the majority of her followers that she was, in fact, alright and no wilting flower. She was ready for the distraction of dinner and found Benedict had returned from a brief sojourn to the King's tent for news. It was clear to her that he was worried about her for the talkative lordling was remarkably quiet at times. He had at first tried to distract her with charming banter, but Luveday was not happy with the disruption in her tent. She had things to do, a daily mental checklist and though she was glad to see him for several days in a row, Luveday was not happy that every step she took had been to dance around her new shadow.

Iain appeared sometime around nightfall. The camp seemed to clear as he took up a seat next to her, a spot that until a moment before had been the home of Sir John Templeton, her other shadow.

They sat in silence for a moment as men departed to their own tents and campfires. Luveday was secretly amazed at how many people continued to come and check on her. Even Jane had sent her well wishes, though Luveday thought it was silly that the Madame stayed away least the connection bring Luveday's character into question. Still, people had been in and out of the healing tents every day; many were men she had seen to or who had someone who was cared for by her own hands. Now the area was nearly deserted.

"You remember your promise," Iain spoke with his head turned toward her, so close that she felt the breath of his words against her cheek.

Luveday didn't have to think about which promise he referred to; there was only one that he would bring up now. "Yes, I remember." In fact, she had been expecting him to remind her of it every day after her stay in the enemy camp, but he hadn't. This last misadventure was apparently too much for him, but she couldn't blame him.

"Luveday," He obviously expected some fight, but the truth was that even she was wary of the task she had set for herself. She sighed, and Iain's gaze sharpened. "'Tis time you went home, lady."

"Yes, My Lord." She stood up and went back into the tent, there was much to do before she left.

Chapter 11

Best be yourself, imperial, plain and true.
~ Elizabeth Barrett Browning

The morning was not as cold as everyone had expected. The sky was overcast, and the clouds had kept the temperature from dropping too low. Fog meandered through the camp, ghosting around tents and the legs of the horses. Luveday's horse was saddled and ready to go. The lady had said her goodbyes the day before, had even finished resupplying the healing tent with the common herbs and ointments. She was confident in her work and happy to go home. The letter she had received from Lady Emmalyn had only made her miss her friends more, and yet she would miss the people here too, but Luveday realized that she had done all she could.

Sterling and the King were in negotiations, though not face to face. After her attacker's capture, many of the mercenaries were unhappy with the would-be King, and his support was failing. Iain watched for treachery as he expected Sterling to pull some stunt before giving over. Word had come that morning that Sterling looked as if he was readying to flee, and the King was ready to give chase. The enemy would receive no quarter.

This morning Iain and the men lingered around her, helping with what they could. Iain watched with a dark expression, and yet he seemed relieved that she was going. Luveday tried not to take it to heart, she knew that her near misses with disaster had worried them all greatly. Even she knew that she was running out of luck and would be unlikely to get away unscathed the next time.

As the sun made a valiant effort to overpower the clouds, Iain finally gave the signal that it was time to mount and head out. As the King's Champion, he was staying behind, and only a few of his men were traveling home with them, the rest of the group were bound for other destinations, some heading as far south as town. Sir John Templeton was at her side, as was Lord Henry, and Lord Grayson Stern, the later was heading home to his wife. The two lords had fared the best out of the captured nobility, Lord Frasier and Duke Orland were still under the weather but improving daily. Luveday had extended an invitation to them when they passed by Lander's Keep. Iain hadn't been upset that she had made such a suggestion without his approval as he thought highly of both men. Iain walked beside her as she neared her horse in the muffled morning air. Iain stopped before her mount and looked at her as if memorizing her appearance. Luveday was puzzled by his scrutiny but didn't interrupt.

"You will keep your promise?" The deep quality of his voice sent a strange pang through her, but she smiled at his reminder.

"Yes, My Lord." She looked up into his eyes. "I keep my promises." She smiled at him in reassurance. "I will stay out of trouble, and head straight home."

Iain seemed pleased that she had called Lander's Keep home.

"Will you keep your promise, My Lord?" And he laughed.

"Aye, Lady, I did not forget." In return for her quiet and quick departure, Iain promised that he too would keep out of unnecessary trouble and when all was done, head straight home. He was touched by her obvious concern for him and his men, though he would not admit how much it affected him.

He helped her mount, and she looked down at him satisfied, but could not help adding, "See that you don't."

"Fare thee well, Lady Luveday." He stepped back as men farther up the line began their journey.

"Be safe, My Lord. My heart will be here with you and your men." She moved off with the rest of the line.

Iain called out, "Sir John, you had best keep the lady safe!"

The older knight smiled, but he heard the threat just the same as he called over his shoulder. "Aye, I will, My Lord." And not a moment later the group was gone.

The journey home was miserable. The weather seemed colder than Luveday ever imagined it being. Inns and Keeps were full of travelers, most heading to or from the King. Luveday being a lady of no consequence was put wherever she could manage which was usually in the stable with a number of other "guests." That was when they had a stopping point for the night. Most of the time she slept on the ground. They had but a single wagon in the group, and it carried supplies along with a few wounded men leaving no room for her. All in all, the trip didn't take as long as Luveday feared, though they trudged through snow and mud in turns. Her mount was calm and steadfast, though Luveday regretted not taking a few short rides while at camp to keep her body used to the saddle. The first few days had been more than uncomfortable for her, but with Lander's Keep in view, she forgot everything except being home.

Cries filled the bailey as Emmalyn and Elli came running. Cassandra and Agnes appeared a few moments later as the women welcomed back one of their own. Word had reached the keep of Luveday's misadventures while on campaign, and the women were eager to see her and hear her tale for themselves.

"Are you hurt? Are you injured? Do you need anything?" Elli looked her friend over. "You look exhausted? How was it in the enemy camp? They say you saved the prince's life!" The girl rattled on.

Emmalyn laughed at her exuberance, able to now that Luveday was safely among them. "Elli girl, let us get inside. She's been traveling for days, and this cloak hardly keeps out such a chill." They ushered the group in, including Sir John. The group was smaller now than when they had begun, as men had broken off to journey on towards their own paths home. Only a few remained, and fewer still would be heading out again toward town and what lay beyond.

"Sir John, can you see to our fellow travelers? See if you can't get someone to help Sir Peter in, I'd like to see to his wounds." The man looked like his old self, the unkempt knight she had first met. The older knight had been her constant companion, and at times his usual chatty self, but it was clear that he took her safety seriously as most of the journey he was ever vigilant, constantly scanning their surroundings for trouble. Her abduction had hit him hard, and it was clear to Luveday that he felt responsible for it though she had assured him otherwise.

All were visibly relieved to make it home in one piece.

Once settled in front of the warm fire, warm spiced ale in hand, Luveday recounted her tale while Cassandra saw to the injured that had recently arrived. "And then Lord De Lane asked me to return home. The road seemed a bit longer in the cold." She smiled over the rim of her mug still savoring its lingering warmth. Luveday looked up to see that many familiar faces had joined them around the fireside. Even Lady Christabel and Adela had found chairs to listen to her tale. Luveday noted two men whose faces were vaguely familiar as they stood by the lady and remembered that they were Sumerland's men who had accompanied Christabel back to the keep. Whether they were some protection for the lady or an incentive for her to behave, Luveday couldn't guess.

Once the excitement of the moment was over, many left to return to their duties though Luveday's adventures would surely occupy the castle for several days.

Many thought the lady was spinning a yarn until several of the knights pitched in to collaborate her story. Sir John's serious recounting was enough to satisfy many of the disbelievers as none could remember the old knight being so solemn ever before.

After the tale, Sir Fuller had a new respect for the little lady and kept a watchful eye on her rival. The retired knight saw the look of hatred that briefly marred the court beauty and knew that while Christabel wanted none of Lord De Lane, she still did not like being outdone. Fuller made a note to talk to the others, best to keep an eye on Luveday lest Christabel's anger find it's mark.

Luveday had never felt so happy to see her small room. She had a proper bed, with furs and a blazer. Her items were where she had left them, though Elli said she had kept the room clean and aired for her. Sleep came quickly, and when dawn broke through the cracks of the tapestry over her shuttered window, she was well rested and eager to return to the familiar routines of Lander's Keep.

Though the weather had changed, coating the landscape in white and dulling the world, things inside the keep were much the same. Christabel stayed inside her rooms or before the fire. She took no notice of anything unless it displeased her. Many thought she might journey to the Abbey, but the weather was too cold for her delicate skin. Not even Luveday could undo her moods, and so she stopped trying. The spiteful child was the only cloud over the castle.

Emmalyn was happy to have her companion back, and Luveday shared the skills she had learned from Thomas Moore. Luveday was surprised when Emmalyn asked her to pen a new entry in the old journal but took it as the honor it was. Luveday took great care with the book and practiced what she would write until she knew the entry by heart before finally adding it to the book. The whole experience made her want to write a handbook about herbs and healing techniques much like the volume by Ody that was still in her room. She finally pulled out the volume to show Cassandra and Emmalyn who had never seen it's like and poured over the book for several days asking Luveday to read the entries to them. Many of the herbs in its pages were unknown to the women, and some resembled plants that grew in the far corners of Anora, but only a dozen or so were familiar to them.

The days moved on at a slow pace. Men arrived bringing news of De Lane's exploits on the field. Sterling had fled the battle and was being hunted down. The mercenaries had turned sides, offering up names and information for their freedom. They were escorted to the sea, and many swore never to set foot in the kingdom again so long as the line of King Edward lived. Luveday thought that was a bit overdramatic, but having seen the outcome of this war, she amended that it just might be true.

Despite the cold, Luveday accompanied Paige to visit Sir Chadric and Catherine. Catherine's health had rallied, but it was clear that the couple was struggling. The few supplies she brought were excepted graciously as Luveday surveyed their winter garden. Paige stayed behind to do the washing, but Luveday returned to the keep after a few hours, chilled to the bone in the old drafty house. Something would have to be done, or she feared the Lander's would not survive until spring.

A week had passed without news. Lander's Keep housed a number of wounded knights who had come looking for aid. With nothing more to do, talk turned to De Lane and the upcoming wedding.

Luveday found herself thinking of the night she had shared with Iain and couldn't quite stomach Christabel on those occasions. A part of her cringed at wanting another woman's future husband, but the reality of the situation was not lost to her. Both parties were being forced to wed, and Luveday tried to make her attraction to the man disappear, but the saying proved to be true, absence did make the heart grow fonder.

Thoughts of their wedding turned to contemplating Elli and Gregori as the girl seemed to be pining for the missing warrior more each day. It was as she ascended the stairs, thinking of ways to decorate the chapel for such a happy occasion that she ran into Adela. Christabel was curiously absent.

The nurse seemed surprised and yet happy to see her. "Lady Luveday."

"You may call me Luveday, if you wish, Adela." The old woman had recently asked to drop the formality with the young woman but still called her Lady.

She laughed, having forgotten herself. "Luveday, if you would be so kind." She pulled from her apron pocket a necklace made to resemble spring flowers. Luveday had always liked the piece; it suited Christabel's coloring more than her own. "I retrieved a bobble for My Lady and found this," holding up the necklace so that Luveday could see that the chain was broken and some of the flowers hung precariously from the rest. She continued, "and I have no notion of how to fix it. I know the keep has no jeweler and though the piece is only glass and metal it is one of My Lady's favorites..."

Luveday got the gist of the plea and took the item to look at it. "This has seen some rough ware." The flowers were an intricate lacework of metal accented by colored glass made to resemble more precious stones though the glass itself was something few could afford. "May I keep it and ask the other women if they have any ideas?" With Adela's approval, Luveday pocketed the necklace and went about her duties remembering throughout the day to ask many about their opinion on how to repair the precious piece.

"Aye, I think I can manage it." Barth had surprised her by admitting that he had been trying his hand a more delicate work over the years. "The link is easy enough, 'tis the fine-work that will take some time. A hard hand could cause more damage. May I keep it for a spell?"

She didn't have to think, Luveday trusted the blacksmith. "Of course, Barth. If you think you can repair it, keep it as long as it takes." She smiled openly at him and was surprised to see the man blush.

"I swear 'tis in good hands, My Lady." Luveday was reassured, but his demeanor was too serious.

Nodding, she tried to encourage him. "I know it is, Barth. Thank you."

The blacksmith only nodded and returned to his worktable near the forge. Luveday left him to contemplate on his own.

It was later that day that riders appeared proclaiming the King's victory. Sterling had fled the country lest he loose his life, his supporters were left to make a stand, but with the head cut off of the snake, their endeavor was doomed at best. Luveday stopped listening when the herald began reporting the list of gruesome deaths and punishments. The two good things she got out of the whole ordeal was that the battle was over and that De Lane would be returning home soon. The riders rested, took a meal and were on their way again before the night was over. Their task was to stop at every keep from the King's tent to town spreading the news of Sterling's defeat.

Emmalyn seemed as happy to see them go as Luveday was. Excitement was in the air as mid-winter solstice drew near and many prayed the lord of the keep would return to join in the festivities.

It was the day after that Barth sought her out to return the necklace. She made the blacksmith blush again as she complimented his work. Indeed, the piece looked as good as new. She put it in her pocket to return to Adela when she next saw her and promptly forgot about it. It was only as she emptied her pockets searching for a bobby pin that Luveday came across the necklace instead. It happened to be in the carding shed, where several women worked to turn the remnants of last year's sheering into thread.

Beatrice, who still held a grudge against the Lady was visiting a friend and one of her men at the keep happened to see the lady pull the jewelry from her apron and quickly shove it back in. Curious, and knowing exactly who the item really belonged to, the tavern wench went in search of the future lady De Lane and conveyed what she had seen with her own eyes. Beatrice was thanked for her information and couldn't help but smile at the cold and hard aspect that had settled over the lady's countenance as she went in search of her missing necklace. The tavern wench almost skipped back to the Boar's Head, laughing all the way, as she thought of what might befall the little-lost lady. Christabel was sure to put her in her place if only Beatrice could be there to see it!

Christabel watched as a small group of women left the weaving shed. It was winter, and a half-dozen women spent the short hours of daylight turning wool to thread and thread to cloth. Proper ladies were found by the fire, sewing cushions and decorating clothing, but not Luveday. No, Luveday wanted to learn how everything was made. She helped to spin and dye the wool, and for once Christabel was glad that she couldn't keep her nose out of things. As the women left Luveday alone in the shed and returned to the kitchen for a hot mid-day meal, Christabel and her two guards moved in.

The room was empty when they arrived, but the rustling and a melodic humming could be heard from the next room where the raw wool was stored. It was with a hard smile that Christabel greeted her rival because that was what Luveday had become in her eyes, everything that Christabel was not. The castle and its stupid people seemed to love the poor woman for it, while she was despised. Christabel had always felt there was something odd about the lost lady, and now she knew. Luveday was a liar and a thief, and oh how the people would hate her when they found out the truth.

"*Lady* Luveday," Christabel emphasized the word, feeling she no longer deserved such a title. "Busy I see."

Luveday was clearly surprised by her presence there and straightened from looking at a bale of wool. "Lady Christabel, what are you doing out here? Have you come to check on the dye colors for the new tapestry? Henna assures me, we will get dozens of shades this season thanks to Tinker Thom's timely arrival." She chatted happily, not really taking note of the men slowly circling behind her.

Christabel sniffed at the odor of unwashed animal the clung to the shed; the wood structure reeked of it. The room was full of bundles of wool stuck in nooks and crannies to keep it dry even as a few rays of light peeked through holes in the roof. Luveday moved to the center of the floor but kept the post that held up the arched roof between them. "I am not here to talk about wool, girl." The widening of her prey's eyes was very satisfying, and so Christabel moved closer. "I'm here to speak of another matter. I will give you a chance, only one chance," she held up a slim finger, "to redeem yourself."

Luveday's look of wide-eyed innocence was very convincing as she protested. "I don't know what you mean. Redeem myself how? What have I done?"

Christabel wouldn't let herself be fooled by this woman again. "This is your only chance, Luveday. Confess, and I will see that they are lenient with you. It will be much kinder this way."

"Christabel, I don't know what you mean." Luveday's informality grated on her nerves, and she ground her teeth. If it were any other woman, she would probably have slapped her by now, but this game wasn't over yet. She still had to retrieve the necklace.

Sir Peter and Sir James were now behind her foe, and she gave the signal. One man grabbed each arm and held her still while Luveday protested and struggled. "Let me go. I don't understand. What are you doing? I've done nothing wrong."

Christabel reached into her apron pocket and was rewarded. She pulled the necklace free, examining it closely, only to sigh a moment later. It was undamaged by Luveday's grubby hands. The necklace dangled from her finger in front of Luveday's face which was a mix of emotions. Confusion furrowed her brow, and Christabel's anger piqued.

"And what is this, pray tell? Helping yourself to my jewelry, Luveday?" She laughed. "Of all the things you could have taken, you chose a bobble worth nothing at all." That pathetic look was still on her face and Christabel couldn't help herself. She backhanded the woman across the face. There were no tears or screaming, only a shocked pain that lent a shimmer to the other woman's eyes. "You will find out what it means to steal from the House of Sumerland." She looked to Sir Peter who had a sparkle in his dark eyes, that was brighter than his usual admiration for her. She had been perplexed when her father had ordered men to stay and keep watch over her, but Sir Peter was perhaps, the best she could have hoped for. The man had a fascination with her, and it took little for him to do her bidding. Sir James looked troubled, but he was too young and too eager to prove himself, he would follow Peter's orders, or her father would hear about his disobedience.

"Get to it, good sirs." And she left the shed, happy to have fresh air in her lungs, as she put the necklace on. *Foolish, girl*, she thought, *if you have taken any other piece, I might have been able to forgive you, but never this.* She stroked along the edge of the delicate flowers. *Never this.* Christabel's hatred burned hot and would only be cooled once Luveday was punished properly. The smile that curved her lips was beguiling and utterly cold.

Luveday fought and tried to call out, but her efforts were quelled by a fist connecting with her stomach. Using their names seemed to only make one of the knight's madder. Sir Peter and Sir James, Sumerland's men. She had wondered if it was a miscalculation on the Lord's part, to let two men so devoted to Christabel be her guards. It was clear that Peter was obsessed with his lady. Luveday had kept a watch on him, fearful for the girl, what a fool she had been.

All the air left her chest in an involuntary gasp. Pain radiated through her so quickly that she couldn't even speak. Her statements of innocence fell on deaf ears as she was bound to the beam in the center of the room. Her two attackers exchanged words, but Luveday was still reeling from the pain they were inflicting and trying to figure a way out of this. She continued to struggle as she tried to catch her breath, but another blow nearly sent her to her knees, if not for the belt that bound her hands high on the support beam she would not have continued to stand. Her shoulder caught the beam as she tried to rise back to her feet and that was when she heard the ripping and felt cold air touch the skin of her back. Pain and panic raced through her as she fought her own mind and body to stay focused and be ready for any chance of escape.

It was only a moment later that the larger man's laughter and words registered in her mind. The young one seemed to have doubts, but the other knight's tone sent another wave of nausea rolling over her. "The lash is the only thing good enough to deal with a thief."

She shook her head, but the first stroke fell. Luveday found her footing and tried to wrestle her hands-free. She opened her mouth to scream in frustration and defiance, but hands clamped around her neck like a vice. Blackness formed at the edges of her vision and stars twinkled in the dim light that penetrated the room. The hands left her, but what was happening to her was strangely distant. Luveday realized she was close to blacking out, had been for some time because the pain in her back seemed far away though she knew Sir Peter had landed several more blows, but how many she couldn't remember.

Though Luveday fought to keep conscious she didn't know how much more she could take and realized that while she couldn't speak or scream, a river of tears poured from her eyes. She refused to beg, she knew it would not help and tried to hold on to herself fearing what they might do to her when she was unaware.

Harsh voices spun around her and then silence. On the wind was a ringing tone that filled her with hope. It was her name; someone was looking for her. Sir James suddenly appeared before her and loosened the belt on her bound wrists; she was bruised and bleeding there. His eyes were full of sorrow and compassion even as he fought off Peter nearly knocking the man out. "You can't do this to a lady. I won't let you." Luveday was suddenly free and sank to the straw-lined floor. Overhead she watched a blurry scene unfold as she drifted towards unconsciousness.

Peter's furious retort was slurred as blood filled his mouth. "She's no lady, 'tis better than she deserves."

"You've gone too far, Sir Peter. Ten lashes are all a woman would receive, and you've given her many times that over." The older knight lunged for his subordinate, but the boy was fast and had more spunk than she would ever have imagined. James landed a heavy blow, but both of them stalled when voices drew closer. Suddenly, something seemed to come over the two. They glanced down at her prostrate form and decided it was time to flee. Luveday heard rather than saw them go, and as familiar voices called her name, she finally lost the battle giving oblivion the field.

Screams filled the kitchen and the hall. Emmalyn ran in search of the cause, troubled that she could not find Luveday at all. As she entered the kitchen women gave way as Sir Fuller and Agnes tried to stop their lady from coming any closer. On one of the large tables was something covered in rough cloth. The form moved slightly, and a pale hand came into view. Ellie who was only a few paces behind her lady had frozen at the sight. The wail that left the girl pierced through the heart of the castle. Emmalyn was galvanized into motion. She pulled back the cloth, trying desperately to find the calm that often engulfed her as a healer, but the bruised and bloody mess that was once her beloved friend's back sent her to her knees.

Fuller caught his lady, supporting her as she looked around. Through the tears and quiet sobbing, she demanded that they take Luveday upstairs. "Get her out of here."

Mistress Adela was exiting her lady's room when she heard unfamiliar sounds erupt through the hall. Looking up, she spotted Christabel coming toward her and noted the almost serene expression on her lady's face. She was caught off guard for a moment, and instead of asking what commotions were taking place below, Adela noticed the repaired necklace that hung around Christabel's neck. Relief swept through the old woman. Luveday had found a way to repair it, and the old nurse owed the lady a great deal for only Adela knew who had given her lady the bobble and why the girl treasured it so dearly. "I see Luveday has given you back the necklace, we must thank her somehow."

Right away, the Mistress knew something was wrong.

Christabel looked at her with a cold gleam in her eyes, something she had not seen aimed at herself in many months. "Why would Luveday have my necklace?"

Adela tried to ignore the lump that formed in the pit of her stomach. "I gave it to her, My Lady. Remember the other day, it got snagged on your dress. It must have broken when you took it off, for when I went to put your ruby comb away, it lay broken in your chest." The old woman watched as a strange expression seemed to wash over the girl's face, as she continued speaking. "I gave the bobble to Lady Luveday thinking she would know some way to fix it. Did she not return it to you?"

A pale hand fluttered to settled over Christabel's stomach. The other was flown wide to brace herself against the wall, but despite the pose of distress, the lady's face remained as smooth as if it were carved from stone.

Voices cried out from below. The sound of many feet running toward the chaos echoed up the stairs. Adela grabbed her mistress in a vice-like grip, whispering harshly, "what have you done, child?"

Christabel grimaced, and Adela rushed them into their room before anyone else could take note.

Luveday floated for a while just beyond the pain, but close enough to the surface that she could occasionally hear the voices that comforted her. She knew that she was safe and that she would not be able to stay in this in-between state for much longer, though she thought that she had not been there very long at all.

Everything hurt. Her head, her skin, her muscles and her bones. Her face and her back throbbed though something had dulled the ache in areas; it was not enough to take the pain away altogether. It took herculean effort to move anything, including her eyelids which felt like lead weights, but she finally managed it.

The first thing that met her eyes was Emmalyn, leaning over her and talking quietly to someone beyond Luveday's line of sight. It took her foggy mind a moment to realize that the room was full, which wasn't hard considering the cramped nature of her chamber. People peered down at her with intent faces, many marred by tears and concern. Hands arrested her movement as she tried to continue rolling onto her back and getting a better look at the room and its occupants. It didn't take her body more than a heartbeat to decide that such an idea was not a good one. Nerve ending shot fire down her spine. She gasped and returned to her stomach, noting the warm sensation on her cheek as her face groaned into the pillow.

Luveday realized that Emmalyn was talking to her, not just talking but was repeating, with infinite patience the same question she had been asking for several minutes.

"What happened, Luveday?"

For an instant, Luveday didn't know. She couldn't remember why she felt this way, but as she turned to the elder lady a face came to her like a ghost out of her memory, and everything rushed at her. Her breath caught in her lungs at the remembered pain echoed in her current state. She felt the heavy hand again and failed to speak. Emmalyn gently moved a hand behind her head and raised Luveday almost to a sitting position, yet slightly more awkward, as she was on her hip as they tried to protect her healing back.

In a voice barely above a whisper, Luveday recounted what she could. Emmalyn blinked back tears as she related the story to those in the room. Only a few people were allowed in the small chamber, but many made periodic trips to stand outside her door to wait, watch and listen.

Emmalyn quietly told the girl what they had pieced together for themselves over the two days that Luveday had drifted in and out of wakefulness since they found her in the wool shed.

"Henna and Paige found you on the floor of the shed. Henna ran to the kitchens, where Sir Fuller and Agnes helped to carry you back inside." Emmalyn swallowed past the lump in her throat and gratefully accepted the cup of water that was given to her. Taking a sip, she helped Luveday drink before continuing her tale, he eyes moving away from the finger-shaped bruises that marred her neck. "Henna remembered seeing two men hurry away from the shed. She remembered them as Sumerland's men, though the girls have not had much to do around the two." She glanced at Sir Fuller who rested just inside the open door, frowning as he continued to growl under his breath. "It was only after we had brought you upstairs that anyone thought of finding..." Ellie burst into the room and squeezed her way up to rest behind Emmalyn who paused until the girl was settled. "Sir John and Fuller went after them, but they snuck away before nightfall."

Cassandra continued when her friend could not. "Mistress Adela has kept Lady Christabel in her rooms, but the castle knows who was at fault here. That woman will pay." The ice in her tone was mirrored by everyone in the room.

Emmalyn nodded in agreement, and Luveday momentarily wondered why she couldn't drum up enough energy to protest. Deep down she knew that they would not hurt the girl, but Luveday knew all too well how miserable they could make the pampered courtesan.

Several days passed in a haze of pain and foul-smelling ointments. Luveday was grateful for her mentor's skill, and no one seemed to grow weary of the constant need to renew the medicines. No one spoke of how badly she was injured, only to say that it was bad and turn pale. Under the concern was a smidge of pity and Luveday knew, without asking, that she would bare lasting scars.

By the time the messenger arrived Luveday was recovered enough that she could sit propped up in bed, though still careful to avoid any contact with her back. The bruise on her face had been treated as well and was now a slight purple discoloration under her left eye. In the potted mercury glass of Emmalyn's mirror, it looked as if she had had a few restless nights and not been backhanded in the face.

Apprehension and a dark expectation settled over the castle as they awaited the lord's imminent return. No one stopped Lady Christabel and Adela as they took only what they could carry on their horses and fled for the Abbey. Even the women had no illusions that this was an escape. Iain would come for them, it was only a matter of time, but Adela knew it was only holding off the inevitable for a little while. Her lady had done something unforgivable in her spite.

The castle prepared, knowing that De Lane and his men had fought long and hard in the King's service. His people wanted to give their Lord all that he deserved on his triumphant return, though what had transpired within the keep did a good deal to dim their enthusiasm.

Emmalyn had dreaded Iain's return, yet wanted the foolish Christabel to feel what she had done to a sweet and innocent lady. Cold, burnt meals and unwashed clothes were not enough in anyone's estimation as Christabel hid in the sanctuary of her rooms. She was glad that they had fled, Emmalyn could not think of a way to tell her nephew what had happened without the full force of his rage being directed at the girl. It was clear to many that Iain had no feeling for the girl but was bound by his oaths and the King's decree and unfortunately, it would take something more than this to void such an agreement.

When the time came, Emmalyn waited in the solar rather than meet him in the bailey. There was no way that her nephew could look at her and not know that something was terribly wrong, and she wanted privacy for what she had to tell the boy.

For the first time in several days, Luveday's room was clear of people, all except Henna who was charged with looking after her. The commotion of the castle suddenly kicked up as echoes traveled up the stairs and in through the open door. It was no surprise that she was left here. Emmalyn had confided her fears, not knowing how Iain would react to this dreadful news but knowing that it would go badly and very badly for the lady responsible.

Luveday had finally found some of her compassion, but only after Adela had snuck in to whisper her deepest apologies. Christabel had stood at the door for only an instant, long enough to see the mess that was Luveday's back and gasp in horror before returning to her room. Luveday didn't understand what the girl had been thinking, but she knew that it was Sir Peter who held the real blame and not a spiteful girl.

Iain's deep laugh echoed down the hall as he carried his belongings to his room, not knowing what was ahead.

Luveday struggled to her feet as pain radiated through her. Her back felt as if it were made of leather, there was no give to muscle and sinew that had once been supple and able to bend. Henna gasped in horror, protesting, but eventually helped the lady dressed in a simple gown. "Luveday what are you thinking? Emmalyn said you should stay in bed a few more days. Lady, you are going to tear open wounds that have only just healed."

The room rocked a moment until Luveday could steady herself. She knew Henna was right, but she also knew without a shadow of a doubt that she needed to be in the solar at that moment.

Henna steadied her by holding her elbow as she made the short journey to the solar door. She didn't know that traversing a dozen or so feet, could be so hard, but she locked her jaw and refused to show just how much pain she was in. Reminding herself how bad it had been that first few days helped. Knowing she could survive that made the pain she was in now a little easier to bear.

Somehow, she made it into the solar and stood before Iain. A sense of calm came over her as a weight was lifted that she hadn't realized she bore. With him here she felt safe and hadn't known until that moment how badly her own peace of mind had been broken. Pale and shaken, yet now better able to stand there, Luveday smiled for the first time in days, a true smile that was more than a half-hearted attempt to reassure her friends. It was a smile with more emotion than she could imagine and one that shocked Emmalyn and Agnes into silence and their injured friend moved closer to their lord who had yet to fully grasp the situation.

Iain was bone weary and happy to be home. He had taken the ribbing from his men that he was getting soft, but it had been nearly two months since he had slept in a proper bed and had a good meal at a proper table. He was eager to get home, and if he admitted it to himself, eager to see his people and his family. Especially one stubborn woman who had never been far from his thoughts since they last parted.

People met them in the bailey, but Iain spared only a thought that it was odd that Emmalyn and Luveday were not there to greet him. He assumed they were busy, no doubt preparing something for him, and his men and the thought warmed his heart against the winter chill.

Inside the men rumbled and laughed as they walked like old men, stiff from too many hours in the saddle, but none had complained when they pushed through rather than stopping to rest. Home and comfort awaited.

Coll ran amuck, happy to be reunited with his friend, Gus. The boy didn't know if he was coming or going, so Iain carried his own bags up to the solar. The subdued greetings and expectant looks didn't really register to his tired mind, though something nagged at him as he was told that his aunt awaited him in the solar. He hoped that Luveday and a hot bath awaited him, and he quickened his steps.

No bath and no Luveday. He banked the sudden disappointment and only half noticed the look on his aunt's face. He busied himself with unpacking a few things, trying to contain the growing sense of dread that was building. He had seen that look before. It was the day that news had finally arrived, and his elder brother was dead.

He turned around sharply at her stuttering words. She couldn't seem to say whatever it was she needed to say, and that was so unlike the elegant and dignified woman that panic raced through him.

The door opened, and Iain thought he might pass out from the lightheaded relief that he felt. Luveday stood just inside the door and smiled at him. It was a peculiar smile, but he felt it from the top of his head to the soles of his feet. He turned away, pulling the small gifts from his satchel as he took a moment to find his bearings.

Emmalyn gasp as she stared at her friend, but Iain had eyes only for Luveday, noticing that she looked a little pale in the dim winter light pouring through the open window.

He found himself talking, suddenly unable to deal with whatever his aunt was about to say, he focused on delivering the items he was charged with and wished, not for the first time, that he had something more to give her. "Lady Luveday. Good morrow." She smiled a bit wider at his happy tone. "I come bearing gifts from your great admirers." He was only half joking, and only willing to deliver the tokens since the men that gave them to him were happily married or very soon to be. A true admirer would have no doubt found his fist to be the definitive answer to such a request. "John, Duke of Orland, Thomas Morris, the Earl of Pembroke, Lord James Frasier, Lord Henry Blackthorn, Lord Grayson Stern, Sir Marcus Drake and Sir Lionel Wick send their most esteemed thanks and these tokens of gratitude to the fair Lady Luveday, healer and fairest champion of King Edward the third, of Anora." Iain bowed with a flourish and offered the lady a satchel solely dedicated to the bits and bobbles he'd carried for her.

Emmalyn gasp again as a hand flew over her mouth. Luveday approached slowly, and Iain saw how tired she looked, but the happiness that lit up her face was beyond beautiful. The lady sighed but didn't take the bag from him. "They made it then. All the men recovered, even Frasier." In true Luveday fashion, she was pleased by the news of their recovery and the bag was forgotten.

Luveday swayed a bit on her feet, but Iain thought it was only a physical reaction to her own relief. He only had a moment to glance over her golden head and see that Agnes, Sir Fuller, and Sir Gregori stood crowded in the doorway before he moved. Their concerned expressions didn't penetrate his happy bubble until it was too late. He couldn't remember the happy words that tumbled from his lips as he grabbed her too him in a fierce hug, but he would never forget the scream that rent the air and tore through him as she collapsed in his arms.

While his aunt gave out orders, Iain moved the lady to his bed. "No don't lay her on her back, boy. Roll her over." She looked to Agnes. "We'll have to cut the gown off her."

Henna came in with Ellie and Benedict as the room suddenly filled with people. "I didn't tie it up proper, we should be able to remove it without cutting this one. I wouldn't want her to lose another gown."

They were able to get the garments off quickly and without causing her too much harm.

Iain and the men hovered nearby asking periodic questions that were ignored for the most part. All the focus was on Luveday. When Cassandra arrived, panic filled the men's eyes. Everyone moved out of Cass's way, even Emmalyn who was an ashen color. Iain followed in her wake and his men with him. What they saw he couldn't fathom.

Cassandra removed the linen from around Luveday's hips and the wrap from her shoulders that held the main bandage in place. The material conformed to her skin thanks to the ointments and pastes that were healing her. Removing the last piece of material, the damage was clear. Though only a few days had passed the lacerations and welts were closing. Her small back was severely bruised, and blood leaked from the high ridges where the whip had laid open her skin.

Iain turned white as a ghost as his stomach lurched. Benedict turned away to lose the contents of his stomach in the empty piss pot. Gregori swore a stream that should have been unfamiliar to a monk, before praying for her quick recovery.

In a voice no one had ever heard from their lord, Iain turned to Emmalyn and Sir Fuller. "Tell me who did this."

Warmth cocooned her in a happy bubble as she floated along. Someone gently brushed a strand of hair off her forehead and behind her ear. She would have done it herself, but it took too much effort, and she had no wish to endanger this fragile place she was in. Voices carried from far away as the warmth suddenly left, her back exposed. The calming voice above her turned deep and harsh as it swore a blue streak not fit for a lady's ears. It was the mix of banked fury and unspeakable pain that made Luveday force her mind away from the tranquilizing fog of the painkiller Cassandra had given her to seek out the cause of Iain's distress.

Opening her eyes had become easier, Luveday noted the fact and wondered if she was becoming immune to the opiate-like concoction or if Cassandra was diluting the doses. It crossed her mind that the later was a good idea. Luveday had no wish to become addicted to the stuff and coming off a drug that powerful was not going to be a pleasant experience. Thinking a moment, she didn't feel addicted, she felt like she was able to think a little clearer than she had been for a while.

"Easy lass." Cassandra's soft voice issued from somewhere above her. Luveday was getting tired of always laying on her stomach. The position made it hard to do anything, especially see and participate in what was going on around her. A hand came to rest on her shoulder, and she settled back into the bed. Cass was changing the dressings again, ready to see what damage her foolishness had caused.

Luveday belatedly realized that she was not back in her little cell of a room but resting comfortably in the warmth of the lord's bed and momentarily panicked. She didn't want to be nearly naked in Iain's bed, but then again, it wasn't as if she had gotten here willingly. She realized Iain must have put her there and was calmed by the fact that he could move her at any time.

The door closed, and the women were left in silence as they cared for her back. Emmalyn commented that Sir Templeton had returned from the abbey. It was confirmed that her two male assailants had fled to town.

Sometime later as she drifted on the remains of the pain killer, Iain appeared at her side. She had enough strength to turn towards him. It was enough to look at each other for a while. Iain's thumb brushed her cheek as the hard line of his mouth turned down at the corners. It was clear that he knew the discoloration was a bruise and not there from lack of sleep. There was a stillness about him that was not usually present, and it took Luveday a moment to realize that he was keeping himself in check with a tremendous amount of control. Luveday hesitated to think of what he would do to Christabel's men when he found them. She remembered the rage that had consumed him when she was attacked in the healing tent. Something told her that what she was sensing now was a more powerful emotion.

"Go easy on her," Luveday whispered.

The gentle stroking of her hand stopped. "I beg your pardon?" He seemed to choke over the words.

"Lady Christabel." He growled at the name. "You must go easy on her."

He swore under his breath, but there was little room between them to hide his slip. "Luveday." Her name was spoken like a plea, full of exasperation and retribution.

Luveday realized what she asked of him, but the lady didn't deserve the full force of his anger, and since the guards had vanished, the girl was the only available outlet for Iain's wrath. "She didn't hurt me, Iain. She wasn't even there..."

"No, Luveday. She does not deserve your mercy." He whispered harshly, and she quieted, looking him steadily in the eye. He sighed, wary. "I will not harm the lady." He admitted begrudgingly. The corners of her mouth turned up; it was all the smile she could muster.

Her hand unerringly found his, to lay atop it in gratitude. "Thank you." More worried for him, than by what he would do to his betrothed. Luveday knew he was a good man, but anger could cloud good judgment, and Iain's anger was a storm that raged below his skin. She feared that the one to be hurt would be him.

His hand moved to hold her own, squeezing it gently. "Do not thank me, Luveday." He looked at her. "I am not a man who would beat a woman, but have no doubt, Christabel will have to answer for her actions."

Someone knocked on the door and stuck their head inside. Iain rose clearly tired and left to have a conversation beyond her hearing. Luveday moved back into a comfortable position, she could hear someone on the other side of the room. The hummed tune was a favorite of Henna's, and with that small mystery solved, her thoughts turned inward. How quickly so many things had changed, she thought as she pondered how these events would influence the ones to come.

Chapter 12

The devil's most devilish when respectable.
~ Elizabeth Barrett Browning

Luveday recovered remarkably well, she bore a few small scars on her back and carried a few more that couldn't be seen and would take much longer to heal.

Luveday spent two nights in the solar, in Iain's bed accompanied by one of the ladies. The lord slept on a pallet before the raised hearth. He came and went throughout the day, never gone for more than a few hours. The stories of what had transpired since they last met were humorous tales of camp life, and routing Sterling's men. Luveday was happy that he came to entertain her but worried about their growing closeness. By the time she was able to sit up and walk assisted down the stairs, Christabel had been brought back from the abbey.

Christabel returned a subdued and quiet young lady. Luveday made no fuss and tried her best to treat the girl politely. The castle was cold toward the court lady, though they followed Luveday's example and treated her with a polite detachment. Mistress Adela was accepted back into the fold, but even she knew to tread warily, for many knew that Lord Iain's mercy had its limits.

Winter wore on, but the women kept busy. Luveday and Emmalyn planned and began work on a tapestry though the design was kept from everyone as a surprise. Word came that the King had returned to town signaling the end of his campaigns for the season. Iain and his men could not be happier for the rest, though that did not stop them from traveling for the Keep's business. As the long winter days continued, thoughts of spring and the wedding grew in everyone's mind. Many hoped that some divine intervention would stop the lord's nuptials, but if the events to date had not sent the lady packing, then they feared nothing would. The current situation between bride and groom was sharply contrasted by the growing relationship between the favored couple of the castle. Ellie and Gregori spend a lot of their time next to one another. The couple's growing affection affected all who saw them with a warm feeling towards the lovebirds.

"It won't be long now," Emmalyn said as they sat before the loom in the sewing room. Candlelight danced in the dark space, making the gray winter day bright.

"Yes, not long." Henna laughed to herself as she continued altering the outdated gowns that had once belonged to Iain's mother. The girl moped around the castle whenever some duty took the knight away from her. The last two days had been horrible for little Ellie as Iain and several men, including Sir Gregori were called to a nearby village to settle some disputes.

Luveday had been spending a good deal of her free time thinking of ways to decorate the hall and chapel for the event. The approach of spring heralded Iain's wedding, and though Christabel was all but ostracized from the castle, the wedding plans remained. Every time the thought crossed Luveday's mind her stomach would roll uncomfortably, so she tried not to think about it at all.

A scramble was heard at the door as heavy footsteps came racing down the hall. Sir Fuller bust through the door, the women scrambled to cover the loom, not wanting anyone to ruin the surprise, but Luveday saw only the look in the old knight's eyes and went running. Fuller had only enough breath to utter one word, and with such a desperate gasp that everyone, but Luveday was frozen to the spot. "Iain."

Benedict trailed behind the group that carried their lord to his bed. He rested against the outer door of the solar and glanced at Luveday with a pale and glassy-eyed expression. Luveday felt it like a physical blow. She called for someone to fetch the healing kit and gathered what courage she had to enter his room. Coll set on his window seat, looking lost. She stopped to place a comforting hand on the boy's shoulder, but he barely looked up. Men argued and swore in hushed tones which scared her more than if they had been yelling. The quiet meant that whatever has befallen Iain was serious.

They parted like the red sea as Luveday entered the room. Someone lifted a candelabra so that she could look her patient over in the waning winter light. His bronzed complexion was pale, with beads of sweat peppering his forehead. His collar was soaked with perspiration and their attempts to cool the fever that raged within him.

There was a single wound in his side, a cloth matted with blood had been pressed into a tight ball and still held its shape as the liquid dried, molding it into place. She didn't look up as a bowl of hot water appeared at her elbow. She asked the room only one question as she began using the water to release the dirty cloth from the wound. "What happened?"

Gregori's voice issued from over her left shoulder, and she belatedly realized that he was the one holding the light for her. "We were on our way home when we met up with Benedict and his men. A few miles into the woods west of Hough it went quiet. We were on our guard, and Iain gave the word to keep an eye out. In the next moment arrows were flying, we kicked the horses and moved out of their range, but Iain was hurt. It pierced his armor, a wicked looking black arrow. Larger and heavier than anything I've seen. I have it still."

"You took the arrow out?" Luveday slowly peeled away the matted material before picking up a knife to cut away at the ruined tunic.

Benedict stepped forward, his voice hard with frustration. "There was no choice, lady. There was still a day's travel and nowhere to go for aid. Iain said he was well and told us to press on. We bedded down for the night, but no one knew how badly he was hurt until the next morning when he didn't wake up. We cared for him as best we could." The lady's brow furrowed more as his tale continued.

"How long since he was wounded?" The cloth had come clear of the wound. An unpleasant smell emanated from the hole in his side. Luveday swallowed hard and looked to Gregori as the knight choked and turned away.

"A day and a half, maybe a few hours more." Benedict continued to answer questions as no one else seemed inclined to. "We gave him something for the pain, some potion Warin had on him." That was some good news at least. Anything Warin carried with him was brewed by Cassandra, and she had no doubt that the man-at-arms knew how to use it. "Luveday?" Benedict's plea held a wealth of unspoken questions. Luveday wondered how their positions were now reversed; Iain was on death's door and Benedict looking on worried and as helpless as Iain had once been months ago.

Luveday considered her course of action. The wound was infected and would need to be cleaned and sterilized. If nothing serious was punctured, then there was hope for a full recovery, but if something in the chest or bowels has torn, then an agonizing death was inevitable. Breathing deep, she focused passed the turning emotions and turned to the room at large. "You did the best with what you had." She tried to reassure him, knowing that only Iain's recovery would truly do so. "Let us get to work. The sooner we begin, the better chances he has. I cannot make promises, I will not, but I will tell you that he is strong, stubborn and in far better hands than mine." Gregori and many others sent prayers heavenward. "We have knowledge and skill, but what is that in this life? All I know is that I will fight for him, I will pray for him, and I know you will do the same." Luveday caught sight of Emmalyn as she hovered in the doorway, unable to take a step farther. Once again, her mentor looked haunted, and well past her years. Luveday could make no promises but hoped her eyes conveyed the depth of her determination to do all she could for Iain. The Lady nodded as if she understood, even as unshed tears made her turn away for a moment.

There was a resolute gleam in their eyes as the men nodded in turn. Some seemed encouraged by her words, which was all the comfort she could give them at the moment. Cassandra had joined the ranks, and the two women got to work. "Hold him down." Luveday projected a steady facade, not letting one ounce of the turmoil inside cloud her logic. Cassandra directed the men on where and how to hold their lord, her brisk tone brooked no disobedience. Iain had remained unnaturally silent through their inspection, but the pain of cleaning his wound would reach him even in his unconscious state. Fuller, Benedict, Gregori, and Warin each took hold of a limb and leaned into the mattress. More men stood by to assist, knowing the unpredictable strength of a delirious knight. Every move was brisk and efficient as Luveday tied the scented handkerchief at the back of her head hoping the style would work to keep the stench of putrid flesh away.

Cassandra handed her a sterilized blade; she'd run the clean instrument through the flame of a candle a few times before she met the young lady's eyes. The silent question that passed between them was little more than a look, but anyone could see that Luveday was determined and the older healer was relieved to have this task taken from her.

Luveday began using a clean cloth to remove the dried blood and debris from the outside of the laceration. The wound was in the abdomen on his right side. To her eyes, the hole looked large and deep, but she chastised herself, remembering that she had seen much worse not too long ago. Pus and blood oozed from the hole as she pressed down trying to gauge the extent of the damage. She washed her hands in water that was almost too hot to stand before digging past the skin. More gore flowed to be mopped up by hastily placed linens. While the wound bled, the stream was not increasing, the arrow seemed to have been halted by Iain's armor and pierced into his heavy abdominal muscles but not punctured his bowels. It was a great blessing. Still, something was not right.

A large bowl of steaming water and herbs was handed to Cassandra who held the vessel while Luveday took a small cup and transferred the water onto the wound. A milder version of the lye soap that was common here was used to help remove any impurities. As the two women conferred on their next course of action, a man appeared at the door. His boisterous voice was followed by a crowd of newcomers. "Step back, women." The room fell silent at the venomous command. "Back I said."

Familiar faces stormed through the door until the room was overly full. Lady Christabel was followed by her father, Lord Sumerland who was escorted by none other than the Mother Superior, Mary Odilia and a handful of other people that Luveday felt were somehow familiar to her and yet she couldn't place them. The man, who has so rudely interrupted them, stormed forward pushing Cass and Luveday out of the way, causing hot water to spill over each of them. Cassandra sputtered her fury, as the old man looked as if he had traveled hard for several days. The journey had not agreed with his rotund physique. He started bellowing orders, but no one moved. "Did you not hear me, girl?" He yelled at the young lady, with clear exasperation he looked to Lord Sumerland and the Mother Superior.

"Do as the Physician says, woman!" Lord Sumerland looked down on Luveday with all the disdain she remembered. Several men looked as if they would move on the Lord at the insult to one of their own. The healing women and most of Iain's men were soon ushered out of the room. Luveday looked around the great hall as if she couldn't quite figure out how she had gotten there. She soon found herself beside Lady Emmalyn as another bowl of water was brought for them to clean their hands. Emmalyn spoke soothing words to Cassandra and eyed the silent Luveday warily, as the other healer cursed the arrogance of court healers.

Above stairs, Gregori, Fuller, Benedict, and Warin held their ground, not leaving their master and brother in arms to this man, no matter who accompanied him. Lord Sumerland took one look at the men and left the room under the pretext of checking on the state of the castle. No one paid his departure any mind, nor that of his daughter as her pale face fled through the open door.

Mother Superior drew close to the physician. "How does he fare, Master Pope?"

"He's lucky those women didn't kill him. The sick room is no place for their superstition and incantations." He grunted and wiped some gore off on to his dirty cloak before using his hands to probe the wound. "An arrow?" He looked at the men, as Warin nodded. "The damage isn't too bad, his armor held. Leather or mail?" He asked.

It was Gregori's deep calm that answered with time. "Both, a leather vest over a mail shirt."

"Good, Good." He said as if too himself. "The arrow would have punctured the bowels otherwise." Pope poked some more before producing a bag from the folds of his cloak. He pulled forth a small tied satchel of herbs and began stuffing the wound. "We'll see how he fares in a few hours, once the herbs had done their work."

The good Mother, escorted Master Pope from the room, but the men heard her words clearly. "It's truly a blessing that you would come to us at our hour of need Master Pope. Lord De Lane could not have asked for better than your capable hands."

No one saw the looks of worry and dread that passed between the four knights as they wondered what sort of blessing the woman spoke of. More importantly, they asked themselves, a blessing for whom?

Master Pope barely made it up the stairs a few hours later. He had spent the last hour before the fire drinking the lord's best wine and recounting his heroic deeds as a healer to the King. Emmalyn kept an eye on Mary Odilia and Lord Sumerland as Luveday stayed clear of the hall and kept busy preparing lodgings for their unexpected guests. While laughter rang through the hall, only the newcomers made marry as most of the castle's occupants were focused on the Lord of Lander's Keep.

By nightfall, the wind howled, and Iain had taken a turn for the worst. Luveday and the women were kept from the room as Master Pope employed darker measures to save De Lane's life. By the next night, a blanket of despair had settled over the keep as everyone prepared for the worst. Sumerland and his men prepared to depart, Christabel begged to be taken with them, but her father refused, still holding to the betrothal until the Champion was dead and buried. Luveday could not muster any emotion at the sight of the young woman pleading and crying to be gone from them. Her father's harsh words fell on deft ears, but many in the castle would never forget the tone and look of fury as he dragged Christabel to her feet. Spit flew into her face, but the girl was too distraught to care. "A woman's place is by her betrothed's side." Sumerland's hold on her arm looked as if it might snap the limb in two. "You will not dishonor my house by fleeing now. You will do your duty to De Lane. Stay here and bury the man, for you will not return to my house until he has breathed his last. Now go, you foolish girl." He threw her away from him as the group turned to leave the hall. Christabel would have landed on the hard, stone floor if Mistress Adela had not rushed to catch her charge.

Mother Superior left not long after her companions, Luveday thought that Lady Emmalyn looked as if she fought the urge to do the woman bodily harm. Two nuns, a few of Sumerland's 'most trusted' men, and two latecomers, another pair of physicians, where all that was left of their uninvited guests. More than one person wished the departing horde good riddance.

Shouts were heard echoing down from the solar. Luveday took a deep breath as the two aged physicians who had arrived a day later than Pope came rushing down the stairs. Word had traveled that the King's Champion was seriously injured, over the last few days they had turned away any number of healers and crackpots that had come to care for the Lord. They were lucky Luveday was generous and let them take a meal before not so subtlety being told to leave and tell their fellow swindlers to stay clear of Lander's Keep. Whether it was Lord Benedict or Sir Gregori who delivered the warning, the threat was like a flame that burned behind their eyes. If not for the lady's presence, Luveday was sure that the healers would have lost more than the promise of good coin.

Pope stood at the top of the stairs shouting obscenities. "Damn you to hell and back, you tottering old fools. Scullions! You practitioners of fallacy, of midnight superstations. Begone!" He wobbled, and a belch echoed through the hall as both men, belongings in tow fled the hall. "Begone!"

Luveday watched as Gregori headed up the stairs a dark look in his eyes. In the light of Iain's doorway stood one of Sumerland's men. The women watched as Pope swayed, turning back to the solar too quickly for his inebriated body to handle and completely unaware of the danger that followed him.

A hand gripped Luveday's elbow like a vice. She turned to find Emmalyn at her side, and the look in her eyes spoke of fear and something that mirrored the darkness she had seen growing in the knights. A thread of unease snaked through Luveday breaking through the numbness that had surrounded her for days. Without thought, she followed Gregori up the stairs and into the solar.

Two men flanked the bed, swords drawn and poised on the tips of their toes. Gregori stood before her, his massive build in a similar fighting stance, sword drawn as a dark growl left him. No words were exchanged as the men eyed each other ready to do violence and yet hesitant to be the first to strike. Maybe they knew Gregori's reputation and were smart enough not to start this fight. Luveday stood in the small outer room where Coll made his bed. The boy stood before her at the edge of the door half in shadows peeking around the doorframe with wide eyes. He watched Gregori's back with intensity as if he might detect the subtle shift of muscle that would precede the attack.

Luveday's small frame suddenly quaked with fury. The void that had grown inside her swallowing emotions as if someone had taken a spoon and scooped out her insides, her very heart, was suddenly full of fire and ice. She stepped through the arched doorway to push Gregori in the back. It was only then that she noticed the man on the other side of the bed was flanked by Benedict who had taken over Iain's bedside watch hours ago. Two on two, the thought was ludicrous, and Luveday had had enough. Master Pope stuttered as Gregori swirled to take her in. Somehow, he must have known the presence at his back was no real threat because he didn't turn his sword on her, merely shifted his position to cover her as well.

"What is the meaning of this, you fools?" Pope tottered on his feet as he stood beside Iain at the head of the bed. The old man gestured wildly seemingly unaware of the small, wickedly curved knife in his right hand. A bowl rested precariously on the edge of the bed, Iain's outstretched arm rested beside it, and blood-soaked linen, dirty with matted clumps rested atop the ashen forearm. "Get out of here woman!" The Healer screamed; his voice cracked, sending the pitch up into regions reserved for hysterical women. "Devil take you, be gone! Sir Gregori, take her out of this room at once." No one moved at his demand.

It was the first time Luveday had seen Iain since she had been kicked out of that same room days ago. The first thought in her head was that he was too close to death; there was no saving him. His skin was so pale it was almost white. His body was coated in sweat, but he no longer moved restlessly or moaned in pain. When Luveday's mind finally registered what the man was about to do, the fury inside her, that had dimmed so quickly upon seen Iain's current state, flared to new life burning inside her like a summer sun.

"Get out." She said.

"How dare you..." Pope sputtered and took a step toward her.

"Get Out!" She cried and flung her arm toward the door as she advanced on him.

The healer lurched to one side nearly collapsing on the man next to him. "Keep her away from me! I am Master Pope! I am the King's physician." He continued to rant about his own importance, but in his drunken stupor, the man-made little sense to anyone but himself. By the time Luveday had wrestled the knife from him and taken his left ear in a punishing grip the two men Sumerland had left behind had sheathed their swords and chosen their side. One took the left arm and the other the right and half carried, half dragged, Master Pope from the room. Coll stood inside the door smiling wickedly as Luveday slammed it shut efficiently cutting off the incoherent rantings of the old man.

She did not spare a glance for Benedict or Gregori as she turned and went to Iain's side. The sheets were soaked with sweat and other bodily fluids. The smell was so foul she had to cover her nose and mouth to stop from vomiting. Tears stung her eyes as she whispered brokenly. "What have they done to you?" A shaky hand reached out to test his forehead. The sweat on his brow was remarkably cold. Cold as death.

Iain didn't stir as she began her work. "Hot water, strong soap, clean linens, Cassandra and the willow bark syrup. Bring the honey and a cup of Sir Templeton's spirits." Benedict rushed out of the room yelling orders. Women were already on their way. "I will need new bed linens, clean bandages, fresh rushes and strong soap."

"You already said that, Lady." Gregori was at her elbow once more. He turned her away from the man on the bed to look her in the eye. "Is he going to be alright, Luveday?" What he really meant was, is he going to live?

Luveday shook her head as it seemed to wobble on her shoulders. In a hard whisper, she told him the truth. "I don't know, Gregori. I don't know…" There was a look of horror before she whispered. "He was bleeding him, Gregori." There was a shared moment between them, a bleak and pain filled look before people bustled in carrying out her hasty orders.

They began by washing Iain and changing the linens on his bed. Pope had let the Lord rest in his own refuse for days. With the foul smell gone Luveday could pinpoint the smell of decay on De Lane's body. With patience and small gentle movements, they removed the ball of dirty linens from the wound in his side. It wouldn't have surprised Luveday if it were the same mound of cloth, she had removed that first day. The wound was worse than even she expected. Red streaks ran across his torso radiating from the hole in his side like an angry sun. The edges of torn skin were black; nothing looked as if it had begun to heal. Cassandra let loose a stream of curses that would have made a sailor blush, but no one reprimanded her tongue. If Master Pope hadn't been thrown out on his arse, the women would have throttled him.

Cassandra saw to the wounds left by the bloodletting, continuing to curse the arrogant bastard of a healer as Luveday probed deeper into the arrow wound. It wasn't her imagination, the wound looked larger than it had before, deeper too somehow. It was swollen and infected. Pus and brown blood ran in rivers over the edge of the bed and into a deep bowl, too much to be stopped with linens. A sinking suspicion left a knot in her throat and a heavy stone in the pit of her stomach. It was disconcerting that through their ministrations Iain did not so much as flinch.

"Spirits, where are the…" Someone handed her the silver mug of firewater that Luveday recognized as something like vodka. It was what she had poured into Benedicts leg wound, and she was about to do something similar to Iain. Men rushed forward, not to stop her but to hold down her patient remembering all too well how violently the young lordling had reacted.

A thin stream of alcohol filled the wound when Iain did not move or moan a strange silence fell over the room. No one seemed to breathe, but Luveday didn't have time for them, she was testing her hypothesis. Even with Pope's lesser skill, the herbs and some techniques he possessed should have helped the wound along a little. After all, it had been cleaned properly before he arrived, but if it hadn't… If it hadn't then… Luveday cleaned her hands again in water so hot she doubted her skin was unscathed. Digging carefully in the depths of the wound that, thanks to the swelling, was now nearly twice as deep as if was before; Luveday felt something hard that should not have been there. She could barely fit two fingers inside and had to feel her way as best she could, but she was finally able to move the object free of the muscle that had tried to heal around it. A moment later more pus and blood flowed onto the floor followed by a small plop. Luveday bent to retrieve the item. A small piece of chainmail, only a few links, covered with blood and dirt rested in her palm. Cassandra looked at her and the chain in wonder. Their features soon schooled themselves focusing once more on their patient, but the nod the older healer gave her was more than one of encouragement, or pride, it was one skilled healer to another.

After the wound was cleaned and packed with honey, herbs and sterilized linen the women turned to other problems. They cleaned the bed linens once more and sent tools and utensils to be washed downstairs. The room cleared of people as the worst of the tasks were finished. Next on the list was nutrition and repairing the damage the bloodletting had caused. Luveday wondered how such a practice had ever come to be, but she knew that similar methods were used to relieve pressure on trauma wounds in her mother's modern medicine. In this setting, it was more likely to kill someone than help them. Not only did bloodletting remove blood from an already depleted body, taking with it nutrients and white blood cells, but more often than not, the wounds inflicted by the healers could become infected themselves. Dirty blades would cause blood poisoning, and once in the blood, there was nothing they could do. Luckily, it looked like the only form of hygiene master Pope practiced was with his tools and so Iain had been spared that at least.

Hours later the two women had managed to get a spoonful or two of a sickly-sweet syrup down his throat with a little beef broth. The syrup was a mixture of sugar and salt which would hopefully help replace some of the electrolytes and other nutrients from his system. They hesitated to give him more willow bark, opting to watch for signs of pain or his return to awareness. Iain remained still, breathing shallowly and nearer to the edge of death than anyone, save the two women who watched over him, knew.

The first thing that Iain De Lane saw was a bright light and, in that light, stood an angel outlined in golden hues. The look in her blue-gray eyes was one of concern and wonder. Shutting his eyes against the white-hot pain he turned away afraid her radiance would burn him, but her soothing voice grew quiet, and he had to turn back afraid she would leave him.

His arm extended out into the white light, but she was not there. Something seemed to break at her absence, and he knew that wherever she had gone, he would follow. He must follow, but before he could move to rise, she appeared again, taking his outstretched arm and moving to his side. It was only as she came close that he realized he lay in bed and tried to pull her closer so that she could join him there, but she did not do as he wanted. Voices drifted to him from afar, but Iain could not bring himself to care for anyone or anything except the golden woman before him. As he slipped back into unconsciousness, he was not troubled knowing without a doubt that his angel would continue to watch over him.

Sometime later, the darkness around him receded and Iain was once again aware of his surroundings. Candles burned around him in the room he now recognized as his own. His mind seemed heavy, slow to move and slower to remember. If his mind was bogged down then is body was made of stone, too heavy for his listless mind to will into action. He tried to remember what had happened to him, something worried at the edge of his consciousness but when he tried to discern its source it seemed to fade away. Slowly his mind took stock of the world around him. His body, stone that it was, didn't move beyond the steady rise and fall of each breath. His legs twitched with the effort to move them but remained where they were. Linen, soft and warm encased him, and for the moment he was content to stay as he was. Something soft nestled in his hand, and one by one his fingers closed around it. His head rolled to one side, and he caught the mass of golden hair that rested at his elbow off the side of the bed. *His Angel.* It was no surprise that he recognized the woman next to him, though her face was turned away. His angel had a name and wasn't it wonderful. *Luveday.*

A warmth spread through him as his eyes closed once more.

"Where is she?" A hoarse voice demanded from the bed flooded with the weak light of midmorning.

Gregori was startled by the direct gaze that pierced him in his chair beside the bed. "Who?" He began, but did he really have to ask. Gregori smiled. They had told him that Iain had had a few moments of lucidity, having improved miraculously since the day they had removed Pope from the keep. "Lady Emmalyn commanded that she go wash and rest. Lady Luveday has barely left your side in a fortnight."

"She was standing guard, my angel." He murmured to himself not realizing that the knight could hear him.

Gregori couldn't agree more but said nothing as he watched his friend get his bearings.

"How long?" There was wariness in the question as if Iain already knew that much had transpired while he was unwell.

"Since the arrow pierced your side, 'tis been twenty-two days." Shocked eyes flew to meet his own. Gregori didn't have to convince him, the monk never lied, and the look in his friend's eyes spoke of days of pain and worry.

Iain moved in bed, but the effort to shift himself higher on the pallet was almost more than he could accomplish. His weakness alone attested to what had befallen him. "The arrow." He tested his side and found it strangely numb.

A moment later Cass appeared to swat his hand away saying, "Stop that, foolish boy." Though there was no sting in her words. She was clearly relieved to see him awake and talking. "We have only just closed the wound."

He nodded, smirking at her. "Some of your dreadful potions to help with the pain?" He remembered some of the foul concoctions he had to drink as a child, but unlike the hacks and charlatans of King's town, Cassandra's potions always delivered on their promise to heal.

She huffed but took the teasing as intended. "Aye, and more still to come." She pressed on his side around the wound that was now stitched shut. The smooth muscle of his abdomen now dipped inward, leaving a permanent well where the arrow had pierced, and the rot had taken hold. "Just you wait, My Lord." She said with no little glee, as the man shuddered like the boy she remembered.

"Lady Luveday sleeps?" He asked seeming concerned.

Cassandra looked to Gregori who held her gaze steadily. There was the smallest smile at the corner of his mouth as if he knew exactly what she was thinking. "Aye, My Lord. She was sent off to bed but a chime ago. The girl was dead on her feet. If Lord Benedict had not dragged her from the room, I doubt she would have been able to make it there on her own." There was a noticeable narrowing of his eyes at the mention of Benedict. Though perhaps it was inevitable, and though Cassandra secretly wished for it, as many of De Lane's people did, she could not stop the prickle of unease that passed through her at the blatant evidence of the growing attraction between her lord and her young protégé.

Cassandra distracted him and herself by outlining everything that had transpired between the time that Lord Iain had been returned to the castle and that moment. It filled up the minutes until the noon meal and more importantly for Iain until Luveday's return.

Days passed quickly. Spring was making a valiant effort, but winter refused to let go of her fury, and despite the mild weather of recent months, snow fell often and in great flurries. It looked as if warmer weather was far off. Iain De Lane recovered quickly. Twenty-two days he spent unconscious in his bed, by the time a week more had passed he was up and walking in the great hall. The scars on his side pained him a little as his body tried to become familiar with the restricted movement. It was a familiar experience for a knight and slowed him down little despite the stern warnings of his three experienced healers.

Luveday was both solicitous and exacting. It was clear that he had scared her, and clearer still that she cared deeply for him, but more often than not, his attempts to draw her out were met with disappointment. One moment they were talking, laughing and the next it was as if a barrier thicker than the baileys outer walls suddenly stood between them. Iain was at a loss for what to do. Not only did Luveday seem to be drifting away from him, and often Christabel would somehow find herself in the way. Iain had not forgotten what his fiancé had tried to do to the lady, and he could not forgive her. Not yet, perhaps not ever. The nuptials were still looming ahead of them, and neither Iain's near-death experience nor his miraculous recovery could hold them off indefinitely.

It was with a great deal of wicked intent that he called her to him one night.

Luveday entered the solar with every fiber of her being protesting. She had passed Cass and Henna as they exited the chambers. Both had given her odd looks. Cassandra appeared concerned for her, while Henna gave her a nod and a smile that was clearly encouraging. Luveday didn't know which one worried her more.

Now she stood before the inner door, his door and debated whether or not she should turn around and... well, flee. The thought left a foul taste in her mouth. She was a lady, a healer, and a damn good one. Opening the door, she reminded herself that she did not flee from handsome men... her mind slid to a halt as she turned toward the fire and the large copper tub there. She did not flee from handsome men bathing in the glow of the fireside, but maybe she really should.

It was hard to swallow with her mouth going suddenly dry and the gasp that was stuck in her throat. His back was to her, and in the firelight, she could clearly see the pattern of scars that marred the skin of his shoulders not that she needed the light to see them. No, the pattern had become very familiar to her over the last weeks of tending to him. She had always made herself scarce during bathing hour. Not that she hadn't seen him nude since his illness began; indeed, the visions still haunted her. It was that she didn't want him to see her reaction to him. She could pretend that he didn't affect her, while he was sick and unaware, she could be professional, but she had no illusions now. Iain could take one look at her and see through the walls she had worked so hard to erect around her heart. Everything had changed between them, and yet nothing had. His future was still planned; his place beside Christabel should have been carved in stone for how little this new-found longing had altered that course.

"Come in, Luveday." She had paused behind him, unwittingly admiring what little she could see. More often than not, he would leave off her title as if to say they were somehow equal. It was those little intimacies that were beginning to drive her mad.

"You summoned me, My Lord." Cold yet polite, rigid yet respectful; that was her goal. She berated herself, once again needing to remind herself to remain professional. Her mask needed to be flawless.

She came abreast to the tub, deciding to face the fireplace leaving the bed at her back. Better to keep the monstrous thing out of view.

The smile on his face was like nothing she had ever seen, and she prayed somehow, she could be spared this one. "My Lady Luveday." Luveday wanted to faint or flee but willed her spine to stay stiff. She knew how he disdained formality, so as he smirked and sipped a goblet of wine, she curtsied to him. The graceful movement had come after months of practice and caused a slight frown to mar his brow. One for Lord Iain and One to Luveday, she counted to herself.

Iain sat the goblet aside, using a simple wooden stool as a table beside the tub. Before he could speak Luveday jumped to fill the poignant silence. "How may I be of service, My Lord?" Service, she cringed mentally wanting to take the words back.

That devastating smirk returned causing her to feel like a rabbit caught between the paws of a lion, or more appropriately, a wolf. "I am in need of a healer's skill." But the way he said it made her think that he had planned his answers well.

"And Healer Cassandra could not help you." It was more of a statement than a question, but she could not help the disbelief that colored her words.

"Dear Cassandra," Luveday almost laughed at the false endearment, "has grown impatient with me. I need a steady hand and a light touch." Luveday was looking anywhere but directly at him, but in that moment when their eyes met, she had the impression that he had been watching her every movement since laying eyes on her.

Luveday was clearly at a disadvantage. "May I ask what ails you, My

Lord?"

Iain seemed to be displeased by her question, though nothing more than a slight narrowing at the corners of his eyes gave it away. "My wound is still troubling me. The stitches are out, but I am concerned I might open it again." Only a few days after leaving his bed, Iain had torn out a few of the stitches. Thanks to the numbing salve they had put on the wound, he had not realized the extent of the damage until Aunt Emmalyn had nearly fainted and Luveday came rushing to his aid. At the moment, Luveday could not tell if he had pulled that excuse out of his arse or if he was genuinely concerned. She suspected the former, but caution prevailed.

For a moment she looked heavenward, but the ceiling provided no immediate solution to this predicament. She would have to take a look at his side, either by circling around the tub or leaning over it. The first option was prudent but cowardly while the second was efficient with temptations galore. Breathing deeply, she knelt on the stool beside the tub and reached over to examine the wound. Iain turned towards her, leaning in and yet somehow arching his back to give her a better view of the wounded side. The skin remained a light shade of pink along the scar and the small dots where the stitches had knitted his flesh together. The color was good, the skin had healed nicely; all in all, everything was as it should be. Luveday said as much, but as she leaned back ready to extract herself and leave his presence his large hand delicately returned a wayward strand of hair to its resting place behind the shell of her ear. Out of the corner of her eye, she caught the movement, and the look on his face was so intent as he watched her that Luveday was momentarily mesmerized.

She felt more than saw him lean closer and before his intent could be made reality she retreated to the end of the tub. He looked startled for a moment, but his gaze became hooded as he watched her fight for composure. The mantra in her head was no help; the words were jumbled and made no sense. "Cold yet ignite, rigid yet resentful." That wasn't right. "Gold met delight, timid yet neglectful." She almost growled at him. How could the man do this to her?

"Luveday." His voice was too deep, too perfect and sinful and he knew exactly how to use it.

It took her a moment to unclench her jaw and reply. "Yes, My Lord?" She asked only a little breathily. She yearned to yell at him, to tell him to stop playing games with her.

"The women have gone, and I am in need of help." He seemed amused by her discomfort and annoyance.

"Help?" She asked exasperatedly.

"With my bath?" He leaned forward to look at her earnestly.

"With the bath?" She echoed dumbly.

"I cannot reach to wash my back." As he held out a soapy cloth, Luveday realized that he was indeed dirty from the day's activities.

Squaring her shoulders, she took the cloth from his outstretched hand and moved behind him. She began at his nape and traveled down his spine. Her strokes were smooth and even, the pressure consistent and in every way as practical and detached as she could make them. A soft moan escaped him, and Luveday thought she might die. She continued the task until she had cleaned the dirt from his shoulders and back.

As she moved to return the cloth to him, he grabbed her wrist pulling her to him. Soon she found herself at his side and face to face with him. "My hair." She couldn't help looking at the mop of sable brown hair in his head. "Wash my hair." She must have looked as if she might bolt for, he threw her a challenging look before settling against the back of the tub. "The water is behind you. The soap is in that bowl." She looked, and sure enough, a bucket of water stood warming by the fire, and a small bowl of soap sat on the raised hearth.

Luveday retrieved both and began to wash his hair, a process she had seen done on more than one occasion. She poured a cup of water over his crown as he leaned his head back, his arms gripping the edges of the tub. She took a bit of the powdery soap in one hand, a small amount of water in the other and began to lather his hair. The tresses were thick and smooth and slid through her fingers with ease. It took her a moment to realize that she was no longer lathering but massaging his scalp in circular motions that made his head rest heavy in her hands. The line of his throat was fully exposed to her, and she had the sudden thought that she had never seen anything so beautiful in her entire life.

Shaking from her thoughts, she took the bucket and slowly poured the contents over his scalp washing the suds away. She took clean linen and dried his hair. Luveday stepped away to lay the cloth over a chair to dry and found him watching her through heavy-lidded eyes when she turned back. He didn't say more, only held out the washcloth to her.

What possessed her to take it she would never know but take it she did. Luveday knew he watched her as she worked, but she didn't falter. Though she tried to tell herself that this was like bathing a child or cleaning the wounded, she could not lie to herself for long. This was nothing like that, and though she wanted to, she didn't linger. Whatever game he was playing with her this night, Luveday was determined to prove to herself that she could do this. Methodically, she bathed his right arm from hand to wrist to shoulder. She moved across his chest, moving under his arms and over his ribs. She moved down one hip to the right leg, which he lifted only a little to give her better access. She rounded the foot of the tub and started up his left leg, left hip, left ribs, left arm until she had cleaned everything she could reach. Face to face she held the cloth between them willing him to take it back, but he just looked at her. Both were breathing heavy which Luveday only noticed as their breaths mingled in the small space between them. Shaking the cloth in her hand, she looked into his eyes, but Iain refused to take it.

"You're not done yet." His voice was deep and little more than a breath between them. "You missed a spot."

Luveday looked at him. There was only one place on his body she had not touched, one place she had refused to look at or acknowledge during this heated encounter. Luveday wanted to swear, throw the washcloth in his face and leave, but the look in his eyes said he expected her to do just that. She paused for a moment, eyes narrowing as she gazed at him. Had he done all this to prove to her or to himself just how deeply he could affect her? Were all the small ways he singled her out, the brief touches, the intimate moments not enough? Did he have to prove that she wanted him? Male ego was not beyond Iain, but she had thought that such childish tactics were, so what then was all this?

With steely eyes and a careful movement, Luveday released the cloth and it sank beneath the water exactly over his groin. She moved as if to rise but moved only halfway to her feet. Instead she leaned over the edge of the tub and followed the cloth's descend with her hand. Iain had been unprepared for that action as well as the moment when her fingers closed lightly around his staff. His whole body jerked in response, his eyes closing involuntarily before opening to stare hard at her. Luveday cleaned the part of him she could not bring herself to look at, instead, she stared at the muscles in his jaw as a tic seemed to develop on the right side. She was as efficient at this as the rest of her task. And all too soon she let go.

Iain moved to grab her, but she anticipated it and moved to evade his grasp. He surged out of the water sloshing suds over the edge of the tub. He looked incredulous, ready to pounce and damned hungry. Luveday flung open the door, Coll stood stunned as he folded extra blankets for his bed, Henna, Cassandra, Ellie, Agnes and Lady Emmalyn crowded the far door. Luveday got the impression that the women had been pumping the boy for information about what he could hear beyond his master's door and was not sure if she should berate them or applaud the success of their scheming. Instead, she addressed them in a voice too loud for the small space. "Kind women, please help Lord Iain. He is in need of drying off, lest he start to smell like a wet dog." She pushed past the women who gasped and chuckled in turns.

Behind her, a furious voice boomed out of the solar. Her name rang through the hall below like a clap of thunder. Luveday smiled as she slammed her door shut with a satisfying crack.

Chapter 13

*With stammering lips and insufficient sound, I strive
and struggle to deliver right the music of my nature.*
~ Elizabeth Barrett Browning

Luveday found other things to focus on, most importantly, the growing affections of Gregori and Elysant. The two had been nearly inseparable since the knight had returned from the campaign in the north. The budding romance was the delight of the castle, and when Gregori finally asked there was not a soul who stood against.

Gregori rose from his chair beside Iain, Ellie sat a few seats down; the knight met the eyes of Iain, then Lady Emmalyn, Luveday and finally his intended target. The hall went quiet, and all eyes turned to the high table. They saw him swallow and take a breath before hoisting his goblet in a salute to his lord, but his eyes didn't leave Ellie who looked on in admiration tinted with dismay. "Good health and long Life to Lord De Lane and Lander's Keep." Goblets raised as the crowd echoed back the well wishes, 'To De Lane.' "It is an honor to serve beside such a man," Iain growled at this show of affection and nodded to signal that he felt the same for his brother in arms. "I would be a great honor if you would give me the hand of Elysant of Lander's Keep," There was a sudden roar of approval from the tables as men shouted and banged their cups and cutlery in manly encouragement. Gregori continued, but only those at the high table could hear him over the ding, "and bless our union."

Iain rose to his feet as silence fell. He raised his drink and clapped an arm around his best knight and friend. "You may have the girl and the blessing, Friend. May heaven smile down on you and yours as you have brought prosperity and some joy to Lander's Keep."

Cheers and congratulations filled the room. Ellie knocked over her chair in her haste to reach her love. The girl, small as she was launched herself into his arms and was caught by the knight who kissed her long and hard. Cat calls were quelled by a stern look from the ladies at the high table even though it took a bit for the two lovebirds to remember where they were. Both returned to their seats and dinner progressed without much ado.

For days Ellie floated around the keep in a daze, the girl was practically useless, but no one reprimanded her. Luveday was overjoyed for her friend, yet alone at night, she couldn't help but feel a twinge of sadness and perhaps even jealousy. So here was Ellie's happily ever after which seemed to contrast so sharply with what lay between Iain and herself.

Luveday was happy for the distraction as preparations for their ceremony began. Since spring had yet to make an appearance, Luveday had the idea of crafting flowers from other items. This wasn't entirely new to her since she had done something similar for her sister Annalisa's wedding several years ago. Luveday's mother had wrangled together a group of women who when they put their mind to it, had fashioned a lovely country wedding for the frugal and creative bride. Luckily for Ellie, Luveday had an excellent memory and some creative ideas to turn twigs and odds-n-ends into decorations that would mirror the girl's cheerful personality.

So, the women found themselves sequestered in the sewing gallery one mild afternoon. Henna and Paige looked through the numerous baskets, buckets, and bins, picking up pieces of this or that. Everyone knew that Luveday had been collecting items for over a week, but while they also knew these things were for the upcoming wedding, they could not help but wonder at the strange things she studiously gathered. There were twigs of varying thicknesses and lengths, wood shavings, dried seed pods, washed bird feathers, bits of string and some sort of paste that smelled strange that Luveday referred to as glue. Luveday had made a special trip to the Abbey to see Father Quinn and came back with the recipe they used to make paper from flax and wood pulp.

"I know this doesn't look like much," Luveday smiled to herself at their doubtful glances as the women continued to peruse the items, "but trust me. I think this will work wonderfully."

Only Ellie was excited to begin, so much so that the girl fairly vibrated in her seat. "What do we do first, Luveday?"

The women finally settled into their usual seats with the newcomers taking up positions around the long room. Luveday positioned herself in the middle, the basket of examples she had crafted the day before at her elbow. "It is a rather complicated process, but once you are familiar with the gist of it, making flowers is quite easy."

"How do we get flowers out of this mess?" Henna looked at a tangle of undyed linen and string and wondered if the lady hadn't lost her mind.

Luveday laughed at the seamstress's scorn. "Some imagination is needed, Henna. Something I know you have in abundance, or you would not be able to take thread and cloth and make such lovely garments." The girl preened at her praise, not really knowing what this imagination thing was, but liking it already. "I have some flowers that I finished," She passed around the basket. Women marveled and awed at the designs; they did look like proper flowers. "Right now, they are their natural color, but Warin and Archer said that they can mix up some whitewash and we will paint them all white. Maybe add a bit of dye in the mix to get some pretty pinks and greens." The sudden impact nearly took Luveday to the floor as Ellie threw herself at her friend in a fierce hug. Luveday just hugged the girl back for a few moments until her friend released her and found her seat again.

Emmalyn took that moment to join them, Agnes in tow. "What are you up to in here?"

Henna answered from her corner, "We are making flowers from bits and bobbles." She stated, but her attention was soon diverted as the basket had finally reached her. "My, aren't these clever." She said to no one in particular.

Luveday beamed at Emmalyn, who returned the girl's enthusiasm. The older lady took her spot, Agnes beside her. "Well then, let us get to work."

By late afternoon they had over a dozen of six different varieties of flowers still in their natural hues, but the women were now on board with the lady's thinking, and many looked forward to gathering the supplies and a few items for themselves.

As the days passed the sewing gallery looked more like a strange greenhouse than the dark room it had always been. The women were often found chatting and making flowers during their free time. The men stayed clear of the room, told that when the time for their help was needed, they would be informed. Lady Christabel often stuck her head in or stayed for a few minutes under some pretext of asking one of the other ladies a question, but Luveday could clearly see that the girl was curious and interested in what was going on. Unfortunately, the whipping incident had not changed the young lady in the least, and even Luveday could not stand her for any length of time. The women's happy chatter would suddenly cease as soon as one spotted the lonely girl. Luveday could find no more empathy for her. Christabel was the only one to blame for her frosty reception.

There was only one other person that troubled Luveday's life and that was Lord Iain himself. The man was waging war against her senses; there was no other way to look at it. Since her moment of insanity during his bath, she had tried to regain the emotional distance between them, but he would not have it. Every look they exchanged seemed to have deeper meaning, undercurrents, and riptides. She was drowning, and he was pulling her deeper. He would appear out of nowhere at moments when she was alone: in the wool shed, in the weaving room, in the Lady's garden, as she walked through the village. Nowhere was she safe from him. It was not that he threatened her or forced her to remain in his company. No, the man was polite, attentive, charming to a fault and Luveday could barely hold onto her composure and remain practical even when he wasn't focusing his attention on her. With desperation, she hung onto her sense of self-preservation, but it was slipping through her fingers with dangerous consequences.

"Ah, Lady Luveday." Speak of the devil, and he shall appear, she thought. Luveday turned around in the corridor that led to the sewing room. The place was empty as dinner preparations were underway, Luveday herself would have been downstairs, but one of the children had brought a basket of odds and ends to add to their flower making supplies, and she had decided to drop it off herself. "How go the wedding plans?" Iain asked though he had shown little interest thus far.

"Very well, My Lord. The women have done wonders, and we will have lovely decorations for the chapel." Luveday was truly pleased, and the feeling colored her expression. She looked at him with rosy cheeks and a soft smile not knowing the effect they had on him. "If you will excuse me," she turned away but was caught by a hand at her elbow. Startled by his sudden nearness, she looked up at him as they stood silent for several heartbeats.

"Luveday." His voice was urgent, and without warning she found herself embraced in Iain's arms. A soft sigh left her as his lips descended to hers, blocking out any protests that her inner voice tried to raise.

She was lost, and she knew it. He demanded her surrender wiping clear her resolve and leaving her a mass of quivering nerves and turbulent emotions. They separated, both breathing hard with heavy-lidded gazes.

The sound of footsteps drawing closer cut through their sensual haze bringing them crashing back to reality. Luveday backed away slowly while Iain looked as if he would protest, but if he took a step closer, she would have no choice but to flee from him. After a half-dozen steps, she turned and continued down the hall to hear Fuller and Benedict engage De Lane in their ongoing debate.

She could only catch her breath once she was safely on the other side of the heavy door to the sewing room. Leaning against the solid surface for support, it took her several minutes before the feel of his lips began to fade, and several minutes more to remember why she was headed there in the first place.

Their next encounter happened in the shade of the castle wall, despite the lingering touches of winter, the day had turned warm. Luveday had taken the opportunity to move outside and chose a sheltered spot for the painting of the roses. Several makeshift tables and ladders dotted the area between the curtain wall and the shorter wall of the Lady's garden. The whitewashing was going well, the ladders were used as drying racks as dozens upon dozens of faux-flowers dried in the mid-day sun. Only a small section of the wall remained in shadow, and that was where Luveday had taken refuge after hours of working in the sun.

Footsteps approached but Luveday didn't open her eyes just yet, she was taking a break from painting and dipping the flowers, and a break from reality. Her mind was far from here, home and trying to conjure up the once familiar faces of her family. She could almost see the image of Annalisa at her wedding. Mark stood at her sister's side with her parents on one side and Luveday on the other posing for photos. It was one of the happiest days in recent memory, and Luveday wondered exactly when she had stopped thinking of the world she left behind and started to think of a future here. It would be a future without Iain, she was coming to realize that her time at Lander's Keep might be shorter than even she imagined.

A hand brushed a stray hair behind her ear, but she didn't need to open her eyes to recognize the heat and smell coming off of Iain. The man was pure temptation and unused to denying himself what he wanted. Luveday had to be the responsible one between the two of them, and for the first time in her life, she hated it. His hand caressed her jaw and slid to play with the delicate chain of her necklace, rubbing the spot where the column of her neck met her shoulder.

Iain looked his fill while Luveday centered her roiling emotions and prepared to open her eyes. She already knew what she would find and wasn't disappointed.

The flame of attraction, of hunger burned in the depths of his gaze and the answering flame that sprang to life within her, was hard to smother. Luveday had never thought of herself as a sensual being. She was practical, cerebral, polite, and underestimated, but never the object of a man's desires, not in this all-consuming way that Iain had about him. The passion that was banked within him singed along her nerve endings. Why, oh why, did it have to be him? She could give in, as she longed to do. She craved a taste of the promise of ecstasy he offered with every look, every touch, but she had made herself follow that action to its inevitable conclusion, and she could not stomach it.

He had said he didn't mean to hurt her, would never do so, and she believed him. Every day together pulled them closer, mind, body, and soul but so much still lay between them.

A large hand came to rest on her hip and the other tilted her head back a fraction so that their lips aligned perfectly. The brush of his mouth over hers was sheer heaven, but as he leaned in, trapping her body between his own and the cold wall at her back, common sense came flooding back to her. She cursed inwardly, wanting to ignore her sensible nature and continue kissing him. The voice of reason screamed at her in a last attempt to get her cooperation, knowing that with each encounter Luveday was paying less and less attention to her own sense of self-preservation. Iain's knee slid north between her thighs and came to rest against the v of her center causing Luveday to pull away and bite down hard on her lower lip. The pain stopped the purr that was moving up from her chest and brought with it a bit of clarity to her addled wits.

Unwittingly, Luveday shook her head still chewing on her bottom lip and considered Iain's steady gaze. Her name on his lips was a reprimand; he was familiar with the look that heralded her withdrawal. "Luveday." The anger and frustration in that one word perfectly mirrored her own thoughts. He had no right to be angry.

"You are playing with fire, My Lord." Surely, he knew that.

"I would burn with you for a thousand years, Luveday." His head dipped to take her lips again, but Luveday forced herself to push at his chest. She knew that it wasn't her strength that moved him, but his own reluctance to hurry her. Iain was infinitely patient in this regard and completely focused on coaxing her to him. Luveday found that quality vastly appealing, he knew when to push her, and just how far before letting her go.

That he knew her so well thrilled and terrified her. "Iain." His name was a plea for things she would never voice to him, to anyone. He tilted her head up again so that they could look at each other, and she knew he saw the working of her mind clearly as the wheels turned behind her eyes. Without meaning to, she spoke her thoughts aloud. "What do you want from me?"

"Everything." It was an admission that startled them both. His hand dropped from her cheek. It was he that put more distance between them, but neither was grateful for it.

Luveday watched as he turned away, his shoulder dropped a bit, his head bowed as he fought with something inside himself. It was not a sight that she took any pleasure in. Indeed, she hoped that he would come to the same conclusions she had and put an end to this before they were torn apart. When he turned back to her, straightening to his full height the look in his eyes made her heart drop to the pit of her stomach and a flash of despair cut through her soul. Advancing on her like a wolf hunting down its prey, he did not stop until they were mashed against the wall once more.

The kiss they shared should have left some lasting sign on the world, like the after images of people caught by a nuclear blast. Their silhouette should have been imprinted forever on the curtain wall, but when voices pulled them unwillingly from their passion, nothing remained to mark the occasion, but the few powerful words that hung suspended in time and space as he strode away from her.

"You are mine."

Emmalyn was casting Luveday concerned looks every few minutes. Gathered around the fireside, they listened to Lord Grayson Stern recount his recent visit to court and once again mention how excited many were for Iain's upcoming nuptials.

Luveday chatted and laughed, but she was not exactly aware of what she was saying. Of course, Emmalyn noticed, but she prayed that no one else did. In her mind's eye, Luveday replayed the moment only a short time ago when upon his arrival, Stern handed over a missive from the King, one addressed to Iain alone. The moment he had finished reading the note his eyes had sought her out. She had never seen that cold look directed at her, and it took Luveday a moment to realize that the content of the letter had nothing to do with her but was a stern reminder of his vows to Lord Sumerland and his daughter. Vows were vows and the King, though beholden to Luveday for saving his son, saw no reason for De Lane to stop the marriage.

Now they sat chatting, while Luveday refused to look at Iain for more than a few seconds at a time and only when spoken to.

"Lady Luveday your presence would liven up the court," Stern commented, not for the first time. "The ladies there have little sense save the Queen." He took a long drink of wine before continuing. "Your skills would earn you some pretty coin and many favors. The King was most impressed with your healing ability and bayed me remind you that should you ever journey to town, he will repay his debt to you in a public fashion." Even Stern sounded impressed by the notion. King Edward was known for making grand gestures for those who pleased him, what more would he do for someone he owned a debt to.

"Perhaps next fall, we might journey to town." Emmalyn looked to Iain but noticed he watched the lady in question rather than paying her much attention, though he must have heard her query.

His gaze swung to her, but he did not look contrite being caught staring. "If you wish, Aunt. The fall is the best time to go, perhaps just after the grain harvest."

Emmalyn turned to Luveday suddenly eager. "Wouldn't that be lovely?"

Luveday smiled, more pleased by the woman's pleasure than by the thought of town. "If you think it best, Lady." Her reply was said to the lady next to her, rather than Iain.

The bell for the mid-day meal rang, and as the group rose to find their seats at the tables, Luveday was halted by Ellie who grabbed her right arm and turned her back toward Emmalyn who took the other. They drew closer and whispered once the men were several feet away.

Luveday caught the look that passed between them, but it was Emmalyn's concerned voice that jarred her from her thoughts. "Is something wrong between you and Iain, child?" Luveday had no words to describe what was between Iain and herself.

Ellie searched her friend's face for some hint for her odd behavior. "You are not fighting, are you? I know there is much going on with the wedding preparations and the spring thaw." She glanced at Emmalyn who was looking for clues as well. "I know Lord Iain confides in you, but if it is not something between you two, then what else...?"

Luveday didn't let her finish. The women were worried, and she had been so caught up in her own emotions that she had yet to see what was going on around her. She turned the conversation back on course, not wanting them to worry unnecessarily but also not wanting to reveal the truth of the matter. "It is merely a difference of opinion between us. Nothing more. I am sure it will be sorted out before the wedding." She reassured Ellie. Emmalyn, on the other hand, looked as if she meant to probe deeper but glanced at the girl and nodded leaving it at that.

Dinner progressed with more happy banter, and when Luveday finally climbed the stairs to find her bed, she felt emotionally battered. Later she would blame what happened next on having to hide her turning emotions since Lord Stern's arrival. Most of the castle was asleep, save her. The hall was dark as the candles had been extinguished over an hour prior and so, she did not see him at first, not until he was close enough to swoop her into a quick embrace before ushering her toward the back stairs near the sewing room. Luveday didn't use these stairs much; they were dark, cramped and too steep for her petite frame. She was surprised once again when Iain ascended the stairs rather than heading down. There was nothing above but a seldom used lookout post. The area was kept clean by the men-at-arms, but Luveday had never had the need to venture up there. Her fear of heights made the view less than spectacular, so she had stayed away.

The hatch-like door was thrown open to reveal a roofed structure. The lookout was little more than eight feet wide square with several of those feet being taken up by the door. Iain pulled her free of the safety of the stairs and towards the railing. The structure reminded Luveday of a boxy gazebo stuck atop a tower. While the view was breathtaking for more than one reason, she had eyes only for Iain. In the dim light of a crescent moon, she watched him look out over his lands and tilt his face up toward the waning sphere. As he stood there a moment longer, she looked around and spotted a bench built into the wall. She sat and only glanced down at the castle gates and farther down the road. From here she thought she might be able to glimpse the spires of the cathedral at the Abbey, but she could discern nothing beyond the woods that lay on the other side of the village.

When she turned her attention back to him, he was no longer looking out but had turned to lean back on the railing and watched her. Luveday imagined he saw a good deal, though only half of her face was bathed in moonlight. She wouldn't have been surprised to learn he could see her clearly in the dark. She sat sideways on the narrow bench, her left arm resting against the railing, her legs folded neatly to one side, one foot touching the floor facing the same direction as he, though she could see little of the fields and orchards below. Her vision was full of open sky, deep and lovely and full of stars though from here they seemed much closer than they usually were from her window.

Luveday waited. She was content to let him make the first move after the mental exhaustion of the last few days. Since his admission beside the garden wall, nothing had been settled between them, and Luveday knew that sooner or later things would come to a head, she just had not expected Stern and the King's letter to be the catalyst.

"I am to marry Christabel." He said it so matter-of-factly that it dulled the sting of the words.

Luveday nodded. "This I know." Her voice was thankfully devoid of emotion.

"I am to marry her a week after Gregori's ceremony. The date has been set by the King." He stayed where he was, not coming closer to touch her or comfort her. And Luveday looked on, noting absently the wind and light that danced in his hair. Their gazes held for a matter of minutes until a sigh seemed to deflate him. Iain bent his head and ran his hand over his face before looking back at her. She had not moved a muscle. "Guests will be arriving shortly, as soon as the morrow even." Finally, he moved to sit beside her, his face in shadow, the moon over his left shoulder caught her gaze.

He turned her back toward him. "What do you want from me?" She asked again, only this time it was a whisper full of little emotion.

His answer was the same. "Everything." He grabbed her by the shoulders and pulled her forward until she rested on her knees bringing her up to his level for the deepest, darkest kiss she had ever received. Luveday struggled with herself, with him. If she let this continue a moment longer, she would be devoured by his hunger. For the first time he did not let her go so she struggled harder pulling her mouth free of his. He seemed to come back to himself though he did not let her retreat, instead, his forehead came to rest on her own with a weary sigh. Luveday's eyes drifted closed as this moment felt more intimate to her than his burning passion a heartbeat ago.

"Luveday." Her name had never sounded so wonderful before, it was a plea and a benediction. "The future had been set, long before you appeared at my door." She sank back, sitting almost in his lap. His hands came to frame her face and dive into her hair; his thumbs stroked the skin from her temple to the curve of her cheekbones under her eyes. "I cannot change it, you know that." She gave no reaction to this declaration but the slight widening of her eyes. "I do not love Christabel." At the sound of her name, Luveday wished to be released, but instead straightened her spine and prepared herself for what was to come. "But I have vowed to wed her and wed her I will." Luveday was already aware of this but hearing the bleak tone of his words brought the truth home in a way they never had before. "I will not break my oaths, but I cannot lose you."

Her eyes flew open; she had not even realized she had closed them.

"Your home is here; your life is here, and I promise you it will always be so. Stay with me, Luveday. Stay and love me. Love me like she never will. Love me as I love you." He begged her.

She had always known the words would hurt when they finally came from him. They hurt just as much being left unsaid every time he tried to seduce her with witty banter or soft touches. Hurt and confusion warred within her. A part of her yearned to answer his pleas with words of her own, but she was smart enough to realize that she would be making promises she couldn't keep. So instead of answering, she kissed him; kissed him with all the love and pain inside her. She kissed him until they both forgot what he had asked of her, and when she pulled away and fled down the staircase, he did not immediately go after her. Luveday hoped that he had taken that kiss as her answer, and leave it at that, but she knew sooner or later, Iain would realize that she hadn't said the words. Luveday hoped that by then she would have everything under control.

Indeed, it took several days before Iain realized that Luveday had made no declarations of her own and no promises. With the arrival of guests and only three days left until the ceremony for Gregori and Ellie, there was little opportunity to talk to her alone. Under the cheerful façade, he presented to his guests burned desperation the likes of which he had never known.

In private he paced and planned to get her free of the crowd that seemed to follow her everywhere. His attempts thus far had failed, earning him only a few moments alone in her company and never the opportunity to extract an answer from her. He felt like he was being crushed under the weight of his responsibilities having to parade around the keep with Christabel at his arm playing the loving couple for the nobility. Failing that, they at least had to appear to get along. He threw his mug into the fire and watched the wine and flame sizzle. The liquid was not enough to quench the hungry flames, and Iain felt similarly. He could not quench his hunger for Luveday, her kisses haunted him. Her kind heart, her humor, and her quiet beauty drew him in and was a comfort to his very soul. Her mere presence drove him mad, and he feared that something would take her from him.

Christabel would have no say in the matter. Once they were wed, he would do his duty and send her back to court. She could rule from his private rooms in the palace, the perks of being the wife of the King's Champion. Luveday could stay at Lander's Keep, she was already the lady here in everything but name. And he could, and he could... but his fantasies fled before him. He could have her and ruin her. Could the child she bore him be any conciliation for her lack of standing? For dishonoring her?

As he paced, he kicked over the chair nearest him. The thud was unsatisfying, and he had the urge to rip the room apart, but everywhere he looked he saw Luveday's touches, her concern for his comfort. So, he picked the chair up and returned it to its rightful place. Belatedly he grabbed the fireiron and retrieved the metal goblet before the hot embers warped it beyond repair, and let it cool beside the hearth.

He was a fool. Iain sat on the chest at the foot of his bed, head in his hands, shoulders slumped and heart heavy. He could not reconcile the truth of what was about to happen with what he wanted. For years, his life had been shaped by his own hand and his alone. Now that the future was so close, he could touch it, it was too late to realize that what he had thought he wanted was not what he needed. He needed Luveday, needed her like his next breath, but at what cost. It was frightening to know, to realize that he didn't care. He didn't care what it cost him, what it cost her, so long as she stayed with him. He would not let her go, he vowed. Not ever.

Luveday searched through her chest. She had meant to do so days ago and have the gift ready beforehand but life these days was not going according to her plans, but she prayed that would soon change. In the warm light of the open window pouring in from above her bed, she found the bag of jewelry she had purchased on that fateful day nearly a year ago before she had been transported to another world. She had bought the necklace for her sister, but while Annalisa would have liked the piece, it would have ended up in a drawer of her jewelry box with a dozen similar pieces she rarely wore. On the other hand, Elli would cherish the piece forever. Luveday placed the heavy gold necklace in the palm of her hand and held it up to the light. The rose quartz stones were carved to look like flowers while small pieces of jade circled the buds mimicking the form of leaves. Around each stone was a bit of gold wire and gold leaf. The piece had cost a bit more than she would usually have spent on such an item, but Luveday had taken one look at the necklace and thought that it was meant for a special occasion. She just had not guessed how special it would be.

She slipped the necklace back in its velvet drawstring bag and picked up the tiny studded hairpins she had only recently found in the bottom of her bag. At first, Luveday had not remembered where the pins had come from, she was sure she had not purchased them, nor did she own such items. It took two days before the memory came back to her. She sat at a table after Sunday brunch with her family. It was one of the rare occasions when everyone was present. Luveday had taken a seat next to Abigail. The five-year-old girl had been dressed in her Sunday best and had rambled cheerfully on about anything and everything she could think of. Luveday had never been as happy as when she was with the girls. Abigail was her best friend, and Luveday hers. After waffles had been consumed and much orange juice drained, Abbey had become impatient with the fancy hairdo her mother had so painstakingly woven. The tiny studded hairpins had graced her dark head like the ring of a starry halo, but Abigail would have none of it. Luveday was barely able to extract the offending items before the pins were lost forever and had tucked them away in her pocket but had forgotten to return them to Annalisa before they left. Now she vaguely remembered putting them in a plastic baggie and popping them into her pack, intent on remembering to return them the next time she saw her sister. Of course, they had been lost in the depths of her bag, and only when Luveday had searched the folds of the bottom of the backpack did she now find them.

Luveday stood looking at the faux gems as they caught the light. The memory of her family was bittersweet but still made her smile. She knew that Abigail would not mind that she was giving the pins away, in fact, the little girl would have been excited to give something to a bride on her wedding day.

Elysant cried when Emmalyn presented her with a woven hair covering as was a tradition for a bride. The golden mesh-like fabric would be passed down from mother to daughter for generations. Henna gave the bride an embroidered handkerchief, the pattern around the edges matched the flowers they had made for the ceremony. Agnes had snuck away from the kitchens long enough to present a small bride cake, another wedding tradition that Luveday was coming to know. Elysant ate it with tears in her eyes. The women had gone out to pick what flowers were brave enough to grow in early spring, and they mixed the real flora with the sturdy bunch that they had made. Luveday had learned that floral bouquets were not one of their traditions, but once the women had learned of the idea, they had insisted upon it.

When it was finally Luveday's turn, she felt her gift might be too grand, but she wanted Elli to have it. "Dearest Elli," the tears were already flowing, and Luveday hadn't even gotten to the gift yet. Laughing to herself and trying to hold back her own happy tears she continued, "we are friends, you and I." The girl nodded enthusiastically. "I hope you will accept these gifts and wear them today." Whatever profound and pretty words she had planned to say were lost as Luveday handed over the bag and placed a dozen or so hairpins in her friend's hand.

Emmalyn came and took the pins, "How lovely, Elli." She said. Luveday took one after another and used them to pin the veil in place.

With shaky hands and a quivering chin, Elysant opened the velvet bag. Its contents tumbled into her open palm, and the whole room gasped. The green of her wedding gown, the same gown that had been altered for Iain's wedding, would show the stones off to perfection. Luveday received a hug that felt strong enough to crush her bones, while Emmalyn wiped tears from her cheeks. Elli insisted that Luveday put the necklace on her, and as the train of women flowed down the stairs, out the door, and to the chapel, Luveday was heartened to see her friend stroke the necklace and hoped it gave her some courage.

Before the doors of the chapel stood Father Quinn, dressed in burgundy attire wearing a priest's lapel as a symbol of his office. To the right was Sir Gregori in hunter green that matched his bride. Iain stood by his side wearing a blue that was similar to Luveday's own gown. Luveday watched Gregori's expression as he first caught sight of his bride and had never seen such a loving look on the man's face. She could not help glancing beside the groom and nearly stumbled when a similar expression shined down on her from Iain's bright eyes.

He smiled, and she hoped that none but her had seen the look in his eyes.

Facing the people amassed there, Iain gained the attention of the crowd. "Welcome friends. We gather here to hear the vows between these two, but before we begin," Iain pulled from his over tunic a piece of paper, those standing closest to the steps could make out the red of a royal seal. "Here I hold a missive from the King. Mistress Elysant of Lander's Keep," the crowd gasped at the title, "Had been entered into the royal registry as an acknowledged and blooded member of the line of the house of De Lane, recognized these three years as a ward of my house." Luveday only vaguely understood the enormity of what Iain had just said. Emmalyn swayed on her feet, her tears coming in earnest. Elli looked shell-shocked and ascended the last steps to her place beside Father Quinn in a daze; it was only Luveday's steadying hand that got her there without incident.

Upon a slight nod from Iain, Father Quinn began vows that were eerily similar to those of her own world. "We are gathered here today in the sight of the Great Creator and the presence of friends and loved ones, to add our best wishes and blessings to the words which shall unite Sir Gregori of Brooke Abbey and Young Mistress Elysant of Lander's Keep in holy matrimony." The priests' voice flowed over the crowd in rich tones. "Marriage is a most honorable estate, created and instituted by our Creator in his love for us, so too may this marriage be adorned by true and abiding love." Silence settled over the area, as the priest's gaze fell on the men and women before him. "Should there be anyone here who has cause why these two should not be united in marriage, they must speak now or forever more hold their peace." It was as if the crowd held its breath. After an appropriate pause, he continued. "Who is it that brings this woman to this man?"

Elysant had asked her friend days ago to be her maid of honor and stand with her, Luveday had been honored to accept. "I do," Luveday guided Elli forward and placed the bride's hand within the groom's and stepped back.

Father Quinn gave her a reassuring smile as Luveday resumed her spot in front of the crowd before he continued on. "Sir Gregori and Young Elysant, life is given to each of us as individuals, and yet we must learn to live together. Love is given to us by our family and friends. We learn to love by being loved. Learning to love and living together is one of life's greatest challenges and is the shared goal of married life." Luveday's eyes met Iain's behind the couple, and she alone caught the flash of pain there.

"But a husband and wife should not confuse love of worldly measures for even if worldly success is found, only love will maintain a marriage. Mankind did not create love; love is the work of our Creator. The measure of true love is a love both freely given and freely accepted, just as His love of us is unconditional and free." Something inside Luveday clicked into place, and she had the feeling that Father Quinn was speaking to Iain and herself. A few moments later she was sure of it. "Today truly is a glorious day the Lord hath made – as today both of you are blessed with the greatest of all gifts – the gift of abiding love and devotion between a man and a woman. All present here today – and those here in heart – wish both of you all the joy, happiness and success the world has to offer. As you travel through life together, I caution you to remember that the true measure of success, the true avenue to joy and peace, is to be found within the love you hold in your hearts. I would ask that you hold the key to your heart very tightly." At that moment, the doors to the chapel opened from the inside, and Father Quinn turned to lead the procession in for the mass and final vows.

Gregori and Elli followed behind the priest, Iain and Luveday were next; Lord Stern escorted Lady Emmalyn, while Agnes begrudgingly took Sir Fullers arm. Others followed behind, but the crowd was too dense for her to see.

Luveday knew the exact moment each person finally noticed the decorations. Candles burned in clusters to light the dark corners as sunshine streamed in high windows and the one stained-glass rose window behind the altar. The knights had helped to finish the decorations and came up with ways to hang the decor as Luveday had imagined, but no one other than Father Quinn had been allowed in the chapel after that. Luveday had spent two days, working from evening and late into the night to finesse the flowers and fabrics.

Elli had confided that she had always wished to be wed during the spring at High Castle, the home of Lady Emmalyn. The walk to the church was down a lane flanked by blossoming trees that had perfectly melded the white of winter and the greens of spring. Luveday had done her best to recreate that here. Men had cut branches the size of young trees and whitewashed the leafless bowers. Luveday had worked to make extra garlands of fabric flowers from natural linen and used a technique much like paper-mache to harden the blossoms and attach them to the branches. The flowers that the women had made were arranged artfully around the large room, the blooms held only a hint of color, while dried leaves had been cut down, whitewashed and tinted to resemble their former selves. The abundance of whitewashed plants should have given the room a haunted, frozen look, but instead, the chapel looked enchanted and elegant.

It was only a glance over the bride's shoulder, but Luveday caught the look of wonder and gratitude that the girl flashed at her. The guests settled into their seats, awed into silence as they observed the decorations. Father Quinn took his place before the altar, with the bride and groom before him, and Iain and Luveday taking their place to the left and right to stand as the witnesses before the Creator and the congregation. Gregori and Elli knelt before the altar, ready to receive the prayer and blessings.

After a long and heartfelt prayer in Latin, the last vows were exchanged. Father Quinn motioned for the couple to rise. "Would you please face each other and join hands." Turning to the knight, he began. "Sir Gregori of Brooke Abbey, do you take young Elysant to be your wife? Do you swear before the Creator to love, honor, cherish and protect her, forsaking all others and holding only to her forevermore?"

The large knight had to clear his throat before he could voice the traditional, "I do so swear."

Then it was the bride's turn. "Elysant De Lane of Lander's Keep, do you take Sir Gregori to be your husband? Do you swear before the Creator to love, honor, cherish and protect him, forsaking all others and holding only to him always?"

Elli's voice was strong and clear as she echoed, "I do so swear."

Father Quinn smiled at the resolve in her words. "Sir Gregori and Mistress Elysant, as the two of you, come into this marriage uniting you as husband and wife, and as you this day, affirm your faith and love for one another, I would ask that you always remember to cherish each other as irreplaceable and unique individuals, that you respect the thoughts, ideas, and suggestions of one another. Be able to forgive one another, do not hold grudges, and live each day that you may share it together – as from this day forward you shall be each other's home, comfort, and refuge, your marriage strengthened by your love and respect."

Luveday had always gotten the feeling that there was something different about Father Quinn, that his views were not quite popular with the church. In her mind she termed it being too "modern," and she had never been so aware of the fact as when she looked to the back of the chapel and saw many of the men and women frown at his phrasing. Talk of equality, of love and respect between man and wife, was not the norm and probably wouldn't be for a few hundred years.

Uncaring about the few looks of censure he received, the priest concluded the ceremony, "May the Creator forever bless this union of two souls so well matched. It is my honor to pronounce you husband and wife. Go in peace."

The chapel was surprisingly full of friend's and a few noblemen, though most had stayed within the keep, unconcerned about the marriage of some lowly Knight. The dinner that followed was not the grand affair that would accompany the Lord's wedding, but everyone had tried to make the occasion special for the bride and groom.

When it had grown late, and the time had come for the couple to retire, Luveday had a moment of concern for Elli but had to remind herself that this was the way of things. Luveday felt out of place as she was pushed along with the crowd toward the room where the two would be spending the night. The knights and woman of the castle hassled and teased the bride and groom until both were laughing and red with embarrassment, but still too happy to care. Hanging back, Luveday merely wished to see that everything in the room had been taken care of before leaving the rowdy crowd and turning to find her own room.

The day could not have gone smoother, and Luveday sighed as she walked down the quiet hall, her thoughts in opposition. Once again, Iain snuck up on her, turning her into his embrace for a fiery kiss. She pulled away as laughter echoed down the corridor.

"Why sneak away? Was the merriment not to your liking, Lady?" Iain's hands moved from the back of her shoulder blades to play with the wisps of hair at her nap.

The gesture was more comforting than sensual. "The last few days have been very long."

Iain laughed though there was a hard note under the mirth. "Aye. You've done this house proud, Luveday. I could not have imagined what magic you performed today. Elli has never been happier."

"She deserves the best." Luveday looked up at him, tired and not wanting to pull away. "'Tis one of the happiest days of her life, I wanted to make it special, and no magic was needed, just a bit of ingenuity and imagination."

"As you say." He didn't look like he believed her.

"Thank you, thank you for recognizing Elli publicly." Emmalyn had briefly explained Elli's elevated status that came with being an acknowledged member of the family. It was a precious gift, one not often given. She wondered why Iain had thought of it now, and not sooner, but she supposed such a gift was better late than never.

"You are welcome, though I did not do it for you." He seemed amused by her gratitude. "Nor for Gregori either, he was happy to take the girl as she was."

Luveday looked at him, confused. "For Elli then," though it was more of a question than a statement.

"Aye," he squeezed her close before turning them to continue down the hall that led back to the one that contained their rooms. "And for myself. I have always wondered about the girl. We could find no record of her parentage, but she is surely my brother's daughter. She bears the family traits and birthmark, a gift that skipped even me." Luveday had wondered, she had heard talk of a birthmark, but having seen Iain in all his glory, she had never spotted one. De Lane continued, obviously, the topic was one he had contemplated for a while. "It is not impossible that Willum had married her mother, but with both dead and no proof. Well, it finally occurred to me that I could change that by claiming the girl. It might not make much difference now, but someday they may be thankful for it."

"I am sure she is thankful now." Luveday let her hand move to his back, as he walked beside her, his own resting in the curve of her spine. They must have looked intimate, an arm wrapped around each other's waist. As they turned the corner Christabel's door came into view, and Luveday's arm fell away.

He looked down at her puzzled by the sudden loss of intimacy but soon followed where her attention was focused. Placing his body between her and the offending door did not erase it from her mind or reality. She would not let him kiss her, not that she did not want a distraction from her thoughts, but she refused to be kissed outside his fiancé's door.

Stepping away and around him, she maneuvered out of his grasp. "Goodnight, My Lord," was said over her shoulder as she closed her own door behind her.

Chapter 14

He said true things, but called them by wrong names.
~ Elizabeth Barrett Browning

Spring had somehow blossomed overnight. Men and women crowded every nook and cranny of the keep. Luveday had never imagined such a conglomeration of nobility. Every room was full, the under-gallery was bursting with knights, and even the sewing room housed a dozen women who had come to help with the wedding day celebrations.

Many were up long before dawn, Luveday included. The kitchens had been cooking nearly non-stop since Elli and Gregori's wedding. Though much of the castle was unhappy about the ceremony that was about to take place, no one stood to contradict the King's decree, least of all Lord Iain. Through the bustle of preparations, Luveday had decided her life and Iain's place in it. Though she had spoken to no one but Lord Benedict and Lady Emmalyn, and separately at that, there was a feeling that something monumental had been set upon the young lady's shoulders. Many friends watched her throughout the preparations, and many nobles watched her out of curiosity or concern, but either way, Luveday felt the eyes of many on her every time she stepped from her room, and today was no exception.

"Watch it, girl!" Lord Sumerland was as mean-tempered as ever, but luckily, he had arrived only the evening before, and so Luveday had little time in his company. She bowed but didn't apologize as if it weren't her fault that she had nearly poured the spiced wine in his lap not that it would make much difference to his attire. He wore deep burgundy velvets, matching leggings and large pieces of chunky gold jewelry. The combination was striking if a little overdone.

Luveday had picked up the pitcher to pour drinks out of necessity as every other woman in the room seemed to be occupied; that Sumerland treated her no better than he treated any of the other serving women had ceased to surprise her. Even Elysant was still condescended to though De Lane's acknowledgments of her had caused a storm of gossip and whispers.

Weaving through the crowd, she had little else to do at the moment as the guests waited for the bell to be wrung and to journey the short distance to the chapel tower. Coll appeared, grabbing her attention by snagging the skirt of her blue gown, the same one she had worn a week prior. Leaning in so she could hear the soft-spoken boy over the din of the crowd, she heard his words all too clearly as they sent a shiver of dread through her.

"My Lord wishes to see you." And a moment later the boy was gone. Luveday had no doubt that Coll had meant right now. Iain's mood had become increasingly changeable as the days had passed. Was it strange that she could sense his desperation, or was she merely projecting her own emotions onto him?

She handed off the nearly empty pitcher and passed by Lady Emmalyn as she headed for the solar. The women exchanged a look. Underneath the concern, Luveday thought she glimpsed a bit of pride from her mentor, which only solidified her own steely determination.

Coll waited at the top of the stairs to open the door for her but didn't follow her in. The sound of the thick wood door closing behind her wasn't surprising; it was almost welcomed as it hushed the noise of the hall to a quiet roar. The inner door was cracked open, light flooded the room beyond, but not from the window in the solar, this was firelight, not the cheerful sun outside. Large candles burned around the room lending an intimacy to the space that seemed to block out the outside world.

Pausing on the other side of the threshold, a single step inside the room, Luveday looked at the alcove that housed the window and wondered why the shutters were closed. Movement to her right caused her to turn toward the fireplace. Iain stood leaning his shoulder against the massive mantle. He wore a pair of dun-colored leggings, no shirt or boots.

In her confusion, she blurted out the obvious. "You are not dressed?" It was a statement and a question.

He glanced at the bed, and her eyes were drawn there as well. The canopied monstrosity was neatly made as it was every day, but atop it were two piles of garments, one hanging off each side of the bed. The outfit on the right was the same blue he had worn a week ago that complimented her own gown very well. The other pile was burgundy velvet that matched Lord Sumerland and, she suspected, Lady Christabel's wedding attire. So here was the dilemma, which to choose. Luveday nearly laughed at the blunt symbol of their current predicament.

"You should have been dressed an hour ago." Luckily, Christabel was still primping in her room, or they would have been waiting on a reluctant groom. Moving to the left side of the bed, Luveday began looking over the garments and readying them to ware. Iain spun her around, ripping the tunic from her grasp and throwing it back onto the bed.

"Tell me you'll stay with me." He grabbed her, smoothing his hands over her shoulders, feeling the velvet that covered them with pleasure. "If you are beside me, I can walk out there. I can do this."

And there was Luveday's fortitude, her spine straightened because she had realized two very important things over the last week watching Elysant and Gregori in wedded bliss. First, that she loved Iain beyond distraction which she knew would eventually cause her demise. If she stayed with him, she would give in, if only to have him to herself for one night, one moment and once tied to him, it would be almost impossible to break free. She had no doubt that if the sorrow didn't somehow kill her, she would end up being a hard and bitter woman. Her second realization had come on the heels of that hard truth. Though many women had repeated the words like a mantra, few believed them. Only now did she understand and believe. She was worth more than this. She was worth being someone's first choice, not settling for what Iain was able to give her, even if it was his heart and his love. She wanted respect, she wanted equality, and if she stayed to be his mistress, his leman, and lover she would have a semblance of those things, but they would not be hers in truth. The respect and honor would be his wife's, Lady Christabel. All the love and lust between them could not dull that sting.

"I will walk out beside you." She heard herself say, but she knew the truth. She could never follow him in the way he wanted.

"Luveday." His breath mingled with hers as he leaned in to kiss her long and hard. Luveday took it as the last they would ever share, while Iain took it as a sign of her capitulation to him. "You are mine, remember that. You swore to stay by my side before we went north, and you will stay now." It was a command, not a request.

Luveday looked at him, memorizing his face, and turned to hand him the burgundy garment. She helped him dress, picked the jewels he would wear on his hands and around his neck. Bedecked in the finest court attire, more handsome than any man she had ever seen, she followed him out of the room. Their hands brushed at the top of the stairs as every eye gazed up at them. Descending the stairs, Luveday was a step behind and still shorter than him; she took advantage and hid a bit behind his shoulders.

De Lane was swallowed by the mass of well-wishers. Luveday stayed by his side despite the looks of censor around her. Lord Sumerland had taken her aside that morning for a talk she knew was coming. Luckily, the encounter didn't last nearly as long as she had imagined. "It is too late, not that you could have stopped this, girl." The hand that was clamped around her upper arm closed like a vice causing Luveday to clench her teeth against the pain. "My Christabel was made to be his match, and with the power of the King's Champion our future is assured." She had never had any illusions about this match; it had always been about what Sumerland needed. The scheming man had taken advantage of De Lane, of that she was sure. "Tread carefully, now. Once my daughter is mistress here a word will send you out into the cold." He jerked her forward as a sickened look of appraisal entered his eyes. He looked her over like he might a piece of horseflesh. "If you weren't so small and manipulative, I'd offer to keep you in town for myself." He looked at her chest with some approval. "Too bad I have enough trouble with these women already." Luveday almost kicked him, refusing to lose the contents of her stomach on his shoes. "Heed my warning girl, the world beyond these walls is cold and hard, and a lady with no fortune, no matter her station, is little more than a whore. This world is ruled by men, if you want to survive, learn to play our games." He had let her go and fled back to the hall where Lord Benedict came upon her.

It took some time for her to ease his concern, and still, Benedict kept a wary eye on her throughout the day.

As bride and groom joined hands to lead the procession to the steps of the chapel Luveday hung back. Iain had caught a glimpse of her as the exodus through the doors began, but the nobility of higher rank muscled their way between them. Luveday took that opportunity to fall behind. Emmalyn appeared at the end of the line as the masses gathered before the great doors to hear the priest and the vows. The village and other guests crowded the area, some stood high on the walls or any place they thought might afford a view. Fortunately, a small path out of the castle gate remained clear.

Tears filled Luveday's eyes as the woman handed over a bundle. "Here you go child, for the journey." She accepted the gift, not knowing its contents and hugged her friend and mentor quickly.

Elli appeared between them, a look of concern and grief in her eyes. "You are leaving?" The girl shook her head and hugged her friend so fiercely that Luveday wondered if she would ever let her go.

"I must," was all she could get past the lump in her throat.

Wide, watery eyes turned up to hers. "I know." Elli stepped back as Emmalyn pulled her aside, not wanting someone in the crowd to take an interest in their exchange. "I will miss you." Wiping her eyes to hold back the tears, the girl raced toward the crowd in search of her husband, in search of comfort.

"We will meet again, Luveday." The lady took her hand and squeezed it. "I am sure of it." Luveday gave her another quick hug and looked to find Benedict at the back of the crowd looking expectantly in her direction. "May you have a safe journey and be blessed."

Luveday stepped away, half turning back she looked at Lady Emmalyn framed by the massive doors. "Thank you, for everything. Blessings on you and all of Lander's Keep." It felt like she ran to Benedict's side, but in truth, they walked casually through the gate with no one taking any notice. Father Quinn had begun to speak, but though neither stopped to listen, Luveday felt that his words were not the same heartfelt vows that he had uttered only a week ago.

As they found their horses on the other side of the village, Luveday thought about how lovely a day it was. Her belongings were already tied behind her side-saddle, her cloak rested against the pommel in case a wind should arise. She looked to Benedict who mounted after helping her to do the same. The four men that accompanied them looked disappointed to be missing the festivities, but Benedict had commanded them, and like the good men that they were, they would obey.

The castle sat on a slight rise, looking warm and content in the spring sunshine. It looked much the same as it did a year ago when she had first arrived. One year, five days was all it had been, and yet her time there had felt like a lifetime.

Benedict called to her, and she flicked the reins and pressed her heeled boot into the horse's side. The journey had begun, as all did, with a single step. This time the unknown that awaited her was not so terrifying. She was a different person than the mousy young woman who had been thrown into this new world. Luveday had changed, learned new skills and gained a quiet confidence. She had a friend beside her and hopes for the future. As every step took her farther away from what she had known, she consoled her broken heart with the knowledge that she had been true to herself and that with time and distance this pain would fade.

As the small band of travelers entered the wood, a rider, running at full gallop came up the road. The horse slowed as the harried man on its back spotted them.

The rider looked as if he had journeyed hard and long. "Please, I pray you. Is Lander's Keep far? Is the Champion's wedding this day? Have I missed the speaking of the vows?"

Benedict spared Luveday a glance before leaning forward in his saddle to answer. "Aye, Friend, you are almost there. If you make haste, you might get there before they finish the vows." But before the lordling could wish the rider luck, the man kicked his mount and galloped past as if all the hounds of hell pursued him.

"He didn't want to miss the feast." One of their companions laughed, but his lord speared him with a disapproving look.

"Shall we continue My Lady?" Benedict asked and Luveday was not sure if he referred to their brief stop or to the journey as a whole. She had made it clear that there was no other option for her.

"Of course, My Lord; we have only just begun." Tapping her mount, they were off again.

Part Two

Anora

Chapter 15

"Will that light come again, As now these tears come...falling hot and real!"
~ Elizabeth Barrett Browning, Sonnets from the Portuguese

Lady Jane St. James steered Luveday by the elbow as they quickened their pace down the hall. Both women were nervous, and as a result, they spoke not a word and looked neither left nor right as they followed the servant. Their demeanor was severe, and their backs ramrod straight as they were escorted to the King's personal chambers.

Luveday thanked God for the lifeline that Benedict's mother provided. She had come to see how she and Lady Emmalyn were such dear friends. She was not sure how she would have managed the separation without her, and especially not this royal summons.

The day the letter arrived was still fresh in her memory. Luveday had arrived several weeks earlier at Lion's Head castle bone tired and miserable from the long and wet journey, though truth be told, her tremulous emotions had more to do with what she had left behind than what lay before her. Benedict's mother had taken one look at her and seemed to get the gist of the matter and had tactfully stayed clear of any talk of Lander's Keep. As the two women became accustomed to each other, their friendship seemed to blossom almost overnight; no doubt helped along by the fact that the young woman had saved her only son's life. Luveday was told to stay as long as she liked, forever even, if that was her wish. She took up the task of being Jane's companion and helped out where she could, though there was a lot less for her to do here than she was used to. Lander's Keep had been short-handed from the start; something Luveday had never fully realized until she saw what a well-oiled machine Lion's Head castle turned out to be. So Luveday spent most of her time sewing and weaving, while Jane indulged her wish to continue to learn the healing arts. Though Lady Emmalyn had told her life-long friend of Luveday's skills, Luveday got the feeling that Jane thought it more a useful hobby than something the young woman would ever excel at. Luveday was simply happy to continue learning and was careful not to overstep her bounds and lose this newfound generosity.

The Lady's solar was the spot of choice for both women. Full of light, fresh air, and laughter, the tower room was the first place anyone would look for them. That day started out as ordinary as the dozen before it. Luveday sat on a settee in a place she had begun to think of as her own. A young serving woman sat beside her darning a torn hem while Luveday embroidered exotic flowers on a pillow cover. The rush of footsteps up the stair was not uncommon, and so the ladies felt no sense of urgency until the young man burst through the door waving a missive, the giant red seal blinking at them with the rapid movement. "Lady Jane a message from the King." The boy was winded and staggered a little before handing over the letter. Luveday tried but failed to remember his name. After nearly a month in the castle, she still saw new faces almost every day.

"'Tis addressed to you, Lady Luveday." Jane handed over the letter with some surprise. More footsteps were heard as Benedict appeared in the doorway looking magnificent and golden in the early morning sun. The young woman beside her, Lily, was a seamstress, and personal woman for Lady Jane having taken over the position from her mother. The girl sighed as many of the young women did when they saw the heir to the castle. As Lily had said, "What's the harm in looking? Beauty eases the heart in all its forms. No need to worry about him turning my head, I have as much chance of catching his eye as a bee is to find a flower in winter. You on the other hand lady..." Luveday almost laughed again at the thought, momentarily distracted by the man despite herself.

"There was a messenger from the King below. What news?" He looked to his mother who nodded towards the girl.

"The letter is for Luveday." All eyes turned to her, while she looked at the piece of parchment as if she had never seen one before.

"Well, Luve?" The Lord prompted, startling her by using her new nickname.

Nodding, she removed the seal and read the sharp lines written there. After someone cleared their throat for the second time, she got the hint and started over, this time reading the letter aloud.

"His Majesty, King Edward the Third of Anora requests Lady Luveday, previously of Lander's Keep, be presented to his royal person at the seat of Kingstown at the Lady's earliest opportunity. The King wishes to discuss personal matters of great importance. Godspeed, Edward the Third, King of Anora and Lion of the North Isles."

Jane huffed. "Is there nothing more?" Luveday shook her head and handed over the letter at a loss for words.

Benedict looked at his friend with some concern. "What could the King want with her?" He addressed his mother as Luveday still seemed to be in a daze.

"I have no notion, my dear." She looked at Luveday with a calculating eye. Her embroidery hoop landed in her chair with some force as Jane rose to her feet. "But I mean to find out." Orders were issued to several people who waited anxiously beyond the solar door. "Begin packing immediately. The best gowns, provisions for four, no, for a week and the new items for Luveday."

Not trying to be ungrateful; still, Luveday protested. "Jane, I told you I don't need..."

"Hush now, we are going to court." She said as if that statement alone was an explanation. "They will eat you alive dressed like that girl; we must prepare." She turned to her son and patted him on the chest. "Benedict…" but she didn't have to finish, for mother and son were on the same page.

"I'll be ready to leave within the hour." He looked at Luveday as she smiled bemusedly at them both. "And if the messenger is still below, I'll see what news I can get from him."

His mother winked at him. "Good boy." She turned to Luveday. "As for you…"

Luveday shook herself and rose to her feet as a storm of servants sprung into motion like a hive of agitated bees. "Isn't this a little soon? The letter said…"

"I know what the letter said, Luveday." Jane calm demeanor gave way as she bent and shoved the mass of thread and embroidery into its basket beside her chair. "At one's earliest opportunity is just the royal way of saying as quickly as possible. They never want to seem rushed about such things but mark my words; there is no time to delay."

Having no experience with court matters Luveday deferred to Jane's wisdom and got her butt into high gear. Within the hour they were in the traveling coach, fully provisioned and starting the three-day journey to Kingstown. Luveday tried to calm her nerves as her worse fears began to come true. She was a fraud, an unwitting charlatan waiting for the one faux pas that would bring her failings to light. She was going to the one place where she would be under constant scrutiny, where the threat of exposure was the greatest; she was going to court.

The door was held open for them, and a deep voice announced, "Lady St. James of Lion's Head, and Lady Luveday of Lander's Keep." Both ladies entered the room and bowed as gracefully as any in the royal court still clinging to each other. Luveday's eyes rose from the floor to find not only the familiar face of the King but that Queen Augusta sat across from him. The simple table and chairs belied the gilded grandeur of the throne room they had passed through several moments ago. This room spoke of comfort, familiarity, and a closeness that the previous rooms had not. Red drapes matched the velvet of the Queen's gown, while the King wore a deep blue. Both royals had gold trim and trappings that clearly marked their superior station, but the gilt was a tasteful accent rather than a show of prestige.

"Please sit, ladies." The Queen was the first to usher them in, and her kind smile was enough to ease Luveday a little. The women sat, and all eyes turned to King Edward who sat in deep thought. "My dear?" His wife prompted.

The King seemed to shake off some dark thought to address the women, but his eyes settled on Luveday with a calculating gaze. "I am sorry to have made you travel in such weather; the roads are still wet with the spring rains. I had hoped…"

"We had hoped that your help would not have been necessary." The

Queen continued when it looked as if her husband would not.

Luveday wondered what could rob such an elegant man of his speech, and what did they mean by her help? The only skills that would mean anything to the Royals were her healing abilities, and the court was full of men whose experience and reputations far overshadowed her own. And yet, Luveday thought she noticed a hint of desperation in their eyes. The unease returned along with a twisting in her gut.

"'Tis not common knowledge but Prince Holden has fallen ill." Lady St. James gasped as the Queen continued. "Of course, we have tried everything..."

"Every crackpot, bone mender, and tinker." The King growled.

A gentle hand came to rest on the King's own, and Luveday got to witness a rare personal moment between husband and wife. "You are our last hope, Lady Luveday. If you cannot help him..." she looked away, for that moment she was just Augusta, a mother desperate to save her son, and not the Queen of Anora.

Jane nudged her companion with her elbow and Luveday grappled with herself to find the words that might give them some comfort. "I wish I could bring you some solace, your majesties. I cannot imagine your worry." The Queen looked at her, gauging her sincerity. "I cannot make you any promises. I will need to see the prince before I can tell you if I can be of any help."

"Straight to the point." He nodded to himself. "I told you, my dear." Edward smiled at his wife before rising to his feet.

The royal couple seemed heartened by her answer, though Luveday couldn't fathom why. "So, you did, husband." The Queen rose to her feet as well, the two ladies followed suit a moment later, trailed along behind her without question.

Luveday wondered how deep into the castle they would venture while trying to distract herself from the doubts and fears that were turning her insides to knots. She looked to Jane as they turned a corner down another long hallway. The woman reminded her a bit of her mother, with her sharp wit, an easy laugh, and a pragmatic disposition. That is where the similarities ended; the woman was tall nearing six feet while her mother was only a few inches taller than Luveday's five-two. Lady St. James was slim, almost athletic in build, with chestnut locks and warm doe colored eyes. Though the two women were physically different in nearly every manner, there was something in their spirit that linked them in Luveday's mind and heart.

The older woman still had Luveday's right arm around her own and would give it a pat or a reassuring squeeze now and then. Luckily, their destination was not too much farther along, and finally, they came to a pair of carved doors. Two guards stood in the hall appearing as if they might be part of the high stone structure, though Luveday detected only the slightest hint of breath from each of them. The Queen let herself in, though Lady St. James moved to do it for her. They entered an anteroom that was dark despite it being the afternoon. The heavy drapes on the window to their right let in a small sliver of sunlight that was almost blinding in the darkness. It was the sudden dimness and sharp contrast with the world outside that distracted Luveday long enough to miss the fact that there was a man in the room, who stood silently waiting by another set of equally massive carved doors. Like the first, the creatures and designs that marked the door's surface were obscured by thick shadows, shadows that hid the man as well. The Queen stopped only when she had reached his side. The two had a whispered conversation; the subject of which must have been Luveday as both occasionally looked to where the two ladies stood just inside the far doors. Momentarily forgotten, Luveday took the time to look around her.

The few candles that lit the room created little vignettes of the life of the person that lived within. The room at first seemed stark, but that was due more to the darkness than design. A single candle sat on a round table and illuminated some books, parchment, and ink. Scribbles and drawings covered cotton parchment and vellum as if the writer's mind where too fast for his pen. Stepping closer out of curiosity, Luveday noticed that the subject of interest was medicine, more specifically the human body and the issue of humors. Luveday's nose wrinkled as the absurdity of some of the notions penned there.

"Not to your liking, Luveday?" Jane came up to bend over the table, studying the scene but touched nothing.

Luveday smiled at her friend; the brief time they had known each other, they had become familiar with each other's expressions. Their rapport was as easy as if she talked to Emmalyn or Elysant. She turned her mind away from that life and all the dreams she'd put behind her to study the thoughts of their mysterious healer. "No, they don't suit me."

"You think you can do better girl?" A male voice reminded her that they were not alone. Luveday turned toward the hostile character.

The Queen put a hand on her companion's arm, and the man stilled. "She cannot do worse. He is dying."

She had turned away, but the whisper carried in the quiet room. The man nodded as he gave Luveday a hard look. "Logan is Prince Holden's man, and he will help you with all you need. You are to take over care of the prince immediately. We are putting our trust in you, Lady Luveday." Her tone said more than her words; do not fail us. The Queen gazed into the little healer's eyes for a long moment and was satisfied that her unspoken message was received before leaving.

Rounding the table, Luveday came closer trying to get a better look at the man, but he turned away opening the doors behind him. The room beyond was large and full of clothes. Male clothes, rich in color and texture hung around the room on pegs. On closer inspection the walls were lined with some sort of dark fabric, a glass lantern sat in the middle of the room on a simple wooden stool that was barely knee height. Luveday realized they were in the prince's closet, but before she could speak the servant opened another set of doors on the far wall.

Following behind, Luveday knew that the prince must be somewhere beyond but how many rooms might lie between them; she had no idea. The next room was much more to a boy's liking, full of hunting gear, old toys, boots, and even a real saddle tossed over the back of an old wooden horse. The prince was growing up but had yet to put away all of his childish things.

"Sir Logan?" Luveday called out as Jane caught up to them. "Sir?"

"It is just Logan, My Lady." He sounded exasperated, or maybe exhausted was a better fit.

"Logan." She stopped as he turned to look at them.

"My Lady." He waited.

Luveday tried not to be put out by his impatient and impertinent manner. "I am truly sorry to hear about Prince Holden's condition, but, please, can you tell me a bit about him?"

The man seemed to grit his teeth. "The Queen has put me at your disposal. What would you like to know?"

If he was not pleasant at least Logan was willing to work with her, she thought. "How old is he? What was his constitution before he became ill? Was there a previous bought of illness? When exactly did the first signs appear?" Luveday looked up; realizing that she might be overwhelming the man, but when she met his gaze, there was a peculiar look in his eyes.

"His Highness has always been a rather active boy, trying to keep up with his elder brother, Prince Archibald. He has seen sixteen summers, and if it were up to me, he would live to see a hundred more." His voice softened for the first time since they had met, and Luveday could clearly see that the man loved his charge. "When he was ten summers, he became ill for about a fortnight but was none the worse for wear." A distant and thoughtful look came over the man, and Luveday wondered how old he was, and how long the prince had been in his care. The lantern in the room did nothing to illuminate the subtle nuances of his face, though Luveday stood close enough to make out many of his expressions. "If I recall correctly, his highness became pinked and easily tired a few days before he was confined to bed. That was almost three moons ago."

Jane gasped. "Three moons and the boy has not improved? What of Master Pope; is he not the best healer at court?"

Logan laughed and sneered at the name. Luveday clenched her teeth remembering her brief meeting with the man. "Master Pope continues to pour strengthening potions down the Prince's throat and swears they are all that is keeping the boy alive. The Queen and King have given up on his fool's errands. He has left his servant behind while he travels to find some silly plant, he claims to be our savior." The derision in Logan's tone left no doubt about his thoughts on the master healer. Luveday had to agree; she had no faith in the drunken lout and was grateful that she would not have to deal with him today. She could not forgive him for nearly killing Iain.

"So, who is left to care for the boy?" Luveday turned to Jane, unbelieving the older woman had asked such a question. Logan took it as she expected and the emotional wall between them was raised once again.

"Who, you ask, My Lady?" The smile on his face was all white teeth and anger, a startling and unnerving sight in the darkness. "Why, let me announce you!" He spun on his heels and threw open the doors in front of them.

The doors banged against the wall as every eye in the room turned toward them. Logan dressed in dark robes swept into the room and in a voice made too loud in the ensuing stillness said, "Good day, healers of the realm. May I introduce Lady St. James and Lady Luveday." Luveday took a step forward into the light cast by the massive fireplace while Jane stayed in shadows. "Lady Luveday is a healer from the North," the men scattered around the room seemed to come to their senses enough to look down their noses at her as Logan continued his dramatic and satirical monologue. "She has traveled here, with what fabulous, unheard of, healing concoctions I do not know. I can but wait with bated breath," Luveday noticed that Logan's voice, though mocking had grown a little horse. "The lady has been given dispensation by the Queen." There was a collective intake of breath, "Her will is the will of Her Majesty; her words are as if they were spoken from royal lips." Now a growl passed through the room, and hate-filled eyes glared daggers at the little healer. Logan, taking great glee in the spectacle, cleared his throat before continuing. "From this moment forward the prince is in her capable hands. Do not glare at me so, gentleman." He said the word gentlemen as if he would rather spit in their faces than call them such. Bowing with mock humility, he said simply, "I am here but to serve," before sweeping away into a dim corner of the room.

With every eye turned to her Luveday took a deep breath and for a moment almost panicked when she could not draw enough air into her lungs. She coughed as thick incense coated her throat, while laughter filled the room. Someone commented on a healer healing one's self, but Luveday didn't stop to think. Lurching toward the heavy velvet drapes on the windows, Luveday struggled to find the opening she knew must be there. A moment later hands came to help as she threw open the panels and opened the pained glass window beyond.

With her first breath of fresh air, the tears in Luveday's eyes subsided. Angry voiced rang in the room behind her, but all the lady could think about was easing her racing heart with deep breaths of the evening air. For a moment Luveday looked out over the crowded city and noticed that the unpleasant place seemed almost magical from the castle window. That was until one of the men came up behind her shoving her out of the way as he tried to close the window again.

Her helper appeared at her arm, and for a moment Luveday recognized something about the young man but couldn't put her finger on it, though he grinned gamely at her, she had no notion of who he was. Her attention was taken up by the healer in front of her as he grumbled under his breath slamming the window closed and locking the latch.

He whirled at her, "You foolish girl! What idiot taught you of the healing arts? You will kill the prince in a week." The man was out of breath and hoarse by the time he finished talking. Luveday's eyes were beginning to sting as the incense started to regain its hold on her.

"Quiet man," A familiar voice said at her side causing Luveday to glance at the bearded man taking up her cause. "This is Lady Luveday of Lander's Keep. Have you not heard of her deeds in the High North? She saved Prince Benjamin's life from Sterling."

"This little mouse? Don't make me laugh." He pushed past them into the room where the rest of the men had gathered to gawk at her.

Luveday didn't hesitate. She opened the window again, took a deep breath and turned to face the crowd. The healer who had just closed the window turned back as if he meant to do her harm, but one of his companions clamped a hand on his shoulder to stop him. She scanned the crowd of fifteen or so men as her vision cleared. They ran the gambit of size, shape, and color, but the one thing they had in common was that they were, perhaps, the bottom of the barrel. These men looked sneaky, underhanded, dirty and far too confident for their own good.

Steel settled into Luveday's spine as she brought all of her determination to bear down on them. A few men had the good sense to fidget at her change in demeanor, but the rest just glared back.

"Their Majesties, the King and Queen, have asked me to take over the care of Prince Holden." Some were disconcerted at the mention of the King; Luveday almost smiled at the change in the room. Her expression remained hard and piercing. "Like this room, it is time to clear the air. Those of you who are here for the King's coin will be compensated..." The grumbling and denials started as if on cue. "...for your time and efforts but let us face facts gentlemen." They quieted as if to listen. "The prince is dying; even the Queen can see that. Do you really want to be here when that happens? Would you rather not take the coin and go than be tossed out on your collective arse?" Some agreed, while others looked around to gauge their competitions reactions. "I am only offering this choice once; it would be wise to take it now." Two stepped forward as if to confront her but Luveday didn't so much as flinch. "I have no wish to mince words with you or prove who has the greater skill. I am here to save that boy's life, God willing." Her gaze swept over the group once more. "I have no time for anyone who does not share that purpose." She walked through the crowd to find Logan in the middle of the room, the great bed holding the frail body of the unconscious prince dwarfed the man and room. "See to it, Logan."

Luveday turned to the bed, and her patient as a fresh breeze washed through the room. Luveday found the fragrance burner and snuffed out the flame. Checking the bed linens, and the emaciated boy inside, she was happy when her friends returned to her side. A male voice chuckled at the room cleared of healers, only the two of them remaining. "What do you need of me, My Lady?"

Troubled by the state of the prince, Luveday turned to him with a furrowed brow. "Thomas, tell me everything you know about the prince's condition and all the treatments he's received. Start from the beginning and don't leave out a single detail."

It was several hours later, and much work that Luveday rested, and finally thought to introduce her two friends. Jane was happy to meet the apprentice of Master Pope, while Thomas was delighted to be included in the regard of such a noble lady. The two chatted quietly in the corner as Luveday made her way back to the small study.

More candles had been lit, and light flooded the room as night settled over the castle. Logan sat at the table scribbling on clear corners of parchment. Luveday chided herself on not realizing the room belonged to him. Logan, as servant and friend to the young prince, had tried to take an active role in his charge's care by writing down the healers' treatments. As the line of failed attempts grew, and new healers came to try their hand, his was the only complete record of medications and crackpot schemes.

"I see it is you I should have asked about the Prince's care and not Thomas."

Logan looked up at her, setting down his quill and folding his hands before him. Not for the first time that night, he studied her with unnerving patience as if waiting for something to be revealed.

Luveday stared back, too tired and troubled to be unsettled by such a direct gaze. "May I see your notes?" The man handed over a handful of papers, still not speaking to her.

As she studied them, he finally asked, "Are you so bold that you think you can do what a hundred healers and wise men could not?"

Luveday briefly wondered if the number of healers was accurate or an exaggeration but batted it aside as it was not his point. She looked at him over the papers in her hands. "I would not say I am bold, or overly confident, nor would I call those men healers or wise men." She looked at him, but he did not react.

"Yet you dismissed them and their knowledge out of hand." He was clearly agitated with her.

She placed the paper back on the table and looked down at him. Leaning in she tilted her head as she often did when she was curious. "Why do you say it was out of hand?"

He seemed surprised by her question or her nearness, whichever one it was she couldn't say, but he started and leaned away in his chair. "They have had years more experience no doubt." He paused to look at the glass doors of the bookcase behind him. The leather volumes there were worth a fortune. "They have studied under great men and traveled the world."

"And that somehow makes them better than me?" Luveday stood up to her full height, short as it was. Logan looked perplexed. "And yet they took the money and ran, didn't they?" Anger colored his face, but he didn't speak. "They lacked heart." She said, before turning away, taking the scribbles and notes with her.

Luveday sat on the floor. A lantern atop a stool sat by her side, a smooth board in her lap, a notebook and pencil case beside her thigh and for a moment she felt a sense of déjà vu. For a heartbeat, she was transported home and several years in the past as she studied for college exams on the floor of her dorm room while her roommate slept not five feet away. Glancing up and across the room's expanse, she could see the bed where the prince lay. His breathing was shallow, a little wheezy and his skin dry but too warm. They had changed the sheets and bedclothes as they bathed the prince. Luveday was chronicling the healers that had seen the prince and the treatments they had given. Truthfully, she was unsure how the boy had survived so long. To her modern sensibilities, half the procedures and a number of the potions he had received were enough to kill a healthy man, let alone the weakened prince.

The wheeze in his lungs was troublesome; being in bed for an extended period had caused a number of unknown complications, perhaps even pneumonia along with the muscle loss. The boy had a fever that seemed to return in cycles, the most recent of which had started the night before. Luckily, Holden could be roused enough to take in some liquids two or three times a day, but the healers had been using those opportunities to pore God knows what down his throat instead of trying to nourish his body.

Luveday pulled out her herbal, the book by Ody was dog-eared, smudged and full of slips of paper with notes about things she had learned from Cass and Emmalyn, but it had proven a lifesaver. She was sure she had memorized its pages, but the volume quieted some of her own doubts. Without a definite diagnosis, she could only start treating the symptoms she could see. Luveday made a list of herbs and the supplies she would need. She needed someplace to work but didn't want to be too far from the boy. She had a list of to-dos an arm long. She prayed for the one thing outside of her power: time.

An unnatural quiet settled over the city as the moon rose high. Logan entered the prince's room to check on the boy. Each time he approached the bed a weight dropped to the bit of his stomach as if his heart had turned to stone and fallen from its mount. Dread caused the hairs on the back of his neck to stand on end, his hands grew clammy, and his skin chilled as if death itself waited nearby. The steady rise and fall of boy's chest released a rush of relief and gratitude each time Logan found his friend still alive. Even though only a few years separated them, Logan felt as if he had aged decades over the last few moons.

Logan stopped to study his friend, unable to see the vibrant and joking boy in the body on the bed. The light of his lantern made the child look too pale and thin. As he was about to return and find his bed, he noticed the light caught something else as well. On the far side of the bed, before the windows whose curtains were open to reveal a starry sky, sat a sizeable winged-back chair. Covered in her traveling cloak and curled into a ball, Lady Luveday had fallen asleep while watching her charge.

The lady looked small and young in such a position, more modest and more youthful than she had when they had first met that evening. As a servant, Logan had no place to go against the Queen's wishes, and as the recipient of their trust and charity, he had not the heart to challenge their decision though everything he possessed told him there was something unusual about the lady. He could no longer say if her presence here would help or harm his friend. So, he decided to watch and wait for he had no other options. She was the last hope, and if she could not help Holden, then no one could.

He returned to his room and the small bed beyond. His dreams were plagued by memories of the prince and the night held no reprieve from his fears.

Chapter 16

"Why, what is to live? Not to eat and drink and breathe,
—but to feel the life in you down all the fibres of being,
passionately and joyfully."
~ Elizabeth Barrett Browning

Luveday worked in the still room that had once been the Prince's horde of toys and gear. The boy had shown little improvement in three days' time, but she hadn't expected much. Thomas was a Godsend and a more knowledgeable assistant she couldn't find. The connection they had seemed to share in the north was still there. The young man worked diligently beside her and without whose help she wouldn't have been able to find the herbs and equipment she needed, whether from the royal stores or local vendors. Luveday didn't know what she would have done without him or the name of his master which he wielded shamelessly to motivate disagreeable parties.

Thomas had returned to town and remained there since leaving the north. Pope had traveled about a good deal, leaving Thomas on his own, which was nothing new. The young healer had not heard of his master's visit to Lander's Keep until Pope's return, and then he had heard every detail for some weeks. There was no love lost between Luveday and the old man, Thomas was secretly pleased every time he heard the story of Luveday throwing him out of the Keep. From Pope's retelling, Thomas could believe that Luveday had chased the man through the gates herself. Luveday laughed as Thomas mimicked his master perfectly, as he groused about the spiteful little woman. Luveday almost didn't recognize herself or her friends in his tales and shook her head that the old man worried only for his hurt pride, and not for almost costing Iain De Lane his life.

Thomas made the mistake of trying to talk about the lord of Lander's Keep only once, briefly mentioning the wedding. He had watched Luveday stiffen beside him and glimpsed the pain in her expression as they sorted through herbs before she had pointedly changed the subject. He had more than guested that something lay between them, and part of him was glad that she was here now, while the other part cursed De Lane for a fool, a damned fool for letting such a woman go. They spoke of it no more.

By the end of her first full day as court healer, she had set up a stillroom to rival any in the kingdom. She was neat, organized, focused and determined to succeed if not for the Prince's sake then for her own. There had been only one instance when Luveday had faltered in her determination. It had been that first morning after she had awoken cramped and aching from the night spent in the chair beside the prince's bed. Throwing off her cloak, she had looked across the bed to see what had awoken her. There stood a man fussing with a small chart and a number of bowls. At first, Luveday's mind was too foggy from sleep to realize what she was seeing, but as the man pulled a familiar looking blade from its sheath, she could not help the yell that had escaped her.

The man looked at her startled as he froze in place like a deer in headlights. Footsteps were heard drawing closer, but Luveday had already rounded the bed to find the man had moved and now faced her, blade in hand ready to defend himself.

"Stay back woman; I mean no trouble to you."

Luveday grew angry at the man's demeanor as if she were the threat here. "No, you stay back. Stay away from the Prince."

Offended he gasped, "I will not. I am the royal bloodletter. I…"

She didn't let him finish but plucked the blade from his hand while he was too distracted with his own importance to resist. "I know who and what you are. You will not come near the boy again while he is in my charge." Jane and Thomas entered through the main doors, while Logan had appeared from his rooms. They looked at the scene in confusion.

"This is an ancient healing…" The man tried to enlighten the woman but was clearly wary of someone who now had his knife.

"I know the history, and I know what harm it causes." Luveday turned as Logan came up behind her.

The look on his face was dark and directed solely at her. "Morgan has been at this castle for decades, leave him be, lady." The bloodletter gasped at the title.

"I will not." Luveday was so angry that tears came to her eyes. "I will not let him drain the prince of his life's blood while he is fighting to survive. God knows how he had made it this long with you backward and ignorant people."

"Luveday! Bloodletting is…" Someone tried to say, but Luveday cut them off.

"Ancient, time-honored and the stupidest thing I've ever heard of." She blinked away the tears and looked at their astonished faces. "How much blood do you think is in the human body? Huh? How much can you take out before the heart stops? Before he stops breathing?" She held the small blade not realizing she was jabbing it at them to emphasize her words. "It's supposed to remove bad blood? How can you tell if it is bad or not? Holden is barely eating enough to stay alive, and you want to make his body work harder to replace the blood it's lost?"

Morgan sputtered.

Luveday turned back to him. "I am in charge here, and I say, out with you." She squared her shoulder and looked him dead in the eyes. "Out!"

Morgan tried to protest, looking to Logan who stepped around the little healer to usher the man out. Luveday heard him say, "She is here by order of the King and Queen. Her word is final."

The man collected his belonging, somehow forgetting the knife she still carried. Before he was escorted out the door, he looked back at Logan. "Let's hope she has not killed the boy already."

Jane looked at Luveday as if she did not know her; Thomas looked equally troubled while Logan just glared. Luveday was beyond crying; she was truly angry now. The two she counted on had not had her back, and while she tried to remind herself that they knew no better, a part of her was deeply wounded by this.

She had spent the day in stony silence, rolling up her sleeves and getting to work. They had much to do and no time to waste. By the end of the day, Jane had softened to her and Thomas's faith was as unwavering as it had once been. She thought maybe even Logan had revised his harsh opinion of her, but it was only a thought. Her attention returned to the task at hand. By nightfall, the stillroom was almost complete, already herbs seeped in pots and ingredients hung from pegs. As the first remedies were finally prepared, word came that the last of the herbs were on their way. She could not have hoped for a better outcome, though some dissension was heard brewing among the castle's population. Luveday could not help their hurt feelings and bruised pride, nor did she care to at the moment. Her sole focus was the prince, and everything else would have to wait.

The two days since that bloodletting incident had not proved fruitless. Logan continued to watch her like a hawk and seemed begrudgingly impressed by her skill and the ease with which she worked beside Thomas. They moved as a team and thought along the same lines. It was almost as if they were back on the battlefield in the north not having been separated for months. They poured over Ody's herbal and their notes. Thomas had been astonished at the book and the detail of the drawings there. There was no way to tell him they were photographs of the actual plants and not handmade drawings, so she let him think what he would. They started treating the symptoms they could easily identify in hopes of eliminating what they could and getting down to the real problem.

Oils, rubs, tinctures, teas, and compresses were concocted and taken directly to the sickbed. Luveday minced, chopped, powdered, boiled and stirred until her arms ached. Some of the herbs would take days to turn into the proper syrups and tinctures while others she could boil in teas which were given to the prince right away. Garlic was a natural antimicrobial and antifungal, catnip and purple coneflower for cold, Elder Cowslip and Eucalyptus to help break loose the phlegm she could hear in his lungs. Lavender, fever-foe, St. John's wart and Vervain Verbena were to help with headaches and fever, an additional antiinflammatory herb for the nervous system. Comfrey and Tyne mixed with essential oils of mint and lavender were rubbed into his joints and put into hot compresses to help ease the ache of being in bed for so long.

Luveday started to help Thomas move the boy's limbs to get blood circulating and keep the muscles from deteriorating further. If anyone were watching, they would think that this treatment was ridiculous, but Luveday knew of its benefits and wouldn't let making a spectacle of themselves worry her one bit.

The Queen and King came and went with little fanfare. Benedict came to collect his mother, reminding her that she should be careful around the sick bed. Luveday was rarely far from it. As the prince's body began to fight off his illness, he got worse before he got better. The coughing started after a few days as the herbs worked as an expectorant to loosen the mucus in his lungs. Weak as he was, someone had to hold the boy in a sitting position while he coughed up green and brown mucus that was at times hard and dense. The more he could get out of his lungs the better he would be, but the coughing fits wore him out quickly.

The prince began to improve in small stages, but Luveday couldn't tell exactly which treatment may have caused it or if the boy was recovering on his own once the crackpots and their potions were gone. After a few days more, Holden had almost lucid moments, and they were able to get more substantial amounts of beef broth and teas down him. He seemed to enjoy the ritual of baths and linen changing that the group did every few days. Now that his body was sweating and releasing toxins Luveday was even more worried about him lying in soiled sheets.

Several weeks after her arrival she sat practically in the prince's bed feeding him spoonful after spoonful of broth as he lay propped up with an array of pillows and looked at her. For the first time, she could tell that he saw her and was not in some semi-conscious state. Often, he would appear lucid asking questions and talking briefly but fall back into slumber only to wake again and repeat himself having no memory of what had happened before.

Logan was overjoyed the first time Holden had opened his eyes and spoken to him, but Luveday could see that the boy's eyes remained clouded and far away. Luveday warned him, but it was still heartbreaking to see the light leave Logan's eyes after the second and third time the prince had called to him asking for water and what had happened to him.

"Who are you?" A hoarse voice asked.

"Easy, your Highness. You have a sore throat from a bout of coughing earlier." She carefully raised the spoon toward his lips. "Here have some of this, and you will feel better." The boy swallowed obediently. "I am Lady Luveday, recently of Lander's Keep. I am a healer, and it has been my pleasure to care for you these last two fortnights."

He looked startled and turned to her. "Two?" He looked down and fiddled with the sheet. He wore only a linen tunic, soft and undyed. He looked at his arms, the bones shown in odd places. Worried eyes looked at her as he had trouble shifting in bed.

"Easy, Love." She said, taking no notice of the endearment. "You have been ill much longer than that, Prince Holden. 'Tis nearing four moons now."

Thoughts raced across the boy's face as he warred with the truth before him. He looked at her again, his expression clearing some. "Benjamin?" Luveday was puzzled by this; she had not seen any of the other princes. For their safety, they had been moved from the castle and city once their brother had fallen ill and no cure had made an improvement to his condition.

His expression was expectant, and then it occurred to her, he was not asking for his brother but about her connection to him. She blushed. "Yes. I am that lady that saved Prince Benjamin in Sterling's camp."

To her surprise, the boy perked up at this news. A door opened as Thomas returned with the ingredients she had requested. "Thomas, please get Logan for me, I believe he is reading some letters in his room." Thomas looked to the bed and met the prince's clear gaze and back to Luveday who nodded at him. With a wide smile and a skip in his step, Thomas rushed off. A moment later both young men returned to the bedside. Luveday continued to spoon broth down his throat as he listened to Logan rattle happily on about everything that had happened since he became ill. The prince drifted off to sleep with a warm and full belly as Luveday promised to recount her time in Sterling's camp the next time he awoke.

The Queen made daily trips to check on her son and had called for the return of his brothers. One day she had arrived to find him napping in a chair by the window and had drawn Luveday aside, back into her stillroom. "There is nothing I can give you that would be worth my son's life, Lady Luveday..." Her beautiful hazel eyes shined with unshed tears. "Ask of the crown what you will. Anything you desire will be yours."

Luveday's heart skipped a beat at such a gift, but her heart plummeted knowing that what she wanted was not in the Queen's power to give. Being practical and rather optimistic, she cautioned the royal instead. "Thank you. Your generosity has been wonderful, but I don't think now is the time to celebrate." Many things were still on Luveday's mind; many questions had been left unanswered. "The prince is improving daily, but there is still work left to do, and I have not yet found the cause of his illness." The Queen's eyes turned dark. "Without knowing the cause, I cannot say that this will never happen again, and the next time might be the last."

"You think the illness lurks nearby." She looked weary and ready to go on the hunt.

Back-tracking, the healer clarified. "I don't say this to startle you. The fact that no one else had fallen ill is a heartening sign, but in my opinion, illnesses do not confine healthy boys to the sickbed without cause." She looked at the Queen. "Despite what many say, it is not some divine punishment but has some earthly reason. The Creator has his hand in many things, just not in this." She thought of her life in Anora thus far, had it all been leading up to this? She shook her head clear and focused on the boy. Symptoms, timing, contagions, nothing had fit in the gap of information she possessed. "I just have to find what it was." Luveday was determined to find out what had happened to Holden. The question had been plaguing her from the start.

"Perhaps you are right." The Queen glanced at the door where the prince lay beyond. "As long as the boy is out of danger, we will hold off celebrating for now."

"Until he can join us." Luveday countered crossing her arms before her.

A hopeful smile lightened her features. "Until Holden may join us." The Queen squeezed her forearm much as Lady Jane would have done before returning to check on her sleeping son. Luveday watched her stroke a hair from the prince's forehead without waking the boy. The Queen left as quietly as she came, and Luveday knew her time in the castle was nearing its end.

What the future would hold, she could not even imagine.

Days later the prince sat up in bed; young Benjamin sat near the foot of the bed with Henry and John curled up between their elder brother and Luveday. The story she was telling was interrupted as a servant appeared to deliver a message directly from the King, summoning Luveday to the royal presence. The children begged, but all Luveday could do was promise to finish the tale later, sleeping beauty would have to wait upon the King.

Henry was pulled out of Luveday's lap with some effort as she tried to rise and go with the impatient servant. The boy did not talk much but remembered her from his visit to the Keep and was glued to her skirts since his arrival; only his mother could pull him away.

Logan took the boy with a chuckle, and Luveday marveled at the transformation. Her harshest critic had become her biggest admirer. His appearance had changed over the last week as Holden steadily improved. When the prince had taken his first stumbling steps across the room and fallen into his friend's arms, the light in Logan's eyes had mirrored the sun. Gone were the dark circle and lines of worry and soon the young man's youth had returned to him. Luveday had been shocked to learn he was merely twenty; she had thought him a decade older at least. Now the two laughed and joked together like brothers. Luveday left them knowing the two could keep the smaller boys entertained. She left a message for Thomas to explain where she was should he return from his errands before she did.

Luveday found herself back in the King's sitting room where Luveday had first gotten the news of Prince Holden's illness. The atmosphere was lighter than it had been over a month prior, but something was still amiss if the frown on the King's brow was any indication.

"Vexing." He mumbled under his breath.

"So, the rumors are true, my King." Augusta sipped her wine from a golden goblet and glanced at Luveday who sat at the far end of the rectangular table.

The King put down the letter in his hand and turned to their guest. His smile was easy and genuine when he looked at her.

Luveday smiled back, at ease with the royal couple after spending so much time in their presence of late. "Lady, my wife has suggested you may be able to help us with another matter." Luveday couldn't help the sinking feeling she got at those words.

Augusta laughed at her dubious expression and sought to comfort the young woman. "Not to worry, Lady Luveday. This task should prove easier than your last." She looked at her husband before retrieving the discarded parchment. "On the coast is a keep of some renown. You may have heard of Briar's Gate."

Luveday nodded her head. "Few ladies have not." She looked to her husband with a smile. "The perfumes and flowers they grow are found nowhere else in the kingdom."

"The keep and lands are held by Lady Claudia, the widow of one of my most trusted lords." His gaze became hazy with remembrance. "Lord Titus was a brave and loyal man, died in a skirmish coming home from battle a few years ago. Never found out who did it." He looked troubled.

"Recently there had been some... unpleasantness surrounding the lady." She glanced at the letter. "Sir Navarro, Titus's best man, has sent this letter asking us to spare his lady while Sir Marcus Reeves is here to plead her cause." The Queen's eyes crinkled at the corners. "We are not hard-hearted and have let the woman grieve, but without heir or issue the Land has returned to the King." Both royals looked at Luveday who only nodded, and the Queen continued. "Though the land is bountiful and their goods in demand, Lady Claudia has failed to deliver her taxes two years in a row." Luveday knew this was an insult to the crown, especially since the King had recently called for aid in his war against Sterling. Lady Claudia had snubbed the King one too many times. "We wish this to be a delicate matter as her husband was dear to us both and can see only one solution."

Luveday swallowed past the lump in her throat. "Me?"

King Edward laughed. "You have proven yourself to be a clever and industrious woman. With what you have done for our son and what miracles you accomplished at Lander's Keep, Lady Claudia and Briar's Gate will be a simple task." Luveday looked to the Queen whose eyes narrowed as they met her own.

The Queen disagreed with that last statement, and Luveday had to agree. Nothing about this seemed simple or easy from where she was sitting.

"We merely wish for you to visit the Lady and get a lay of the land as it were. After a short stay, return and tell us what you think of the lady. We trust your judgment, and with Sir Benedict at your side, we hope that a fortnight or two there will let Lady Claudia see some wisdom. Perhaps even consider accepting a new husband." She looked at the King who nodded sagely. Meaning Luveday was sent to persuade the lady to behave or risk royal punishment. "We will have to hold off your court celebration, but surely the weather will be better in a few weeks as well."

The King agreed. "By then the court will be in full bloom."

Luveday smiled weakly. She did not like the royal court nor it her. She was a celebrity of sorts, having healed the prince and her misadventures in the north, but there was far more dislike of her then there was support, despite having friends in high places. Or because of it. The court ladies were mostly two-faced, smiling at her and joking about her behind her back. Luveday had been happy to stay with the young princes, but even she would have to attend the royal celebration, especially if it were partly in her honor. The thought was unpleasant. Luveday thought she saw a sparkle in the Queen's eye who was fully aware of the healer's dislike of the courtesans. Augusta often marveled at the way the little woman maneuvered the women with her polite demeanor. The ladies thought her simple, country-bred and little more than a passing amusement, but when pushed the Queen had seen Luveday hold her own. With time and a little confidence, the young woman would be a force to be reckoned with, and she hoped, a good friend.

Luveday accepted, what else was there to do? A few days passed, and Holden's full care was given over to Logan and Thomas. The latter of which was wary of leaving the Lady alone. Rumors at court had not spared Lady Claudia, and Thomas was hesitant to leave his friend in the clutches of such a conniving woman. Luveday reminded him that they still had much to do as she worked out a schedule to help the prince regain his strength and adamantly wished Thomas would stay and make sure that nothing else happened to impede the boy's recovery. Especially not the impending return of Master Pope. Thomas eventually gave up and accepted that he would stay behind, both pleased and wary with the weight of this responsibility.

Saying goodbye again felt somehow final. Luveday hugged the boys and men and teared up saying she would return in a moon and expected them all to be playing in the gardens on her return. The boy's promised to teach her all the games they knew next time they saw her. For all the animation of the exchange, there was a sad undercurrent held barely in check. Thomas felt as if she were slipping through his fingers once again. He felt a as if he stood at a crossroads. He could choose to hold on to her or let her go forever, but he couldn't express exactly what he was feeling. From the prince's chamber window, he watched the small group of the King's men ride out, Lady Luveday ringed by knights and men at arms. Thomas admitted to himself that he had fallen in love with her, but he knew he had missed his chance and nothing more would come of it. Turning, he smiled at the boys and thought of something to entertain them and get everyone's mind off this loss.

Of all the things that Luveday missed while being sequestered in the sick room, riding a horse was at the top of the list. On the other hand, the ache of several days in the saddle was not. How quickly she had forgotten the discomfort of it all. Riding away from the city left Luveday with a sense of relief, and yet the uneasiness of an unknown future rode with her. Benedict was constantly by her side and his usual chatty self, filling her in on his mother's activities and everything she had missed since coming to court while ignoring its goings-on. She listened half-heartedly, more amused by his colorful retellings than any desire to hear of people she had never met. The men with him were familiar faces, somewhere his own and some the King's guard. The group left with no fanfare, but well outfitted and as ready for the journey as anyone could be. They kept a steady pace, as fast as any dare go but still a moderate jog for the horses. Five days in the saddle to Havenwood Castle where they would rest a few days on Lord Grayson Stern's hospitality. Then there was another five days to Briar's Gate. Luveday looked forward to meeting the lord and his wife, as well as seeing the coast and its milder weather.

Days passed as the weather grew warmer and the colors of spring more abundant while they drew closer to their destination. Luveday spent most of her days quietly in the saddle. Benedict had run out of news, and finally realized that she didn't need him to fill the silence. She was happy to be for a while.

It was with a startled look one night that Benedict had let it slip that there were rumors of trouble at Lander's Keep. Something had happened not long after the wedding, but no one knew the details except that the animosity between Sumerland, his daughter, and De Lane had grown.

Luveday studiously considered her cup of stew, while Benedict stuttered for a moment trying to find a different topic. Nothing coherent came out of his mouth until one of his men sitting across the campfire came to his rescue. "We should reach Havenwood on the morrow, My Lady."

Luveday looked up to regard Rolf, a man at arms. He was old enough to have a daughter a few years younger than herself and had found during the brief conversations they had shared that he was a kind man, honored to hold a high position as one of St. James' senior men at arms. Luveday sent him a half smile, grateful for the lifeline, but also realized that Lander's Keep was growing farther away with each day and her heart was mending. The dreams of what could have been began to grow distant, and soon, she realized, she could start dreaming again.

"I am eager to see how Lord Stern fairs. He seemed a good man." Luveday took another bite of stew.

Rolf huffed. "A good man indeed."

Benedict cut in. "I sent word ahead, so they should be expecting us." He watched the lady warily.

Another man spoke up, "We have made good time, so hopefully they will be ready."

"There was tell of some trouble with Sir Peter going missing." Someone said as they took their place beside the fire. Luveday stiffened and looked to Benedict who said nothing. The man continued, one of the King's guards who spoke low and gruffly. "Strange thing that; he disappeared without a trace during the battle with Sterling. Greyson had men searching for him for days. But he was not among the injured or the dead."

"That is concerning." Benedict offered thoughtfully.

"I hope nothing tragic has befallen him," Luveday spoke into her cup as many nodded in agreement. Talk flowed around them until Luveday finally got up to take her rest.

As she settled into her pallet amid the roots of a large out tree, Benedict found his place not far from her. She curled into her cloak and watched him roll out his blankets and set his weapons at the ready as he prepared for sleep. The glitter of his eyes caught hers, but she couldn't quite discern his expression with the firelight at his back.

A loud whisper met her ears. "I am sorry, lady."

Luveday didn't need him to clarify but wished he wouldn't apologize. "There is nothing for you to be sorry about, my friend." She couldn't know how the bittersweet curve of her lips affected him. "It is I who should say how sorry I am that you have been torn from your blood brother to take on my burden…"

His harsh whisper cut her off. "You are not a burden, Luveday."

Luveday wanted to laugh, but it was a bitter taste in her mouth, so she pulled her cloak up to hide behind it for a moment and compose herself.

"You are not, Luv." He stared hard at her as if the force of his words would make it so.

The familiar endearment on his lips no longer startled her. "I thank you, Benedict." She paused a moment before voicing her thoughts, and he went back to settling down on his palate. Her words caused him to turn and look at her sharply, though they were spoken for his ears alone. "Neither of us could have changed what happened." Over the few feet that separated them, she could see that his eyes were questioning. He did not interrupt though it looked as if he wished to argue but saw that speaking of this was hard for her and so kept silent. "I do not believe any words could have changed De Lane's mind." In the long nights since she had left Lander's Keep, she had thought much on it, though at times she had begged her mind to stop its insistent circling; only time had proven the cure. Only time had provided her with an answer, though it was not one that she liked; it had not changed since that night in the upstairs corridor with De Lane. "Only he could choose his path, for right or wrong, love or honor." She rolled on to her back and mused a moment before continuing. "It is all anyone can do, to choose a course, even deciding to do nothing is a choice. I could have stayed, you could have stayed, but I feared what would become of me... or him. If we decided to keep circling each other." Luveday sighed. "I know in the marrow of my bones what that future would have looked like."

"Luveday," Benedict whispered harshly.

She turned back to meet his gaze. "I saw it for a heartbeat, reflected in his eyes." His eyes darkened. "It wasn't a bad thing, Benedict. It was the wrong place and the wrong time." She almost laughed at that. She out of place and time, what irony. "And I want to be his first choice, the one he could weather any storm beside. But he didn't choose that, and I couldn't live with what was left."

A growl escaped Benedict, and a hand suddenly grasp her own. "Luveday..." she heard a question in his voice somewhere amid the anger and frustration. "Did Iain, did De Lane..." he pressed her hand trying to ask what he couldn't get past his lips.

"Nay, Benedict." His whole body sagged in relief. Luveday didn't want to admit how much had passed between De Lane and herself because it felt too intimate and too raw. "What was between us was strong, and I felt that eventually, desire would win over everything else. Like a stone worn away by the ocean, my resolve would have eventually succumbed." Benedict didn't look happy at this. "What is it?" She asked.

Was it her imagination or could she hear the grinding of his teeth?

"He knew better." A frustrated breath left him and ruffled the hair on her brow. "He had more honor and sense than that. At least I thought so." His blue eyes turned distant, and she knew he didn't hear her muffled protest. "As a knight, we are held to a line above other men. Flirting, stolen kisses, and embraces from women who are free is one thing. It is a game played at court, but this." He looked at her again. "I knew he was going too far. I saw that what he felt for you was more. Though I prayed he would find his way to you… you are right, Luveday. He chose his course and could have changed it. He wanted you, and prosperity at Lander's Keep. I am not sorry that I chose to help you. I merely wish…" There was so much that he had to tell her, and yet it changed nothing.

"That it is what it could have been." She finished for him. "I wish it was what we wanted, what would have made us happy." Luveday finished in a melodic whisper, "but that is not what it is."

They were silent for some moments, realizing the camp had gone quiet around them.

"Rest well, My Lady." He whispered.

"Rest well, My Lord." She turned away, settling on her other side and found sleep sooner than anyone else.

Benedict watched as her breathing evened out into the depths of sleep and not for the first time wished they felt more for each other, or he less for her. Sometimes he wished that this deep friendship between them would blossom into something more, and sometimes he wished that he were as good as she thought he was. Never did he wish that he had never met her, nor that he felt nothing for her, but he knew that though they could journey through life together and be happier than most, there was one man out there that suited her even better than he.

Laying there, part of him wondered if his reasoning for helping her still rung true. He had wanted to give her whatever assistance she needed because he knew her to be a worthy and extraordinary lady, but when Lady Emmalyn had come seeking his help, he had told himself it was more for Iain that he did this thing. Benedict had thought to look after the lady on his behalf, fully expecting Iain to come to his senses and realize that here was his other half. So, he had taken Luveday from Lander's Keep with the surety that Iain De Lane would not be far behind, but as the journey grew longer and they reached his lands, his confidence wavered. Finally, after weeks and no sign of his blood brother, Benedict had admitted the truth, if only to himself. Iain De Lane was a damned fool, a bloody damned fool for letting the lady go. And if his friend did not send some word soon, Benedict feared he would prove to be just as foolish and make a bid to keep the lady for himself.

Havenwood castle was stark in the midday sun. The walls were lined with men of arms who stopped them to ask their names and purpose before allowing the group entrance. Somehow, the castle was less than she expected, though she would never voice such. Compared to the three other castles she had visited; this castle was plain, though its fortifications were greater. Luveday thought it appropriate for a family with the last name of Stern. Looking around as they traversed the outer bailey, she and Benedict were granted leave to take their horses up to the gate of the keep. She learned the keep was also referred to as the dungeon, though she had always thought that was a name for the place where they stored prisoners. As honored guests, she learned that this was a privilege, as mounted and armed individuals were kept far from the hall.

Benedict helped her to unmount, as an older knight watched from atop the steps. Luveday could see the frown as he noticed her split skirt, the only option to save her modesty while riding astride.

"Sir Bernard. Greetings!" Benedict called out as they reached the man.

"Lord St. James. 'Tis good to see you again." The knight's eyes looked Luveday over. He was a large man, and tall. Very tall, she conceded as Luveday tilted her head back to meet his gaze.

"May I introduce Lady Luveday, recently of Lander's Keep. Lady, meet the most skilled of Stern's household knights, Sir Bernard." Sir Bernard's frown and look of interest were replaced by a welcoming smile.

"Dear Lady, you are most welcome here." He seemed to start as she tried to reply and ushered them in through the massive doors as a porter held them open. Sir Bernard called for the refreshments to be taken to the hearth, as Luveday got a glimpse of the hall. It was well appointed and spacious. The tables were being cleared, signaling they had missed the noonday meal, but there was a well-ordered feeling to the place that Lander's Keep had lacked until well into her stay there. "Come Lady and rest yourself." Luveday's attention turned from the shields on the wall, a common enough sight in a castle, to the hearth where Sir Bernard, and Benedict talked while she was out of hearing.

"Damn," she heard Benedict mutter as she came closer. Sir Bernard cleared his throat, and Benedict looked a little sheepish at her raised eyebrow.

"Forgive us My Lady, but I informed his lordship that Lord Stern and Lady Margaret were called away not two days ago to Heath Castle to be present for the birth of her daughter's first child." Luveday nodded understandingly. "'Tis why there was only me to greet you."

Luveday thought a moment, "So they left even before your messenger arrived." She looked to Benedict who nodded and shrugged.

"I'm afraid they will not be back for a fortnight at least, My Lady, but you are most welcome to stay as long as you like. The solar is being prepared for you, and Sir Klein's room for you, My Lord." At that moment, the food and drinks arrived, and they sat to talk. Luveday brought the pewter cup to her lips and was pleasantly surprised to find cider instead of ale. She drank carefully non-the-less. Every bite that came to her lips tasted better than ever thanks to the hasty meals of dried food she had consumed over the last few days.

The men talked while Luveday listened drowsily, happy that she was in a comfortable chair that did not move beneath her. Luveday listened to Benedict talk with the knight, serious and jesting in turns. The two men seemed old friends, then again, if Stern was a sworn blood brother to, he and Iain, they must have been in each other's company often.

"Would you like to freshen up and rest a bit before the evening meal, My Lady?" A young woman asked seeming to appear at Luveday's shoulder.

"Yes, thank you." Luveday rose to excuse herself. Benedict looked at her, and Luveday realized that the two men had completely forgotten about her for a moment. If that was the case, she didn't feel bad about leaving them to their talk.

The young woman, Ann, led her to the solar where a large pitcher of hot water, scented soap, and towels were laid out for her. Ann helped Luveday out of her traveling dress, marveling at the ingenuity of the split skirts. Once in her chemise Luveday bathed as much of herself as she could, including her hair. Ann thought they might be able to get the small tub up after dinner and she could have a proper bath. Luveday sighed at the idea and accepted as long as it wasn't too much trouble. Fed and washed she crawled into the big bed and fell asleep almost instantly.

It seemed but a moment until Ann woked her for the meal and helped her dress in one of three other gowns she had brought with her. Hair braided prettily atop her head. Ann insisted upon a veil, and though Lady St. James had made sure she carried one, Luveday had never warn it, not even for the Queen. Veil in place, Luveday thought she must look every inch the proper lady. Dinner progressed uneventfully, though Sir Bernard who sat at her left, kept looking at her with something between nervousness and awe. His conversation seemed stilted compared to earlier. In fact, he had turned to her as if he had something to say, only to halt, cough, change the subject and grow silent. Several times he apologized before turning to the man on his other side.

She looked to her right, to Benedict for an explanation. He laughed softly and bent to her ear. "I may have shared your healing of the young prince with him before dinner." She heard rather than saw the smile in his voice. "He is rather in awe to have such a renowned and honored lady sit at his arm for a meal."

Luveday attempted to get the knight to speak to her before the meal was over, and Sir Bernard settled a little before they retired to the hearth. Not long after the meal was cleared and the tables were taken down, Ann appeared to take her upstairs.

"Sleep well, My Lady." Sir Bernard offered.

Benedict warned, "Be ready to rise early. We leave not long after dawn. With Stern gone, there is no need to tarry." Luveday nodded and said her goodnights.

As she undressed and readied for her bath, Luveday wondered if Benedict didn't have some message he was to carry to Stern for the King or Queen. They had planned to stay two days at least, to rest the horses, but now there was no delaying the King's business.

Clean from head to toe, she pondered what she had come to learn of Briar's Gate. It sounded like a wonderful and magical place, except for the shadow its lady cast over the domain. Falling to sleep, she had time only to as God to give her patience and help preserve her and guide her. Once again, she felt overwhelmed, a ship lost at sea while a storm moved across the horizon.

They left with the suns waking. Sir Bernard wishing them Godspeed, and their packs full of a generous amount of provisions, which Luveday took as a thank you for her help in saving Stern months ago.

Though she was disappointed that their stay was so short and that Stern and his wife were absent, Luveday felt as if something waited for them. It was as if that storm she felt on her horizon was not just a metaphor; its heart was settled above Briar's Gate and growing stronger with each passing day. There was no way to skirt this storm, the only path lay through, and she prayed they weathered it well.

Chapter 17

"Quick-loving hearts ... may quickly loathe."
~ Elizabeth Barrett Browning Sonnets from the Portuguese

Color and beauty filled the fragrant air that swirled with the scent of flowers and sea salt in turns. The sweet and the salty only complimented each other rather than jar the senses. Men and women worked in the fields which, more often than not, wore a profusion of flowers rather than the first crops of spring. Luveday expected a castle behind the ivy-covered stone walls, but what she found was a large manor house built off an old stone tower. Round, rather than square, Luveday wondered if it was some lighthouse or something unfinished as the shape didn't seem to fit with the wood and stone structure that had grown up beside it.

It had taken some moments before the doors to the walled bailey were opened to them. Only the name of the King granted them access which Benedict and the other men were not happy about, perhaps as unhappy as the people of Briar's Gate seemed to be with their presence. Luveday was certain that something was afoot.

Luveday dismounted, once again with Benedict's help. They shared a look she knew meant the game was on. While Lord St. James was there in the name of the King, Luveday was there to gauge the healing properties of the flowers and plants the area grew in abundance, some of which seemed to flourish only here. At least that was her cover story. They had agreed that the less official her stay appeared, the more likely it was that Lady Claudia might confide in her. That it was extremely unlikely that a woman, who was as shrewd and cunning as this lady was told to be, would confide in a total stranger was a thought that Luveday had kept to herself.

The wealth this family possessed was evident in every corner of the hall. They waited by a large stone hearth though the structure was mostly paneled in rich dark woods. It looked as if she was in one of the manor houses on the east coast, something like the old families of New York still possessed. Fabrics were on almost every chair; heavy drapes covered a large glass window. Luveday had heard that the flower trade had been extremely good to Lord Titus's family, and his wife had a mind particularly suited to expanding her trade, even across oceans.

Looking around, Luveday admitted that the talk wasn't all exaggerations as she had seen this level of luxury only at the King's Court. Luveday perched lightly on the edge of a heavy carved chair as Benedict stood with his back to the room gazing broodingly into the fire. He was one hundred percent Lord St. James at that moment, none of the charming courtly knight could be seen.

Minutes ticked by, stretching out as quite settled over the hall. Luveday heard the distant whisper of servants, but still, no one came to greet them. The middle-aged woman who had ushered them into the hall had seemed harried by their arrival, though they both knew that a messenger had been sent by the King to inform the lady of his man's impending arrival. Only Benedict knew the content of that missive and said it would not interfere with the rolls they were playing, but Luveday could see that this visit had put everyone on edge.

Finally, the woman returned and another woman, dressed in a lovely rose-colored gown, with flowing sleeves and long flowing golden locks barely covered by her modest veil, came gliding in behind her.

Luveday was taken back by the woman, who reminded her of sleeping beauty, as she sincerely apologized at having kept them waiting. "I am sorry to have kept you waiting for so long. Bea had trouble finding me in the west garden." The women's smile was soft and kind, exactly like a fairytale princess should be. "We were not expecting you for two more days, Lord St. James. And who is this lady?"

"Lady Claudia, may I introduce Lady Luveday, she is currently in favor as the King's healer." The other lady looked intrigued but waited patiently for an explanation. "When I knew I would be journeying here, the lady said she had heard of Briar's Gate and wished to see the plants you grow and study their healing attributes."

The smile on the other's lady's face widened. "You are most welcome, Lady Luveday, a lady healer, how extraordinary." The lady took Luveday's arm and patted it; the gesture was motherly though Luveday thought they were near the same age. "You are most welcome to stay here, Lady and avail yourself of what help and knowledge we can provide." The lady turned away, and Luveday exchanged a perplexed look with Benedict who only shrugged as the lines around his eyes grew more pronounced. The smile he gave her was as sedate as she had ever seen on his face, a bare twitch at the corners of his mouth. "Bea, Bea?" She called the serving woman who had disappeared through a far door a moment ago and now returned.

"My Lady?" She curtsied.

"Bea, are the rooms ready for Lord St. James and Lady Luveday?" At the woman's nod, Claudia looked quite pleased. "I hope your men will not find it too lonely in the warehouse. It's warm and dry, and much better than the barracks this time of year."

"Warehouse?" Luveday was curious that why they would need something so large as the word warehouse conjured.

"Why yes Lady Luveday." Claudia looked at her as if she were a little slow. "We store much through the seasons, bulbs for spring, dried flowers for winter, and so on."

Glancing at Benedict, Luveday saw a softening in his eyes and grew worried. "Of course." The words fell from Luveday's lips without thought.

Lady Claudia took charge. "How lucky that our recent guests have departed and the two of you may have the best rooms in the hall." Two women appear through the far door. One carrying Luveday's backpack and Benedict's pack. Claudia continued nodding to the young women. "Gemma and Clare will show you to your rooms to freshen up and rest; I will have something brought to your rooms." Bea waits almost impatiently just beyond the doorway through which her lady had entered.

Dismissed by the lady's back, Benedict and Luveday followed the women uped a carved stair and through several rooms until the came to a hallway. Luveday went right, and Benedict left, glancing at each other as they parted ways.

The water was cold but not as cold as the room even though the spring sun shone through large glass windows. Outside was a colorful garden, but there was something gloomy about it that Luveday couldn't shake. Looking out the small diamonds of glass, she couldn't help but think of sleeping beauties cottage and almost snorted at her penchant for acquainting Lady Claudia with the fabled princess.

Wiping down as best she could, Luveday wasn't surprised by the quick knock or the door opening to admit Benedict though she had yet to answer.

"Clever," He retrieved the scarf from the floor and laid it on the bed. After Clair, the plainer of the two young women had left, Luveday had purposefully placed her scarf in the door as it closed so that Benedict could find her room. Hopefully to a passerby, it would look as if it were merely an accident.

"Anyone in the corridor?" Luveday asks, he looked puzzled for a moment and then a look of knowing shined from his eyes. He hadn't thought she would notice such things, but Luveday had watched enough spy movies to know what to look for.

"I heard and saw no one, though I had expected someone stationed atop the stairs." He turned to see Luveday's gowns hanging from the open wardrobe and glanced back at her. "Let us rest tonight; my inquiries can start tomorrow." He looked at the notebook and several items on the foot of the bed.

Benedict had been curious about some of the stuff from her time, and so Luveday had tried to keep them out of sight, but Clair had started to unpack her backpack before Luveday could usher her out with the reassurance that she could finish by herself and rcally, just wanted to rest. In the push to rush the girl out, Luveday had forgotten to put the items back. Luckily, Luveday had kept much of her belongings in a locked trunk in her room at Lion's Gate where she had every intention of returning after this ordeal.

"She is not what we heard or expected." Luveday offered, not sure how to tell Benedict to keep up his guard, but the man was eyes and ears for the King, so she shouldn't need to tell him that. Right? She was here on her own mission and remembered that she to would report to the King. She hoped this was some sort of misunderstanding and that she could help Lady Claudia, but she wasn't sure that the lady needed help. At least not the kind she was offering.

"No, but we have only just arrived." He countered.

"My thoughts exactly." She murmured.

"I'll leave you to your rest, lady." He turned to leave. "I will check on the men before the evening meal." He added as he turned to close the door behind him. "Rest well."

Luveday was sure she would need it.

The gardens were exquisite. There was no other word for it. Part of her was sad that such splendor sat hidden away from the world. Another part was glad that masses of people didn't tour the gardens trampling its solitary beauty. Here not only blossoms scented the air, but herbs like lavender, mint, basil, and cloves. Orange trees and lemon trees peeked over the garden wall. Clair, who had awoken her this morning had hinted that other spices were brought from afar to add to the complex mixtures in the soap and perfume houses.

Luveday itched to know how everything worked, but her curiosity had to come second to her reason for being here. Last night had been uneventful. Dinner was rather solitary at the high table with Lady Claudia. Except for a few people the hall had been empty. Luveday was told that most servants went home in the evening, and those that lived in the hall ate in the kitchens. The men at arms and household knights ate in the hall in turns and currently most were away on errands.

"Sir Navarro," The young woman said his name on a sigh, and Luveday got the idea that he was a handsome young man from her moony expression, "has been touring the land for Lady Claudia. Spring is our hardest time of year, getting the flowers to bloom and all. 'Tis a short time we have to get the work done, My Lady. It is so much harder than planting the spring crops." She whispered.

"I can imagine," Luveday muttered. A variety of flowers were seasonal, and annual meaning they would have to be replaced every year, unlike roses and other bush or vine perennials. Many plants were temperamental, liking only the right soil and amount of water to bloom. Luveday wondered how they managed to keep the soil full of nutrients and made a mental note to ask as she bent to smell a fragrant pink rose, making sure not to touch the blossom for fear of bruising it.

Lady Claudia's voice was surprisingly near. "You are careful with the flowers." She said thoughtfully, obviously having watched Luveday for some time. "They bruise so easily…" the lady seemed to be speaking to herself more than to Luveday who only nodded her agreement. "Few know or care how fragile they are. It's rare to find a guest who takes such care, Lady Luveday."

Not sure they were talking of just flowers Luveday hazarded a reply. "Life can be hard enough; I see no need to harm something so beautiful or so fleeting."

Something in Claudia's eyes said that she like her answer. "Come Lady and let me show you around some more of the gardens."

As they walked, and Claudia pointed out a patch of this herb or that plant, she asked Luveday some probing questions. "How does a woman such as yourself become a healer, let alone one favored by the King?"

"Learning to heal seemed a practical skill to have, though I am often told that ladies are not suited for it." Claudia almost growled under her breath, and Luveday wondered if she hadn't met another medieval feminist. "I seem to have a talent for it, or so I have been told." Luveday didn't mean to boast, much. "As for gaining the favor of the King, I have to say that was not my doing or intention but a small miracle and my own stubbornness."

Laughing, Claudia took her arm, the first truly friendly gesture she had seen from the woman yet. "Now that sounds like a story indeed, My Lady. Share and I will take you out to our flower tables to talk to Leah, she is the healing woman of the village, and perhaps the most skilled with the use of flowers."

So Luveday told her tale and told it well as they journeyed beyond the garden walls until they reached a series of buildings set beyond the house grounds. People bustled around carrying baskets, jars, pots, and buckets.

A rank odor wafted from an open door, and Luveday looked inside, animal fat was being rendered to cure into soap. Not all of which seemed to make it into the final product at least judging from the smell.

"Sometimes making the sweet comes from the bitter," Claudia lifted a delicate hand to her nose as they passed.

Luveday quickly moved on and noticed that what she had thought were additional buildings were worktables covered like the public picnic areas back home. The structures were large and well built, able to shield the workers from all sorts of weather. Braziers heated areas while women could be seen crushing plants into mortars with pestles.

"Do you know much about the making of perfumes, Lady Luveday?" Claudia asked.

"I know the basics, but it was not something we did at such a scale; nor were our soaps so fine." Luveday looked to Claudia who was quietly speaking with a woman.

"Leah," Claudia called aloud a moment later. An elderly woman left a far table to stand before them. "Leah, I must see to something in the house, Lady Luveday has questions about the healing properties of our plants." Noting her brisk tone, Claudia softened it a bit to look back at Luveday. "Please see to her during her stay."

Luveday was shocked at how quickly she was dismissed. One moment they were in the middle of a conversation and the next Claudia was gone. The finality in her words made Luveday wonder if the lady was coming back. Whatever trouble was in the house seemed urgent, then again Benedict was starting his task today, and Luveday was suddenly sure that the lady had never meant to linger so long with her, if at all.

"Good morning, Leah. I am Lady Luveday, one of the King's healers."

"Good morning, my..." she seemed to start and look at Luveday's fine but simple attire. "Lady Luveday you said. There was a Lady Luveday, a lady healer that saved the young prince during the battle with Sterling in the north.

That be you My Lady?" The older woman was thin and wrinkled, yet something about her seemed kind.

"Indeed, the very same," Luveday admitted a little sheepishly. Though she had told Claudia of the tale, the woman had acted as if she had never heard of Luveday, and that had been fine with her, but it seemed that the tale had reached farther south and much wider than Luveday had ever expected. Then again, she wouldn't be surprised if some bard were, at that moment, singing about her, which caused Luveday to cringe at the thought.

"Oh, now lady." The woman gasped, and others looked around to murmur amongst themselves. "The woman who saved Prince Benjamin is most welcome here. Yes, My Lady, most welcome." She turned to look at the others, some smiled back, and some grew silent and watchful. "Anything you need, My Lady, you ask me." She corrected a man who tried to plop a bucket down on a worktable. The man grumbled and took the pale off to another area. "Now, lady, what is it your wanting to know."

Luveday liked this woman. "Everything."

She was changeable. At least that was what Luveday had come to think of her in the three days that had passed since their arrival. Lady Claudia was as different from Lady Christabel as night from day, but sometimes she saw the childish pettiness, and an unrealistic desire to have ones every want fulfilled. While Benedict went over the accounting books for the domain, and his men not so discreetly made inquiries around the hall and fields, Luveday was behind the scenes. Claudia was under scrutiny, and she knew it, but sometimes her temper got the better of her.

Smack! The sound reverberated down the hall it was so loud. It wasn't hard to recognize Gemma, though the girl cowered and gulped as she fought back the tears. Luveday couldn't make out what was said, but Claudia's hard and angry tone spoke volumes that morning when Luveday came down to take her morning meal. It was the little things that made Luveday suspect that the people were afraid of their lady.

Having spent the last few days among the men and women working the perfume house and some time spent in the fields, Luveday noticed a decided change whenever Claudia appeared. Even when spotted at a distance the people around Luveday would grow silent, turn away, or watch their lady with an intensity that bespoke their fear, like watching a snake devour a mouse. Many watched to make sure their children or daughters didn't upset the lady. No one spoke ill of the lady, and what praise left their lips was too enthusiastic, too shallow, and repeated too often to feel natural.

Luveday followed her prey at a leisurely distance, shadowing Claudia's movements for the second day in a row. Something slammed into the back of her legs and almost knocked her over. Luveday caught her balance but tried to grab whatever had hit her, and the effort of holding on to it caused her to go over.

Suddenly sitting on the ground, Luveday found herself gazing into a pair of beautiful hazel green eyes shimmering with tears.

"Easy now," Luveday assessed the damage. She was fine, though her bottom was a bit sore and her left leg was at an odd bend, she had managed to sit herself down with the child in her lap though she was not sure how. "Easy little one." She heard a sniffle and arm came up to draw a sleeve across the boy's face. "What's your name?" Luveday leaned back a little, getting a whiff of the boy.

"Artair." Came a gruff voice, she hadn't expected from such a skinny kid.

"Artair. I am Lady Luveday..." The boy panicked before she could finish speaking. He tried to get up, legs and arms scrambling. Luveday took an elbow to the face, while a hand braced against her chest and a knee struck her thigh. The boy trampled her skirts leaving behind muddy footprints as Leah's voice was heard calling both Artair and the lady. Luveday watched the boy disappear none the worse for the collision but noticed a few men throwing him dirty looks as he passed in a dead run. Leah reached her side to help her up.

"My Lady, what happened? Are you hurt? Do you need..." Gaining her feet, she looked herself over and the child's footprints were clearly visible on the gray gown. "Oh, my. Your dress, My Lady. Oh, no." Leah looked perplexed and glanced where the boy had gone. "Can it be saved?" She whispered.

Luveday looked it over, shaking out her skirts, the medium gray wool was light and yet kept out the lingering chill. It was the gown that Ellie had given her the first day she was at Lander's Keep, and it had seen much worse than mud. "Aye, it will clean up fine. I have gotten some stubborn spots out of this gown. No worries, Leah."

"Oh, thank goodness, My Lady." She moved Luveday aside. "Artair isn't usually so clumsy."

"Was he looking for his mother?" She asked, worried about the little urchin despite the mayhem he had wrecked upon her person.

Leah's chuckle lightened the mood. "Nay, if he had wanted me, he'd have not been shy about it." Luveday did a double take, not believing that Leah, who had seen sixty-eight years was the mother of a boy who looked to be no more than five. Then again, she mused, women had no protection, so it was completely possible that Leah had birthed a child so late in life. "Oh, now I know what you are thinking, My Lady, but Artair is my own miracle, sent to ease my heart so late in life." She grabbed and patted Luveday's arm affectionately as she was wont to do when they walked beside each other.

Luveday took her words at face value and would have thought nothing more about them, except for later that evening.

"Keep the boy out of sight, Leah. I'll not tell you again." Claudia's words were hard as steel, and though Luveday caught no more of the conversation, she knew a threat when she heard one.

"Are you sure we aren't a bore, Lady Luveday?" Claudia asked that evening after Benedict had made it clear that he and his men would be gone for a few days and that Luveday would not be accompanying them.

"Bored? Hardly Lady Claudia." The fact that neither of them had assured the use of titles was a fact not lost on Luveday.

Benedict laughed. "No, I fear, Lady Luveday is much too enthralled by her studies to be bored." The fact that his words were only half in jest was not lost to either of them as Benedict locked eyes with her. Luveday was quite interested in the use of flowers to soften or flavor the common remedies and didn't wish to leave yet, though this parting was a farce to give Luveday some time and space to befriend Claudia. It had not taken either of the spies long to see that Benedict was too much of a distraction for any sort of friendship to blossom between them. Though Luveday doubted such a thing would occur in his three-day absence, she was certain that his absence would change the tide, but she also feared that Benedict was the only reason Claudia was on her best behavior.

"The blossoms are more than just color and pretty smells, Benedict." Countering, "they have soothing and healing properties. These varieties do not grow anywhere else in the kingdom, so here is where I must study them." She heard rather than saw his eyes roll as Claudia stifled a laugh that was not as fake as some that left her lips.

"Yes, but you need not be so eager about it." He shot back.

Luveday humped. "Eager as a lad with a wooden sword?"

Benedict laughed outright. "Touché! Lady." His laughter was always contagious. "At least such eagerness has a use."

"And here too, My Lord." Claudia cut in, though her merriment was less evident.

"Aye, Lady Claudia is right, My Lord." Luveday agreed. "Who knows what ailments we may learn to cure. These flowers may hold untold answers." The gleam in Claudia's eye did not go unnoticed, but Luveday wondered what it meant.

'So tired,' thought Luveday as tried to work the kinks out of her back muscles from hours spent over a worktable. Today wasn't just for show. Luveday had helped make perfumed soaps and oils and brewed a few batched of syrups for common ailments. The mild seasons and coastal weather brought on lung congestions in many of the workers. Fever Foe and healing salve were the first she had started. Adding a few calming flowers to the mix made the salve more of a balm, and Luveday wondered if she couldn't start making something like the creams back home.

Home, she paused looking out as people cleared up the work areas and prepared to go home. Home was not something she thought of much anymore, except for the longing to see her family, the life she led in that other world seemed so far away from the woman she was now. Not for the first time, Luveday counted her blessings while she imagined what kind of life she might have had if she had been born here. She could have been Leah's daughter, or granddaughter because with a certainty she couldn't shake, she knew that she wouldn't be part of the nobility. That truth was one she would never voice aloud. It bothered her; the gaps that raised up the few and sunk the masses into servitude. What could she do, but show compassion, spread kindness and hope that someone would take note and carry it forward?

Leah's voice came from somewhere behind her, and Luveday turned around a smile lighting her countenance, but it was not Luveday the old woman was after. No, she saw her talking heatedly with Bea. Grabbing the last of her things, Luveday headed toward the hall, but took an indirect path, so that she could get closer to the two women without being seen. Since they had moved off the main path back through the hall's gardens, she was able to gain the shadows of the gate unseen.

"This is foolishness, girl." Luveday's new friend berated the younger woman.

Near tears, Bea whispered, "I know, Leah, but she won't see reason. I try to talk to her, I do, but she's set to do what she wants, and there is no one to stop her. Oh, if Sir Henry would return, or Sir Marcus, she would be calmer." Bea's eyes overflowed with silent tears as her breathing grew heavy under the weight of her emotions.

"You hush now." Leah tried comforting the distraught woman. "Hush, child."

"What will happen to us, Leah?" Bea pleaded. "What will happen?"

"Oh, dear. I don't know." Leah looked out over nothingness, "but I do know that we can't keep going on the way we are." Leah sighed as if the future were too heavy a burden for her, though Bea practically wept in her arms.

"She won't stop, and him…" But Leah cut her off without letting her finish, shushing the whimpering woman. Luveday watched as Leah's back went straight and she stepped further into the shadows. Following Leah's gaze, Luveday could see that her absence was finally noted. Quietly and as quickly as she dared, Luveday picked her way back to the hall, stopping into the kitchen to collect her tray and ask that hot water be brought to her room as soon as possible.

Pieces continued to fall into place, but something worried Luveday, and she couldn't put her finger on it. As she ascended a back stairway to take the long way to her room, Luveday had a sinking feeling that she was running out of time.

Early morning and evening were the times when most people were about, and Luveday knew she was taking a chance by being where she was not supposed to be so early in the morning. Dressed in simple garb and with a work cloth around her waist she hoped that at a glance she would appear just another servant about their duties. It was the tower she wished to get access too, as it was the one area of the manor that she had been politely, but continuously steered away from.

A heavy outside door opened silently as Luveday let herself into the tower. The base was larger than it looked, from the outside and seemed to have little room as it narrowed toward the top where it ended with a battlement and a cone-shaped roof. There was an anteroom of sorts that met the tower; a narrow hall led to the room at its base. Traversing the hallway, she was shocked when she realized that the stairs went up and down. Thinking that going down might be better, Luveday was shocked again when she realized that the way down was already alight.

Fear tingled up and down her spine, but Luveday silently descended into a room with a stone floor which was empty except for a stool, and three sets of manacles that hung off the perimeter of the round walls. The room must be at least twenty-five feet in diameter as this was the widest area of the tower. The manacles were blessedly empty, and Luveday was ready to leave the dungeon behind, but her steps echoed through the cell, and a muffled voice called out.

The sound came from the room, and not from somewhere above, so Luveday steps closer and only then did she see the large wooden door set in the floor. Hurrying closer, Luveday looked over the door. It was too large to open and too heavy for her alone. Only a bolt held it closed, but if it were as heavy as Luveday expects, it would probably take two men to open the hatch.

Whoever was below called out again, and banged against the door. Leaning over it, Luveday finally saw a small hatch cut in the door and open it calling out. "Be still, shush." The man below stilled instantly. Luveday couldn't see anything beyond the darkness, but she heard splashing and knew that whoever this prisoner was they were in serious trouble. Never did Claudia mention holding someone. Never did she or Benedict hear of someone held at the hall. "Who are you? Why are you here?"

"You are not Lady Claudia." He whispered and Luveday could barely make out the glitter of eyes beyond the small iron grill that made it impossible for him even to reach her.

"No, I am Lady Luveday, now answer quickly." Should she tell him that she wasn't supposed to be there?

"Lady Luveday, Luveday..." He murmurs. "Lady Luveday of Lander's Keep." He asks hesitantly.

Shocked at not having been called that in some weeks she answers cautiously, "Aye. The same."

A gust of wind lefted him, and Luveday was hit by a blast of foul breath. "Lady, it is I, Minstrel Hardin of Northelm."

Luveday had to think a moment and gasp. "The minstrel from Ellie's wedding, the young man from Northelm. You brought news of squire Coll's family, no?"

"Aye, Lady you remember me." He sounded so relieved.

"Why are you here, Hardin?"

"I but tried to leave after singing for my supper for a few nights. The Lady grew angry and raged at me." He whispered as if she might hear. "I never saw a face so changed." He spoke to himself more than to her.

"Hardin," Luveday moved to cover the few fingers on the grate with her own. "Hardin, listen carefully. I am not supposed to be down here, but I will not forget you. Lord Benedict of Lion's Gate will return in a day or two." She could see that while the mention of Benedict hard heartened him, the time he must wait was a heavy burden. Lord, how long had he been down there, she wondered. "Stay strong; I will come back for you."

"Lady," He whispered desperately, and she grasped his fingers, and Luveday squeezed with all her might, hoping to impart some strength to him.

"I will be back, Hardin." She moved to back away, sorry she must close the little door on him to leave him in the dark again, but she never got the chance. A large hand clamped onto her left shoulder. Luveday nearly jumped out of her skin when a sickly familiar voice whispered from behind her.

"Aye, back to keep him company." It rasped, and Luveday felt the brush of lips over the shell of her right ear. "Only after I am done with you, little healer." It was barely over the sound of her dread that she heard the screaming and rattling of the hatch as Hardin bellowed below them, venting his impudent rage.

It was the face of a man too smug for his own good. The face of a man who was never to set foot on this soil as long as King Edward's line lived. It was a face Luveday had hoped never to see again, but Ladislaus Sterling was standing before her. Her hair still hurt where he had grasp handfuls of it to drag her up the stairs.

Luveday had called out for help and received a fist to the gut for her efforts, but her screams met with the noise that carried up from below and footsteps had come running. One look at the situation and Bea had fled to find her mistress, but Luveday guessed no help would come from that corner. Was this the mysterious 'he' the serving woman had mentioned to Leah last night? How long had Sterling been there? How long had Claudia been cavorting with the enemy?

"Well, little healer," he looked down at Luveday as she tried to scramble to her feet but ended up throwing herself into a large oak chair in what looked to be a man's study. "What providence has delivered you to me?" He mused darkly. Luveday had no trouble identifying the gleam of violence in his eyes as he moved closer. "You have evaded my grasp, but it was only a matter of time before you were mine." He licked his lips as if looking at a choice piece of meat and savoring the taste. "Yes, time; passed time you paid for the wrong you have done me." He moved forward and grabbed Luveday by the shoulders, she was fumbling, having already lost her meat dagger, the small blade she kept strapped to one ankle would have to do, or perhaps there was something around her, but a glance revealed nothing within reach. Sterling was pulling her to her feet when the door burst open, and Lady Claudia came gliding into the room, followed by a distraught Bea.

"Ladislaus, my love, please unhand the lady." Claudia's blasé tone merely slowed the man.

"Not this time, my darling." He turned his head only enough to speak to her over his shoulder. "I have waited too long to get my hands on her."

Claudia came near enough so that Luveday could see the hard gaze leveled at her. In a sweet tone, the Lady of Briar's Gate opposed the treasonous earl. "Ladislaus, you cannot harm the lady when we need her to make sure that Lord St. James leaves here with Edward's men."

There was a deep growl as Claudia moved to put a hand over his. "To spare her friends, Luveday will tell Lord Benedict that he may leave without her, she had more studying to do, with the new shipment of spices coming in a few days. Benedict will leave after I promise to see the lady safely to court with the first batch of perfumes of the season." His anger dimmed at Claudia's calming recitation of this new plan. "What are a few more days here, my love? St. James went with his men and none the wiser to your presence."

"And after..." He removed his hand to take Claudia's and kissed her knuckles looking deeply into her eyes as they both took a step away from Luveday.

Steadying herself on her feet, Luveday longed to make some retort, but her instincts, along with Claudia's cold glance told her to be silent. Swallowing hard, Luveday inadvertently brought his attention to her, and a moment later she was thrown back into the chair by the force of the slap that connected with her face. She couldn't help the whimper that escaped her or the tears that stung her eyes. Through the pain she tried to listen as the couple left the room, giving orders that she be moved to the upper tower room and put under constant guard.

Chapter 18

Think, In mounting higher, The angels would press on us,
and aspire, To drop some golden orb of perfect song,
Into our deep, dear silence.
~ Elizabeth Barrett Browning

Leah tsked as she gently applied the healing salve to Luveday's cheek. Laying still in the bed, she surveyed the canopy above her. The circumference of the tower room was in shadow, except for the bit opposite the one window. The swelling was affecting her vision in her left eye, but more troublesome than the blur was the throbbing in her head. How she wished she had some of that nettle plant to numb the pain if only for a little while. Before coming to Anora, only one other time in her life had Luveday seen someone slap another person. Luveday had been present once when a girl at school had backhanded another girl. The bruise and swelling were noticeable for several days after, but then Sarah did have a very pale and delicate complexion. How much worse was this going to be? There wasn't a comparison between the backhand of a hundred-pound cheerleader and the full force from the blow of a grown man, was there? The pain of her whipping had been worse, but luckily, Luveday had been unconscious for the majority of the first days of healing. She knew there would be no reprieve from this, not if she wanted to survive this ordeal.

Leah sighed, bringing her back to the present.

"Leah," Luveday had so many things she wanted to ask.

The older woman stopped her, "Now, child. You know I cannot say what our Lady has been about." Leah finished her task and stepped back. Luveday could see the concern in her expression, but she knew she would have to press her friend. There was too much at stake to go through this blind. Right now, she was a liability to Benedict, a ruse at best, bait or worse should Sterling have enough men to fight St. James. She could easily imagine that odious man deciding it was better to kill the King's knights rather than chance it.

Luveday was no fool; she knew that Claudia had only spared her for the moment, and she wasn't sure the act had been entirely self-serving. Still, she couldn't guess why Claudia seemed to care. The woman hid behind a beautiful mask, and try as she might, Luveday had yet to see the woman behind it.

"Leah," Luveday tried again, this time taking a direct approach. "Sterling has been denounced after his acts of treason against the King. Lady Claudia is in a lot more trouble than just missing taxes."

Leah looked shocked. "Missing taxes?"

Eyes widening, at least one eye in Luveday's case, the lady had thought that that was a major reason for the secrecy around the hall and village, but maybe she was wrong. "Yes, King Edward sent Lord St. James and me to Briar's Gate to ascertain why Lady Claudia has not paid them for the last three years." The older woman stumbled and dropped to a stool beside the bed. "You didn't know about the coin?" Leah pressed a hand to her mouth as she shook her head. "Sir Marcus Reeve is at court asking for the King's leniency on your lady's behalf, but the King is not so tolerant as he may wish. His Majesty thought that I might be able to help Lady Claudia and with reason, find a solution acceptable to the King."

"His majesty sent you, sent you in person."

"Do you mean, did I see him and speak to him? Yes, he and Queen Augusta believed we might be able to come to terms in such a way as to spare the lady any grief. No one imagined that Sterling would be involved." Luveday's mind swam with the complications, or the pain she couldn't quite tell. "Leah, I need your help, or I fear something terrible will happen here." Leaning out from the bed, she grabbed the woman's hand and squeezed. "Please Leah."

"You will help Lady Claudia?" She fervently asked Luveday, almost pleading.

"As much as the Lady is willing." Luveday could promise nothing.

Sighing wearily, Leah nodded and considered the rafters a moment before nodding once again. "Lady, how can I help? I cannot take you from this room, she's told the house and workers to keep a lookout, and if you did manage to flee and she found out 'twas me, she'd hurt my Artair."

"Is she so cruel Leah?" Luveday couldn't understand why Claudia garnered such loyalty, it seemed to be more than just fear.

"Nay, at least, not until recently..." She harrumphed. "Not before the Lord's death did, I become aware of most of it. Then, I had Artair, and my work kept me busy enough." Leah looked Luveday in the eye. "She was a good lady, and he a good lord, much better than his father ever was, not to speak ill of the dead, but Titus's father was a hard man, stern and never pleased. Our Lord was kind, and though his marriage was not one of love, they got along well enough."

"But that changed?" Luveday prompted when she grew silent. They didn't have much time, Luveday was sure the guard would call the woman out soon.

"Aye. Lady Claudia's always had her moods, but most lady's do." Leah looked out the window. "She's cunning, cleverer than most men I'd wager." Leah smiled at that. "She fought with her husband about the way we make perfume until he told her that if she thought she could do better; she should prove it." Nodding and smiling smugly, Leah continued. "Changed almost everything we had been doing for a century, but with her notions and her letters, she found ways to do it better from all over the lands. Made the house richer than ever old Titus thought he could be. A bright future lay ahead for all of us." Admittedly, Luveday was impressed. She imagined Claudia as the CEO of the medieval version of Dior, or some cosmetic brand. A colossal achievement considering the obstacles she had faced.

"Leah," Taking her hand again, Luveday drew her near. "Yet many of the workers fear her. Something must have changed."

She nodded sadly. "The Lord and Lady began quarreling more."

"About the money or perfume?"

"Nay, more matters between man and wife?"

Luveday thought a moment. Did Lord Titus not like the power his wife possessed? Was he the type of man who couldn't take the success of a woman where he had failed? Possible, she mused, she hadn't heard enough about the Lady's husband to hazard a guess. He was called a good man, but what did that mean? A good knight, a good lord, a good husband or a good human being? Something struck her, and Luveday asked, "They had been married for some half dozen years, but the lady never bore Lord Titus any children?"

Something passed over Leah's face, only to be replaced by utter sorrow. "There was a babe, five years back, but it was born without the gift of breath. The wee thing was buried in the old churchyard."

Wondering about the flash of emotion she saw before Leah told of the babe, Luveday felt she was treading through murky water. There were layers and layers of secrets to this place.

"How is Sterling involved?"

"The Earl and Titus trained as knights together."

"Sterling? But firstborns…"

Leah shook her head. "Had an older brother, and several sisters, before the lady bore Ladislaus late in life. He was a spoiled child and became more so as he grew into a handsome man."

Luveday snorted. There was something a little too, well, too evil about the man to be called handsome though she had briefly thought it upon first seeing him. "That explains a few things at least."

"Not an excuse, but his mother doted on him something fierce." She nodded. "He has some lands not far from here and stopped by to take advantage of our lord's hospitality. There was talk of some debt owed to him, for saving our Lord's life, though I never learned the details." There was movement heard outside the bolted door, and Leah grasped Luveday's hand, but after a few moments, they released the breaths they each held.

"What else?"

"That was before My Lord married, but after a visit, well after the Earl got sight of our lady, he seemed to make more regular visits."

"Ah, the lure of a beautiful face." Luveday wondered if it had started out innocently or had Sterling had darker feelings for another man's wife? Seeing comes before wanting, or so she had always heard.

"Aye, and I think too, a meeting of minds. As he was still the second son and she a married lady, My Lord let it go a bit farther than other men would, but he was a kind man, and wanted to keep nothing from her that gave her pleasure. At least in the beginning."

"Before the Lord's death, were they in good terms or maybe Sterling stood between them?"

Growing thoughtful for a moment Leah answered truthfully, though it was not what Luveday wanted to hear. "Since the babe was lost, they hardly spoke a word to each other and were rarely in my company together. You see, the lord was gone when she went into labor. Some falling out between them and she was so aggrieved that she birthed too early."

There was something stilted in the way the older woman relayed this that confused Luveday. Here is another secret, she thought, something about the child.

"Since his death, the lady hasn't openly supported Sterling's campaign against the King..." Luveday thought aloud.

"Do you think that is where the coin has gone, lady?" Leah asked earnestly shocked.

Nodding more to herself than her friend, "It looks that way, Leah. There is no sign that she has spent it frivolously or put it to use here at Briar's Gate. Benedict could find no accounting for it, yet the villagers he questioned assured him the taxes were always collected on time."

"Aye, we paid in full more likely than not. As I told, the years have been good to us." Though her words held a touch of pride, Leah was clearly troubled. "Oh, what has that child done?"

Touching her hand, Luveday tried to give comfort. "She is not alone in this; Sterling is to blame as well. I am sure of it."

"She was such a quiet and clever girl, reminded me of my Ann when she married. I took her under my wing and showed her the working of perfumes. She was so quick. And when she took over, she made me head woman even though I was a widow and not more than refuse to the head man." Luveday could see that Leah owed her so much.

"Leah," there was movement outside again. "Leah, I need to know everything you can gather about Sterling and his men. Where they are staying, how many men there are with him. Can you..."

"All right now, what's going on here?" A gruff man with a sword on his belt entered the room.

"Just finishing with the lady, Sir..." Leah asked.

"Sir Owen of Bryce Castle." He looked over the simply furnished room. "Out with you woman. The Earl wants this one left alone." He looked at Luveday's face and grimaced. Turning away, he held the door open for her and watched as Leah grabbed what things she had brought and left the room without looking back.

He was late. Benedict had said three nights, just three, but five were near to passing, and he had not returned. She knew that he would, but she also knew that something he found might have been worth the delay. Or Sterling could have done something, but the more Luveday thought about it, the less likely that seemed. Her captors wouldn't be so watchful, or she still breathing if something had happened to the King's men.

Waiting was growing tiresome. Sterling came to threaten and manhandle her, but the bruise on her face was fading quickly, thanks to her salves, and they wanted her in top form to dupe her companions. Three days in the tower room with nothing to do but think was emotionally, if not physically, exhausting. She had paced, assessed her surroundings, paced, thought up the ten most likely scenarios for what was to come, paced, checked the door, paced, checked the window, paced, checked for hidden passages, paced and paced some more. She supposed she had slept in their somewhere but sleeping and eating were not on the top of her to-do lists. The fact that Sterling could accost her while she slept, or that someone could put something into her food, was not far from her mind, but she also needed to be ready to fight if or more likely, when, the time came.

And now there was only the sound of her pacing and the voices in the courtyard below, and a strange scratching sound but she couldn't find where it was coming from. Rats, she shuddered, it was probably rats. Finding rodents at your local pet store cute was one thing, but free-range plague carriers were something completely different. Luveday's skin crawled just thinking about it. She plopped down on the bed and pulled her knees up.

Luckily, the sound stopped, and she was left to thinking again. Falling sprawled over the made bed she stared at the canopy. Something grabbed her foot as it dangled off the side of the bed, Luveday bolted upright ready to scream but came face to face with a wary looking child. It took a moment to find Artair in the dirt-covered, cobweb-sporting boy.

"Artair?" She asked as the boy threw something at her to land on the bed. A moment later she heard scraping, but by the time she had gotten off the bed, the boy was gone. Looking back, Luveday picked up the missile, which turned out to be a scrap of parchment and read a simple word, men with six lines underneath. Luveday could only assume this was Leah's way of counting Sterling's men. So, either there were six altogether or six plus Sterling. With the men of the village and house, there were probably a dozen or so who would fight, but only a few were trained with weapons as the house Knights were still abroad on one task or another. No wonder Claudia didn't seem perturbed that the hall was undefended, she had Sterling and his men in reserve.

Looking around Luveday tried to spot where the boy had disappeared to, but there was no sign of him. Then again, he had been covered in dirt and cobwebs, so maybe whatever hole or shaft he had climbed was small enough to be unused, and thus no use to her. But now she had a way to pass information; the problem was that Leah had only a basic grasping of writing and reading as she helped keep a tally of who was working and what goods were going in and out. The books were basic row and columns with tally marks to count out each item. Leah says she had memorized the order of items more than she could read the words running down and across the page. What could she ask for that Leah might provide? Luveday sat down. Nothing came to mind. Anything she needed to know would have to be delivered quickly and sending Artair would take time, while putting the boy in danger. "Urgh," She groaned to herself and fell back on the bed again.

An hour later Artair reappeared looking ready to bolt.

"It's alright, Artair. I won't hurt you." Luveday just smiled at the boy who had appeared from under her bed.

"Momon told me," he nodded as if agreeing with her, "but Lady Claudia is mean, and I don't like her. Momon said Lady was nice, but I've met only Lady Claudia; so I didn't know." Some of the words rolled together, but Luveday clearly understood the boy. Perhaps he was older than he looked, though small for his age. Failure to thrive or something else, she wondered, or perhaps a difficult birth considering Leah's age. "Take." He held out another scrap of paper and a piece of charcoal.

"What is this for, Artair?" She asked taking the items.

"Momon said you know letters and to write a message for the Lord." He looked at her with narrowed eyes. "You know your letters, right?"

"Yes," she laughed at his doubtful expression. "Yes, I do." Luveday wrote quickly on the side of the parchment that wasn't as dirty.

"Do all ladies know their letters?" He asked watching her.

Wrapping up the scrap so that the writing would be protected, Luveday returned it and leaned over to look at him. "No, just some really special ones." The boy only looked at her thoughtfully before nodding and bending down to disappear beneath the bed.

This time Luveday knelt to watch him and was surprised to see one of the square panels in the headboard give way, and the boy looked to slide through the gap and down into darkness without fear. Luveday almost called him back, but she remembered that Artair had done this before. It was no wonder she had missed the hidden door. The space beneath the bed was probably larger than her modern beds at about eighteen inches giving her a clear view of the clean space, but the opening in the panels of the headboard was barely big enough for the boy to slip through. She wondered what it had been used for and made a mental note to ask Leah eventually.

Leah appeared not long after Sterling had left, at least once a day he visited her to make himself felt, and she guessed that he was anticipating what he would do to her. Claudia had not been with him on this last visit; she hadn't liked to look upon Luveday's bruised face. Luckily, she couldn't see her arms, or the lady would see the marks her lover's rough handling had left. Luveday wasn't one to bruise easily, but you would never know it looking at the damage he dealt her.

Leah silently applied the salve to her face, but the glances they exchanged were full of unspoken words. Luveday mouther her thanks for the messages. Leah smiled and nodded. The last day or so the guard had not allowed them to talk in private, now often standing in the doorway while Leah or Bea accomplished their task. Luveday guessed that the tension was mounting as the hall grew impatient for Benedict's return and no one more than her.

"Out with you woman." The guard called.

Leah quickly gathered her things and gave the man a look. "Keep your hands off her Sir Knight. She is a lady and if anything happens to her..." Luveday knew she threatened the guard with her closeness to Lady Claudia, being only one of two women in her confidence concerning Luveday. The guard seemed to take her bluff seriously and glared at both women before closing the door behind them.

Luveday almost laughed at the nonsense. It was strange that Claudia did seem to care for her well-being. Luveday wondered about it and thought it was most likely that Claudia respected another intelligent woman to some degree. If her concern was truly self-serving than Luveday really shouldn't care, but there was something fragile about the woman at times. From what Leah had said Luveday feared that Claudia was mentally unstable. More than once she had heard of or witnessed severe mood swings, taking the lady from pleasant to wrathful in a breath. Claudia's anger, once riled, what like a rabid beast that bit anyone who came too close.

It looked like some of the house was still in denial about their lady's instability, while others took the route of least resistance, and chose to avoid her as much as possible, which was rather easy for an operation of this size. Those most loyal to her, those closest to her were the ones that took the brunt of her anger but were also the ones that tried to hide her deterioration. What some wouldn't do for love, she mused.

Dawn came as bright and crisp as ever, finding Luveday up and ready for the day. A part of her still feared that Sterling meant to do her more harm, catching her when she was most vulnerable and force himself upon her. Luveday's stomach rolled at the thought of such a violation. Her nerves quivered, and her palms sweat just thinking about it. She wouldn't put it past him to forgo Claudia's warning and hurt her anyways.

The first hours passed until she heard the strange scratching noise once again. Luveday knelt beside the bed and waited. It was not long before the small door popped inward and a small head immerged in the shadows under the bed. The small head turned toward her and Luveday was surprised to see a grin split the boy's dirty face. Soon he was out from under the bed and standing beside her. Luveday wondered that there was any grime left in the secret passage after the boy traversed it; all the dirt seemed to be on him.

She smiled at him and wiped something off his head. "Good morning Artair." She whispered.

Whispering back, the boy informed her of some good news. "Momon said John brought news your lord is coming back today." He grinned. "John said he heard last night that Lord Benedict," he stumbled over Benedict's name, "...was de-laid, and was on his way."

"Thank you, Artair, that is great news." She smiled. "Is there anything else?" The boy just shook his head. "Oh, can you tell your mother that we will have to signal Benedict somehow before he enters the hall. Sterling's men might be waiting for them." Luveday didn't doubt that Sterling meant to frighten her when he threatened to kill Benedict and his men before doing worse to her, but she couldn't say if he would follow through. For all his words, Luveday doubted that the traitor dared to stand and fight, especially when his enemy had larger numbers. She pegged him for the type to let money pave the way and let someone else handle the dirty work. After all, hadn't he used the mercenaries to fight the King and run at the first opportunity? He was a bully, a man who only hurt those weaker than himself; something sneaky and underhanded was exactly his style.

"Momon sent John this morn'. He's to wait at the crossroad for your lord, even if it takes all day."

Luveday quelled her relief. "John has my note, my letter?" She asked patiently. Artair grinned and nodded. Luveday felt like hugging the boy, and she would have, if he weren't so dirty. "Wonderful." She thought she heard something outside. "You had better go, Artair. They've not brought my morning meal yet, and I don't want them to find you." She whispered her thank you as the boy slid under the bed, but the door opened before Luveday could get entirely back to her feet.

Startled, Luveday did turn to the boy hoping, but no. The guard yelled and dove for the bed. Luveday moved to wrestle with him, but a solid shove to her middle sent her flying backward. Falling hard on the floor, she barely missed striking the post at the foot of the bed. Luveday kicked out, but the knight caught the boy in one hand and her ankle in the other.

"Who do we have 'ere?" Artair fought like a wild thing though the knight held him upside down by his leg. "Little miscreant." The man grunted as Artair's foot landed a kick to the man's chest.

Luveday looked around, but Bea only stood in the doorway shocked and torn about what to do. There was no doubt that she recognized Leah's boy and only when the knight shook him did both she and Luveday yell for him to stop. Luveday was released, but the boy was not. Bea looked as if she might turn and flee but a moment later the tray she carried was tossed at the Knight causing him to drop the boy. Luveday lunged, but Artair was already moving. He landed hard on his side, and thankfully not his head. Scrambling to his feet, the boy dashed through the door, the Knight in hot pursuit. Unfortunately for Bea and Luveday, the scuffle and the crash of dishes had alerted another man, who, unable to stop the boy running down the stairs moved to lock the two women in the room while they chased the runt down.

Bea and Luveday only looked at the locked door before turning to each other. "I am so sorry, My Lady!" Tears brightened the woman's eyes but did not fall. Luveday only nodded. How many times had Luveday looked at the woman only a few years older than herself or Claudia and wondered at the woman's torn loyalties. Time and time again, Bea had sided with Claudia by choosing to do nothing rather than doing what was right. Now the woman had, consciously or not, thrown in her lot with Luveday. She didn't see Claudia going easy on her trusted friend's betrayal.

The stairs beyond the door had been silent for some time when both women moved to pick up the ruined breakfast. The only thing that had survived the tosh into the knight's face was the wooden tray. The clay teapot and mug, the flatbread trencher full of meat and eggs with their toppings lay scattered on the floor. They scooped up bits and tossed the ruined meal out the window, leaving the shards of pottery in the empty chamber pot. Washing up in the basin of water Leah had left the other night, both women settled onto the bed, Luveday taking the head near the window and Bea taking the foot near the door, so the stretched out looking diagonally across the bed at each other.

"You know this cannot go on for much longer?" Luveday asked after a few moments.

Bea nodded sadly, looking down and pinching at the skirt of her gown nervously. "My Lady, she is not thinking clearly. I fear... I fear she has called down the King's wrath on us."

Luveday didn't know what to say to that. She had the urge to comfort, but too much had happened for her to give platitudes and she did not want to tell this woman something that she knew was untrue. "Sterling's presence here changes everything, Bea."

"'Tis Beatrix, Lady Luveday. Only My Lady and Leah call me Bea." Beatrix spoke with her head down glancing up at her every once in a while. Luveday nodded, not liking the use of a nickname, they were not friends.

"Beatrix, if Lord Benedict and the King's men are hurt or even killed," Bea looked up, startled and shook her head violently, but Luveday continued. "Then there will be no helping you." Almost looking distraught Luveday watched the emotions and thoughts flash across the serving woman's face. "Help me," Luveday begged. "Help me to help your lady and save my friends." Luveday looked at her, and for once their gazes held. "Please Beatrix. I need to find a way to warn the men of trouble. I am sure they will arrive today." Luveday watched the woman nod as if she too had heard the news.

"I will, for My Lady." Luveday watched as determination settled over the woman like a cloak before Beatrix moved off the bed and rose to her feet. They looked around, but there was nothing to help them escape. The serving woman looked back to the bed. "The sheets My Lady!" She gasped.

"They aren't long enough to form a rope to climb out of the tower," Luveday said matter-of-factly. She had thought of fashioning a rope and repelling down the three stories to the ground, but not only was there not enough material, Luveday doubted that she had the upper-arm strength needed to hold onto the rope.

"Nay lady, we would fall to our deaths, but if we dangle the sheet out the window, then the men might be able to see if from the road..."

"And think it strange at least, maybe enough to look around?" Luveday got up, and they quickly stripped the bed. "Good idea Beatrix." A few moments later the bedclothes were securely tied to the bedpost on one end and flapping in the spring breeze on the other. Luveday thought she heard some commotion below, but no one raised the alarm.

If Benedict did not hurry, then she was sure someone would come to take down the sheets. Looking at the door Luveday assessed her chances. Even with the items Beatrix had brought there was nothing to open the door which latched from the outside, but a thought occurred to her. They might not be able to get out, but perhaps she could keep them from coming in. Luveday had passed on the idea days go as being left without food or water was only marginally worse than focusing Sterling's wrath on her defiance. The guards would eventually break through the door, but perhaps they could stall them long enough for her friends to arrive.

"Beatrix, let me see the tray." The serving woman retrieved it from its place on the only stool looking confused. It was a solid piece of wood, oak if she guessed right. The iron handles on the end were heavy and twisted to give it an ornate design for something so simple. "If we can find a way to wedge this beneath the door, it might keep out the guards long enough for Lord St. James to see our warning." Luveday glanced at the sheets. Beatrix looked at her and nodded.

"I've nothing better, lady." She shrugged.

Luveday approached the door, listening but heard nothing on the other side. Part of her expected it to be thrown open at any moment. As she approached and was thinking of how to wedge the tray in the gap between door and floor or door and jam to best stop it, the latch scraped on the other side, and the door opened. Rather than the violent movement that would have slammed into Luveday the door opened only a crack and a small dirty face peeked inside. Upon spotting Luveday, Artair grinned impishly.

"Artair!" Luveday explained and met the boy for a quick hug which he returned. "You're not hurt, are you?"

"Nay lady, they can't catch me." The boy looked sheepish as he let go of her.

"Oh, thank the creator, you escaped." Bea expelled a breath. "I feared he'd beat you, child."

Artair seemed wary of the serving woman but didn't run. "Only if they catch me."

"Artair, where are the guards?" Luveday asked, not hearing any movement in the hall.

"Gone, Lady." The boy looked wide-eyed for a moment. "Lots going on down in the hall."

"I bet," Beatrix mumbled.

Luveday looked at the crack in the door. Escape was not the best option, but perhaps fortifying their position was. "Beatrix, Artair, I need your help."

Both looked to her, and she saw a note of eagerness in their eyes. "It's foolish to think we can escape, especially since Benedict is not far off." She mummed over the slip of using his Christian name. "But there is someone else who needs to be rescued." They looked at her questioningly. "Now here is my idea."

"Nothing yet, m'lady," the boy's whispers echoed down the stair.

"Pull Beatrix, on three." Each woman grasped one of the handholds on the heavy wooden door in the floor of the cell below the tower. "Get ready to push Minstrel." Grunts were her only answer. "One, two, three." It was a miracle that the three of them could move the door at all. As the door rose high enough that a body might slip through, Luveday used her knee to wedge the stool into the space, keeping the door from slamming back down should they lose their grip before the minstrel could get free.

The man slithered out of the cell, his lower half soaking wet. Hardin crawled on all fours until he heard the door close rather softly behind in. Though he smelled foul, each woman grabbed an arm and helped him gain his feet.

The lady whispered, "Quickly, Hardin," as the three tried to negotiate the stairs. At the first landing, Artair kept watch. The boy took one look at them and ran ahead. A moment later he waved them on and ran up the next flight of stairs. On the second floor, another passage linked the tower to the rest of the house. Once back to their room, and with a few items pilfered thanks to Beatrix intimate knowledge of the house and Artair's speed, they quartet was back into the tower room without anyone the wiser.

Luveday looked around, thinking someone must have come while they were gone, but the sheet was still tied to the bed where they had left it. If anyone had come to find they had escaped, surely, they would have thought that the lady would make a run for it, and not go below to rescue another prisoner, and thus, Luveday hoped, it would take them some time before they thought to come back here.

"On the bed," Luveday guided.

"Nay, My Lady." Minstrel and servant spoke together. "The stool, Beatrix countered, and the man agreed.

Not wanting to argue, Luveday helped to settle Hardin on the stool, before going to close and wedge the door shut. Testing it, Luveday couldn't move the door though she used her foot as leverage against the jam. It would have to do, she thought.

"Good, My Lady." Hardin looked too thin, bone warry and bedraggled.

"Beatrix help him undress. We'll wash him as best we can and see to any wounds." She watched as a look of determination came over the other woman's face. Artair looked on from the end of the bed as the serving woman helped the man take off his soaking clothes. Among the items they had procured from the rooms closest to the tower room was Luveday's backpack and healing bag. Both of which had been in the study on the first floor. Sterling had combed through the items setting aside somethings from her modern time. Luveday had swept everything back into her pack along with a knife and some bread left over from what she assumed had been Sterling's morning meal. Artair had procured several pitchers of water, and one of ale. The water would help clean up the minstrel; the ale was to drink. Luveday's healing bag was full of bottled salves, bandages, knife, scissors and an assortment of other items.

Searching through the backpack, the lady pulled out the wad of clothes from the area once reserved for her laptop. Her old boxer shorts and t-shirt would have to do. She looked at the foot of the bed and saw the folded coverlet. It was all they had. Washcloth in hand, Hardin was wiping down as much as he could reach, while Beatrix washed what he couldn't. It took only a few minutes, but there was already a vast improvement.

Luveday grabbed the scissors, holding them up as she asked permission. "May I?"

The startled look on his face quickly turned to gratitude with an eager nod. If Luveday remembered the man correctly he had been handsome, well kept, and polite despite the hard life he must have led.

Luveday trimmed his beard and cut his hair. Without the grim and ratty mess, she glimpsed the charming man she remembered, though the smile on his face no longer had the roguish charm that had bewitched some of the serving women, it was full of emotion. "Better," Luveday said as Hardin's eyes brimmed full. Beatrix dried off the rest of him in an economical fashion. Sitting wrapped in a bit of cloth the man shivered but looked human once again.

"Now, let us look at your feet." Luveday started at the bottom and worked her way up. As expected, the skin of his feet and legs were waterlogged from hours if not days in the hole. "Were you in the water the whole time?" She whispered under her breath.

Clearing his throat, he answered. "Nay, Lady." He coughed. "The water drained slowly. Every few days they would open a gate, and water flooded the hole through an opening below." He shuddered at the memory. "They wouldn't open the door above me, just let the water fill it up until there was almost no room left." Luveday grabbed him by the shoulder, and the gesture grounded him in the present.

"There might have been a small blessing in that." Though he didn't answer, Luveday could feel he wanted to object. "I doubt they let you out to relieve yourself; the water would wash away some of it, so you weren't sitting in it for long." She received thoughtful looks from the two other adults while Artair moved to listen at the door. Once wounds were cleaned and bandaged, Luveday offered her clothes. Hardin put them on. Both garments were large on his skinny frame. Luveday worried about the weight he had lost since she had last seen him.

Dressed in her night things and cocooned in a blanket, they settled the minstrel on the ticking since the sheets still fluttered through the window.

"Someone's coming." Artair looked ready to bolt.

Luveday looked to the others, who wore equal looks of concern and defiance. She wondered what had taken them so long. Had they found them missing and started a search? She didn't think so; there had been no alarm. So, they had finally come to collect her.

The door was tried but didn't budge. Luveday looked to the small washstand and Beatrix must have had the same idea for a moment later, while men yelled, and heavy objects banged on the door, they placed the small washstand in front of the door wedging it under a metal band. They moved back to the bed, Beatrix rounding it to stand on the far side holding on to a post like her life depended on it. Luveday gave a knife to the minstrel, while she perched on the side staring straight at the door. Artair climbed the bed and came to rest at her back.

Luveday willed the door to hold as she heard Sterling scream curses at her. Beatrix gasped at the vulgar things they could hear clearly through the door. Hardin growled while shifting closer. Artair wrapped an arm around Luveday's right arm and set his head on her shoulder, but she didn't look away from the door. Luveday clutched the meat knife Emmalyn had given her all those months ago in her right fist. The blade was little use against the weapons in the hands of the men on the other side of the door, but its presence was somehow reassuring.

The door shook and jerked, but despite all odds, held.

More cursed traversed the space between them, but soon more voices, urgent and compelling sounded, though they were less clear. Sterling vented his rage at the door, bellowing his fury she had no doubt the pounding of the door was his last effort to get to her, but still the door held.

After a moment, the voices quieted, footsteps receded, and the tower grew silent. A few moments later the courtyard below their window was full of people who ran about with panicked activity. Beatrix moved to the window while Luveday and Hardin still stared at the door.

"Down there, lady. That's Sterling's men." She pointed, her arm moving to follow the men below. "They're leaving." She gasped in suppressed joy.

Still, they watched the door, afraid it might be some trick. Minutes passed with not a peep.

Sterling's voice echoed from somewhere below the window, and only then did they breathe easier.

A gentle knock sounded at the door. A knock everyone seemed to know.

Getting to her feet, Luveday removed the washstand and stared at the tray. Its handle was wedged in the gap between door and frame. The metal handle was bend with the effort of the guard to enter the room, and for a moment the lady wondered if she would be able to pry it free or even if she should.

Hardin stood on week legs and shuffled over to her. His hand on her shoulder startled Luveday out of her thoughts. He only nodded.

"Lady Luveday." A soft voice called with a note of question.

"Coming, Lady Claudia." She answered as she tugged the tray free.

A heartbeat later the two women faced each other over the threshold. Luveday noticed the slight widening of her enemy's eyes as Claudia took in the minstrel and her serving woman. The boy took her attention for a moment, and a flash of something dark colored her expression before it was gone as if it had never been.

"It seems you were more of a challenge than he thought." She smiled a bit bitterly, but there was also a ruefulness there. Claudia must have warned her lover not to underestimate a woman. Clearly, he had not taken her advice. "Your escort has returned."

"Lord St. James is here?" Luveday asked, not sure if she should close the door in the woman's face and barricade themselves in that room until Benedict himself came knocking at the door or trust her that Sterling had fled. Speaking of which, she asked what had changed the tide. "Sterling decided to run from the King's wrath?" And this time there was a small twitch at the corner of Claudia's eye, before she sighed releasing a large breath.

"Nay, Sterling has never feared the King, more fool him." She seemed to give him up as a lost cause. "St. James is hardly enough to make him balk.

Nay, he would relish the challenge of defeating the sworn brother of the King's Champion. What a blow to the Wolf that would have been; Aye?" She laughed a little under her breath at the thought. "Nay, Lady Luveday. That would not have been enough."

"What then?" A raspy voice asked over her shoulder. Hardin's voice was hoarse, no doubt from days of screaming, crying and pleading for his release.

Claudia smiled though it was much more subdued than her usual alluring turn of the lip. "It seems Lady, you have quite a number of champions."

Looking confused, she was about to ask before Claudia stepped away and gestured for them to follow. "Come."

Instead of descending the stair she ascended a small set tucked out of the way. At the top of which was a small door that stood slightly ajar allowing a shaft of mid-morning sunlight to dazzle their eyes. Claudia led the way, followed by Luveday who groped a moment in her blindness. Hardin was behind her and grasped her to steady himself. Luveday turned to help him, though the staircase was not large enough for them to stand abreast, she turned until she rested under his arm to act as a human crutch. The minstrel paused in the doorway where there was a slight landing and a bay cut out of the cone-shaped roof. Before them was the battlements atop the round tower and a view that took Luveday's breath away. Fields of flowers, corps of trees dotted the gently rolling landscape before her. Below were the courtyard and the South wall, the same wall the chamber window looked upon. Luveday followed Claudia with her eyes as she moved toward the east side and the main courtyard with its gate lay below. The road was a long ribbon of hard packed dirt that cut through the land. Luveday thought it should look out of place in all the greenery, but instead, it looked more like a garden path moving easily amid the garden the creator had given them.

"Come and see for yourself, Luveday." Claudia gestured down the road where Luveday could see a mass of riders approaching. Their number was much greater than her escort, and yet Luveday swore she could make out the familiar outline of Benedict and the King's men. Calling over the breeze, Claudia beconed once again, forgetting their titles. "Come Luveday. Your release is at last at hand."

Hardin grabbed a fist of her skirts as Luveday started to move closer. Turning back, the minstrel gave her a warning look and shook his head. He was breathing hard but fought to take the last steps to join her. For a moment her concern was only for him. Days spent in the cramped hole with little food or drink submerged in putrid water for hours on end she marveled that he still had the strength to sit upright let alone stand beside her.

The two advanced on the Lady of Briar's Gate as she stood a golden silhouette amongst the beauty of her lands, hands clenched tightly at her waist. She looked hard, and beautiful and then she turned toward Luveday and the vision shattered.

Hatred, pure rage distorted a face too lovely into something horrible. Luveday took an involuntary step back, Hardin bumping into her back. Words, half hiss, half scream left Claudia's lips. "Everything is gone. Taken from me, everything because of you!" She lunged, but at the same moment, several things happened.

Something darted passed Hardin and Luveday though the edge of the tower was perilously close. The breeze which had been playing with their hair on and off went still for a heartbeat before a large gust swept around them hitting Claudia full in the face. In the lull between the wind's breath, Luveday and Hardin reached for Artair as he went by them afraid the boy would fall to his death. Claudia lunged and revealed a small container in her hand and squeezed it. The liquid made a fine mist on the air, but before it could travel the few feet between them, the wind blew hard, throwing the mist back into the lady's face.

She was screaming, screaming as Luveday had never heard as angry red marks appeared over Claudia's face. Holes were burned into her beautiful gown as the mist settled over her. Luveday watched in horror as realization dawned. Acid, that little container had held acid and Claudia had meant to burn her.

"Horrible, miserable child." She screamed looking at Artair and blaming him. "Devil take you, I should have buried you the night I birthed you." Hardin gasped, as Luveday drew the boy to her. He shook in her arms as they stared up at Claudia's ruined face. "It wasn't enough that you took him from me? Always worried about your future and not me, not what I had done, but what he would leave you." She laughed bitterly and smeared a hand across her face. Skin fell in patches leaving muscle and bone exposed. "All gone." She whispered to no one. Looking Luveday in the eye with every ounce of hate that could be condensed into such a small frame. "If you had never come it all would have turned out right. Years of planning would have made it right!"

Shouts from the courtyard heralded the opening of the gate. Suddenly, Claudia's expression was full of panic as if one emotion had erased the other. "What will they do to me?" She turned back to look at Luveday who saw something in her eyes.

"Claudia!" She called and took a step forward, but the lady was already moving. One moment she stood at the edge of the battlements, and the next she lay motionless on the stones below. Luveday gasped, her stomach and mind rolling. Artair turned to huddle in her embrace as Hardin leaned heavy on the roof and placed a hand on her back. Moving the boy to stay with the minstrel, Luveday carefully moved to the edge and looked down. The courtyard was full of people, screaming and crying. Men looked from the broken body up to the tower roof and back as if they couldn't quite believe their eyes. Benedict had dismounted and stood just a few feet from the fallen woman, but his eyes met Luveday's and held all the horror she knew mirrored in her own.

Questions, answers and more questions. Beatrix, Hardin, Artair, and Luveday sat in the great room under interrogation from Benedict and Lord Grayson Stern. It seemed that the two had met on the road, and while his wife had stayed behind with their daughter and new grandchild, Grayson had received Benedict's letter thanks to Sir Bernard's foresight. Rather than journeying home, the northern lord had come to Briar's Gate to offer aid. What they had found was far from the gentle scene of domestic tranquility they had expected. Grayson, looking at the Lady and the boy huddled in her lap, could not believe that little more than two hours ago he was convinced, as Benedict had been, that the rumors about Lady Claudia were nothing but vicious gossip and that something had to be done to help the lady.

"And this Leah woman, can swear to your words?" Grayson asked. The lady looked up to him a bit of heat showing in her bleak eyes. Stern didn't believe the lady could fake that sort of stunned grief. She might not have had cause to care for lady Claudia, but all could see that she was sorrowful for the woman's death.

"Sterling," Benedict growled, not for the first time. When Beatrix had tearfully told her end of the tale, it seemed all Benedict had heard was the traitor's name and not much more. "We should go after him, before he…"

Grayson clamped the younger lord on the shoulder. "He is already to sea by now Benedict. That is if he's a smart man. And the one thing Ladislaus is good at is …"

"Saving his own skin." Luveday finished for him.

Again, he looked to the young woman, and not for the first time thought that Iain should have scooped this one up and locked her in a tower and thrown that courtesan out on her spoiled little arse. A Northern Lord needed a woman who could hold her own and lead their people while her husband dealt with any threats by the sword. Christabel had never been such a woman, would never be. "Hum…" He thought that if he were unwed and a little younger, he would have liked the lady for himself. Then again, he had heard the mess De Lane was in and wondered what the future might hold for both of them.

"She's right," Benedict grumbled under his breath.

Grayson felt the disappointment of his prey slipping through his fingers, but the group was focused on the tragedy of Lady Claudia, and the story had come too late to give a timely chase.

"Where is momon?" A small boy asked again.

Luveday looked over the boy's head to Beatrix, who stood in the corner talking to servants in hushed tones. The serving woman gave her a tear-bright stare and shook her head. Leah had not been found, and Luveday feared that Sterling might have taken the woman with him, or something ill had befallen her. Sir Rolf appeared with a handful of parchment, and all eyes turned to him.

"What do you have there, Sir Rolf?" Grayson asked as the knight shifted through the papers trying to put them back in order.

"I searched the tower with the men," he looked to the minstrel. "It's as was said, a cell in the floor of the tower's lower room." None had doubted their words, but Grayson had hoped that there was a limit to the dark secrets this place held. "I found these in the… study, you called it, Lady Luveday?" She nodded as he handed over the documents.

A deep frown grooved Stern's face before he handed the parchments to

Benedict. "The hand is too curvy; I can't make sense of it." He admitted with no shame.

Benedict looked, but a similar expression soon settled over him. He looked up, but the other men in the room looked wary. A few shook their heads indicating that they would be of no help until Benedict's gaze landed on Luveday who looked up at him expectantly. His lips quirked at one corner, a slight smile that was all he could muster given their circumstances. "Would you be so kind, My Lady?" He didn't have to ask, Luveday eagerly accepted the stack of thick paper.

Luveday flipped through the parchment and looked to Sir Rolf as Artair moved to settle in beside her. "Are these as you found them? You didn't shuffle their order?"

The knight looked as if it took a moment to understand, but he caught her meaning. "No Lady. They are in the order I found them."

She nodded and scooted a little so that the firelight and the candlelight in the room better illuminated the parchment. Luveday read and reread the papers, looked to the boy then Benedict, then Beatrix who nodded at her unspoken question then back to Artair before scanning the papers again.

"Well, My Lady?" Stern asked impatiently.

"Leah is much more involved than I had thought, and you too Beatrix." The serving woman stepped forward, head bowed and hands twisting her shirt into nervous knots. "Leah had the old Priest, one Marcus Prim, write down and swear to the truth of these words."

"The priest passed on a few months ago; the church has yet to send a replacement. He and all his belongings were taken to Kern Abbey a few miles off." Benedict had discovered this in his investigation and had journeyed there to look at the registry the villagers said the man had kept fastidiously. "What does it say, Luveday?" Benedict asked growing equally impatient.

"The short version," Benedict had heard this saying from her before, but Grayson laughed at the term, "...is that Lady Claudia bore Lord Titus, a son."

"Who died before or shortly after his birth." Grayson nodded having heard the sad news years ago.

"Nay," Luveday countered. "It says that the boy lived, but that Lady Claudia was so distraught and angry at her husband that she thought to punish him. She took the dead child of a village woman and claimed it to be her own and gave the boy to the woman to nurse. The young girl was given coin to stay silent and care for the child." Luveday looked up at them. "Leah says the girl was her daughter, Rose. And that after giving birth to a stillborn babe Rose became sick, never truly recovered, and some months later died. The girl would have taken her secret to the grave, but she was burdened by it and told her mother the truth as she lay on her death bed."

Beatrix flushed out the tale. "Lady Claudia and Lord Titus had been fighting for some time. The child was all he talked about and the lady, she didn't think right. She told me a year after the babe was buried. We were standing over the grave, and she said something strange. Something like 'What is buried there isn't deserving of tears.' I asked her what she meant, but she wouldn't tell me, not till I told her that her soul was growing hard as stone. She laughed and said it had done that a year past, the night she stole away her husband's future." Beatrix gulped and brushed the tear that ran down her cheek. "I thought she meant she had killed the babe, but she explained that she had given it away, and taken Leah's girl's dead child as her own. A serving girl's bastard doesn't deserve tears, she said. A better fate it could not have wanted, laying among the house of Thorns."

"Thorns?" Benedict asked.

"Aye, My Lord." Beatrix glanced at him. "The house of Pillar, it's the name the family gave to the roses that climb the garden walls. Have you never heard us called the house of roses?" She asked.

"Aye," Grayson answered. "Many who live along the coast have called Briar's Gate the house of roses." He looked to Luveday and then Benedict. "So, she changed it; rather the house of thorns?"

Beatrix nodded. "I begged her to reveal what she had done, but we both knew that the Lord, rest his soul, would never have forgiven her."

Stern eyed her. "So, you kept quiet?"

"I loved My Lady." For once, Beatrix looked him square in the eye and stood at her full height.

Nothing more than curiosity marked the man's face as he asked, "Yet you helped Lady Luveday despite her wishes."

Beatrix looked to Luveday; apology clear in her eyes. "By helping her, I was helping My Lady."

Grayson nodded. "A loyal heart, despite the difficult circumstances, I think you did the best you could."

Benedict looked as if he might protest but caught a look from the lady that quieted him.

Luveday drew their attention having listened to Beatrix as she continued reading the documents. "Leah has other startling news to impart." All eyes turned to her; she looked to Beatrix who she feared would not take what she was about to say well. "There is another letter, only a year or so old, while the others were penned only a month or two after Leah learned the truth." She paused, and all eyes turned to the boy.

Benedict gasped, and Grayson grunted as they realized the heir had been present all along.

"Some months before the Battle in the north, not long after Lord Titus's death, Leah overheard Sterling make some comments to his men." Beatrix shook her head and moved away slowly as if she didn't want to hear any more. "I am sorry," Luveday whispered. "Leah is sure that what she heard implied that Sterling had Titus killed and made the death look like the act of bandits. The priest confirms in his note that the Lord's death was odd, that no body was ever found, only his bloody cloak and sword, his horse and belongings were found days later. Many had suspicions about the likelihood of the unprovoked attack." Luveday looked up. "Prim believed that Leah had heard true, which was why they added this to the parchments."

Grayson turned deep in thought. "She was a clever woman to write all this down."

"Prim says that Leah hoped that one day she would see the heir returned to his rightful place, and her part in this would be forgiven."

"It was my hope as well," Beatrix whispered. "The lady's anger towards the boy only grew as he did. The more he looked like Titus, the angrier, just the sight of him, made her. I fear something was not right in her mind or her heart." The tears the woman shed were real.

Luveday wondered how much the woman must have loved her friend and lady to show such loyalty despite all else. She could not say she had done right, but Beatrix was only a servant, and as the other woman had fervently whispered to her, she had only wanted to protect her lady; sometimes even from herself.

"That is the gist of the writing," Luveday said. "I think the priest must have illuminated manuscripts in his youth for the penmanship is so flourished it is almost hard to read." Handing over the six pieced of parchment; she gave Benedict a look. "Leah must have thought to give them to us, before..." she didn't finish but looked to Artair.

Grayson moved to crouch before the bench that Luveday and the boy shared. Artair watched him with sharp eyes. He was not sure how much the boy understood, but the older man was certain alot was about to change for the boy. "You did well young man." Grayson's large bulk was almost level with the boy's gaze. "I would like to clasp the hand of the young man, who bravely helped My Lady."

The boy straightened in his seat and scooted forward a little to grasp Lord Stern's arm. In one quick movement, the man swept aside the cloth covering the boy's dirty left arm. Once again, Luveday looked down with the thought that she would scrub him from head to toe at the first opportunity, but she saw a mark on the boy's forearm that was too dark to be dirt. Angling her head, she met Grayson's gaze as he let go of the boy with an affectionate pat on the head. Luveday marveled for a moment. What were the chances that the birthmark Leah and the priest had alluded to in the letter would be shaped like a rose with leaves?

It was easy to catch the nod Grayson gave his friend before Luveday looked to the grinning boy. "You were very brave, Artair." The light left the boy's eyes as he whispered for his mother. "You will have to be brave a while longer." She said, and he nodded taking on an expression she thought too stern and knowing for a boy of his years.

Claudia was buried in a quiet ceremony only two days later. Her body was taken from the courtyard to a chamber off the kitchen where she had been cleaned and dressed and prepared as was befitting of a lady. Villagers and servants lined the small chapel as the priest from Kern Abbey made an impromptu service having arrived unexpectedly that morning baring documents for Lord St. James. Luveday thought the words were simple and heartfelt though she couldn't judge from the atmosphere surrounding them. She thought that many were grateful that their Lady was receiving her due weather she was deserving or not. While many had seen the scene before their lady had fallen to her death of her own accord, many pondered whether it was suicide or an accident. While many talked of the former in hushed words, several strong voices suggested it was an accident caused by strong winds atop the roof and that no one could have saved the lady. Luveday took a different approach and was satisfied with their silence on the matter. She honestly believed that Claudia had not been in her right mind and that her actions were not really of her own doing. Thus, this service was justified in the eyes of the church and people not for the woman she was, but for the woman she had once been. Several things had come to light in the last few days, and Luveday pondered them in the back of her mind, keeping her thoughts to herself.

Artair stood by her side, dressed in simple but fine clothes and as clean as a well-washed boy could be. He fidgeted, and Luveday looked down to whisper, "Almost done." He quieted and took her hand in a gesture that had become all too familiar in the last days.

"May all blessings go with you." The priest intoned the last line of what Luveday had begun to think of as their version of "Amen."

They walked back to the Hall in silence as Luveday looked around. For some reason, she had thought that Leah, if she were able, would appear amongst the gathered people, but her now familiar face was not there. After reading the letters to Grayson and Benedict in full, Luveday thought she understood the woman a bit more and guessed that part of the kindness she had shown the lost lady, had been in part for the daughter Leah had lost years ago.

As word spread of Artair's parentage, the boy became a curiosity to many and stuck beside Luveday like a lost puppy. How she wished she could promise him that Leah would return, but deep down Luveday wondered if the woman hadn't disappeared to make this transition easier on the boy in some ways.

"I think it best we journey to court and tell the King ourselves," Luveday suggested as they sat before the fire in the great hall. A repast was served in the garden, per Luveday's wishes. It seemed that a reception was not something they practiced, but the food was appreciated and may gathered to ease their grief which was all the lady had hoped for.

"I don't..." Benedict started.

"She is right, St. James." Grayson used his surname to gently remind of his station. "The missive we sent will not satisfy him. It would be best he hears it from the Lady. After all, she is the one he sent." Another reminder that his friend didn't take so well.

"Artair will come with us." The lady stated. It was not a request.

"Momon?" He asked suddenly appearing at Luveday's shoulder.

Luveday looked at him. "No news of her yet, Artair, but the men can search for her while we are gone."

"And perhaps she will be back when you return." A man offered, and Luveday glared at him while she tried to remember the knight's name. Failing that, she glared harder, and he had the decency to look chagrined. She had told them they would not give the boy false hope and pretty words to distract him from his loss. It would only be worse if Leah were not found or was not found alive. As days passed, she could not help the doubts and fears and knew that what little she did for the boy were only momentary distractions.

"Really?" He looked almost eager at the thought.

Luveday didn't have the heart to answer and so the deep "Perhaps" came from Lord Stern. Luveday gave a slight nod to the man.

A moment of silence fell over them as Artair returned to play with a cat near the hearth. "Can you be prepared to leave on the morrow?" Stern asked. "I can leave a few men, and Benedict as well," the latter nodded in agreement. "Word has gone out, and Sir Henry Navarro should arrive this afternoon." The man would be devastated by his lady's death and more so by the tragic details they would soon impart.

Luveday tore her gaze away from the boy. "Aye, we'll be ready."

Amelia M. Brown

Chapter 19

"My patience has dreadful chilblains from standing so long on a monument."
~ Elizabeth Barrett Browning, Letter to Mary Russell Mitford, 1836-1854

King Edward, the Third of Anora, watched her a moment, unblinking atop his throne. Queen Augusta sat beside him, stiff with a hand pressed to her middle and looked between Luveday and the boy at her side several times. Luveday had finished her tale, and the reactions of all present were similar to that of the royals before her.

Luveday missed the informality of the royal chambers and tried not to stare at the nobles gathered around her. The court had cleared except for two dozen or so, the majority of their numbers made up of the Lords most loyal to the King. A few of their wives were included in the group, but there were not enough women to soften the hard line of warriors.

"And you say, this is Lord Titus's heir?" He asked a moment later. "Come here, boy." Artair went without much hesitation and proudly displayed the birthmark that was the trademark of the House of Pillar of Briar's Gate. The King looked at the boy who looked uneasy but held his stare without fear. He had seen the proof for himself after hearing their tale and receiving letters from Lord Stern who had returned home, the priest who had spoken rights over the lady and a message from Beatrix, whose words Luveday had neatly copied verbatim as Stern had insisted. "You may go back to the lady." He said after a thoughtful moment.

Artair returned to her side with a small smile. They had talked about what might happen before the King and Luveday had schooled the boy in etiquette as best she could over the ten days it took to return to court.

The royal couple exchanged a look that communicated volumes, but Luveday couldn't decipher its meaning. Augusta smiled kindly down to the pair before them. "You may retire to your room while we think over this issue." The Queen looked to a servant who stepped out to show their guests the way. "And once you are rested, Lady, I am sure that the princes are eager to see you again."

Luveday bowed and left Benedict with a look as he stood off to one side. There was a lot of floor to traverse behind their guide, but Luveday was not sure she had the energy for it. They had barely had time to settle their mounts before they were summoned before the court to account for their time on the coast. Now all she wanted to do was rest.

Luveday heard the knocking at her door, but her groggy mind couldn't remember where she was or why the noise was important, so the harried servant burst in before she could pull her wits together and get off the bed. The small frame tucked up against her atop the bedclothes stirred a little, then opened his eyes. Artair looked so small for his six years that it sometimes broke her heart.

Exasperated, the servant looked at the two of them, humped and said in a crisp, clear voice, "Their royal majesties wish to speak with you in their private chambers." Luveday scooped up the sleepy boy and carried him as they made their way from one side of the castle to the other where the royal chambers were located separately from the wing which housed their guests. Luveday was hoping that they would return to the informality and comfortable room she had first met the Royals. She was not let down.

Luveday took the familiar chair at the end of the table, Artair sat in her lap, his head nestled against her breast, sleeping soundly once again.

The royal couple shared an unreadable look, and Luveday secretly wished that she had a husband that she might speak to in such a fashion where words were unnecessary. Queen Augusta smiled that maternal smile at Luveday and nodded to the boy. "He need not stay, Lady Luveday."

Luveday was loathed to let go of him. "He will sleep through our talk."

The King nodded and let the boy remain.

"It is no surprise to you that your letter and the turn of events this last fortnight was not what we had expected." The Queen started, but the King almost laughed at her understatement.

"Indeed." He said sarcastically and looked to Luveday with one arched brow.

Luveday didn't know where to begin, so she said what was on her mind, not entirely sure how wise that might be. "I assure you I did not imagine I would be sitting here with the lost heir in my lap and a slew of trouble behind me. Sterling had not crossed my mind in several months, and I had hoped never to see that man again."

The King glowered and shifted in his chair at the mention of his enemy. "We too had hoped the next time his name was spoken in our presence that it would be to announce his death, preferably by the Wolf's hands, but alas." The King wrapped sharply on the table only once as a sign of his anger.

Augusta sighed and covered his fist in a loving gesture. "Alas, it is not so." She looked to Luveday. "I believe there are some things that Lord Stern has left out of his letter." Luveday looked confused by this, having known that the Lord has added some private message to the parchment that he had sent to court, but she had not been curious about its content until that moment.

"Such as, Your Majesty?" She asked in confusion.

The King answered. "Stern thinks you have an eye for detail and may have learned something of the woman's nature or illness before you left the coast."

Luveday looked startled. She had been thinking about many things since that horrible day on the tower roof. Her bruises had healed, but her heart still felt raw. She had kept a lot of her observations to herself, but on more than one occasion she had caught Stern looking at her thoughtfully. Perhaps he had seen more than she thought. "While Lord Stern and Lord St. James put many of the puzzle pieces together, I found some other interesting bit of news that may or may not explain Lady Claudia's illness." They only looked at her expectantly. Luveday swallowed, licked her lips nervously and continued. "The work to make perfume could not be stopped for long, and Beatrix along with another head woman, took up work in the absence of Lady Claudia and Mistress Leah."

"The woman is still missing?" The Queen asked.

"Yes." Luveday looked at the sleeping boy in her arms and shifted him slightly without waking him. "While I oversaw a bit of the work, I also found that the lady had been doing some work of her own." The couple looked confused, and a bit intrigued by this news but didn't interrupt. "In one of the sheds, which I was not allowed into before, I found Claudia's private workroom. It was set up much like a healer's workroom, with exotic plants and equipment to mix and brew any number of..."

"Potions... brews..." the couple finished for her.

Luveday nodded. "I spent several hours in the room trying to see if I could discern Claudia's notes and find what she was studying." The look of interest grew keener. "While I wasn't able to find out what her purpose was, I was able to look at some... trials she had done in the past and found some very troubling things. Some of the plants and spices she used were brought from overseas. Several of which were poisonous. Many could be the cause of her illness, having dangerous effects on the mind and temperament."

The King asked a logical question, one she knew had been coming but was not entirely sure she wished to answer. "Do you believe the lady was aware of these effects?" Both royals had a hard look in their eyes.

"I am sure that she did, as she made notes of where the plants originated from and what she could learn about them. It seemed that she paid a large sum of coin to have them brought to her. Claudia was changing doses, adding small amounts to perfume and lotions." Luveday took a breath. "While I am sure that the plants are deadly, from what I could see, she was trying to distill them in such small amounts that they would not be harmful to anyone who used them. It is true that while poisonous, many of the plants have healing qualities in small doses."

"You believe she didn't intend to brew a poison for her lover to use?" The Queen asked cautiously.

Luveday had thought the same upon learning about the workroom and the experiments that Claudia had been running for years, but the fastidious nature of the woman had pointed to a scientific mind, not a murderess. Though that had clearly changed, Luveday would have called Lady Claudia a chemist if she were born in her modern world, but she didn't know how to explain that to the two before her. "Lady Claudia left a journal, her notes though not complete, suggest she was looking for an edge. Something new that would make the perfumes of Briar's Gate the envy of the world, not just the talk of court. Somewhere along the way, something changed, but I don't believe she ever thought of brewing poisons for Sterling or using her skills to harm others."

"Not even this burning potion she made?" The King scoffed.

"She did write about that. It was an accident. She poured together some things that should not have been mixed and found that the brew made her metal rods brittle and burned to the touch. She was later able to recreate the incident but thought of using the liquid to etch metal or glass, and to dissolve minerals to add to her brews."

"And what do you believe happened to the lady's mind?" The Queen asked.

Luveday looked at them both. "She was not as careful as she should have been. The workroom was dark and hot, and I think she handled the more dangerous plants improperly." A look passed between the couple again, and they nodded for her to continue. "Claudia began her trials a few months before she found out she was pregnant. Many of the things she procured are dangerous when ingested, but they are also harmful if they come into contact with the skin. She limited her exposure to the poisonous plants, but I believe that over time the effects built up in her system," she saw their confusion and tried to clarify. "It's like filling a pale, a drop at a time. A drop doesn't seem like a lot, a drop of water is so small it might seem like it would make no difference, but if you were to add a drop each day, or each hour, how soon could you fill a pale." Light dawned in their expressions.

"And she worked for years..." The Queen said to no one in particular.

"Yes, years going through the trial and error of trying to improve her work. There is a clear change in her notes; her thoughts become harder to follow. This change happened about six months before Lord Titus was killed." Luveday noted. "I don't doubt that the potions, even the fumes from brewing the plants could have caused a serious change in how her mind worked. The lady became fearful that people were trying to steal her secrets, that her husband no longer loved her and was seeking the arms of other women. Her ramblings go on. I think the sudden changes in temperament and signs of anger were only one of the effects of handling these herbs."

The King grew thoughtful for a moment, but the Queen had another question. "What did you do with the workroom?"

Luveday sighed. "I tried to touch as little as possible, washed my hand thoroughly after leaving each time. I gave instructions to Beatrix and the women that the room was to remain locked and no one was to touch or take anything from it. I made it clear that I thought something in that room had harmed their lady. They looked suitably fearful. Hopefully, they will heed my warning and the room will be as I left it when I return." Luveday looked to them. "I have no wish to take up after Claudia; I have no doubt my fate would be similar. I had thought of sending a missive to Lander's Keep and Lady Emmalyn to talk to the local healer there by the name of Cassandra, or even send a letter to Father Quinn, who is knowledgeable in all sorts of plants and ask how best to go about destroying the herbs. I am afraid that if I bury or burn them somehow, they might poison the soil or some animals that come across the remains."

The King looked pleased by this answer. "So, no wish to use the herbs, Lady?"

"Nay, your majesty. I am not skilled enough or foolish enough to risk it."
Luveday thought a moment. "I have to admit that what she hoped to do, had it
worked, would have more than the desired effects, but I think that our methods
and means are not knowledgeable enough to accomplish what she wanted
without causing serious harm."

The Queen looked at her thoughtfully, while there was a narrowing of the
King's eyes as he asked, "You admired her, Lady Luveday?"

Luveday thought about it for a moment. "I think the woman Lady Claudia
was years ago and the woman I met were not the same person. The first, I think,
I could have befriended while the lady I met could never have been."

The Queen nodded, and the King only looked at his wife but seemed
satisfied by the answer.

A few moments of silence passed before the King moved on. "Now, what
to do with Briar's Gate?"

Luveday looked up while the Queen and King shared a conspiratorial look.
A frisson of uneasy went down the Lady's spine as she watched the flash of
amusement pass between them. "What indeed, my dear husband?"

They both looked to Luveday who instinctively pressed herself tight
against her chair, squaring her shoulders and raising her chin.

"The boy is not old enough to take over his duties, and given the mental
state of his mother," Luveday was about to protest that last statement, "We think
it best to install someone of our choosing to oversee the house. The loss of such
a thriving venture would be a detriment to the kingdom, don't you think my
dear."

"Yes, I do." The Queen looked at her steadily while answering the
question.

"Briar's Gate needs a new lady and new blood." The King continued, and
Luveday panicked.

"Your Majesties, if I may." She interrupted.

They looked a little taken aback by the emotion in her tone but they
nodded for her to continue.

Taking a deep breath, Luveday tried to counter what she feared was
coming as politely as she could. "I am honored that you would think to offer me
such a great gift, but I believe that Artair will grow to be a man worthy of his
Father's name if he has a strong and steady hand to guide him. That being said, I
would be happy to be his guardian, to preside over his household until he comes
of age to marry or take over those duties for himself. I can't take his inheritance
away from him. So much has been stolen from him already… I would watch
over him, but I can't take Briar's Gate from him."

The Queen gasped and looked to her husband who looked thoughtful rather
than wroth. After a moment he smiled again. "You never cease to amaze, Lady
Luveday. You do know what we were prepared to offer you?"

Luveday nodded. "The lands and all the wealth they would provide. While
I think I could continue the work there, probably with some ease, my heart
would never settle knowing I had supplanted the rightful heir."

Laughing, the Queen shook her head. "I believe any other woman in your position would have said thank you and left without looking back, Lady."

"You are probably right your majesty, but as you have found, I am not like other ladies." Her nod was almost solemn.

"If not this, then what are we to give you for everything that you have done for us?" He asked earnestly.

The Queen looked at her knowingly. "Husband, perhaps we should think on this more. The lady is too modest for her own good." Luveday looked startled. "We have every intention of fulfilling our debt to you, Lady, but I see it will take more cunning for us to find something worthy of you." The Queen gave her husband another enigmatic look, and both rose. "You may retire to your room before the evening meal and join us in an hour or so. If the boy is well, I am sure my sons wouldn't mind sharing a meal with him. Your short visit to them this afternoon was all they could speak of." Once again that maternal smile graced her face. "Do try to have some fun at the meal Luveday." The couple looked at her as she rose and bowed gracefully despite the boy in her arms and fled.

It was during dinner that Luveday realized the Queen had addressed her without a title and she was somewhat heartened by the fact. Augusta seemed to like her, but she found the Queen quite likable as well, though she had no hope of them becoming friends. Friendship with a Queen was something she didn't even dream of aspiring too. The thought was almost laughable but seated next to Benedict and the Duke of Orland, who had asked her to call him John, Luveday felt a surreal sense, almost like an out of body experience. She looked down to the King at one end and the Queen at the other and chatted with nobility on all sides at what was a rather intimate dinner party. Her gown was plain, but by no means less than any other lady present, and Luveday smiled to herself with a slight twist on her lips.

"What is the matter?" Benedict leaned closer as he took a sip of wine.

Luveday almost laughed. "Nothing. Just not sure if I am here or still asleep."

He seemed to get her drift and smirked. "This is no dream, My Lady. You are officially a court favorite." Now Luveday really had to fight to keep from laughing. She was far from a court favorite as many of the players were putout that she had no time or interest in political maneuvering. Court favorite equated to the flavor of the week in her mind, then again, when she thought of their royal highnesses, she didn't get the feeling that their favor was bestowed on anyone undeserving. They were a shrewd and steady force that governed the kingdom with a fair but strong hand. She imagined that they gave a man his due, whether it was praise or punishment.

A voice spoke from down the table drawing their attention. "Not joining the Wolf on his hunt, Lord St. James?" A man asked, and Luveday remembered him from her time in the enemy camp, in fact, most of the men captured by Sterling were present. Lord Henry Kilgrave waited for an answer from the man who stiffened beside her.

Luveday tried not to react; she knew that news of De Lane would be forthcoming, after all, he was the King's champion.

"Nay, Kilgrave, not this time." Benedict hid his discomfort fairly well.

"Keeping the lady company, instead?" Another unfamiliar man asked. Luveday wondered if any were privy to the events surrounding De Lane's wedding and their disappearance.

"Damned remarkable, the way he can track his pray to ground. One might think he had a bit of wolf in him in truth." Orland's laughter had many around the table joining in. Luveday was happy that the conversation was back to discussing the hunt for Sterling.

"How long do you think it will take him this time?"

"A reliable sighting, and a fresh trail..." Kilgrave calculated. "A fortnight, two on the outside." Luveday wondered if they were placing bets.

"So soon?" a lady asked around a bite.

"I have seen him on the hunt, Lady Olive, and he is every bit as keen as the rumors say."

Luveday commented to herself, "that would make them facts, not rumors." She was unaware that many heard, but they laughed and agreed. The Queen was the most vocal and gave her a strange piercing look. "Indeed, Lady Luveday, they are not rumors, but truths." She looked across the length of the table and caught her husband's eye. "Nothing less should be expected of our champion, am I not right, my King?"

"As always, my Queen." He raised a glass. "To the Wolf and his hunt. May is prey be taken swiftly to ground!"

Calls came from around the table. "Aye, to the Wolf." "To De Lane." Luveday raised her glass and felt more than one pair of eyes watching her as she echoed the cheer and sent up a silent prayer.

"Are we sure this can be believed?" Luveday looked at the missive that Beatrix had handed her, though the writing was little more than chicken scratching, she could make out the meaning of the letter.

"Aye, the tinker said he had it from the priest himself." Beatrix nodded reassuringly.

"See the man here and prepare him a meal if there are any leftovers from the midday repast."

Beatrix smiled at her as she left out the workroom door. "Aye, My Lady."

Luveday looked at the scrap of parchment in the light before her gaze sought out Artair where he trailed behind Sir Marcus Reeve like a puppy.

Luveday still remembered the morning over a month ago when she and Artair were summoned to the throne room where Sir Marcus Reeve soon joined them. The look of anguish that passed his face broke many a heart. The fact that it was he who was charged with presenting her as Artair's guardian, and the new, if the temporary lady of Briar's Gate was a hard fact for him to swallow, but the man had proven to be beyond reproach. Though there was a brokenness about the man that she suspected was more than just the loss of his lady. Luveday thought it might have been love, love and betrayal. The truth about

Artair seemed to have doubled the man's pain. Now she looked at the letter in her hand, from the same priest who had helped Benedict with his search. News had come and from a very surprising person.

The tinker was rushed in, and Luveday recognized him immediately. "Tinker Thom, How wonderful! Good morning." She greeted, happy to see him and wondered briefly, if she couldn't send a letter to Emmalyn.

The man removed his hat nervously but smiled at her. "And to you Lady, it's been a good while since Tinker Thom had the pleasure of setting eyes on you." He looked to the missive he had hidden in his cart for many a night. He had not been tempted to read its contents, not that he knew many words by heart. He was good at trading, and numbers, letters were not easy for him. All he had known was that the priest had been adamant that he delivered the missive as soon as possible, having heard Thom say he knew the lady for whom it was intended.

Gesturing toward a chair in the eating nook, Luveday had commandeered for her study, Luveday looked at Beatrix and nodded in reassurance.

"It isn't bad news, is it Lady Luveday?" He nodded to the parchment before her and looked at the items scattered over the small round table. "I mean, it's none of my business, but I always hate to be the bearer of ill tidings."

Luveday nodded. "Aye, don't shoot the messenger and all that," Luveday said absently to herself, but the tinker nodded solemnly. Luveday shook herself out of her thoughts to focus on the man. He looked as hale as ever, and not too wary from the journey. "It is not bad news Tinker, just very unexpected. I don't know what to make of it."

Thom seemed to perk up. "Tinkers are a crafty lot, Lady; perhaps I can help." He looked very eager.

"Well," Luveday sighed. "From what I can make out, there is a priest traveling from overseas; he has found a man who seems to hail from Briar's Gate."

"Seems to?" The tinker asked. "Doesn't he know?"

"The man had been wounded some years ago and lost his memory of anything before that time."

The tinker nodded. "I've heard tales of men getting hit in the head and forgetting their life before that moment, even their name."

"Yes," Luveday looked at the letter and the scribble of a drawing on the bottom left-hand corner. "It appears that the man has some knightly skills and has been protecting a village there. What things he had on him tell of a knight of Anora and a man of rank. But there is one thing the priest points to that ties him to Briar's Gate specifically."

"What is that My Lady?" Tinker asked expectantly.

Luveday turned the parchment to show the man the priest's design. "It seems he bears a peculiar birthmark. One very familiar to me." Luveday moved to show the rose to him, only to hear Beatrix gasp. The clatter of the tray as it hit the stone floor peeled like a bell and Luveday briefly wondered if it was a death knell, and for whom it tolled.

The hall was filled with servants, knights, and workers. Luveday looked to Sir Navarro, the household knight, and Sir Reeve to calm the clamoring masses. Their raised voices only added to the noise, until her head began to ache.

"NOW SEE HERE!" Reeve shouted hand on his sword hilt, but no one was afraid of his idle threat, they knew the man too well.

Luveday looked around, spotted a metal soup spoon, and moved to the empty pitchers. The peel of the metal on metal was satisfying and brought back memories of another time.

"Now," Luveday spoke in a loud and clear voice that carried over the hushed gathering. "This is what we know thus far." People settled onto wooden benches and looked up at her, a little awed. "A brother of Father Heim who was sent to us recently," the crowd remembered the priest who had buried their lady, "has sent word of a man from a village in Canthus who bears the mark of the rose. He is of a similar age and physic as Lord Pillar." There was a murmur rising, but she held up a hand. "This man has no memory of his life before six years ago, and yes, we are aware that Lord Pillar was killed during that time, though no body was ever found. Those who know this man, say he came from overseas, and he speaks with an Anorian accent." She looked at Navarro who nodded. "There is a strong possibility that he is Lord Titus Pillar."

"But how can that be?" A man called out.

Navarro answered in a deep, yet exasperated voice. "We don't know. Perhaps he was picked up by smugglers off the coast, perhaps the men that were said to have killed him meant to ransom him instead, but wounded he got away."

"But didn't return?" A man-at-arms asked, dumbfounded.

Luveday spoke. "The wound to his head that took his memories would have been severe, and he could have forgotten everything, even his name."

"You think it is he, Lady Luveday?" There was some unrest, and Luveday wondered if they wished her to stay or go. They were just getting used to her, and no longer balking at her orders.

"We will wait and see." Luveday countered. "The priest and this man are journeying here. If it is Lord Pillar, then we hope that being at Briar's Gate again will help his memory to return. If it is not Lord Pillar, but perhaps some kin, then we will see what the King says about his claim to the land. Artair is the heir, sanctioned by the King, and that will stand, but what this man's arrival will mean to us, I don't know."

"Sir Navarro and Mistress Beatrix will know if he is an imposter." A woman pointed out.

Luveday nodded.

Sir Navarro stepped forward on her other side. "Any number of us will know if he is our Lord with just a glance," many nodded at the knight's words. "Have patience."

They looked to Luveday. "It is all we can do, have patience and pray for resolution for whatever is to come." They nodded and looked grim as they talked among themselves. Luveday moved to the head table to take her seat and motioned for the meal to begin.

The return of the solemn atmosphere they had only just abandoned seemed a blow to Luveday. Was she never to find a place for herself? She looked to Artair and smiled at the tentative look he gave her.

"Do you think it is my father, Luveday?" He asked as she cut off a piece of meat and shredded it for him.

A troubled frown crossed the boy's brow, and she longed to smooth it away. "I think it may be possible that he is."

"Is he a bad man, like Lady Claudia? Do you think he will try to hurt me?"

Luveday couldn't help herself and hugged the child with her left arm. "I don't know the answers to those questions, Artair, but I do know I will do my best to protect you." He looked at her and nodded. "You believe me?"

She was surprised by the seriousness in him sometimes, especially when he replied, "Yes, I do," and started to eat his meal. Luveday looked up to find Sir Reeve who looked at her and gave a sharp nod as if to say; he would too. Luveday turned back to look at Sir Navarro on his other side and found the man gave a similar gesture. Not by word but by deed, a sacred oath, she thought solemnly.

Days passed much like any other; Spring turned toward Summer. Luveday filled each day with work, building out a routine for herself and her household and waiting with a growing seed of doubt. She feared the day when the awaited man would arrive. With one breath she prayed it was Pillar, and with the next, she asked to hold on to what she had. With each day she came to love Artair more, and the boy seemed to thrive under her care.

"Higher, young lord." Navarro cautioned as the boy paced off against a lad twice his size. "Arms up, and steady." Luveday wondered how the stick like limbs of her charge could hold aloft the mock sword and shield he was learning to wield. While the knight had assured her that such training began around such an age, the two had both wondered how such a scrawny and ill-nourished boy would fair. Artair had surprised both with his gameness and fortitude. While he spent time, each day, being beaten by the older lads, Luveday also began the work of teaching him to be lord one day. The boy was young, smart, and eager, so she took advantage of it for however long it would last. By the time he was of age, Luveday planned for him to be both a cunning and powerful lord.

"Eyes forward, boys." Both lads had turned to acknowledge the lady's passing and missed a swift attack from the knight acting as the referee for their training. "Keep alert." He admonished while nodding a greeting to Lady Luveday.

Luveday was heading for the perfume stores when a call rang out of riders approaching. Men around the courtyard rush to defend and protect the house. Briar's Gate had changed a good deal since her arrival, as Luveday was ushered back inside the house, Artair running at her side. Luveday couldn't help but wonder if her expression mirrored the look of anxiety on the boy's face.

As she glanced out of a glass window, her hopes and fears battled within her. The black robes and colorful cloaks attest to the fact that the priest and his would-be lord had finally arrived.

Chapter 20

"I love you not only for what you are, but for what I am when I am with you..."
~ Elizabeth Barrett Browning

Men crowded before the hearth as people moved restlessly in and out of the great room. Luveday sat, not in the great wooden chairs, but with Artair at her side on the cushioned loveseat. They both watched and waited, as the newcomers across from them stared back. Instead of taking the lord's seat by the fire, the priest, one Father Julian, and the man who resembled Titus Pillar enough to startle even stoic Sir Navarro had sat opposite the Lady and her charge. The silence that had fallen after Luveday's brief greeting was hard to break.

Several deep breaths were taken, but no words had come forth from either side. Where to begin, was the main question that kept circling through her mind. Luveday took another breath after Beatrix had left the wine before the men and stepped away. St. James had returned, meeting the group on the road, and escorting them to Briar's Gate and Luveday was not sure she had ever been happier to see Benedict in her life. He now stood just behind her resting on the back of the bench, and his solid presence reassured, though it didn't alleviate the stress of the moment.

"They tell me you are not my wife." The returned lord said as if needing confirmation.

Luveday glimpsed the arm that bore the rose birthmark, as he took a drink from the ale with white knuckles. It was strange for her to realize that he was as nervous as she.

"My Lord," Navarro began solemnly, but he was cut off.

"So, you are sure of my identity?" Titus asked with an intent expression. The knight nodded and looked to the rest of the group.

Luveday watched as Beatrix dabbed moisture from her eyes, but the feel of Artiar's tightening hold on her right arm brought her attention back to the boy. She was surprised to hear Benedict speak next.

"I have no doubts." Luveday looked to him quickly. "I have to say we were not good friends, but I know enough of you to be utterly convinced, you are Titus Pillar."

"You knew enough of me in my previous life?" Titus looked thoughtful. "But not well?" St. James nodded again.

Reeves chimed in, "I am convinced as well."

"And you, Lady Luveday?" Pillar asked.

Luveday had known that question would be coming soon. "I am sorry to say that we have never met before this moment. Thus I cannot say aye, but if they are convinced with only setting eyes on you, I must agree. You are Lord Titus Pillar of Briar's Gate."

"You say you are not my wife, but this is my son?" He asked, looking at the boy who was now doing his best to wiggle behind Luveday and out of sight.

She couldn't bring herself to reprimand the boy but leaned forward a bit to make it more comfortable for both of them. "That is right My Lord. This is Artair."

"And yet many know that Titus Pillar had no heir." The man spoke of himself in a third person.

Luveday and several others straightened at his words, but Luveday realized they were not meant as an attack, merely a statement of fact. "It seems that both lord and heir have returned from the grave," Luveday replied. Pillar gave her a quizzical look, Luveday could swear she saw the wheels turning behind his gaze.

"A coincidence?" He asked, and Luveday felt that her answer held more weight than it should.

"Justice, long overdue." He nodded at her words and seemed to settle.

The lady could not know how much his stomach turned at this meeting. She sat, lovely as her name implied, and held court in this grand house while his life hung in the balance. They called him by another man's name, one that sat a little too comfortably on his shoulders like an old cloak, but he still thought of himself as Anon, the man without a home, a family, or a name. They called him Anon as a short form of Anorian, for his accent gave him away, though his command of foreign languages, languages he couldn't remember learning, was superb.

How long had he searched trying to find more than a hint of his past? He had never come close to revealing the truth, knowing only that a ship of unsavory characters had dumped his bleeding corpse on the docks of a city in Canthus and never looked back. The fact that the mark on his arm had held all the answers to his secrets was not surprising to him, on the other hand, the fact that glimpses of this place were more than familiar, was astonishing.

Everything about him cautioned him to be patient, lest he be disappointed, but to be so readily recognized and accepted was beyond belief. It seemed too good to be true after years of living by the sword.

Sir Reeve and Sir Navarro ushered him out of the great hall, as they proposed to walk him about the lands, his lands, his hall, his home.

"Long overdue." She had said.

And it rang in his head, even as these men he could not remember, his men, began to pump him for answers he didn't have. "Justice, long overdue."

Father Julian looked on her with wonder, a small smile peeking at the corner of his mouth. He was middle-aged, and more than a little handsome despite the severity of his robes. There was something kind and very focused in his gray eyes, while his sable hair was rich, thick and showed not a hint of his age. "That went well. Indeed, better than expected, My Lady."

"Did you think you might be disappointed, that we would turn him out?" Luveday asked, turning from watching the men exit the hall.

Benedict moved to take a seat, surprising everyone and taking the spot just vacated beside the priest. He angled his body to see the man beside him and Luveday across the low table between them. The boy, Artair, still hid behind the lady, making the Lord smile at them both. "I must admit, meeting him on the road, I thought I was seeing a ghost." Benedict confided.

Luveday nodded, as the priest looked them over.

"What plans do you have, Lady Luveday?" Father Julian startled them all by getting down to business.

"Truthfully, it is hard to say." She hedged, as she didn't have any set course of action. So much had depended on this first meeting. The way forward was complicated, and she needed to act with caution.

Benedict cut in, no doubt trying to firm up her position in the household. "The King has given the lady control of Briar's Gate." He floundered, realizing for the first time everything that had changed. "At least until Titus's title is restored. He was declared dead three years after he went missing." Looking at Luveday, he suddenly realized they had not had *that* talk yet. They had discussed much since learning Lord Pillar might still live, but not what would happen to her if he regained his lands and titles. Benedict could admit to himself that he had not taken the news of Pillar's return seriously and had only speculated as the rest had done. As their eyes locked, he knew that she had been thinking over the matter a great deal. How he wished he knew what went on in her head. How much had she worried about the future? Once again, the road before her was shifting. Would it ever be this way for her?

Luveday sat forward, Artair standing behind her and wrapping his thin arms around her neck. She padded the arms gently, and Benedict felt the gesture like a blow. Luveday, with a child of her own, was a sight he almost longed for. While Benedict could admit that he loved the lady, he was not *in love* with her. He would save her any hardship, but he could never give her the love she deserved. He thought only Iain could do that, and the daft man had made a royal mess of it. He still hesitated to bring up his blood brother's name, knowing that the memories still hurt the woman, but there was much she needed to know, much had changed, yet he still waited.

"I was given guardianship of Artair and these lands until he is old enough to care for them himself. I suppose there is no reason we cannot teach father and son together."

"Teach?" The priest asked surprise clear on his face.

Benedict laughed. "She is teaching him to read and write and manage sums." Artair nodded and smiled as if confirming their talk but didn't interrupt.

"Languages and knightly skills are taught by others," Luveday supplied, "but what I was referring to is the working of the land and the making of perfume."

"And why would Lord Titus need to know such things?" The holy man was not condescending, merely curious.

Benedict only smiled as the man looked at him. Luveday continued, "The land produces the usual crops to supply the house and people, but the main product is the production of lotions and perfumes. They fill the coffers more than any other trade." The priest looked stumped. "The goods are highly sought after, even in court, and some are taken overseas." This news seemed to impress him. "It was Lady Claudia that oversaw everything to do with the perfumes, and it will have to be taught to Lord Titus and Artair, so that they will be able to do the same." Luveday looked to Benedict. "If they wish to pass that knowledge over to their wives or daughters, then they will be fully able to do so."

Father Julian nodded in understanding. "So, you are saying; it is not entirely a woman's domain."

"Exactly," Luveday exclaimed. "To be ignorant about the workings of such an enterprise would be foolish." She looked to Artair as he finally stepped out from behind her and settled down. "A lord would not be ignorant of the business of wool, or cattle. With the money and complexity of the process, it is unwise to leave it to others, just because it is thought to be a woman's domain."

Beatrix returned from wherever she had disappeared to, and whispered something in Luveday's ear, smiling apologetically at the priest. Luveday nodded. "Artair, would you go with Beatrix. Gemma needs your help again." The boy eagerly excused himself and ran off, Beatrix chuckling behind him.

"The heir doesn't usually help servants." Father Julian stated.

Benedict laughed softly. "Lady Luveday has found a way for the workers to teach Artair the workings of perfume making by having him *help* them."

"Artair's upbringing thus far has been... well..."

"I am aware of some of the details lady." The priest nodded for her to continue and from the look in his eyes his companions thought he was probably aware of more than either of them knew.

"Well... yes, then. I have found that Artair learns things better from certain people. He has a great fondness for Gemma and is willing to sit and *help* her for several hours if need be."

"That is impressive for a boy of his years." The kind smile the priest gave, was settling to Luveday's chaotic mind.

"Indeed," Benedict laughed again. "I don't think I sat still for a whole chime when I was his age."

"Nor I." Father Julian admitted. "So," he got back to the point, "you will accept him?"

They both knew he was no longer talking about the boy. "Aye and try to help him take charge of his lands. Perhaps being here will bring back some of his memories."

The Priest looked skeptical. "Do you truly believe that is possible after so long?"

Benedict looked to her. "As a healer..."

Luveday's gaze turned inward and her brow furrowed. "I have heard tales but have never met someone who has lost their memory so completely. I believe anything is possible."

"Tales?" The priest asked. "I have heard of your healing skills, the tale of your service to the crown has spread far and wide."

Luveday blushed and looked uncomfortably to Benedict for assistance. He smiled at her and tried averting Father Julian's penetrating gaze. "No doubt the story has grown with each retelling." He laughed. "Luveday is a skilled healer to be sure, but to hear the stories she routed Sterling single-handedly."

"It was not only the battle in the north I was speaking of but of the prince's illness as well." He looked at her. "You have saved two princes, no other woman in the kingdom can claim that."

Luveday laugh. "Believe me, it was a distinction I could forgo, but I was doing my best to help others, not thinking of the tales that would be sung about me."

"I don't believe they do you justice." The holy man said thoughtfully.

Luveday tried changing the topic and succeeded in turning the jovial mood sour. "Yes, well, don't believe everything you hear. And speaking of carrying tales, when do you believe we should head to court?" Scowls crossed the men's brows, and Luveday almost wished she had let them tease her a bit longer.

Later that evening, the quartet of Father Julian, Lord Titus, Lord Benedict and Lady Luveday had gone to the study to speak in private and to make plans. "Why the delay?" Titus asked, more curious than concerned when he heard they would not be traveling to court for a few days.

"Resting here is hardly a delay." The priest offered. "And the lady believes that familiar surroundings will help your memory."

"I have heard of your healing skills lady." He looked at her hopefully. "Do you think there is a chance...?" His voice caught.

"There is always hope, My Lord." She smiled at him gently. "As you were so far from home, it is not entirely surprising that nothing seemed familiar to you." She handed him a mug of hot tea, happy to share her evening pot with him as the other men sipped a fine vintage. "On the other hand, I don't wish to give you false hope. It has been several years, and there is a real possibility that your memories will never return."

Benedict sat forward, his easy manner turning serious. "Is there nothing you can do, Luveday?"

The other men in the room exchanged glances, noting the familiarity between the two.

"I am afraid not. The mind is a strange and wonderful thing." She looked at Titus speculatively, but he didn't seem to mind. "The best course of action is to recreate some of your daily routine as Lord of the manor."

"His what?" The priest asked.

"Routine?" Benedict scoffed at the same time.

"Yes," Luveday asked. "Some of the knights mentioned that you would do several different tasks almost daily. If we can recreate your day, as it was, before you lost your memories then perhaps the actions will bring to light other familiar things."

Titus nodded slowly, clearly in thought then offered, "Some things about this place are very familiar already." The other men looked at him with hope.

"That's wonderful, isn't it My Lady?" Benedict asked while Father Julian chided his friend, "You didn't say anything, Anon... sorry, Titus."

"It's fine." He didn't mind the priest's slip, even he still had trouble thinking of himself as Pillar and looked to the woman.

"Yes, that is good news. I would be troubled if nothing seemed familiar to you." She looked into the fire for a moment and nodded to herself before turning her attention back to the men. "It's best if we do not try to push you to remember, but let things progress naturally. I suggest we send a messenger to court with the tidings of your return, but as for a bit of leniency before going before the King. We can start with you getting to know the land again," she looked Titus in the eyes, and captured his full attention, "Spend part of the morning touring the lands, or working with the knights." He nodded. "I have heard you did that often. The afternoons can be spent working in the perfume storehouse and getting to know the people. I will talk to them before we begin."

"You want them to treat me like before?" He asked.

"No,' She answered surprising them all. "I want you to get to know them, and to learn everything, every step, every concern, every measurement, and detail of the process, and that means working beside them, and sometimes following their lead." Brows furrowed. "The relationship between Lord and peasant is not one conducive to this process, but I still wish for them to know who their Lord is. You will gain some of their respect by working beside them, while others might try to take advantage." Now there was understanding in their eyes. "I merely wish to make sure a balance can be made."

"It sounds easy enough," he leaned back in his chair. "Where do we begin?"

"At the beginning of course." Luveday laughed at their confused expression but would not answer further as she was called away to take care of the night's chores so that the house could find its rest.

"The beginning indeed," Titus muttered as he and Father Julian looked over the fields the next morning. Mist floated over the ground in soft wisps as the sun began its climb, not yet cresting the trees in the distance. After a stout but simple breakfast that mirrored the dinner of the night before, men and beasts began their tour of the lands surrounding Briar's Gate. At first, it all looked so mundane; crops filled plots of land like any other across the kingdom as they journeyed back towards the main road. But as the group cut across empty fields or over paths on the circumference of his lands the landscape began to change. As they came around to the east, suddenly vistas of color arose. A garden of flowers stretched out before him; this was no lady's bower, cultivated to appeal to the eye, but flowers growing in profusion on trellises like a giant maze that stood before him, covered in leafy vines. The occasional salty breeze was countered by sweet aromas of mint, jasmine, and honeysuckle.

Men were clearing a portion of field amid the blooming chaos, while Sir Reeve led the way. "The lady is adding a new mix."

"A new mix?" Father Julian asked before Titus could voice his thoughts.

"Lady Luveday is a healer, and she asked if there was a space to plant healing herbs to add to the lotions and soaps." He humped. "Nothing like Lady Claudia that one." He looked up as if realizing what he had said. "Beg your pardon, My Lord; I didn't mean…" He stammered and turned red, then pale.

Father Julian noted the man with some interest, while Titus turned to put him at ease. "As I don't remember my late wife, be at ease Sir Reeve." It wasn't the first time someone had marked the difference between the ladies. Titus was about to ask a question, but once again, the priest was there before him. Rather than be annoyed, Titus thought it might be helpful if the other man asked most of the questions as they seemed to be of a similar mind.

"In what way do you mean? Are they physically different? Their temperaments? Their minds or attitudes?"

While Sir Reeve seemed to squirm in his saddle, Sir Navarro chuckled. "In almost every way, Father." It took a moment of silence, but the man elaborated. "Except looks, I think they are rather similar in that regard." Navarro seemed to be looking back in his memory. "Lady Claudia was a hand taller; her eyes were more blue than grey. She was slender and graceful." An image of a woman flashed through Titus's mind, one he had seen before in fleeting visions, glimpses which he could never tell if they were dream or memory. The woman looked on him with a curious expression in her eyes, they were neither cold nor welcoming, as if she expected something from him. He had seen the visage smiling lovingly at him, and raging, which only filled him with a bone-deep sorrow. He could finally put a name to the woman, but somehow the knowledge did not hurt as much as he expected.

Navarro continued, "Lady Luveday is…"

"Common." Reeve supplied, but every other man in the group made a noise of disagreement or protest.

"No, Reeve. Though you think a lady should act as if she were above the rest of the house, there is nothing of the commoner in her."

"Nor common, in the sense that she is like other ladies." Sir Charles Templeton, youngest brother to one John Templeton, added thoughtfully.

"Aye, there is something unusual about the lady," Navarro added as if still searching for something.

Titus prompted, "Is it something in her attitude?"

"Maybe," the knight hedged. "There is something in the air around her that puts one at ease. She talks intelligently. I'd say her mind is as sharp as Lady Claudia's ever was, but she listens when you speak…"

Father Julian countered, "Lady Claudia didn't listen to her knights?" he asked rather incredulous.

Sir Reeve snorted. "Of course, she did. She wasn't a fool!" Sir Navarro gave the younger man a quelling look, reminding him that he was speaking to his betters. "She listened to us when we brought matters before her." He said stubbornly.

"But she had little time for matters outside of our duties, or how we performed them." Sir Templeton ventured. Reeve glared at him.

"True, Charles. She only wanted to hear from us if we had something to report about the safety of the lands."

"A lady can hardly care about the personal life of her household, as long as they do their duty." Reeve scoffed.

"But it wasn't just her knights." Templeton countered. "She didn't like hearing from anyone about anything outside of their duties, no matter the suggestion."

"Aye," Navarro chimed in again as he looked to the thoughtful expressions of the Father and Lord Pillar. "I think that some people just have a feeling for the welfare of others, and Lady Luveday is like that. She cares what is going on outside of our duties. She cares if we are well and... Aye, I would say... she cares if we are happy." The older knight seemed to be confused by this and yet pleased.

"Do you think that it is because she is a healer?" Templeton pondered aloud.

Father Julian smiled. "Or perhaps she became a healer because she has such a care."

Titus pondered that.

"She seemed to care a great deal for Lord St. James." Anyone could hear the spite in Reeve's voice, just before the man grunted. As the younger man road on the far side of the group, abreast with Sir Navarro as they paused to look over the fields, Titus could only wonder what reprimand the older knight had dealt him. If it were Titus, a swift side-kick would be just the thing.

The priest took up this suggestion and offered a bit of information making Titus wonder just what the priest was doing there. "Lady Luveday was a brief companion to St. James's mother, Lady Jane, and to that Lady's friend, Lady Emmalyn of Lander's Keep."

"The maternal Aunt of the King's Champion, Iain De Lane." Sir Templeton added with a bit of awe.

"The two have known each other for some time, and I've never seen a sign of anything more than friendship between them." Sir Navarro supplied. "He comes and goes, mostly to check on her and bring messages from the King."

The horse shifted restlessly, and Titus knew the group would move on at any moment. "What was she to the champion?" Even he had heard the tales of the battle with Sterling.

Navarro looked thoughtful, while Reeve turned to him with a piercing look. "Now that is a good question, isn't it, My Lord."

Navarro urged his mount forward. "Move on," he called behind him as the rest fell in line.

The Father and he exchanged looks. It was a troubling reaction, but telling all the same, and once again Titus got the feeling that the priest knew a lot more than he was letting on.

Artair wiggled on his perch atop the outdoor bench and stared at his father across the table. Luveday watched the two out of the corner of her eye. Three days had passed since Titus had returned, and Benedict was once again on his way to court, carrying letters from Luveday, Titus and the Priest. Luveday looked toward the Father as he stood back and listened as Gemma and Beatrix recited the types of flowers in each growing season. Artair liked memorizing things as if it were a game. Titus looked like he had some idea of what was going on and why, or if he was a bored as Luveday expected him to be, he hid it well. Father Julian seemed more interested in the dynamic between father and son than in the lesson. Luveday had expected to see the Priest depart, if not right away after seeing Titus settled, then surely when Benedict left for court and offered to escort the man if he were headed in that direction. Luveday couldn't figure the man out. He was polite, pious, and seemed kind yet his eyes were ever watchful, and Luveday constantly got the feeling that he was assessing the situation before him. For what reason, she couldn't guess, but her gut told her that he was no ordinary Priest.

"What, you don't drink it?" Titus's shock dragged Luveday's attention away from Father Julian.

"No, sir you don't drink it," Artair said solemnly, his usual enthusiasm banked. Luveday couldn't tell how the two were getting along. They were strangers, and Luveday wondered if they would ever be family. On top of the Lord trying to regain his memory, he was contending with a child who she wasn't sure, even wanted a father. While Artair new that being lord one day meant a life far better than the one he had led thus far, could a six-year-old comprehend what that entailed? On the other hand, could Titus?

The women looked up as Luveday came closer. Gemma looked as if she was handling these sessions well while Beatrix looked as if she were ready to throw up her hands and walk away. Having been Lady Claudia's right hand, Beatrix new far more about the workings of Briar's Gate, both inside and outside the manor, than anyone else, that didn't mean she had the patience for it.

Spotting Luveday, Titus moved to his feet looking more the lord than ever these last few days. "You make spirits and don't drink or sell them?"

Luveday smiled knowingly. "That's right. The stills are in a separate work shed." She gestured to the building around them. "These are for the storage of flowers and infused oils as they cure."

"I am missing something, am I not?" Titus stepped away from the bench, looking at Luveday, who turned to Gemma and Artair who was now standing atop his bench so that he was included with the adults.

Gemma smiled. "You see, My Lord. The stills produce small amounts of drink. It's not worth it to sort them and cart them to town."

Titus looked back at Luveday doubt written all over his face. "Gemma, why don't you continue the lesson with Artair, and I will walk with Lord Titus out to the distillery."

"Of course, My Lady." Artair smiled at them, not unhappy to see them go. Luveday winked at him, causing him to giggle, as she walked beside his father. Passed the row of warehouses built one on top of each other as the production expanded, passed the hedgerow that marked the end of the manor property. They followed a path that led away from the rest, it was paved, well maintained and easy to traverse.

"What is this?" He asked one it was clear they were alone. He gestured to the path before them.

"I hear it was your idea." She commented and then turned to him a little shocked at herself. She wasn't usually so tactless. "I am sorry."

He laughed at her shock. "No apology need, lady. I know it is a hard thing for others to get used to, yet I would say you have done so better than most." He liked the honey gold of her hair as it sat atop her head in a braided bun. He liked the plain and practical blue gown she wore, and how it reminded him of spring and cool water. He liked that she looked at him as a man, and not as if he were an oddity even after hearing his tale. Overall, he liked the lady too much.

"I would like to think that is because I am trying to see the world through your eyes."

"And how does it look from where you are standing?" He asked as she looked ahead of them, not realizing he watched her so closely.

"New and yet familiar. Friendly, and I hope," she turned to glance at him with a smile, "full of potential."

"All of that?" he smiled softly at her.

"We are here," she meant figuratively, "and there is no way but forward. I may not know the man you were, and I am only getting to know the man before me." She stopped then to look at him, catching him off guard. "I can only think that, despite all you have lost, the man in here," she lightly placed her right hand over his heart, "was made a long time ago." She stepped back as if realizing how close they were. "The things you learned long ago like your skills as a knight, your gift with languages, those did not leave you, and I am sure that the heart of you is still in here whether or not your memories return."

Titus had no idea who this woman truly was, but he had the sudden urge to sweep her into his arms and kiss her. He took a step forward intending to do just that when a gruff, accented voice rang out over the bit of orchard they walked through. "My boy, there you be."

Without thought, Titus called over his shoulder, "Not now Ham can't you see I'm talking to a bonny Lady." They stared at each other for a moment, wide-eyed.

A deep chuckle reached their ears, as both brows furrowed. Luveday spoke, uncomfortable, and trying to change the subject. "I didn't know you had been introduced to the brewmaster."

Titus's brown had furrowed for a different reason. "I have not." They both turned to see the large man standing just beyond a clump of trees. He was older, taller, and wilier than most men around the manor. He hailed from overseas, and his accent reminded Luveday of a brogue, though there was something a little different about it. Ham had spent more years brewing than most people lived, having learned the craft at his parents' knees. It was said he was breastfed on the stuff and only weened thanks to sips of the spirits his mother brewed. Luveday almost believed it.

The two approached while Titus looked at the man in wonder. "There ya are, boy. Took you long enough to return to us." The man slapped large hands on the Lord's shoulders and gave him a good looking over. "You don't look too changed, despite what they say happened to ya." He humped and greeted the lady with a nod. "Forgot about all this aye, well I say there are some things a man might want to forget." He looked at Titus knowingly, and glanced at the lady with a wink, "And there are things a man surely wants to remember." Titus caught the wink, and the stern look the lady gave the brewmaster. "Come on in and take a seat, I had a feeling you would be coming by today." The man led the way to a large house made of stone and opened a smaller door in the large gate on this side of the building. Titus followed, noting that the paved road led directly to the stillroom doors.

Luveday followed, watching the bemused expression on the Lord's face with some concern. It was clear he had remembered Ham, but why this man and no other? Perhaps the old man was correct, and there was something that Titus wished to forget. Luveday paused just inside the doors to accustom herself to the darker interior, and to brace herself for the warmth of the stills. The set up was impressive. Copper and iron wove together to create a system of cylinders and pipes, that was a large still for hard spirits. If Luveday's memory was right, the alcohol created was closest to gin. She had had a gin and tonic once, and her mother had been rather fond of the stuff. While it could be consumed, the potency of the batches they used for perfume making was too high to do so wisely.

Once her eyes adjusted, Luveday saw both men seated beside Ham's long worktable; three copper cups were lined up as the brewer poured out a dram for each of them. Luveday approached as Titus picked up his drink and eyed it warily. "There you go, My Lord." Ham turned to her and held out the last cup. Luveday took it gingerly as the man looked at her knowingly. The lord hesitated a moment and threw back the liquor. He didn't cough but smiled and held out the cup again. Luveday sipped her gin and watched the play between the men.

While Ham talked about his work, from forging the equipment that kept the distillery running, to brewing the mixes that became the gin, there was an easiness about the two she hadn't witnessed before.

Luveday left to check over the supplies, noting that the two men talked animatedly while mentally making a list for the Brewmaster. While Ham was comfortable asking for herbs, spices, and items for the distillery, he didn't ask for much himself. Luveday had taken it upon herself to send over a few things that would make his life a little easier, like burn salve, new thick leather gloves, and the like. He was a good man, and rightfully proud of his work, but without a woman to care for him, it was a rather spartan way of life.

"You brew the grain, and turn it into spirits for perfume?" Titus's voice was closer as Luveday made the run along the back wall and the shelves that held the majority of the distillery's supplies.

"Lady Claudia, rest her soul, left nary a drop for a drink, but ya know I always make a bottle or two for testing the brew." He looked at Titus, "or maybe ya don't, boy." He shrugged and continued. "Her Ladyship here has let me mix a few of my spirits. Juniper berries are plentiful, and the spices she had in her stores are something else, boy. They come from places I have never heard of." His deep chuckle made them smile. "What is it you're looking for, My Lady? You know my place is right in order." He stood tall before her, but despite his size, she wasn't intimidated.

"I didn't expect anything less Master Ham." The man always got a charming smile on his face when she used his title. "We are making a trip into Court in a fortnight, and I wanted to know if there was anything you needed."

He thought a moment, "nothing that I can reckon. You keep me well stocked." He seemed pleased by this, knowing that Lady Claudia often hoarded her ingredients in her final months. Luveday wondered that no one had commented on how changed the woman was. Paranoia leading to irrational behavior and secrecy, hoarding, violence, and drastic mood swings were some of the symptoms she had pieced together post humorously.

Luveday shook her head to dispel the depressing thoughts. "If you think of anything send a message to the house, and I will see what we can do."

Ham smiled showing a crooked grin. "I will, My Lady." They both looked to Titus. "Can I keep the boy..." he cleared his throat sheepishly, "Do you mind if My Lord stays with me a while? We've got some things to talk about." She got the hint and excused herself, noting how content the younger man looked. Somehow the idea that Ham and Titus had been some form of confidants was not as surprising as it should be. After all, the man had worked as a brewer on the land well before the current lord was born. Luveday walked back to the house wondering what secrets they were sharing, but she also feared that Ham had more than a few hard truths for the boy and she was afraid some things would not stay buried.

Titus was somber on his trip to court, and while many attributed it to feeling anxious about meeting the King, those closer to Lord Pillar knew that his mood had changed some time before they prepared for the journey.

Luveday watched his back as they were shown to their accommodations inside the palace. Their rooms were next door to each other, which was convenient since Artair was staying with her, even though the relationship between father and son was progressing. Artair often clung to Luveday, and she understood that the boy had lost too much of his old life too quickly to feel comfortable despite the luxuries of being the long-lost heir. Titus was making an effort to bridge the gap but was still too new to his role to proceed with grace.

Luveday often thought that was what they all needed, a little more grace, in every sense of the word.

Artair was left to play with the princes, and some of the noblemen's children as the adults gathered in the throne room to stand before the King and their peers. The hall fell strangely silent as they entered reminding Luveday of her last visit. Many of the same faces surrounded her. They looked on in wonder and confusion. The whispers started as they advanced, Luveday was attired in her best gown, the blue velvet that Henna and she had completed so long ago. Titus was dressed simply in a fine dark blue tunic and hose that did not match her but were in the same color family. They stopped a respectful distance from the King, who had come to stand at the end of the dais. He looked on his subject with wonder.

Titus bowed as Luveday curtsied a step behind him, after all, it was not she they were here to see. Before the man could say a proper greeting, the King was holding him at arm's length. "By all that is holy, it is you, Titus." The King seemed flabbergasted. "I have had word, even fresh from St. James's lips, but I couldn't credit it." Edward stepped back and returned to the dais but didn't take his seat. "And you remember nothing, not even your King."

A pained look crossed Titus's face for a moment before he answered. "I am remembering bits and pieces my liege, but they are little more than flashes of the past." He turned to Luveday and held out a hand. She took it reflexively. "The Lady Luveday thinks that there is a possibility they may return in time, but no one knows for sure, least of all me." She let go of his hand after a reassuring squeeze.

The King smiled kindly at the lady, a smile that was echoed by his wife. "Lady Luveday has been invaluable to this court though she once hailed from foreign lands." There was a mumble through the crowd which caused her to look around. She spotted Benedict, and her heart almost stopped to see the man beside him.

Iain stood tall and as handsome as ever in the hunter green tunic she had made for him. His face was expressionless, though there was a hardness around his eyes she didn't remember seeing before. Was that expression pointed at her or did it have something to do with the fact that she stood beside another man? She forced her attention back to the dais, but the cause of her distraction was noted by many.

"We will, of course, return your lands and title to you in full and wave the taxes that your lady wife owed and will give you a three-year grace period, diminishing your taxes by half so that you may get your house in order." The King spoke as if these gifts were nothing out of the ordinary but many marveled at the generosity of the crown. Titus and Luveday were both astonished, but Titus's gratitude was waved away as the King returned to his throne.

"The legitimacy of your heir is assured, and by all accounts, Lady Luveday has taken great care with the handling of your household." Queen Augusta remarked as the King nodded in agreement while exchanging a look with his wife. Luveday didn't know where this train of thought was going, but she noticed the King look pointedly over her left shoulder, to the approximate spot where De Lane stood. "If she is willing to continue in this role as you settle into your seat, Pillar, then we are happy to let you return to Briar's Gate in a few days with our blessing."

All eyes turned to Luveday, who sighed internally, while she tried for a graceful smile. "It would be my pleasure, Your Majesty." What else could she say? Luveday thought the nod the Queen gave her was telling but didn't dare voice the questions she had. She prayed a private word with the monarchs was somewhere in the near future, though she feared the meeting would not go to her liking.

"We look forward to seeing you prosper," The King spoke to them as a couple, which made both uncomfortable for different reasons, but they were dismissed without another word.

They moved to a place near the back of the room, and the King's voice rang out across the hall. "As for your summons, De Lane. Let us speak in private and finish the matter of your betrothal to Lady Christabel once and for all."

Luveday caught the words over the murmur of voices, and her eyes flew to De Lane and St. James. The champion was already approaching the dais and moving on to the private rooms beyond. Benedict locked eyes with her but didn't come close as a group of noble descended upon her and Lord Pillar. Had it been her imagination of was there a look of apology or guilt in her friend's eyes? What did he have to be sorry for and why was Christabel not referred to as Iain's wife and not his betrothed?

Chapter 21

How do I love thee? Let me count the ways.
I love thee to the depth and breadth and height My soul can reach..."
~Elizabeth Barrett Browning, Sonnets from the Portuguese

The next few days at court were longer than any other. Titus was an attraction, though many assured him he had never been this popular at court. Luveday heard bits and pieces about the time the young Lord had saved the King's life which confirmed the unlikely friendship between the two. While they were given leave to go, the Queen sent word that they were not to depart until she could have a private word. Luveday had thought that audience would be swift, but days had passed, and no summons came.

The topic of Iain De Lane was bantered about, but never openly. Luveday caught tidbits of conversations where she gleaned that Sumerland had somehow run afoul of De Lane and thus, the King.

"What a mess that is!" One woman whispered loudly.

Another tittered. "Can you believe it?"

There was a masculine harrumph as a man joined his wife. "A boon for De Lane no doubt."

"Sumerland left with his tail between his legs." A woman giggled under her breath. The sound grated on Luveday's nerves as she tried to listen in.

The man chastised the women. "What do you expect after he decided to sit out the battle in the north. With his friendship with the other Sterling calling his loyalty into question he was lucky the King didn't demand more of him."

Titus returned claiming her attention. "Your goblet, My Lady." He offered her the acquired beverage and watched her a moment. Luveday realized he was fully aware that she had been eavesdropping and perhaps why she had been so interested or had an inkling why.

"Thank you, Lord Pillar." There was a tightening around his eyes.

Luveday decided to take pity on him. "Would you like a walk through the garden?" She offered with the idea of getting him out of the line of fire, but he shook his head.

"While I would enjoy few things more, I am told the King will be returning any moment." No sooner had he spoken when the council heralded the return of the King. For once the Queen was not at his side.

There was a devilish smile on the monarch's face, and many mirrored his expression with anticipation of the news he bore. He did not leave his audience waiting. "It is with great satisfaction that I can announce to you, Ladislaus Sterling was killed in the Hunt to recapture the traitor, by none other than my Champion. The beast was brought to ground!" There was a noise of approval, and finality, though not an outright cheer. "Ladislaus died of wounds attained while trying to escape. The bastard tried to burn down Kilgrave Abbey as he fled, but the knights helped to contain the damage and brought back the body." There was a pause. "We wished to verify the identity of our foe and have removed Sterling and his cousin from the line. Reparations will be made to the crown and the nobles for his treachery." There was movement on the dais. "Lord St. James," the man stepped forward at the King's gesture, "will accompany Lord De Lane to Sterling Castle and deliver the news to Lady Sterling post haste."

"Godspeed," rang out across the crowd. Benedict briefly whispered something to the King, before giving a quick bow and cutting across the Hall. Luveday locked eyes with him for a moment; she had been unable to speak to him at all since her arrival. He nodded to indicate something to her, but he was gone just as fast.

Titus was at her side and took her arm. "They are gesturing toward us." He said close to her causing Luveday to tare her gaze from the closed doors to find a royal page beckoning them to the private chambers. They were summoned at last.

Luveday looked on the Queen with utter shock. The woman laughed at the blank expression on the younger woman's face. "I think we have finally outwitted her, my love." The King said kindly, but with a hint of humor in his voice.

Titus had left a few moments ago having outlined their plans to repay the crown, claim his title and guide the prosperity of Briar's Gate for the near future. He and Luveday had spent a few hours each day outlining what the equivalent of a modern-day business plan of the long-term goals for the house of Pillar. Luveday had even designed a logo they would start using in soap molds and on the perfume labels. The crown was more than impressed, but they dismissed Pillar and asked Luveday to stay with somber expressions.

Their stoic delivery had not prepared her for their words.

"Reparations? How much?" Luveday shook her head.

Both Royals laughed, the Queen got to her feet coming around the table to gently take Luveday's hands. "Silly woman, you are rich."

"But..." Luveday began.

The King cut in. "The sum from Sterling's coffers is only a pittance; we have not even gotten to what we are bestowing yet." He laughed too.

"Luveday," Augusta said softly.

Shaking herself out of her bemusement, Luveday hugged the Queen. "Thank you. Thank you from the bottom of my heart and I gladly accept."

"Finally," The King sighed and sat back in his chair as his Queen joined him.

"I am not sure I deserve…" But Luveday was cut off as the Queen looked back at her.

"Dear Lady, do you not know we would have given you so much more…"

"If we thought you would except it." The King harrumphed good-naturedly.

"You are worth so much more to us." At August's words, Luveday felt tears gathering in her eyes and had to hurriedly blink them away while nodding quickly.

"Now," The King grew serious again, and Luveday composed herself to listen attentively. "Beyond the reparations due you, we have debated it, and we both believe that a portion of land is a suitable gift. As you are unwilling to take something entitled, we have settled on one of the properties that was returned to us with the last of their line. The last of the family is without issue, and too old to bare any heirs." Luveday settled her arguments. "The land is too the north, but not unworked." He looked to his Queen who continued.

"There is a manor house, though I heard it is in much disrepair. There is a good-sized wood so that lumber will not be an issue, and I am told there is also some stone available if you wish to use your funds on the manor."

"We don't believe that the task would be any hardship for you." The King smirked at her.

Luveday nodded, "Oh, no, your Majesties. I should do well."

"As for your safety," The Queen looked to Luveday and back again.

"Ah, yes. A lady needs knights…" The King looked thoughtful, but there was a gleam in his eyes.

"Is there no household for the manor?" Luveday asked.

Augusta looked sorrowful, "not any longer."

The King seemed to have made some internal decision as he rose from his chair causing both women to look at him curiously. "We will summon you again when the writ is complete." Augusta rose a moment later. "And will bestow upon you lands and gifts before you leave."

Luveday rose, bowed and made the appropriate gestures before exiting though her mind was still spinning.

She wandered, lost in thought, not knowing exactly where she was going until Titus stopped her a moment before she exited through the door to the gardens.

Grabbing her elbow, he turned her back toward him, clearly anxious. "Lady Luveday." She got the feeling he had been calling her for some time. "Lady, what did the King have to say to you?"

Looking up into a rugged yet handsome face, Luveday noted that his hazel eyes were more golden than green when he was troubled. "I'm rich." She whispered in awe.

"I beg your pardon?" Titus stepped aside to let a lady and knight pass into the garden, but he was talking to her.

Luveday wondered if the shock on her face matched his own. "The King is including me in the reparations from Sterling's coffers." She caught his muttered under his breath, "As he well should," but continued. "They are also making a writ for land somewhere in the north."

Titus looked pained. "A dowry." He stated flatly.

Something cold raced down her spine at the thought. "I do not believe that is its purpose." She stated coolly trying to ignore her growing doubt. "They have not mentioned marriage, and am I not too old?"

"Hardly," he said as if the idea of her being too old was laughable. "Do not think they will not meddle in your life just because you are a favorite, in fact, it makes you more of a target." She swallowed loudly. "Wealthy, young, kind, intelligent, resourceful and beautiful," her head snapped up to look at him wide-eyed at the deep timber in his voice. "What man wouldn't want you." It was a rhetorical question, but Luveday could now identify the mysterious emotion she had seen in his eyes of late. It was longing, and not for what he had lost, but for her. Before she could make some reply, a man called Pillar's name shattering the tension of the moment as they both turned to greet Lord Greyson Stern and Father Julian.

"I hear some congratulations are in order, for the both of you." The two newcomers looked from one to the other. Luveday's stomach flipped, suddenly wondering if they meant there was some rumor about her marrying Titus. Pillar said something but Luveday couldn't hear over the pounding of her heart in her ears. Something slammed into and wrapped around her waist. It was Artair, whose small body had filled out a bit thanks to several months of good eating. He beamed up at her and began to drag her into the gardens, not taking no as an answer. The Princes were waiting just beyond, and Luveday couldn't help the laughter that spilled from her dispelling the panic.

She was unaware that the men talked and watched her intently. Lord Greyson had not meant marriage, but he knew that the crown had plans for the little healer. Father Julian looked on her curiously, having only met one other woman with such kindness, intelligence and fortitude, and knowing that the other now graced the throne, he wondered what future this one might grasp, if she were bold enough. Titus looked on, feeling more for the woman and boy than he had ever imagined possible and wondering at the feeling of loss that gripped his heart. Was it the foreshadowing of something or the echo of memories trying to make themselves known?

A cheer went up from the crowd. "And it is with great pleasure that I bestow upon Lady Luveday this writ which marks that the lands and monies thereof will henceforth belong to her solely." Luveday excepted the rolled parchment while wearing a light blue gown of soft velvet that the Queen had gifted her for the occasion. "May she go with our gratitude and blessing." There was a short pause while he looked over the crowd. "And now," the audience held their breath, "Let us eat and celebrate!"

The Queen descended the steps taking Luveday's arm as they swept across the throne room and made their way to the dining hall. "You did well." Augusta patted her hand and escorted her to her seat while the other guests lined up behind their chairs waiting for the Royals to take their places before doing the same.

Lord Grayson Stern was seated beside her and Luveday was happy to finally meet his wife, while Lord Frazier seated himself on her right. The familiar face put her at ease. Titus was seated across from her, but one of the two women at his elbows, constantly engaged his attention. He seemed to be enjoying himself, though the smiles he flashed at her were a touch mocking.

Luveday barely caught the comment Stern made and looked to the subject in question. Father Julian sat at the left hand of the Queen. "I didn't know they were so well acquainted," Luveday commented to no one in particular.

"Why girl," Frazier laughed, "Father Julian is an old friend of both the King and Queen. Christened their children, rather than that disgrace of an Archbishop." The gruff laugh made Luveday smile.

Lady Stern leaned around her husband and nodded. "He's older than he looks but had known the crown since he was a lad. From a noble family that one, though some think he might be related in truth, a distant cousin of some such." The lady imparted the information in a soft yet matter of fact way which made Luveday think that the soft little lady was well suited for such a large man.

Stern added, "If anyone could be said to have made a business out of the church it is Julian." Luveday looked puzzled, but before she could voice her questions, he elaborated. "Not riches, Lady, but the influence he wields is great. He is seldom in one place for long."

"Why is that?" She asked.

Frazier took up the conversation causing her to turn toward him. "The good Father is sent to take care of whatever is troubling the powers that be." He commented snidely.

"What?" She asked as Stern grunted under his breath. The sound was somewhere between an agreement and a snort.

"He means that Father Julian is used to settle the disputes and other delicate business of the Archbishop."

"And to keep him out of old Ironfist's sight." Frazier laughed.

"Ironfist?" Luveday asked while Lady Stern laughed softly.

The lady nodded. "The nickname most popular for the Archbishop. Mostly for his immovable views."

Her husband clarified. "And the fact that he has a habit of hammering the tables when he disagrees with someone, though he isn't in council often. Usually, Father Julian fills that role when needed."

Luveday sat back in her chair while nodding her understanding as wheels turned in her head. "So, he is rather powerful then…" She thought aloud. "Then why was he sent for Pillar?"

"That's not a surprise, Lass." Frazier took a sip of his wine and turned to her. "The return of a lost Lord, coming back from the dead is definitely something they would have sent him to look into."

"And the fact that Titus was a favorite of the King." She put the pieces together.

"Just so," Stern looked at her with a small smile, and they both knew the wheels were turning. The questions she didn't ask aloud were perhaps the most pressing. What else might Father Julian have been sent to Briar's Gate for? And what tales might he have told the Queen?

Luveday counted herself lucky or was it a miracle that she had made it out of the royal court without a marriage proposal. She had been dreading nearly every moment since Titus had suggested it to her. Artair rode in front of his father deciding it was better to split his time between the two of them. They chatted amiably together, though Titus had proved he could handle the child's rare meltdowns, she still felt the space between them.

She had been left to her thoughts for a while as they journeyed home. Titus's words had settled over her, and Luveday wondered about the future and avenues she had never considered before. How many times had she looked into Artair's upturned face and loved him as if he were her own? If she married Titus, she could have that. She could have a beautiful home, a beautiful and messy little boy and perhaps even more children to come. She could step into those shoes with ease, becoming Lady of Briar's Gate in truth would take only a ceremony, and a few spoken words. So, why was she hesitating?

The fact that she had yet to talk with Benedict was a big issue. He had become her sounding board as of late. Was it the fact that there were no other women she trusted to guide her? Was it something to do with De Lane? Though she had heard hints of the trouble with Christabel and her odious father, she had not been about to glean the truth of the matter, and she was too emotionally involved to ask outright. Truthfully, she wasn't sure she wanted to know. Her hand went to her girdle, the wide cloth road higher on her waist for traveling than the hip-hugger she wore with her daily gowns. Pressed between it and her gown was a letter, one from St. James that she hoped would answer some of the lingering questions. It seemed Stern had forgotten to give it to Luveday until it was time for them to depart. He had passed it surreptitiously to her and Luveday had slipped it behind her girdle without thought. They had stopped once already, but Luveday didn't feel she had the privacy to read it yet.

Why was she even hiding the missive from the others? They knew she spoke to Benedict often. The fact that he wrote to her would be no surprise, especially since he left their group on the King's errand so quickly. She vowed that at the next break she would see what the letter held.

Two hours later she sat under the branches of an oak tree; the leaves shaded her from the hot midday sun. She watched father and son filling waterskins from the cool stream winding its way through the small wood. She pulled out the letter and opened it as men milled around under the canopy of trees, not hurried to return to the heat of the dusty roads.

The wax seal held the imprint of St. James's ring and was just warm enough to make removing it a little easier. Luveday had gotten used to their style of writing letters. People didn't waste space or fine paper by formatting a letter as she was used to. While the missive had all the usual elements, it was one large paragraph, with Benedict's signature at the bottom in a flourish. She began reading, not sure what to expect.

"Written the afternoon of the fifteenth day of Thane's Month, mid-summer at the royal court of King Edward the Third." Luveday noted that would have been the day she had last seen him. "Dear Lady Luveday, I am sorry to be writing this so hastily, but as you know by now, I am at the mercy of my King. De Lane and I will travel to Sterling Castle to deliver the news of his death to his mother, to set men to guard the castle and to install a Lord there until the King's final decision is made, but that is not why I wished to write to you. I have hesitated too long, and that is my fault. I wanted to spare you talk of anything unpleasant as I know your emotions are still raw after leaving Lander's Keep. For over a moon I have known the truth and yet have not confided in you. In fact, I went so far as to make sure no rumors reached your ears. Many know that you left the keep before the marriage ceremony was completed. What happened afterword is a tale I do not have the time or space to recount, other than to say that Iain did not," and here he underlined the word not, "marry Lady Christabel that day, or any day since." Luveday looked up, not seeing the happy brook before her, but envisioning her last glimpse of Iain and Christabel standing on the steps of the Chapel. The vows were spoken before the church, but the ceremony wasn't complete until the blessings were said inside the chapel. What could have happened in so short a time? "I pray you will be patient and wait until the tale is told. I know the King and Queen had plans in store for you, and while I know they look to bettering your future, I ask that you wait a little longer and trust me. Ever yours, Benedict St. James."

Luveday turned the parchment overlooking for some postscript, anything more that might clue her into what was going on, but there was nothing.

"What is that My Lady?" Artair asked plopping down beside her left knee, sprinkling water across her and the letter as he shook out his wet hair.

Luveday mentally shook herself and turned to the boy smiling at his happy face. "Did you take a dunk in the stream?"

He laughed. "Didn't you see? Father dumped his waterskin over my head when I said I wished the stream were deep enough to swim in." The boy looked at the letter and over to his father who stood not a few feet away from Luveday's outstretched legs. The look of concern on his face was quickly replaced with a smirk. "The boy leaned in and asked quietly, "Maybe someday *you* can teach me to swim?" The hopeful expression on his face was endearing.

Luveday nodded a little and looked to Titus. "I am sorry I missed it, but I was reading the letter." She flapped the parchment she still held in her right hand as Titus dropped her full waterskin at her feet and settled on her right. The three of them lounged on her cloak between the large roots of the tree and looked to the letter. Luveday could tell that Titus read it quickly and his frown was deep as he settled back to look at the men around them.

"Whose it from?" The boy asked.

Luveday smiled at him. "Lord St. James. He was telling me that he was going to Sterling Castle and so he couldn't escort us home." Though Benedict hadn't sait those words exactly, she thought it would help to settle some of the boy's questions.

"Will he come home soon?" Artair asked in that childish way where they believe that their home is everyone's home.

"I don't know when he will return to Briar's Gate, but his home is at Lion's Head. He was sent to Sterling Castle on the King's business, so it might be awhile before we see him again." The boy nodded and got up to run off toward the stream again. Titus's hand closed over her own crushing the paper. She looked at him a little startled.

"Is it he or De Lane you are waiting for?" He asked but didn't look at her. He watched the boy, and she turned to do the same, though he didn't let go of her hand. "What is between you?" His voice was pitched low so as not to carry.

Luveday decided to answer truthfully and in full, not knowing what would happen, but was tired of the tension between them. "I would say that the relationship between St. James and myself is more familial than romantic." Titus didn't relax. "We care for each other but not enough to call it love, as in the love between a man and his wife."

His voice was gruff, contrasting with the joy for the boy running before them. "And De Lane?"

Luveday took in a deep breath, to steady herself and to expel her own emotions. "That is harder to say. I left because," she was wary of what this man might think of her but continued. "there was more emotion than good sense. I knew that if I stayed, he would marry another, and yet I think... No. I know, I was the one his heart wanted. He was the one my heart wanted, but I wasn't what his people needed. The King had already blessed the betrothal between them, and they were counting down the days until the wedding when I arrived at Lander's Keep."

"You didn't stay." It wasn't a question, but she answered anyway.

"There would have been shame and heartache." She said simply and raised her other hand to wave at Artair as he chased a bird beside the stream, still holding on to Titus.

"And now?" He asked the hardest question, and she finally looked at him, to find he had been watching her for some time.

Luveday didn't look away; she was committed to telling the truth. "I don't know what happens now, but I will choose a path I can live with, and hope the future is brighter."

Titus finally let go of her as Artair rushed back to them, stumbling into Luveday's lap laughing all the way. His father rose and patted the boy on the head. "A few more moments and then we must move on."

They nodded, and Artair wrapped his arms around Luveday in a fierce hug. When they had untangled themselves, and Luveday started to rise, the boy asked what they were talking about. Luveday's answer was truthful if purposefully vague, "Things that men and women talk about." She ruffled his hair and asked him to help her gather her things and brush off her cloak. Happy chatter accompanied her as they readied to continue their journey, and Luveday wondered if Briar's Gate would truly be home.

Days passed, and by the time the familiar field of Briar's Gate appeared before them, the travelers where worn through and more than ready to be home. The group seemed quieter without Benedict and Father Julian; both had lent intelligence and charm to the conversations on the road. Luveday found it hard to entertain Artair and herself for the entire journey. Titus shared some amusing adventures of his time in Canthus, where he lived by selling his sword arm. More often than not it seemed he ended up doing more than he was paid for a true knight in shining armor. Luveday liked the tales though she thought that he was leaving out a good deal to make them age appropriate.

By the time they entered the gates, and were ushered into the hall for refreshments, several things had happened. One, Beatrix had indeed prepared a meal thanks to the rider they sent ahead, two, another rider had arrived saying that a large group of the King's men would be arriving in a few days. Titus commented, "The rider could have overtaken us on the road," thinking that the writ the King had promised him was finished and being delivered.

Luveday wondered about that, but they had stopped many times to accommodate herself and Artair, where a single rider could have made much better time if he pushed through. Beatrix also whispered that there was some news of Leah and Luveday's heart lodged in her throat. Beatrix's expression was somewhere between sorrow for the boy and concern for her friend, or at least she hoped it was nothing more serious. Luveday said she would take a moment to look over her study as Father and son went to their rooms to wash and change out of their dusty travel garments. Titus looked at her questioningly, but she waved him away but mouthed she had something to see to once Artair's back was turned. Pillar nodded, letting her know they would talk later.

News of Leah took priority over Luveday's need to be clean. They made their way to the little nook that was Luveday's office, or study might had been the right word. She had not been able to use the one in the tower after associating it with Sterling, and Claudia, she had left it alone, and was happy to see Titus using it for his own purposes now. Beatrix wore an apron which she was twisting into knots as a man Luveday had seen about the manor came into the area. "This be John, My Lady." She introduced the man and Luveday wondered if he were the same John Leah had set to wait for Benedict on the road. "He has news." A tall, lean and anxious man nodded a greeting to her. Luveday looked at his workworn hands, his downcast eyes and his patched clothing and took a breath to remind herself to go slowly and not demand the news from him.

"Aye, My Lady, I be John Farrow, I keep the south-west field and see to the fowl of the keep." He said as a way of introduction.

"Thank you, John," the man blushed at her words as he twisted what she assumed was a hat in his hands. "You have news of Leah?" She prompted after a moment.

"Yes, lady." He jumped nervously, causing Luveday's anxiety to double. Their nervousness was making her nervous.

"I took a trip over to Pyne-on-the-Abbey while you were away." He began. "I was visiting my sister and taking them a piglet for the new baby when I was stopped by a woman who works at the abbey." He paused to look at Beatrix,

"She remembered I was from Briar's Gate, you see, and said there was an older woman who arrived not long ago who claimed to be from here, asking for sanctuary at the abbey." Luveday nodded for him to continue as she looked at Beatrix who nodded vigorously back at her as if to verify John's every word. "Well, I talked to her a while, but she wouldn't tell me the woman's name, only asked if I knew someone who she said looks a lot like our Leah and asked if the woman had any family as she was not in the best of health."

"Oh, Leah." Beatrix covered her mouth with the hand that still clutched the apron, fighting tears.

She had to prompt him to speak again as tears were gathering in the man's eyes as well. "What happened then, John?" She blinked fighting back the collective emotion.

"Well," he thought a moment. "We parted ways, I visited my sister and stayed a night and came back home as planned. I stopped by the kitchen early the next morning and told Beatrix what I heard and asked if you had returned, but she said you were still at court," John said uneasily. "Did I do wrong, My Lady?"

"No, John." Luveday tried to reassure him. "You know we have been looking for Leah since she left," the man nodded, "but she is not in any trouble. We will have to send someone to the Abbey." She thought a moment and knew she had to ask Titus before making a plan of action. "How far away is the Abbey?" She asked, knowing Pyne-on-the-Abbey was a nearby village not too far north on the coast. It was rather large thanks to the Abbey's influence and the fishing harbor. She had hoped to visit if soon, but the return of Titus had changed all of her plans.

"Oh, all most a full day on foot My Lady." John offered.

A stray thought had Luveday asking, "You walked the pig?" She looked to the man who answered with a smile.

"No, My Lady, it was a little thing, so I carried him in a shoulder basket." He seemed to finally settle in her presence. "May I go now, My Lady?"

Luveday shook off her thoughts to thank him. "Yes, John, and thank you for bringing news. Beatrix send him off with something from the kitchen if the meal is done."

John tried to protest, but Beatrix nodded to her lady and shooed him out.

Luveday left for her room noting that someone had left a note on the piece of slate she used as a chalkboard. A messy hand had written something about Ham and Gemma; she'd have to figure it out later.

Once cleaned and changed she met Titus on the stairs down to the Hall. He looked her up and down before inquiring about the news she had hinted to earlier. Of course, he already knew about Leah and her role in Artair's life. She made sure the boy could not overhear their conversation, and filled him in on the rest, finishing with the suggestion that they retrieve the elder woman. "Leah should be brought home, especially if her health is as poor as the woman in Pyne-on-the-Abbey suggested." Titus nodded but was still thinking it over.

"And if she dies?" He asked abruptly.

Luveday had a visceral reaction, not because she had become so fond of the woman, but on Artair's behalf. "Then she can die and be buried here," Luveday said softly.

"Do you wish to go, or should we send someone else?" It was not something Luveday had thought through. Her first reaction was to say of course she should go, but was their someone better suited, and how would they keep the news from Artair until they knew how Leah faired?

Beatrix was too emotional; she would cry so much Leah wouldn't know what was going on. Luveday would be missed, but she could go, and perhaps take Gemma with her, though the girl was working hard making perfume, and she wasn't sure the girl could be spared. Coming to a decision, she answered, "I will go, tomorrow. Early, I think." He nodded. "I will take Sir Templeton, John and Clair with me, it that sound good to you."

"Of course, I hope you find the woman well." Titus was about to turn and head down the stairs, but she stopped him. "Do you wish to come as well?"

He thought a moment and looked at her but shook his head. "No, I will be of more use here."

Luveday nodded, not sure but thinking she understood his reasons. "And if she is well and I can bring her home, would you like to speak to her?"

Titus's eyes were piercing, "Yes I would."

Pyne-on-the-Abbey was a bustling metropolis compared to the country villages she's seen thus far. The Abbey was not a cloister, so there were more friars and Fathers than nuns, though the building and gardens were similar in enough ways to make her think of Lander's Keep, she was not as nostalgic as she had feared she might be. Sir Templeton was not as gruff as his older brother, but then again, there was more than a decade separating them. Clair, small and quiet had been overwhelmed by the news that they were traveling to retrieve Leah. Luveday got the feeling that many of the young ones looked at the older woman as a mother or grandmother figure. John drove the cart, but the ride to the Abbey was rather somber, and Luveday hoped that it was not foreshadowing things to come. She fervently prayed that the woman had rallied, and they were not bringing back dark tidings.

Sir Templeton and John disappeared, seeing to the horses and chatting with the Friars as she and Clair were led into the visitor's wing once they said they were there to see Leah of Briar's Gate. The aged Friar didn't pretend not to know who they were looking for but took them right in without even a word.

Luveday had her bag of healing supplies having spent some of her time stocking up and making new medicines that the manor didn't seem to have. She was a prepared as she could be, but both women hesitated outside of the little door. Neither wanted to open it for fear of what they might find, but Luveday squared her shoulders and pushed onward. Leah was pale, the light from a high window not enough to brighten the room. A candle burned in the dark space though it was still late afternoon. It took a moment for her eyes to adjust before Luveday could see the other woman in the room. She was younger, but still well past middle-aged. Luveday nodded to her and introduced herself waving the woman to stay seated as she did so. "I am Lady Luveday of Briar's Gate, this is Clair," she gestured to the girl who followed her in. Luveday saw Leah's eyes flutter and open. "How is she?" She asked softly.

The other woman gestured, but before she could speak her patient answered for her. "I am still here young Lady." Leah's voice sounded hoarse but stronger than she expected. "Found me at last, have you?"

Clair rushed to Leah's side and took up the older woman's hands. "Oh, Leah, we have missed you." She whispered, and Luveday thought she saw tears trek down the girl's cheeks. Luveday looked to the other woman and motioned for the two of them to step outside for a moment. She didn't have to ask again.

"Leah had a hard journey here." She said, looking the Lady square in the eye, but Luveday only nodded. She could imagine Leah fleeing after her secret had come to light. Luveday wondered if she had heard the news of Titus's return or if her illness had kept the story from reaching her. "She is strong for her age, but her lungs didn't fare so well. We've been giving her teas to drink, and though they help, I can't say if she will ever fully recover."

She thanked the woman, who seemed a bit surprised by the gesture. "I have some healing skills; I will see if she is well enough to take home." Luveday paused, "Thank you…" The woman had not offered her name.

"No thanks are needed." She looked inside at Leah who met her gaze and nodded. Turning back to the lady, she said, "Home is where she belongs," and the other woman left without another word.

Luveday and Clair spent the night in the room. Luveday's medicines worked no better than the ones the Abbey had provided, but by morning she was sure that Leah was strong enough to travel. The woman was determined to go home and doubly so after Luveday had confirmed that the rumors that Titus had returned were true. Luveday told the tale as she helped the woman sit up and eat the hearty broth brought to all of them. Tears had rolled silently down from the woman's eyes as Luveday finished her tale while Clair sat silently in the corner, eating her meal. "Thank the Creator he has returned. I worried for the boy, though I knew you would take care of him." She took Luveday's hand, and she squeezed it back. "Not long now." She said and repeated the same phrase as they nestled her onto the pallet of blankest for the journey home.

The courtyard was in an uproar as they pulled the cart to a stop before the front doors. It was times like this that Luveday wished the house had a proper curtain wall, like a real castle, as shouts of riders approaching rang out across the way. The gate was a heavy affair with a watch atop it, but the walls to either side were no thicker than the average stone wall and didn't encircle the house. They stopped a few yards to the right where it met an outer building and carried on father to the left where it eventually met with the garden wall, which was a hedgerow and no wall at all.

Leah was up and looking toward the gate as riders can streaming in, many moving off to the side toward the stables to make room for the men behind.

Luveday was tired and was in the process of helping Leah out of the cart when the riders filled the courtyard. At the front were three men she had no trouble recognizing. Iain De Lane stopped his mount on the other side of their cart. John had to steady the old mare who was agitated by the arrival of so many warhorses.

Benedict St. James was to his left, and Sir Gregori to his right, and all three men looked down on her with mixed expressions. Beatrix ran out of the hall to help Clair get Leah inside. They had decided to ready a room for her in the house if her health was a poor as was told, and Luveday was suddenly grateful for the forethought. John moved the cart out of the way, saying something about taking it the back way to return it to the warehouse.

Luveday found herself with nothing to do, and no one around, and so turned back to their guests wondering what in the world was going on. The men had yet to dismount and still sat watching her. Luveday breathed through her nose, lowered her shoulders and looked at them head held high. "Good day! Lord De Lane, Lord St. James, Sir Gregori," She nodded as she acknowledged each in turn. They each nodded back, though St. James beamed at her, while Sir Gregori tried to keep the smile at the corner of his lips from spreading, his eyes twinkled at her. Iain frowned, but moved to dismount, making his companions follow suit. Luveday had a brief thought to look for Coll, but the men had her full attention.

Just as the trio came to stand before her, Lord Titus Pillar came through the front door to stand beside her and greeted them as well with little more than a 'Good Day.' There was a distinct separation between the two groups. Artair took that moment to find them and grasped first Luveday's hand, and then his father's making it three against three. Iain's frown deepened as the smiles evident on the other men's faces disappeared. Artair looked at the adults, greeted St. James as was appropriate, nodded to the other men as men often did and ran off, but not before Luveday suggested he find Gemma and Beatrix. No one had yet told the boy of Leah's return, and Luveday was loath to do it in front of these men. She briefly wondered how the two women would fare through it and mentally cringed at having rather heavy-handedly given the task to them.

"Please come in." Luveday gestured inside, but no one seemed to move. Turning back, she gently chided, "your missive didn't state who was coming, only that the group was large." St. James looked sheepish as her eyes fell on him, Iain's expression didn't change though Gregori smirked a bit making Luveday wonder at him.

"Do come in, the Lady has only just returned herself." Titus moved towards the door taking Luveday's elbow, while a grunt was heard from behind them.

No one looked back to see the cause of the sound, though Luveday wouldn't be surprised if someone got an elbow to the ribs, that someone being De Lane. The real question was which one of his blood brothers had dealt it.

Inside the cooler hall, they stiffly sat as Luveday drank fresh spring water and the men gratefully downed mugs of chilled ale. Titus watched from his bench with St. James beside him. Iain and Gregori took up the other bench, their weight making the furniture creak. Luveday finished her cup, but no one had taken the opportunity to speak, so she waded in. "I hope the journey was uneventful." She offered.

All eye swung to her and Luveday swore she heard necks snap and tempers crackle as the group turned the tension on her. No one answered. Sighing internally, and not really knowing what to do or how she felt about the situation, she tried again. "You left men at Castle Sterling?"

Finally, St. James answered, though Iain looked as if he might stab the man. Sir Gregori didn't look much happier. "We escorted Lord Cain and Sir Gareth Tate and their men to Sterling where they will remain in residence until the King rules on the title." He took a sip of his ale, eyeing the two men across from him.

Luveday finally figured out that both men were waiting for Iain to speak, in fact, almost refusing to talk until he did. She nearly laughed at the childish gesture. Titus didn't seem amused, though perhaps he had yet to figure that out. She was sure that the men had positioned themselves so that she sat in the chair alone, neither on one side nor the other. It was clear that Benedict had taken the seat next to Titus to keep her from sitting there. Luveday had quickly stepped to the back of the hall to wash her hands and her face, removing the dirt from the summer roads. In the meantime, the men had seated themselves, and she had returned to find herself the odd man out.

A crying Beatrix arrived almost begging Titus to come to Leah. The old woman was asking for him. Titus looked put-upon, but with one look to Luveday he gave in. Benedict only gave her a look, but she answered the unspoken question. "Leah, the head woman, was found at Pyne-on-the-Abbey." He briefly filled in the men, who seemed to know the gist of the tale, before she continued. "There was news of her on our return. Word came that she was in poor health, and I went to bring her home the day after returning from court."

Iain finally spoke, "That is little rest." The comment seemed cold, but Luveday wasn't sure what she expected.

"Leah has been Artair's mother since he was born, and I feared that if her health turned, she might pass before we could retrieve her."

Gregori tried to help the conversation along after a pause. "You wished to speak to her?"

Luveday knew what he implied. "Not personally. I wished her to be home. I feel a bit as if I am responsible for driving her out."

"That was not your fault." Benedict countered earnestly. "They were actions outside of your control." He looked to Iain who watched him closely. Sighing he settled back. "The woman fled her own sins, Luveday. It wasn't your doing."

Gregori stirred and settled as the conversation died again. Everyone except Iain looked uncomfortable, while the King's champion looked as if he were made of stone.

"Oh, for the love of cheese," Luveday exclaimed startling the trio. She leaned forward and looked daggers at Iain. "What are you doing here? What is all this about?" She gestured to Gregori and Iain, "Why are you here if you are going to sit there like a bump on a log?" She looked to Benedict who smirked at her. "Don't give me that look!" He tried to squelch the smile, but it didn't work. "You give me a letter that explains nothing at all and show up with these two," she gestured wildly to the other bench, "and then sit here like you all can wage war with Pillar just by staring him down." She pointedly looked to Iain. "Are you hear to talk to me, or glower at me?"

Gregori and Benedict burst into laughter while Iain scowled at them, but even Luveday could see the twitch at the corner of his mouth. He finally gave in, letting the laughter roll out of him. Luveday smiled too, forgetting how much she loved the sound.

Gregori looked at her, grinning wide. "I have missed you, Lady." The man moved suddenly and smoothly and lifted her off her feet in a hug and sat her gently back down before anyone could stop him.

Iain's gaze met hers, and she could swear that he wanted to do more than hug her, but she looked away, trying to not turn warm at his look. Her eyes fell on Benedict who seemed to know exactly what had passed between them.

Luveday composed herself as the other men settled. "You have a lot of talking to do," was all she said as she looked from one man to the next, waiting for someone to begin.

Benedict began as if the others thought that hearing things from him would be easier, "As we rode away from the wedding ceremony, you remember meeting a man on the road." Luveday nodded, vaguely remembering the harried rider and wondering what he had to do with anything but kept silent. "The vows had been spoken, and the crowd moved into the chapel for the blessing before he reached them." Benedict's gaze flickered to Iain, though Luveday fought the urge to look at him, and waited as patiently as she could, trying not to guess what happened next. "During the blessings, there was a pause waiting for anyone who wanted to have their say; it usually remains an expectant silence." Luveday remembered if from Gregori's wedding, acquainting it to the "speak now or forever hold your peace" moment. "Iain stood during the pause," Luveday's eyes flew to him and back to Benedict. She remembered that the groom knelt beside his bride until the blessings were finished and the priest told them to rise. "Before he could speak, the door flew open." Gregori huffed, at his friend's dramatic gesture as Benedict's arms went wide. "And the rider came running in, asking if he were too late."

"All hell broke loose," Gregori chimed in, "Excuse the language, My Lady."

Benedict glared but waited a moment to see if Iain wished to take up the tale. "Exhausted and wary, he stumbled to the front of the chapel to take a crying Christabel in his arms."

"You forgot the passionate kiss," Gregori added with a helpful tone.

"Am I telling this, or are you?" he asked, but Gregori just shrugged smirking. Iain didn't move, just watched Luveday intently. "Sumerland and his men yelled and threatened to pull swords, but Father Quinn's voice rang out over the chaos, quieting the crowd." Luveday could imagine it. "Sumerland cleared the chapel though many protested, Iain, the stranger, Christabel, Mistress Adela, Emmalyn, Gregori and Emma, two knights and Father Quinn were all that remained." Benedict took a sip of his ale to wet his pallet for the rest of the tale. "Father Quinn let the stranger go first, but eyed Iain." There was a look between the two men, "Well he did, didn't he?" Gregori nodded, laughing while Iain finally admitted it with a nod of his own. "The stranger tells his tale. He is Sir Everard of Bryce Castle thought dead for several years and secretly married to Lady Christabel." Benedict laid out the punch line, and Luveday sat back in her chair but didn't look at anyone for a moment. Her gaze returned to Benedict, and she told him to continue. "Everard had only just returned to Anora after finding some fortune overseas to hear that his wife was betrothed to another. He rushed off to get the papers from the church to legitimize his claims and barely made it to Lander's Keep in time." Benedict almost laughed. "I can only imagine how furious Sumerland must have been." Luveday smiled knowing there was no love lost between any of these men and Christabel's father. "Father Quinn confirmed the seal on the letter was real, and even Mistress Adela spoke up to prove that the marriage was... true." He turned a bit pink as Luveday realized he was talking about consummation. "Sumerland swore and stomped about but left quickly taking his men with him and publicly disowning his daughter."

A brief frown closed the Lady's face, but Gregori reassured her. "She seemed more than happy to have him out of her life. If I recall she was too busy kissing Sir Everard to notice much else." He laughed.

"You mean Lord Everard." Iain cut in.

Benedict smiled. "Right, his cousin, the Lord of Bryce Castle, sided with Ladislaus and was killed on the battlefield. Everard is no longer the poor cousin, but Lord Everard Pryce of Bryce Castle."

"You just like saying that," Gregori grunted.

"I do indeed," Benedict admitted. "I remember him being a good fellow, and liking him better than his cousin, though I admit I am biased against anyone who called Ladislaus a friend." He was not ashamed by this admission, especially when the other men nodded in agreement.

"So, Christabel and her husband are at Bryce Castle?" Luveday asked, but before she could get an answer, a cry went up from somewhere in the castle causing the group to surge to their feet. A moment later as they took a step toward the noise, a small body hit Luveday. Artair went limp as she tried to pull him into her arms, Titus was not far behind him. With the boy clinging around her neck, and his father blinking back the tears in his eyes, it wasn't hard for Luveday to guess that Leah had passed.

"She..." but the words didn't come, nor did they need to. Titus nodded and turned to leave going back the way he had come.

Luveday comforted and rocked a crying Artair for what felt like hours until the boy fell into an exhausted sleep and she laid him down in her room. It was only as she quietly stepped into the hall that her brain started to work again. Had someone shown the men to their rooms? Was dinner prepared? Was it time to eat? She looked to find the sun still up but low in the sky. The days were long, and she guessed that dinner should have been served a while ago. She made her way down the back stairs to the kitchen. Red eyes were seen on every face she met, and so she didn't bother about her own. She had someone prepare a plate for the two of them but said she would walk in the garden before coming back to pick it up.

It was there, walking among the flowers that Iain found her. She was staring at a rose, not really seeing it when his deep voice slid around her. "You love these people." It was a statement yet held a touch of sorrow.

"Did you think I wouldn't?" She asked out of nowhere.

Iain turned her to look at him. He saw her red eyes, her flushed cheeks, and red nose. He also saw that her hair was more golden than he remembered. Her eyes, though red and watery, were sharp and exactly as he recalled. She was thinner, and the gown she wore was unfamiliar to him. He had thought he remembered everything about her and yet she was so much more. He couldn't help taking her in his arms and comforting her. "Of course, you would, Luv. You have worked beside them; you fought with them; you grieve with them." She looked up at him, having settled into his embrace. "Your heart is too large not to have room for all of them and more." She took a step back, and they both felt the loss. "The question is," he paused to take a deep breath as if he needed the strength, "Do you still have room in your heart for me?"

Luveday didn't answer but took a step back and turned away. Iain felt it like a blow to his chest. It gutted him, but he was frozen to the spot waiting for a word from her. Luveday walked to where the paths crossed and turned to face him, then moved back quickly encircling him in her arms, letting him breathe again. "Why did you stand?" She didn't have to elaborate; he knew what she was asking him.

Iain's voice was thick with emotion. "I was listening to the blessings of prosperity, peace, longevity and I couldn't imagine Christabel at my side. At Father Quinn's words wrapped around us, I turned to look at her, but I saw you instead, smiling back at me. My eyes opened, literally, I looked at her and knew that it was impossible, and I thought it was too late, but Father Quinn paused, and I realized it was my chance to change everything. Sumerland be damned." She laughed tears gathering. "If Everard hadn't interrupted, I would have called it all off, but I looked for you, and you weren't there. In the chaos of the moment, I thought I had missed you, and you were ushered out with the crowd. By the time everything was settle hours had past and only when I had searched high and low for you, only when desperation was turning me into a madman did my aunt confess." Iain hugged her tightly. "It was only then that I realized you had never answered me. You had never given me your word, and I understood why." He kissed her cheek to find it wet, she was crying silently. He kissed the other to clear it and rested his head atop hers. "You meant to leave me, all along, you meant to leave me." His voice broke at the remembered pain. "I know now that it was the only thing you could have done, but at the time I thought I might tear down the very walls with my rage."

Luveday looked up at him and wiped a tear away from his cheek. "What took you so long to get here?"

"Emmalyn begged me to let my anger cool before hunting Benedict down," Luveday cringed at the words, but he continued. "Truthfully, it was the King. I had to come to court to inform the King that my betrothal was broken. Sumerland raged as well, but he should have known that it would get him nowhere." He chuckled deep in his chest, and it shook Luveday in his arms. "I think the King was looking for an excuse after the bastard refused to send any men to the north. Short of siding with Sterling, there wasn't a surer move to gain the King's wrath."

"There was something about him paying something?" She asked.

"Edward couldn't outright punish him for his disloyalty, nothing to accuse Sumerland of, but the King could make sure I kept the dowry promised me since, in truth, it was not *I* who broke the engagement." Luveday laughed, knowing Iain had already spent most of the coin paying for labor on the walls, new livestock, and seed for the fields.

"So that was why he was so angry." She nodded. She leaned back so that she could see him better in the fading light, while not actually stepping out of his arms.

"Then you were at court healing the prince, and while I made several journeys there, I never saw you."

"I never knew." She hadn't guessed, "though I rarely left the prince's side while he was ill."

He laughed. "I know, and the King would send me away again so swiftly I didn't have time to find you." He looked as if he might have tried to hunt her down.

"And Sterling?" She asked quietly and saw the mask of ice and death slide over his features.

Through gritted teeth he told her the truth. "I had wanted the man dead for taking you, but when I heard he had come close to killing you, I swore I would not stop until he was mine." Luveday shivered though the air was warm. He looked down at her, catching the movement and his expression softened. "I swore no man would lay a hand on you and live." He kissed her hard, and it ended too quick for both of them. "I had him cornered, and if it had not been for Gregori yelling at me that the King wanted him alive, I would have taken his head on the spot." He sighed. "As it was, I got him in the side. We bound him, cursing and screaming, but I didn't care. The bastard had tried to burn the healing rooms at Pyne-on-the-Abbey." Luveday started having just been there. "There were nuns and men inside, but he thought only of escape." Luveday reached up to brush the grimace from his lips, and he kissed her fingertips. "When I returned the King had come to a settlement between Sumerland and me, which you saw." He looked to the house, and Luveday caught movement out of her peripheral vision as lights suddenly shown in the windows. "Pillar was back, you were to be given coin as reparation and a boon, and I was once again sent away without a word to you."

"Yet you and Benedict surely talked." Luveday thought a moment. "He had word from you, I mean before the last visit to court?" She asked, once again remembering the letter she had received and Benedict's apologies.

"Of course, you would consider that. Are you mad at him, or at me?" Iain asked gently, pushing a stray hair behind her right ear.

Luveday had to think about that for a moment. "I am not mad that you spoke to him… Though I might be a little upset if you spoke to him about me, and neither of you mentioned it," Luveday admitted it was silly that the two sworn blood brothers would never talk to each other again over a woman. If Benedict had known what had happened at the wedding, why hadn't he said something sooner?

"Don't be cross with us." He tried to move her along, farther from the house, but she didn't budge. "I was waiting on the King to settle the matter with Sumerland, and hoping he wouldn't suggest another betrothal…"

Luveday cut in. "Do you mean the King *suggested* your betrothal to Sumerland?" Iain nodded but said no more. "Well, shoot." She had learned quickly enough that the King didn't suggest anything. If he had given the green light for Christabel, then it was a done deal.

"That wasn't the only reason I didn't break the betrothal, Luveday. You know the rest." He cautioned, not putting the blame on the King but taking responsibility for his actions, making her love him more even though the reminder hurt. She nodded not able to speak past the lump in her throat. He pulled her close again. "Luveday, it was never you I… I wanted it all, and for a while I thought I could bend everything to my will, not realizing it wasn't bending, I was breaking you." A pained gasp left her, and Iain held her closer speaking into her hair, into her ear. "I thought if I could keep my vows to you and her separate, but it was… I was a fool, and I realized it too late." She shook her head, but he clarified. "I hadn't yet married Christabel, but it was still too late because you had gone." He breathed. "I just hadn't known it yet."

The stood for a moment holding tightly to one another. A voice rang out from the manor, and they walked back hand in hand. Titus looked stoic beside the fire, Benedict, and Gregori with him, and Luveday got the feeling that they had been talking for a while. Everyone was silent until all but Luveday's eyes turned to Iain. He moved her with a hand at the small of her back until they were near a growing group of people. Feeling the pressure, Luveday turned to find Iain gazing at her. He took a knee, and the shock that filled her expression was mirrored in Beatrix and Gemma's eyes.

"I know this comes on grim tidings, but I cannot let you go again. Lady Luveday, will you do me the honor of binding your life to mine for this day forward, from this life to the next and forever." Luveday felt the world start to tilt but righted herself. She blinked back tears that refused to stay behind her eyes and pressed her right hand against her lips to keep them from trembling. She couldn't speak but nodded vigorously and fell onto him, ignoring the ring he held, and never noticing that the band encircled a particularly important looking document, baring the King's seal.

"Finally, little cousin." Gregori tore her away as soon as the couple parted. She was spun around in a room that was already spinning.

"Long overdue!" Benedict laughed and kissed her on both cheeks.
Congratulations came from every corner as serving women, the household knights and even some familiar faces from Lander's Keep chimed in. Lastly,

Lord Titus stood before her, his expression had lightened, but still held a hint of stone. She knew the emotions he was holding in check and couldn't fault him.

"I am happy you have found your place, Lady Luveday." How often in their talks had they both admitted to feeling out of place despite all they had? "Your happiness is long overdue." They both remember the words she had spoken to him on their first meeting.

"I wish the same for you, Lord Pillar." She said earnestly. Iain swept her away for a moment, but Luveday extracted herself, there was plenty of time for stolen kisses later, she was still the lady of the manor, and she had things to do.

Chapter 22

"You were made perfectly to be loved- and surely,
I have loved you, in the idea of you, my whole life long."
~ Elizabeth Barrett Browning

Luveday laughed and waved at familiar faces, blinking back tears to keep them in focus. She sat in front of Iain, for as soon as the village was in sight Gregori had taken her reigns and her betrothed had swept her off her own horse and into his lap. "Easy, Luv." He chided as her attention swung from one side of the horse to the other. People lined the road, lined the wall of the castle's bailey and waved frantically as they shouted their welcome.

Luveday laughed whole heartedly laying her own arm atop the one surrounding her waist. She thought she would never hear that endearment enough to satisfy her. "We are home, Iain." She leaned back against him and tilted her head back. A warm mouth kissed her right cheek.

"At last, my Luv." He growled into her ear so that only she could hear.

Before the horse came to a stop Ellie was at her knee almost climbing her skirts to hug her. Lady Emmalyn was more sedate, but she looked as if staying atop the stair before the keep was costing her. Luveday was lowered into Ellies arms. Both young women crying as they stumbled over to add Lady Emmalyn in the mix. The men chuckled and laughed, teasing the women for their soft emotions, but more than one man stealthily wiped away a tear amid the roaring welcome.

"Oh, My dear." Emmalyn gasp. "How we have missed you!" Luveday was pulled inside and she greeted and hugged anyone she met. Iain looked on, for once, not riled by other men's attentions towards her. As tears continued to flow from the female population, he looked around and smiled to himself.

Gregori came up to clamp him on the shoulder. "Is it as you imagined?" Like always, the abbey trained knight knew exactly what he was thinking.

"Better." Iain returned the gesture and looked out to his people, all colorfully dressed in scarves and midsummer flowers eagerly welcoming his future bride home. How many times had he imagined this seen as a lad? How different it was from the first time around. He walked shoulder to shoulder with his best knight, that was until Benedict separated them, laughing as he put an arm across each of their shoulders, though he had to be on the tips of his toes to do so. They looked at each other. Iain and Gregori turned to look at their mates, as Benedict quickly stuffed flowers in their collars before escaping towards the ladies. Iain pulled his free knowing they were favors from hopeful young women. There was only one women Iain was concerned with at the moment, and she had eyes only for him.

Two months had passed since Luveday's return and the castle was full to bursting. Tents circled the outer walls and people filled every free space around the outer bailey. Luveday looked out of the solar window from behind a curtain and tried to keep her light meal down. It was late morning and the mild weather for so late in summer was refreshing to everyone except the bride and groom. Iain had given over the solar as her own small chamber, where she had sworn to spend the nights until the wedding, was not large enough to accommodate the host of women determined to see to her preparations. No one needed to calm her innocent nerves as she was a healer after all, and more knowledgeable about the male body than some men. Instead they laughed and joked and teased those yet to marry.

"Now, come away, Luveday. You will do fine." Emmalyn grabbed her arm causing the bride to release her white-knuckled grip on the velvet curtain. "We have practiced this dozens of times." The soft voice of her mentor was soothing to her overactive nerves. Luveday's innated fear of public speaking had vanished over the years, or so she had thought, until glancing at the gathering masses that morning. Emmalyn continued to pat her arm and talk to her, but Luveday didn't hear a thing as the door swung open. Both Lady Janes, Benedicts mother and Lady Jane whom she had met in the north, parted to allow Queen Augusta to enter. The room curtsied as one.

"Lady Luveday." Augusta's outstretched arms beckoned her closer. Luveday took the offered hands before the Queen continued. "You look as you are named, Lovely." Luveday smiled despite the sappy words. The other women grew quiet. "I cannot say how happy we are by this outcome." She looked at Emmalyn and nodded. "I thought Christabel might grow to be a good wife, for under the courtly veneer I thought I had seen a strong spirit." Many frowned at mention of Iain's first betrothed not knowing where the Queen's thoughts would lead. "But had I met you, I would have known you to be his true mate." Smiles brightened, and heads nodded their agreement. "We wish all the blessings this life may give, on you and De Lane." The Queen pulled her close and kissed each cheek, while someone gasped behind her. "May the Creator give you strength, in times of weakness, may He give you love, in times of anger, may He give you wisdom in times of folly, and may He give you peace in times of tragedy." Murmurs followed her words. "Now," she smiled broadly. "What is this I hear about you not opening our gift?"

"Luveday." Emmalyn chided, not really knowing what the Queen was referring to, but well aware that to refuse a gift from royalty was unheard of. "Why would you not accept it, child?"

She visibly cringed but the smile on her face grew wider. "It is not that I don't except it." She talked to Emmalyn over her shoulder and turned back to Augusta who still retained one of her hands tracing the pattern of silver thread around the cuff of her velvet sleeve. "It is that," Luveday paused causing the Queen's attention to return to her, as she dropped the pilfered hand. "It is, your majesty, that Iain has decided to take me as I am. Before we know how your gifts…" not many caught the s on that word, "… can change me."

Augusta laughed. "No gift that I can give could accomplish that, dear Lady," but she nodded, approving of the romantic gesture. "Then let you be as you are… and let Iain be what he wishes, and for now, be only a man and woman vowing to love as the Creator made us to love and be loved." She looked at the women in the room. "The scroll will be there when you have need of it."

Saying goodbye, the Queen left to another wave of curtsies, but grabbed the younger Jane's attention before departing. Both women walked out the door as it closed behind them, but a moment later Jane returned. Though she had little experience with brides, Madame Jane Kilgrave was secretly elated to be personally invited to attend the wedding. Luveday treated her like any other woman, and Jane watched with ramp interest the goings on of the bride. She knew with was as close as she would ever get to the alter herself, and she savored the bittersweet experience.

By the time the first bell tolled, the group had ushered the bride down the stairs. A moment later they were out the main door and like the proverbial Moses, the crowd parted to reveal a path before them. Luveday looked for only one man, because she knew her place was beside him and as she came to stand at the foot of the chapel, a reverent silence fell over the crowd. Father Quinn said a quick blessing, but it was Father Julian who cultured tones carried over the masses. The blessings and intonements commenced as if he sang them to heaven. He said the vows, and Iain repeated as if none stood before him but Luveday, "I, Iain Hargrave Fitzwilliam De Lane, take you, Luveday Marie Bennett, to be no other than yourself as the Creator made you. I take you as my wife, with your faults and your strengths, as I offer myself to you with my faults and my own strengths, to help you in times of trouble. The shelter you when you are wary, and to have faith in your abiding love, through all our years and in all that this life may bring us."

It seemed only a heartbeat before Luveday found herself repeating. "I, Luveday Marie Bennett, take you, Iain Hargrave Fitzwilliam De Lane, to be no other than yourself as the Creator made you. I take you as my husband. Loving what I know of you, trusting what I do not yet know. I have faith in your integrity, your patience and compassion, and your abiding love for me through all our years and in all that life may bring us."

Together they intoned, "I vow my life, my happiness, my trust, and my love do bind us together from this moment forward, so long as we both shall live."

"What the Creator has bless by bringing together, let no man rend asunder." There was an expectant breath. "With these vows, in the sight of the Creator and before these people, I name you husband and wife." There was a roaring in Luveday's ears, but she couldn't tell if it was the crowd or if it was the blood pumping through her veins as Iain kissed her. If Father Julian had more words, she couldn't hear them.

The crowd moved and so they moved to enter the chapel. There was a space between the couple and the first pews, but every other inch or seat of floor held a warm body. Even the King and Queen were pressed closed to each other. A roar sounded outside even through the closed doors as Father Julian finished the vows and the blessings over both of them. By the time the door opened once more. Tables lined the bailey as lines of guests paused to greet the newlyweds. Iain stood on the steps and said something about sharing their prosperity, but too soon Luveday found herself seated at the high table, drinking down a goblet of wine as if she were a man in the desert.

Time had no meaning for the marry makers. Luveday looked to her right and met the smiling face of the Queen as their husbands commented on something that was going on below. A moment later Augusta asked her in a stage whisper, "You look as if you are dazed, my friend, drink and eat something." Suddenly there was a goblet at her lips followed by Iain pressing a bit of meat in her mouth. Luveday looked to him as he smiled knowingly down at her.

"You are right your majesty," her husband said over her head. "I will see to it."

Chewing she thought the moment through not knowing what was going on. "See to what?" she asked as soon as she swallowed.

"To you, my Luv." He whispered in her ear as he kissed the lobe quickly. "You haven't said a word since your vows." He laughed. "I've seen men on the battlefield with such a look."

"I am not in shock." She stated matter-of-factly, but it only produced a puzzled look.

"You've called it that before," he muttered and let it go. "Whatever the word, you look faraway, and utterly tempting." He added that last bit as he replaced the food at her lips with his own. The crowd below roared, and the King said something about holding it together over the riot.

It was some time before she looked farther than the couple next to them. On Iain's left were Lady Emmalyn, and Lord Frazier, followed by Lord Titus and Lady Jane St. James. Lord and Lady Stern finished off that end of the table. On Luveday's left sat the Queen and King, followed Gregori and Ellie, as Ellie had traded places with her husband being too timid to sit next to the King of Anora. Cassandra and Warren sat at the head table, both stoic and looking as if they longed to join the masses and yet honored to be seated at the high table. Cassandra was well known to the King for she had treated his wounds on several occasions as a young man before finding her way to Lander's Keep. At the end of the table sat Benedict and Lady Jane Kilgrave, but Jane kept her eyes mostly on the merriment below talking only when spoken too and looking for the world as if she were utterly absorbed in the food in front of her.

"He'll be getting up soon," Benedict commented as he drank another long draft of wine.

"Who?" She asked a mixture of surprise and confusion on her face.

Benedict had done little flirting that evening, having taken the seat next to her in order to get away from partnering his mother. Lucky for him, Titus was willing to trade spots and his mother was polite enough not to make a fuss, though he was sure he would be getting and earful later.

"Pillar." He huffed, clearly on to her. "You have looked at the other end of the table many times, you watched him get up and talk to Sir Navarro earlier." His cocky smile was almost visible behind the rim of his cup.

"Not so, My Lord." Jane began to protest.

"Not to worry, My Lady," He cut her off, "he has looked your way a number of times as well." He let that sink in. "Have you two been introduced."

Jane stiffened. "Not yet."

"Would you like me to do the honors?" He offered half in jest.

"No." She stated flatly.

Chuckling he sat back. "You can't say you aren't interested, Lady."

It was her turn to huff. "Not for the reasons you think."

Benedict only smiled, a twinkle in his blue eyes. "Your reasons are your own, My Lady. I merely wished to help a friend."

"I don't think he will see it as helping." She muttered under her breath.

In Benedict's nearly drunken state his senses were strangely acute. "It's funny that you thought I was referring to him, Jane." He commented huskily.

Jane looked at him, startled. She didn't know if he was drunk or merely remorse. Benedict's wit was sharp, and they had known each other for years, often meeting in unexpected locations. They had had each other's back on more than one occasion, though they never met in popular circles.

Leaning in she looked him in the eye. "I can bring down my own quarry, St. James." She whispered through her teeth. "I don't need your help."

"Never said you did, Jane." He scanned the crowd briefly. "You have it just the same." He rose and put his goblet down. A woman beckoned him on, a moment later he was swallowed up in the turning masses dancing below.

Jane groaned in frustration. She hadn't even noticed when the tables had been removed to make way for the dancers. She was in trouble. Her eyes found the familiar figure of Titus Pillar and his young son who darted between the lower tables and the high. Why was he even a draw for her, she wondered? He had never even looked her way before now, they had seen each other in passing less than a handful of times. It must be curiosity, she thought. Anyone would be curious about a man who returned from the grave, but that explanation didn't ring true to her and she was not one to lie to herself, to others yes, but never to herself. Since laying eyes on him the day before, just after arriving for the wedding, she had subconsciously been seeking in out in every gathering. She couldn't stop her gaze from resting on him.

Why did it seem that every time she looked at him, he was looking right back at her? She had never met a man with such a direct gaze. Not even the King looked at her thus. What did it mean?

Jane found herself leaving the high table and mixing with the crowd, not having a destination in mind, but knowing sooner or later, she would find her way before the large hearth and into the company of Titus Pillar.

Iain watched the crowd, happy but stiff. Luveday got the feeling that while the man next to her was celebrating their union and anticipating the night ahead, he wasn't completely relaxed. A part of him still swept the room looking for trouble. She smiled, settling into his side. He tucked her close, but still looked across the room. She didn't interrupt but waited until his attention returned to her, as it always did.

"What is that smile for?" He asked warily. He was done with revelry and was ready for the night to be upon them.

"For you, why do you ask?" She said, and he kissed her.

"It wasn't the same as the last few." He said. Looking down at her.

Luveday laughed, exhaustion making her a little loopy, or was it the never emptying goblet of wine talking? "Do they have to be the same?"

Iain looked at her closely and smiled another smug little smile. "No," he paused, "but I know when you are thinking about something."

"Oh, you know do you?" She offered an opening he couldn't resist.

"I do." He said and kissed her. A moment later the crowd roared again, a mixture of cheer and not so subtle innuendos.

Edward raised to his feet and the room stilled. "I believe it is time to put the couple to bed."

Luveday thought the ceremony was bad, but what was to come made her want to sink into the floor. A moment later she was pulled to her feet and swung into strong arms. Through the laughing faces and lude comments, she saw that Titus and Lady Jane were seated before the hearth, deep in conversation, but didn't have time to wonder about it, any more than the fact that Benedict had a woman on each arm.

Not a half hour later she laid, scantily clad in the dark depths of the curtained bed. The King and Queen had already surveyed the room and remarked approvingly on its lush contents. Iain stood, stripped to the waist looking as if he might murder the next man through the door.

Neither remembered Gregori's wedding guests being so bold, but still friends tried to inspect the wedding bed, and give their good wishes. Finally, Gregori, Benedict, Titus, Iain, Fuller and King Edward cleared the room, and hall beyond. No one but Titus glanced at the bed, and he only for a moment before departing wordlessly. Gregori and Benedict whispered sage advice while Fuller and the King merely nodded and went their way out the door. Iain threw the latch, and for good measure wedged a chair against the door. Luveday almost laughed, but her embarrassment kept her hidden behind the covers.

She could see him clearly as he turned in the candle lit room. The soft light bathed his bronzed skin turning it a golden hue. The sudden silence of the room lent an unearthly feeling to the moment. She didn't blink as he removed his boots and came to the bed. When their eyes met neither looked away. Iain didn't bother removing the rest of his clothes, he crawled across the comforter to get to her, moving smoothly like a prowling jungle cat. He didn't stop until their lips were sealed. Luveday lost the hold on the comforter, and let her only protection go. Her modesty and embarrassment were forgotten.

He almost growled as she pulled away and he followed the retreat. "Luv." He breathed out on a ragged breath. A heartbeat later they were entwined. The blanket running for the end of the bed. Iain wanted her in his arms, Luveday wanted everything. Every kiss, every caress, every breath, and thoughts, every day and night. Everything. If felt as if she had been waiting her whole life for this man, and once she had found him again, she had come home.

"Iain." His name was a reprimand as she tried to move to reach more of him, but he blocked her. A moment later they were skin to skin and her frustration was replaced with a contented sigh. That soft emotion didn't last for more than a heartbeat as the wolf came back to feast. Iain was everywhere, touching everything, taking everything and giving it back to her. They fought to get closer to the other, one moving and the other countering, until they rolled and bucked, the friction adding to their need.

They gasped for air, too focused on other things to breathe. This was better than either had imagined and they had imagined much the last few days despite the hectic preparations. They had sent little time together since the King had blessed their union and that absence had made them creative.

Iain shaped soft skin and rounded curves and loved every hollow and every inch. He had planned to make this last, but he couldn't wait and by the noises that were like music to his ears he knew she was not waiting either. He rose over her, "Are you with me, wife?" He was asking so much more than that simple phrase suggested.

Luveday bucked against him, eliciting a gasp and growl as she pulled him down to kiss him soundly. They separated only enough for her to give her replay against his lips. "Beside you, from eternity, my husband." He smiled and kissed her again. He would show her with every action and word from that moment onward just how much he loved her, and how wonderful eternity could be.

Luveday stretched as rays of dawn came through the open window and groaned for all the right reasons. Her body was sore, and if felt as if she had but a moments sleep, but her body told her it was time to be up, and not even a night of Iain's lovemaking could quiet it. She moved, and realized that the bed was empty, though still warm. Once her hazy mind began to work, she realized that the window should have been closed, and so she sought out her husband. The fire in the hearth was smoldering, and a candle rested on the small table beside Iain's chair. She moved, in the light of day, not bothering to hide behind the blankets. After that night, she was sure Iain was more acquainted with her body than even she was.

He sat before the hearth, in one of the two chairs that remained. The table they had installed for the meeting with his brothers had been removed days prior to make room for the women, and guests that flocked to congratulate Luveday as the happy bride.

He didn't lift his head when she moved up beside him, but she knew he wasn't asleep. He looked at something in his hand and held it up as she moved to grab the sheet from the foot of the bed, not because she was shy, but because there was a slight chill in the air. Iain wore only a cloth around his hips. It was part undergarment part loin cloth, and Luveday hadn't yet learned what it was called, but she likened it to a kilt and put that question in her mind for later, as she took the letter from him.

Settling in his lap, she was immediately drawn closer, back into his warmth. She held the letter, careful to not wrinkle the parchment. They sat for a moment in contemplative silence, staring at what would change their lives, no doubt for the better. "The King is generous, Luveday." Iain spoke as if to reassure her.

He couldn't see the smile on her lips as he kissed her neck, but it was in her voice when she replied. "I know. They are both generous for their friends." She said, knowing they asked as much of those closest to them as they gave. It was not a bribe, but an investment.

The seal broke with ease and the parchment crunched a little as she unfolded it. The outer paper was thick and made to protect the finer parchment within from the elements and curious eyes. Iain waited as she shifted until the light was best for reading. Luveday dropped the letter, but he hadn't gotten very far, his reading skills no match for hers.

"Luveday." He prompted after a moment of silence. "Luv, I can't read it in your lap." He tried lightening the mood, but when she turned to him with a look that said she had forgotten he was there he grew worried. "What does it say, Luv?" He asked gruffly and pulled her back so that he could see over her head. The good thing about his small wife, was that she was an armful, but one perfectly formed for him. He wrapped around her as if she were barely there.

The letter was raised but Iain's worry made the words jump and tumble around the page. "Read it to me."

She swallowed audibly. "From King Edward of Anora and Queen Augusta of the Northern Isles. To our most beloved lady. Lady Luveday, soon to Be Lady Luveday De Lane of Lander's Keep. We write this missive with a joyous heart, and grand all the blessings that are within our power to give." Iain huffed at the flowery sentiment, knowing the King's fondness for exaggeration at such times. "At every turn you have shown your loyalty, steadfastness, strength of character and will, and your skill. All that we have asked of you, you have accomplished and more. At every turn you have exceeded our expectations." Another huff, but with a note of agreement she couldn't help but notice. "How are we to repay one who has given us so much, and asked nothing for herself?" Luveday swallowed and moved restlessly as Iain rested his cheek on her head and nuzzled her. It took a moment for her to realize this was his way of asking her to continue. "While we were prepared to give you much, that which you truly wanted is not ours to give." She faltered a moment knowing it was Augusta that spoke to her in that moment. "And though we would give you whatever you asked of us, we know you will not ask for much at all, and so we have thought long on the matter. For your tireless efforts to return our son to us, we give the title of Royal Healer, and Master of the Healing Arts, and all the appointments and benefits thereof. We know you will not think this much a gift as it means you will have to spend more time at court, but we know your presence will do much good." Iain laughed.

"They have given you a title you've earned twice over, all the trouble and intrigue of court, in exchange for the Healing Rooms in Kingston. You will have more work monitoring the healer's guilds than you will ever need." Luveday's ears perked up.

"Monitoring how?" She asked, and he groaned at the interest in her voice.

"The royal healer sets the laws and procedures for the healing arts, for the last dozen years it has been Master Pope." They both almost spit at the man's name. "Now it will be you, but I doubt that old fool spent more than a few days at the Healing Rooms in all that time. The guild has regulated itself for the most part, it is why they are more focused on coin than learning the true art. Anyone is allowed in these days." Iain laughed again, and she couldn't help but notice the bitterness in his voice, but that didn't stop her from thinking. She had heard about the Healing Rooms in passing, though what she had heard never seemed to make sense. She had thought the place a kind of hospital or house where healers learned their skill, but in the next instance it sounded like a guildhall where wares were bartered, and prices set. Perhaps it was both, she wondered and thought to remind herself to ask Cassandra more about it later.

"So, I will get all the responsibility and nothing else?" She asked, not knowing what kind of gift that was.

"You will get a steady stream of Healing supplies, the newest and rarest items from overseas, and rooms at court as well others as near the Healing Rooms." He stated unimpressed.

"How much will that cost us?" She asked aloud.

"Nothing so long as you remain the Royal Healer, it is your duty to learn everything you can to keep the royal line in utmost health, and maybe some court favorites too." He added as an afterthought.

"Books, and herbs, and..." She looked over her shoulder at him.

"And anything your little curious mind desires. No doubt the steward will have trouble keeping up with your demands." He laughed seeing the gleam in her eye. She nodded in agreement and tried to distract him, but he kept bringing them back to the matter at hand. "What else does the letter say?"

She held it up again, "Where was I? Ah, for rescue of our other son through the battlefields of the North," Iain laughed aloud startling her, and himself. He didn't think he would ever laugh at what Sterling had almost accomplished, but the letter was too much. "Can I continue?" She asked trying to be stern and not to laugh as well. He kissed her and after a heady moment bayed her continue. "Through the battlefields of the North, we grant Sterling's personal stock. Two dozen cattle, four war horses, eight gray belly pigs, fifteen geese, three goats, five purebred Northvale wolfhounds of both sexes and four peacocks. The animal and Warhorse were taken during the victory in the North, Lord Frazier has been housing them and Sterling's squire since then and will deliver said gifts a fortnight after the wedding." The hum in her ear was thoughtful.

"I've heard of Northvale wolfhounds, are they not prized for something?"

"Aye, their intelligence and loyalty. Their hunting skills are unequalled. They are a fine prize in themselves."

"Isn't Sterling's personal stock the animals he carted around with him so that his plate was always full?" She asked having heard tales of the lavishness that the man had demanded always surround him. "Vain, selfish, vicious bastard." She said aloud causing Iain to laugh and rock her in his arms.

"Aye my Luv, he was all that and more. May he rot in hell." Luveday concurred knowing that she should learn to forgive, but his crimes were still to fresh for her to even think about such things yet.

She turned back to the letter. "For your return of our dear, lost, Lord Pillar." Iain snorted, not yet deciding how he felt about the man. Luveday knew that much of his animosity for Titus was the fact that he had almost taken her from him. Luveday wasn't sure how true that statement was, for though she felt for Titus, and knew in her bones that they could have built a wonderful life together, a part of her would have always belonged with Iain. She had not come to care for the returned Lord as much as Iain might have thought. Those feelings were only just forming when Iain had stepped back into her life, and she only thought of them in the light that she knew she had hurt Titus in some way and was saddened by it and the loss of Artair's happy presence.

She missed the boy terribly and their reunion had been tearful and hurt her all the more for she knew it was short lived. She cleared her throat and the weight that settled there. "For Pillar and the delicate handling of the House of the Rose, we grant as portion of its produce, with Pillars blessing, to continue your work started there, and a portion of the coin your new potions will bring for three harvests. Pillar speaks highly of your suggestions and already there is much interest here at court."

"What suggestions? What potions?" Iain asked somewhere between confusion and ire.

"I learned a lot while I was on the coast." She started and turned in his lap until she was sideways and able to see him clearly. The sun was up but only their nearness kept them warm from the castle's chill. "I learned about perfume and lotion making." The furrow in his brow was charming instead of irritating. "I tried to mix some healing plants into the mix, to help with ailments as well as beauty."

The frown dissolved. "You were trying to make some of those god-awful potions more palatable?" He asked.

"They weren't to drink, but yes. I was trying to soften the harsher mixtures to make them more pleasant to use, and with some success." She confided.

He nodded as if he expected nothing less from her. "How much coin do you think it might yield?" It was not a mercenary question, but a curious one.

"If it goes as well as I had hoped, next spring might produce, if we get the usual, king's portion, with the yield I had planned." She did some quick math. "Around 20 silver coins, maybe more."

Iain coughed. "Twenty silver coins, what will be your portion, three?"

She smiled, "No, that is my portion." He looked at her. "The perfumes and lotions are the best the House of Pillar offers, and if they plant the three fields along with my healing plants, they should get somewhere near 150 bottles of finished product. At 25 coppers a bottle," he nearly choked, "the end result would be equal to...say... 130 silvers."

"From Four fields of flowers?" He asked incredulous.

"From flowers, and oils, and herbs and spices. Beauty is not cheap, my husband." She mockingly scolded.

He kissed her hard. "Seeing yours every day is worth any price." She couldn't laugh at such a charming sentiment, even though he grinned wickedly at her.

"There is more." She waved the letter hoping to distract him, it almost worked. There was a few more moments of kisses before their attention returned to the Royal missive. "And last, for the wedding gift in honor of the union between our Champion and Healer, we give the lands and titles of the house of Landers, where upon the loss of that line, all property and heraldry will be bestowed upon Lady Luveday and her children."

"The Lander's." Iain whispered.

"Catherine and Sir Chadric?" She asked not understanding.

"Aye." He had to clear his throat. "Though the manor is all but falling down in the woods, the pastureland beyond and the lake beyond that all belong to the Lander's line, a gift from Edward's Father when Sir Chadric was a young knight."

Luveday looked at the paper once again feeling the sorrow of their loss. "There is no one to carry on the line." She stated.

"Nay, Luv." He said. "And my father did not help when he bought the land and unfinished keep. The shift left the village to decide who to support and they felt the Lander's to themselves."

"So close, and yet so far away." She said.

"Aye, Luv," he wiped a stray tear from her cheek. "No need to cry, Luveday. What's done is done, and we will remember them well."

"Aye, that we will." She said and smiled at him.

"What do you think of your gifts?" He asked, knowing she was not impressed with the wealth she had been handed, though she had earned much of it.

"To tell the truth..." She paused and shifted until she straddled him and could look him in the face, with her legs pressed into the side of the chair. She didn't look him in the eye but ran her right hand over his collar bone.

"Aye, the truth, Luv." He countered wondering what she was thinking. When her face turned up to his, her blue gray eyes shone bright.

"Truthfully," she moved to kiss him, and then pulled back, "Truthfully the only thing I wanted was you."

The letter was forgot as Iain took his wife back to bed, despite the sun rising, they didn't leave it for many hours yet. Eventually they found some rest.

Epilogue

"If I leave all for thee, wilt thou exchange, And be all to me?"
~ Elizabeth Barrett Browning

Luveday walked through the orchard of Lander's Keep, looking over the buds of spring. She and Iain had been married in the late summer, not long after his proposal. She had returned to her home to fanfare and tears, but she had never felt better in her life, except maybe when Iain kissed her after Father Julian had pronounced them man and wife.

It had come as a shock to her, though perhaps it shouldn't have, that King Edward and Queen Augusta had bestowed upon her the house of Lander's and the surrounding forest making whole the lands once again. Sir Chadric had been elated at the news and had enjoyed the wedding feast. He had died in his sleep several weeks later, and Luveday had moved Catherine into the keep. She had died sitting in the Lady's garden as the first buds of spring opened. Luveday had left the house, letting Paige keep whatever she wished from the manor. They moved the garden first, then what furnishings could be salvaged. Luveday had plans to demolish the house, little by little moving the wood paneling into the keep, making the two dwellings one.

Between her plans for the castle and her time at the Healing Rooms in Kingston, her days were full up. She was moving mountain to whip the Healing guilds into shape, and when she was done, something like the modern system of medicine would exist throughout Anora, even if it took her a lifetime to accomplish it.

Today she walked for the peace though she wasn't alone in the wood. Warren flanked her as he usually did when they were out but kept his distance as Luveday had wanted to be alone. The letter rested under her breast, tucked inside the high girdle she wouldn't be able to wear for much longer. She was sure now, not only of her place here and her love for De Lane but that a new life would be joining theirs in a few months.

The letter was long and thick, several pieces of her notebook concealed with a heavy bit of vellum. It was addressed to her parents, and many would call it an expensive waste of paper, she hadn't been able to stop herself from writing it. Luveday had told her family as concisely as she could everything that had happened from the day she disappeared until the moment her pen touched paper. Iain had seen her writing and wondered where she had gotten such strange items but had left her alone and she was grateful. One day she might tell him the truth, but she still didn't know if she ever would.

All the love she felt was wrapped in those pages, but she didn't know what to do with them. The writing had started as a cathartic exercise when she realized that a baby was on the way, more would probably follow, and her family would never see any of them. She couldn't leave the letter lying around. She had no one to send it too, and while the idea of burning it had crossed her mind, every time she had attempted to toss it into the fire she had frozen and put it away again. Today she thought she might bury it or toss it in the stream or somewhere where it couldn't be retrieved and possibly used against her.

So, she walked the orchard, deep enough now that no sign of the castle could be seen, and only rarely losing sight of her shadow. The leaves where green and the light shone just so that it reminded her of something, but she couldn't say what. Her left hand rested on a low limb that was almost parallel with her shoulder, and her right hand came to cover her belly and the letter and baby there. She heard Warren's voice and took a step forward, and the world shifted.

One moment she was in the orchards of Lander's Keep, the next she was in the backyard of her parent's house. The large picture window was open before her; the back door was open wide so that fresh air and spring sunshine highlighted the scene inside. Her mother and father were gathered around the dining table, her sister, brother-in-law, and nieces sat around talking adamantly while having a late Sunday brunch. Tears formed in her eyes, but she didn't cry. Luveday didn't know if she wanted to cry for them, or for herself. Was she truly back? She looked down. The gown was still the one she had put on that morning, her cloak rested on her shoulders, keeping off the spring chill. Everything was as it was, just like the moment she had stepped from this world into a new one, but looking at the picture before her, Luveday knew this wasn't her home anymore. She retreated, pray that like the last time, that retracing her steps would somehow return her home. Unlike those years ago, as she turned away, she heard it, as if from a distance, voices calling her name, not her family, but Warren and another drawing closer. Luveday wanted to cry out, but she was not yet in that world again, and fear that she might draw her family's attention kept her silent. Breathing deeply to calm her racing heart Luveday covered her rolling stomach and once again felt the familiar edges of the letter. She knew, with a sudden undeniable clarity that this was her chance, this was what the longings for home had been preparing her for. Taking the letter, she looked back at the window unnoticed. She looked at the fruit trees around her and got an idea. Hastily she pulled the ribbon tying back her hair and tried to tie the letter to a branch, but it didn't work. The voices calling her grew louder while she fought to keep down her rising panic, reminding herself that it wasn't good for the baby.

The sun glinted off the broach Iain had given her. The gems were semiprecious stones, but the large clasp was just what she needed. She unfastened the cloak and used the broach to skewer the letter and pin the two ends of the ribbon together before closing it. Stepping away, she hugged the cloak around her and watched her missive dangle from the tree branch.

A heartbeat later she stumbled into Iain's arms, his frantic cry cut short as he held her close as she cried.

"Luveday," he chanted over and over again. Warren was waved off as he held her close, the other men mumbled but disappeared assured that the lady was found. "Luveday," he finally got her attention. "Where were you?" He asked raggedly, and Luveday looked into his eyes and saw a starkness there she hadn't seen before. She couldn't answer. "You appeared..." he tried again. "You appeared out of thin air." He held her close again. "I rounded the tree and saw a shadow of the corner of my eye. You were gone, then there but like a ghost. I could see through you." He swallowed hard and separated them to cup her face. "Then you stumbled into my arms and you were real." He kissed her hard. "Creator above, what happened to you?" His voice shook, but he looked at her needing to know.

"Let us go back inside, Iain. And I'll tell you everything. It's a long story, and some things are unbelievable, but it's true." She held on to him. "It's all true." They left the orchard and didn't stop until they were in their solar. Luveday asked that they not be disturbed and sat before the fire in Iain's lap as she recounted her life in another world.

Terry Bennett glanced out the oversized picture window catching movement in the orchard. Looking closer, she spotted something hanging in a tree branch. "George, did you finally get that tape to put up in the orchard?" She laughed at her husband of thirty years, thinking only one thing would make her life complete as she looked over at her family, eyes resting on her eldest daughter. Their eyes met, and each knew that the other was thinking of the empty chair at the table. Luveday had gone missing almost three years ago. The local police and federal agencies had done all they could, but no one knew what had happened to their daughter. The family had nearly been torn apart by her loss, but they had come together even stronger, finally realizing how much it mattered, and how much she had mattered to them.

"No, Honey, I still need to go to Home Depot. I was planning to go this afternoon." He tried placating her, not wanting to hear about the tape one more time.

"Then what is hanging in the orchard?" She asked putout. All the heads turned to see the sun glinting off something in their small grove of trees they referred to as an orchard.

George looked stumped and ran a hand through his graying hair. "Was that you Annalisa?"

"No, Dad. You know we don't use plastics," but she said it off-handedly as she squinted, trying to bring the mystery into focus. No one asked Mark if he had done it, they knew he only went into nature to please his wife.

"What is it grandpa?" the girl's asked.

Terry turned to look at them but scolded her daughter instead. "Annalisa you'll hurt your eyesight squinting like that." Her daughter's expression looked eerily like her own when she was exasperated, but no one ever said so. "I've told you; you need to get glasses."

"I will mother, but I can't afford the frames right now." Annalisa climbed to her feet holding onto the table and the pack of her daughter's chair for extra support.

"Frames?" her father asked. "Why? How much do they cost?" But the words were out before he saw Mark's gesture to leave it alone.

"Most stores don't carry the biodegradable bamboo frames," she started as she waddled out toward the door. She was still talking when her mother asked her what she was doing. "I'm going to see what it is." She answered as if it were a silly question.

Terry told her grandchildren to sit down and finish breakfast, as they watched the pregnant woman reach the tree. A moment later Annalisa was yelling and waving something as she hopped across the yard. The men were up, but no one had made it far when she came rushing through the kitchen door. Out of breath she slapped the envelope down and rested both hands on the table; one held a light blue velvet ribbon, the other an antique looking broach. The envelope was addressed to *Mom & Dad* in the same swirling script Luveday had used on every card and note since she was thirteen.

No one moved for a moment until Terry cleaned off her butter-knife and gently pried off the wax seal.

"Is it from her?" Annalisa asked still breathless.

Mark moved closer, but asked from the other side of his father-in-law, "From who?"

"It looks like her handwriting," Terry said in awe and handed the cover letter to her husband. The thick paper was leathery and bore only the words *Mom & Dad*.

"Well," she asked impatiently, shushing the girls as they squirmed in their seats.

"Oh, my goodness." Terry dropped the letter her hands suddenly weak.

Annalisa made a grad for it, but her father was faster. The two men scanned the pages reading fast. "You've got to be kidding me," Mark whispered, running a hand through his hair. He looked to Annalisa dumfounded, a look she had only seen on her husband's face when she had recently announced that she was carrying a boy.

"What? What is it?" She asked, and for once the little girls didn't chime in. "Is it from Luveday?"

The girls squirmed and settled knowing the subject of their aunt was important and serious since she went away. They were as eager to hear news of her as the rest of the family, though they were starting to forget what she looked like and sounded like; though they still remembered that she had smiled a lot, and that she had loved them bunches.

Terry and George exchanged confused looks, as he handed over the sheets of paper.

"That can't be real can it?" Mark asked again, pointing to the letter.

The women read the letter slowly, drinking in every incredible word while George rifled through a drawer of the built-in desk in the kitchen until he found an old notebook. He brought it to the table as they read the final lines. He laid the open book next to the letter as everyone gathered around to see. The lists Luveday had copied for her father and instructions on how to care for the orchard matched the writing on the letter perfectly.

Annalisa swallowed hard. "If this is real, and she left it for us, why didn't she come back?" There was a catch in her voice.

"Honey." George gathered his daughter close as the two girls left their chairs to take comfort from their father. The adults exchanged glances.

It was Mark who lifted up the obvious answer. "Don't you remember, she said she was happy, loved, and pregnant." They looked at him, tears in their eyes. "She had a life there, and maybe..." he looked down at his daughters who clung to him and knew they didn't really understand why everyone was so sad. "Maybe this was all she could do. She let us know she was okay, that she was happy and safe."

"She didn't think we would ever see this letter," Terry said aloud.

Once again Mark, logical to a fault, gave the answer they all needed. "Maybe she got an opportunity and took it before it was too late."

They all looked out the window to the orchard and for a moment they saw, not the orchard and the back fence, but a man and woman embracing. A moment later the couple separated and walked off hand in hand. They had been dressed in medieval garb, looking very much like Luveday and the man she had described as her husband.

"George." She gasped, as mother and daughter held onto him.

"I saw them." He replied as Mark did the same.

"I saw them too," echoed one girl and then the other.

"Where did they go?" asked little Seraphina.

Annalisa cleared her throat as her mother turned to cry quietly in her father's arms. "You remember all those stories Auntie Luv told you about princes and fairies?" The little girls nodded excitedly. "Do you remember how they ended?" She asked and looked to Mark; a tear rolled down his cheek as he blinked more away but didn't let go of his girls as they answered. "That's right. Well, that was Aunt Luv and her prince, in her happily-ever-after." The couple looked at each other across the table, looked to their parents and found that they were all smiling through their tears. "Just like she said."

ABOUT THE AUTHOR

Amelia M. Brown. Author, Artist, Dreamer; she goes by many names. If you were to ask her the really important questions in life, she would answer thus. If she were a dragon, she's be a sapphire Wyrn with a book horde big enough to fill a mountain (maybe two). If she were on a popular Sci-fi starship show, she would be a blue shirt. *You know the one*. If she were a tree, she'd thank you for buying kindle additions, but she'd not be too worried since California oaks are protected by law. If she were an animal, she'd be a fox, because they are a surprising mix of cat and dog. Loyalty, intelligence, snuggly and needs some alone time. That's her to a T.

She went to school and collected papers on the way. Books, Diplomas, and such that say she is a master of her craft from places like CSU: Sacramento.

She's written her own books because some stories really want to be told. They're waiting for you patiently on Amazon. Her first novel, Ties of Fate, was a Herculean labor, while her second novel, The Beast of the Ruin, was a NaNoWriMo challenge. She won in more ways than one.

Her alter ego is as a receptionist at an Insurance Service where she spends her days when she's not riding dragons, fighting dark forces and conquering worlds in the name of Love and Justice.

Amelia M. Brown

Coming Soon:

The Chronicles of Odde: Of Riddles & Ravens

The Kingdom of Stormhelm has an abundance of princes, seven to be precise. None is so loved as the youngest, Ayden. When still in his crib, Ayden was gifted with an extraordinary power. Luckily, other royals seemed to be excluded from the gift, but for everyone else, it only takes one look for them to unconditionally love the young prince. His subjects love him so well that they would give him anything he asked for. Truly, it is not as good as it at first sounds, especially when his subjects want him to rule Stormhelm, but Ayden wants nothing to do with the crown. If only he could get everyone else to believe that, especially his elder brother. The eldest prince, Alexander, has recently been cursed with the features of a wolf. Having only just taken control of the kingdom from his crusading father, Alex feels betrayed by the turn of events, and not just by the curse. He's having to rely on his brothers, and has made Ayden the face of the crown, though using the wretched gift to deflect the court from his own problems has left Alexander with a bad taste in his mouth. With Stormhelm's princes dispersed throughout all of Odde, what is left to stop an even greater disaster from befalling the kingdom?

It's not all sunshine and happily-ever after for Kelly after being transported from our world to the Kingdom of Stormhelm on a continent they call, Odde. She's found a job at the royal castle and is moving her way up the ranks. From kitchen girl to lady's maid, she has her eye set on the royal chambers in hopes of finding something that will take her home. When finally able to move among royalty, Kelly almost blows it when she's unaffected by Ayden's gift. The incident catches the eyes of many, including the cursed prince. Unknowingly, Kelly befriends Alexander, unaware that magic doesn't seem to work on her like it does on everyone else. Kelly's desperate search for a way home is sidetracked when she sticks up for the Prince at a critical moment and earns the ire of a wondering wizard.

Now Kelly's on a quest as the King's champion, having to solve riddle after riddle to find the sorceress Zula Milburga and break the

Prince's curse. If she succeeds, she will be greatly rewarded, and Kelly sees it as her opportunity to find a way home. But even though she was a tough city girl, Kelly can't make it through Odde without help. She has Alexander's best friend and trusted Captain of the Guard, Reece Kaiden whose stoic wit gets her through some tough scrapes, but when he goes missing, she realizes that he has some secrets of his own. The remaining Princes are called on to help aid her through the Quest, but not all is what it seems, and Kelly fears time is running out for all of them.

Will Kelly find the Sorceress and somehow break the curse? Where has Kaiden gone? Can she trust anyone when they all seem to have secrets of their own, herself included? The tasks before her will test her wit, but really, what's up with all these riddles? They get harder with each task. She fears that the last one will be her undoing. Is she smart enough to outwit a Sorceress, or is it all a lost cause?

An excerpt from the next book in The Chronicles of Odde:

Of Riddles & Ravens

"How precious, dear Queen! Another boy to grace the line of Stormhelm." A tinkling laugh rang out as the Queen blinked in surprise; she was sure she had been alone a moment ago. "No need to fear fair Sophia, Queen of Stormhelm. This boy is special, a seventh son, and so my kin has sent me to bestow the traditional gift." The short hair did not give away her fairy heritage more than her petite statue and the strange silvery eyes that looked from the baby, back to the Queen.

"You are a fairy then?" She asked hesitantly. Fairies were strange creatures, some took offense at the oddest things, and a mad fairy was a terrible thing to run into.

"Yes, yes ... Fairy, I know, no wings in this size. But how troublesome they would be, wouldn't they? Always bumping into things, very troublesome." The fairy seemed distracted.

"Yes, I suppose they would be." The Queen's mind was reeling as she looked down at her son. Another gift, how extraordinary. Her first encounter had been with a vastly different looking creature. He had been tall, thin and rather sever as he gave Alexander, the crown prince, gifts to help him rule over Stormhelm with wisdom and grace.

"Now, what gift to give? That is the question. I know you let my predecessor pick for the first born, wise of you that, but what to give little seven?" The fairy brought a glowing stick to her pursed lips, thinking and the Queen remembered that they sometimes carried a wand to channel their power. "What to choose?" She hummed to herself.

The Queen looked at her son lovingly and spoke wistfully. "He needs nothing grand, all I could wish for him is that he would be loved as I loved him, the first moment I laid eyes on him, the first moment I held him in my arms."

"That's perfect, your majesty." The wand sprinkled glowing dust over the baby and the fairy continued. "Your wish is mine to grant and from this day forward all of his subject will love him as you do." The wind picked up and with a flutter of the curtains the fairy was gone. Sophia picked up her son and looked him over. The only sign of the magic cast over him was a faint glowing in his eyes that anyone else might mistake for a happy twinkle. The Queen was in high spirits and sang and danced the baby around in her arms. It was not until several hours later that the Queen realized what a mistake she had made.

Look For: **At First Sight**

(Persephonii Waters Book 1)

by <u>Melanie Brown</u> (Author)

Persephonii Waters' life as a consultant of the preternatural might be the perfect front page cover for a supermarket tabloid, but the savvy, smart, recently turned thirty pseudo detective is happy with her single, nearly non-existent personal life, her charming if frustrating handler/partner and solving the crimes and mysteries of the paranormal world. As a private consultant, her life resides in the zone where the mundane and supernatural collide, two forces that often leave devastation in their wake. She's seen more than anyone and knows firsthand the wondrous and horrific power of all things paranormal.

She returns to the states and finds herself in the middle of escalating cases of violence, leaving little doubt that something inhuman is involved. As the death toll rises the random crimes begin to paint a horrible picture of killer instinct and ruthless purpose.

Persephonii's wayward gifts, honed skill and encyclopedia like knowledge, maybe the perfect mix to piece together the facts and find the force behind the murders before the situation escalates to an all-out war between the two worlds.

As tensions rise, it's up to Persephonii to step out of the shadows and help solve this deadly puzzle where everything is more than it seems at first sight.

Made in the USA
Middletown, DE
18 August 2020